MURDER
ON
OLD MISSION

Books by Stephen Lewis

Mystery Novels

The Monkey Rope
And Baby Makes None
The Dumb Shall Sing
The Blind in Darkness
The Sea Hath Spoken

Textbooks

Focus on the Written Word
The Student Critic
Writing through Reading
Discovering Process
Philosophy: An Introduction Through Literature

MURDER
ON
OLD MISSION

by Stephen Lewis

Arbutus Press
Traverse City, Michigan

Murder on Old Mission

Arbutus Press
Traverse City, Michigan
www.Arbutuspress.com

Printed in the United States of America

Library of Congress Cataloging-in-Publication Data
Lewis, Stephen C.
   Murder on Old Mission / by Stephen Lewis.
        p. cm.
   ISBN 0-9665316-9-8
1. Curtis, Julia, d. 1895—Fiction. 2. Old Mission Peninsula (Mich.)—
Fiction. 3. Murder victims—Fiction. 4. Murderers—Fiction. I. Title.

   PS3562.E9755M87 2005
   813'.54—dc22

                    2005001435

cover photo: Dietrich Floeter
www.dietrichfloeter.com

Dedicated to the memory of
Walter Johnson
who first told me about Woodruff Parmelee

And, as always,
to Carol,
my guide in this as in everything

Author's Note

      I began work on *Murder On Old Mission* at the suggestion of my wife Carol's father, Walter Johnson, the local historian of Old Mission Peninsula in northwest lower Michigan. One day in August, 1997 he took Carol and me for a walk among the graves of Lakeside Cemetery off Eastern Avenue on the north end of the Peninsula. He paused before the rather grandiose monument to George Parmelee, and said, "There's a story here. This man's son was convicted of murder in 1895."

      Just after Christmas that same year, he sent me the newspaper stories of the trial. In a note, he said, "Don't you think this would make a good story just the way it is?" I recall thinking, with a shake of my head, no it won't. It needs to be shaped. The challenge in writing such a book is to remember that in the pull between what actually happened and the imagined story, the demands of the fictional narrative must prevail. An excessive allegiance to the facts will inevitably sink the story. I know this pitfall very well, having written heavily researched historical novels. The tendency is to make use of the material the research has produced, perhaps to justify the work. And in this instance, where the story not only takes place at a certain time and place, but also recreates a specific event, the temptation to repeat the known facts can be overwhelming. No doubt, that is what my father-in-law had in mind, for he was trained as an engineer and placed a high value on getting the facts right.

But I knew I was writing a novel, and I had to find the focus that would organize my telling of the story. Once I found that focus, I used the facts that fit and changed or discarded the ones that didn't. Still, I understand it might interest the reader to know what those facts are, as best they can be determined, and then consider how successfully the novel has risen above them. Here, then, are the facts.

In April 1895, Julia Curtis, 22 years old, basket on her arm, told her parents with whom she still lived, that she was going out to pick arbutus flowers. She did not return. The next day, her body was found in a hemlock swamp near the eastern arm of Grand Traverse Bay. There was a half empty bottle of laudanum on the ground near her. Her neck was bruised. An examination revealed that she was pregnant. A photograph taken by S.E. Wait, and now in the possession of the Traverse City Pioneer and Historical Society, shows her lying with her arms across her chest and a cloth over her face. Before long, Woodruff Parmelee was arrested and charged with her murder. Woodruff, a sometime house builder, and small time farmer, was the son of George Parmelee before whose monument in Lakeside Cemetery we first heard this story. At the time of the murder, George had been dead for ten years, and the huge holdings of his Ridgewood Farms on the north end of the Peninsula had been sold off. Woodruff was living on a small farm close to town, a mile or so north of Julia's family.

Woodruff was twice divorced and twice Julia's age. He denied having anything more than a neighborly relationship with her. Most importantly, he asserted an alibi: at the time she disappeared, he claimed to have been clearing brush for a new road heading toward West Bay. He knew nothing about the laudanum. At trial, Louis, his fifteen-year-old son from his first marriage, supported this alibi.

The prosecution's case rested on weak physical evidence and very questionable eyewitness testimony. The physical evidence consisted of footprints found near the body, which were said to be Woodruff's. This contention loses credibility in light of the fact that some thirty or so men had been tromping around the same ground where these footprints were found as they looked for Julia. Furthermore, there was no definitive forensic procedure at the time to establish a match between the prints and Woodruff's footwear. The eyewitness testimony came from a man who offered his testimony for sale to both sides. Julia's parents and her married brother testified to her relationship with Woodruff. This fact was the most solid evidence presented by the prosecution and no doubt offended the sensibilities of the twelve men of the jury, who most likely also heard about Woodruff's stormy marital career. It is also possible that his family's prominence might have encouraged a guilty verdict as a way of bringing down the proud Parmelees a peg or two. Whatever the combination of reasons then working in the minds of the jurors, he was convicted and sentenced to life at hard labor.

He served twenty years of that sentence, but then was pardoned by Governor Woodbridge N. Ferris in 1915. He returned to Traverse City, took up his previous occupation as a carpenter and lived another twenty-seven years, dying in 1942. Louis, the son who testified in his support, left town shortly after the trial and became a sailor on the Great Lakes. When he died, shortly after his father, he was captaining a car ferry out of Mackinaw City. Woodruff's obituary describes him as a member of one of the pioneering families on the Peninsula. It does not mention the conviction for murder. The one for Louis does not mention his father. That in outline is the factual basis of this novel. It, along with other incidental information culled from Woodruff's second divorce proceedings and other historical documents, is the raw material out of which I composed this fictional account.

While I have followed the broad outlines of this story, I have made a number of alterations. Most obviously, I have changed names to underscore the fact that this is a novel and not a report of the murder, so Woodruff Parmelee is now Sam Logan, and Julia Curtis is Margaret Cutter. I wanted to keep certain landmarks: the site of George Parmelee's Ridgewood Farm, the Congregational Church and its near neighbor the Old Mission Inn, all three in Old Mission Village, on the one hand, and the Curtis and Woodruff Parmelee farmhouses, still standing on Center Road about a mile and a half north of town, on the other. The distance between the Curtis and Woodruff Parmelee farms to Old Mission Village is about fifteen miles, and yet I wanted it to be reasonable for Sam to walk from his house to both Ridgewood and the church. So, I shrank the Peninsula from eighteen miles down to six to accommodate the needs of my narrative.

I kept George Parmelee alive so as to provide Sam with another layer of emotional stress: a father who insisted Sam farm rather than exercise his talent as a carpenter. I have no idea if that conflict has a basis in fact, but it appeals to me as a way to intensify and complicate

8

the story. For much the same reason, I gave Margaret a much younger brother, and had him drown, leaving her scarred. Isaiah, the Louis character, is older and romantically interested in his father's mistress. I incorporated certain facts, simply because they were too good to leave out. For example, from the divorce proceedings that ended Woodruff's second marriage to Euretta McDermotte, I picked up the wonderful tidbit that Woodruff had Mrs. Curtis, aided by Julia, do his family's laundry when Euretta would not, or could not, do that task. Both women testified as to the nature of the clothes in that laundry on Woodruff's behalf to demonstrate that he was adequately providing for his wife. On a more serious note, those same divorce proceedings provided several intense moments, which I have woven into the narrative. Conversely, though, I have given Woodruff's first wife, Eliza Brinkman, a very small (but structurally significant) role, when in fact her marriage to Woodruff was much longer and played a larger role in Woodruff's life.

Woodruff had three sons, two with Eliza and one with Euretta. The oldest, Louis, Isaiah in my story, is the star of the book. However, I did not find a part for Maurice, the second son of Eliza and Woodruff, so he does not appear in the story. I did provide a cameo for Carl, the child of Woodruff and Euretta, but of course I changed his name to Jonathan.

The details of my trial adhere closely to those reported from the actual courtroom. I have used some of those. But here is a most important point that illustrates how I depart from fact to create my fiction. At Woodruff's trial, he denied having a sexual relationship with Julia. Sam fully acknowledges his relationship with Margaret. His defense, therefore, rests entirely on his alibi, and his alibi stands or falls on the testimony of his son. This is the heart of my story. The contemporaneous newspaper report mentions Louis's support of his father's alibi in a sentence or two and then moves on as though that testimony were not terribly important, and perhaps it wasn't in the larger context of the trial. I, however, saw it as the primal conflict, and the driving force of my story. What does the son whose father is on trial for murder do, especially if he has reason to believe his father might actually be guilty, and furthermore is in love with the victim? That is the dilemma I gave to Isaiah.

One incident that occurred during the writing of this book creates for me an almost mystical aura. One evening I was imagining how the prosecutor would present his case, and I decided that he would prepare a map to show where the body was found and the path Woodruff would have taken to it. I wrote the scene, imagining what the map would look like. The very next day, I received a phone call from Mr. Robert Mitchell, of Mitchell and Associates, Surveyors in Grand Traverse County, telling me that the actual map, presented at trial, was hanging on his wall. He had rescued it from the garbage, and remembered reading something about my novel in progress, and so got in touch with me. That map now appears on pp. 12-13.

Rather than a retelling of the factual story, as my father-in-law thought I might produce, *Murder On Old Mission* has its roots in actuality but its fully developed form in the realm of the imagination. I trust that Walter, who died two years ago, would not have been disappointed.

—S.L., Old Mission, 2004

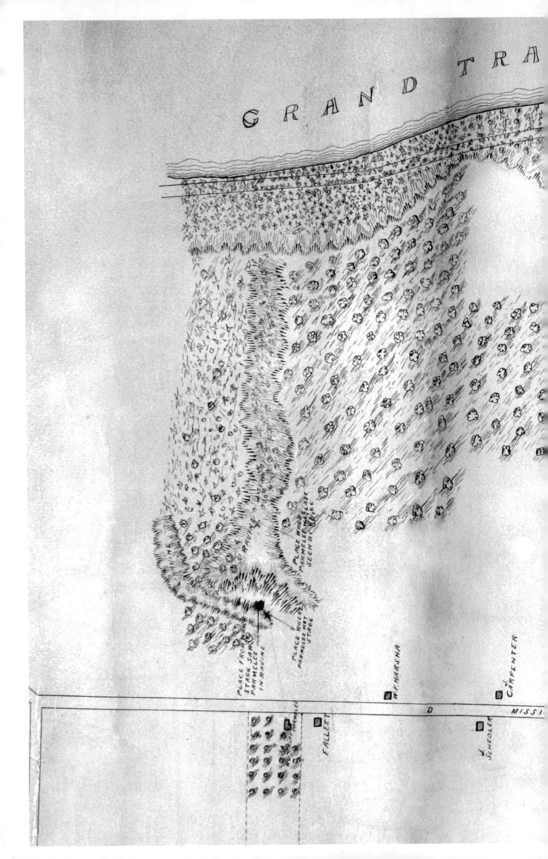

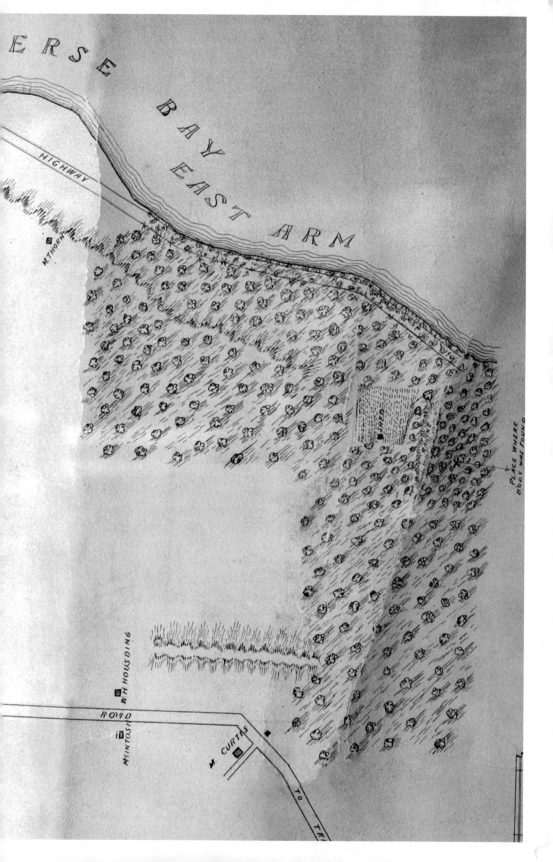

1

—◆—

I saiah Logan, fully dressed in his good suit, lay in his bed this Sunday morning waiting for the first rays of the sun. A mourning dove cooed outside of his window. He had not slept more than an hour or two. Saturday nights had become, of late, interminable. With his eyes closed, Margaret Cutter's face appeared as he would see it later that day. When he opened them, he stared at the cracked plaster of the thin wall that separated him from Sam Logan, his father. Isaiah's expression hardened. The dove, now perched on the window sill, cocked its head and then flew off.

He was now eighteen, the same age as Margaret, but he was sure she still thought of him as the boy who trailed after his father as he had done not so very long ago. At that time, she had looked through him as though he were no more than a shadow cast by the large and handsome figure of Sam Logan.

He reached under the bed and pulled out a small wooden box. He opened it and lifted out a handkerchief with his initials embroidered on it that his mother had given to him on the day she left. With short hair, bright blue eyes and a warm smile that she seemed to reserve for him, she had stood on the front porch, dry eyed, suitcase in hand, looking down at him as he asked her why she was leaving. Opening her mouth to speak, no words came out, until finally, she just shook her head, her eyes moist. He had thrown his arms around her waist, as high as he could reach, and asked her to stay just one more night so she could come to his bed as she did every night. He thought she wouldn't have to read him a story, just tuck him in, but she continued to shake her head, thrust the handkerchief into his hand, tears now welling in her eyes, and said, "Think of me, especially on Sundays when you go to meeting." He watched her climb into a buggy and stared after it until all he could see was the cloud of dust it left in its wake and still he stared. After a while, he imagined he heard the faraway whistle of the train leaving the station in Traverse City. He never saw his mother again, but every Sunday, just like this one, he remembered her parting words.

Isaiah stood in the doorway, drinking a cup of coffee. It would be time to leave soon. He heard his father's heavy tread coming down the steps. A big man, with broad shoulders, blue eyes and a shock of curly brown hair, just beginning to gray at the temples, Sam was wearing denim pants and a work shirt that had once been white, but was now gray and sweat stained. He held a baseball bat.

"I guess you're not going today," Isaiah said.

"I have other plans."

Isaiah downed the rest of his coffee.

"I'd better be going," he said.

"Say hello to Margaret for me. Tell her to come out and watch me play."

Sam flashed a bright smile, and swung the bat back and forth as though he were waiting for a pitch.

Isaiah closed the door behind him, harder than he had to, and he felt its frame shudder against the impact. He was long legged, like his father, but lanky, and he set out in long, deliberate strides that carried him to the crest of a hill a half mile north of his farm. He looked down at the tops of the fruit trees, all green, but not yet flaunting flowers, at the rows of corn just rising from the ground, at the lower foliage in the potato fields, everywhere the earth renewing itself and giving forth life energy. And then he gazed beyond the land to his right and to his left to the waters of the east and west arms of Grand Traverse Bay and the impenetrable surface in shades of blue ranging from turquoise near the shore to shimmering silver in the distance.

Maybe one day he would find an opportunity to tell her of his dream to leave this earthbound life behind and see where those waters would take him.

The white paint on the clapboard of the Methodist church was still fresh enough for angel's feet, Sarah Cutter liked to say. Its foundation stone read 1891, the same year her Benjamin had been born. The building sat on the west side of the road that curved toward Old Mission Harbor, and anybody who had the temerity to climb to the top of the bell tower would see the headland and the blue waters of the bay, and maybe even on a clear day, the horizon showing where the sky joined the great lake. It was altogether a beautiful spot, but Sarah no longer paid any attention to this picturesque country church. Instead, she walked past its front to the cemetery behind it.

The cemetery had been cut out of a stand of maples. The trees on its perimeter towered over it and blocked the sun most of the day except for an hour or two in the early morning. Even on the coldest winter day, after traveling for hours over the snow covered road in their horse and sleigh, Sarah made certain to arrive early enough to kneel at the grave while the rays of the sun still illuminated it. She would bring a small shovel to clear the snow away. She needed to read the inscription, sometimes even to run her fingers over the letters and numbers of the abbreviated life of Benjamin Cutter, born 1891, died 1893. These constituted the bare facts that she felt she must feel with her fingers, but they did not offer an explanation of cause. For that, she had turned to her husband, and when he failed to provide an adequate answer, she opened herself to the ineffable mysteries of God's will. But nothing she did softened the hard core of grief that had turned to anger against the deity Himself, then her husband, but most of all, her daughter Margaret.

Kneeling this morning in the leaves still covering the ground from last autumn, now that the snow had melted, she placed her forefinger on the wreath above the name and then onto the wings of the seraph that floated between clouds directly above the B. She had paid far too much for the engraving on the stone, she knew that, but she had not cared. Henry, as he usually did, stood off to one side. Margaret looked from one to the other. Her father nodded toward his wife, and Margaret walked to her mother's side. She placed her hand on her mother's shoulder. Sarah looked up, her eyes fierce.

"It's late for *your* caring," she said. "You should have been there that day, you know."

Margaret shook her head.

"That's not fair, or right."

"It's too late," Sarah repeated. She took Margaret's hand, and removed it from her shoulder.

"I can make it up to you," she said.

"Don't talk foolishness," Sarah said.

"I can," Margaret insisted, but her mother's face, drawn into a mask informed in equal parts by anger and grief, deterred her from continuing. Margaret turned instead to her father.

"A grandchild," she said to her father. "I'm talking about a grandchild. When I get married."

"With him?" Henry said. "Sam Logan?"

"Of course, who else would I mean?" She looked at her mother.

"You know it's not right, how she blames me," she said.

"It's her grief talking," Henry replied.

"Still, it's not right."

Sarah rose and took Henry's arm. They took a few steps toward the path that led to the entrance at the front of the church. Margaret did not follow. Her mother stopped.

"Come along," she said.

"In a moment," Margaret said.

"As you like," Sarah replied, and she and Henry continued onto the path.

Margaret knelt where her mother had been. Benjamin's grave was next to her two other brothers, both of whom had not lived long enough to be baptized. Their modest headstones rose barely six inches above the ground and simply said "Baby Cutter," and the year each was born and died.

But Benjamin was going to be different. He would make up for the loss of the other boys. He would be the male heir. Margaret remembered the joy in her parents' eyes when he reached his first birthday. And she, too, had rejoiced, relieved of the burden of being the girl child in a farming family. Benjamin continued to grow and to thrive, a bundle of energy and curiosity.

She, like her parents, struggled to make sense out of the death of a robust toddler whose eyes danced with the joy of new discovery. It was, of course, that curiosity that drew him to the creek behind their barn, into which he wandered when backs were turned, and there flailed his arms, unable to scream his distress with a mouth filled with water. Much too late hands plucked him up, laid him on the grass of the bank and pressed in futility against his chest. The question of whose back should not have been turned, whose eyes should not have left him, remained unanswered.

She heard a halting step shuffling through the leaves and coming toward her. Another mourner, she thought, and did not turn around. The steps stopped and a leaf floated past her and onto Benjamin's grave. She leaned forward, picked up the leaf, and crumpled it. She felt a hand squeeze her shoulder.

"Notice the dust," a deep bass voice said. "Just like the poor flesh of these babes, to dust have they returned much too soon, but their immortal souls are at peace." She waited for the hand to lift off her shoulder, but it remained.

"Minister Lapham," she said, "I thank you for those words."

She started to rise and the hand released its hold.

"The ground is hard and unforgiving," he said.

The bell tolled and he started to walk toward the rear door. She watched how he planted his one good leg, and then swung the other one after it. She turned back to the headstone and brought her lips to the rough stone. She imagined Benjamin lying beneath the ground and staring up at her, accusation in his eyes. When she stood up that image was still in her mind. That is why she did not notice the man in her path. He was short and round with a red face and a warm smile that seemed to suggest he knew people he was meeting for the first time.

"Excuse me," Frederick Gorschen said.

As the bell finished tolling, she hurried past him to stand at the back of the sanctuary. There was a center section with aisles separating it from narrower areas on either side, and at the front a wooden platform rose a foot off the floor. The pulpit there was a simple wooden lectern. The windows were clear as were the walls empty. Her parents were in their accustomed seats in the right side seating area. Still, Margaret waited. She saw her mother turn around to gaze at her, and she read the displeasure in Sarah's glance. As she started to walk toward her parents, the door behind the platform opened, and she hurried to slide into the seat next to her mother.

"You didn't expect that he would come, did you?" Sarah asked.

Before Margaret could answer, a thumping sound came from behind the open door, and first a wooden leg appeared, and then Minister Lapham strode onto the platform. Margaret cast a glance toward the seats in the center, which were reserved for the more prominent members of the congregation, such as Charles Logan, Sam's father. If Sam himself arrived, she would then move over, and he would have room to sit beside her, right where he belonged. Her parents' eyes turned to the minister, but Margaret searched the pews to her left to see if perhaps he had slipped in from the aisle on the other side of the center section and taken his seat. Her eyes stopped at the old man and woman directly across from her. Charles Logan looked at her as though he knew her, but she had never been introduced to him. Livonia leaned forward to see around her husband and offered a polite smile. Margaret saw that there were two seats open next to the old man.

Minister Hiram Lapham paged through his Bible to find the text he would base his teaching on. He opened his mouth to speak, but before his words began to fill the room, the front door creaked open. It hung a little askew on its hinges and announced its movements.

In her seat, Margaret wanted very much to turn to see if he had decided to come after all. Her mother seized her hand and nodded toward the minister. Still, she swiveled her head just enough to determine that the late arrival was not Sam, but his son Isaiah. The young man walked by her pew and looked at her. She willed the disappointment out of her expression. He seemed about to speak, but then contented himself with a quick movement of his head, a barely perceptible acknowledgment of her greeting. He found his seat next to his grandfather across from her family. The old man offered him a flicker of a smile, and then whispered a question into his ear. The young man shrugged, and his grandfather scowled.

Margaret had met Isaiah several years ago when he accompanied his father to her parents' house but now that he was grown she rarely saw him except on Sundays. Once or twice she had seen him in town in the company of his father, and he had been friendly enough in a kind of distant way, but there had been something in his manner that made her uncomfortable. She attributed his uneasiness with her to the unusual nature of his situation, being the child of her lover's first, failed marriage. In fact, she felt a kind of empathy toward him, both of them living with parents whose minds were elsewhere, hers with her dead brother in the ground, and his with a father who, she knew very well, spent little time thinking about his son.

Minister Lapham had not moved. Margaret watched as he rocked forward. She feared that he would lose his balance, and she began to raise her arms as though to try to catch him, but then he stepped back, and the sound of wood against wood rang loud in the silence. She looked about her and saw how almost everyone's face turned away from the sound as though they feared looking at the wooden leg protruding from the bottom of his black trousers.

"Let me tell you how the Almighty spoke to me that day thirty years ago in the Wilderness when He sent a cannon ball to take away my leg. The Lord knew He had to do something dramatic to get my attention, and He did. I was a poor sinner then, and the Lord reached out and saved me, and I'm here today to teach you how to grasp the hand the Lord holds out to you."

Listening, she wondered how indeed she could be saved, how her sins could be forgiven. Her brother and her lover. The images of one superimposed on the other jumbled before her, the little face as she imagined it in the water, her lover's smiling above her. She shut her ears. She must be damned. So how could she beg forgiveness when she knew she would continue in sin? She had vowed, sitting in this very seat, Sunday after Sunday, to either give him up or demand that he do the right thing. She could not, and he would not, although he never answered her directly, just a smile and a chuck under her chin as though she were a child asking for a piece of pie before dinner. As furious as it made her to be so treated, yet there was something in his eyes and the way his lips curled back that melted her resolve. Let the old, white haired man preach his heart out, his words only inflamed her to want to sin again, and yet again. If that way lay damnation, so be it.

Across from Margaret, Isaiah positioned his head at an angle to the minister so that it appeared he was listening to him while he studied his father's young mistress. He noted the red in her cheeks and questioned whether its source was religious enthusiasm. He chastised himself for not doing more than offering her a nod as though she were only an acquaintance and not the subject of his dreams every night. But her smile had been like an excess of chocolate, too sweet, and it rendered him unable to form a simple sentence. Now, as the preacher moved into his sermon about the need for sinners to cleanse themselves in the warm bath of God's holy word, he felt an irritability of such magnitude that he had to will himself to sit still when every fiber of his being desired nothing so much as a touch of her hand in his. Only by turning his thoughts to his father, with a kind of self satisfied superiority, could he quiet himself enough to endure the service. At least he was where he was supposed to be. And so was she, that is, not in his father's arms.

None of the players at the crude baseball field, carved out of a meadow between two hills, took notice that a quarter of a mile away, the fierce old preacher would be finishing his sermon. When they played on Saturday, they could expect fifteen or twenty spectators sprawled either on the hills or standing on the level area behind home plate. But on this Sunday, only two boys, one tall and lanky, wearing an engineer's cap, and the other chubby and bare-chested, plus a thin, barefooted girl of about twelve, dared skip meeting to watch the game. The boys stood on the first base line, aping the motions of the fielders and hitter. The girl sat behind third base and stared at Sam Logan on the pitcher's mound. There was a click and the ball spun behind the catcher.

A wooden leg placed itself in the ball's path and it stopped with a soft thump. The minister knelt with care to pick it up. The catcher called for the ball but Lapham held it. All the players stood with their eyes on the white haired minister.

"It is the Sabbath," Lapham said.

"We're just having a little relaxation on the Lord's Day, preacher," Sam said. He waited. The next batter strode toward home plate, taking practice swings with his bat.

"I'll take that," Lapham said.

The batter looked to Sam.

"Give it to him," Sam said.

Lapham approached the batter, and without a word grasped the bat. Sam stared at the preacher.

"Do you know which end of the bat to hold?" he called.

Lapham stared down at the bat. He held first the barrel end, with the handle pointing toward the sky, and then reversed his grasp and squeezed the handle.

"Well, sir, I am not quite certain of which end of this implement to hold," he said. "But I assure you I know in which direction lies heaven, and in which hell."

Logan tossed the ball a few feet into the air, and then caught it in his little glove.

"Do you want to take a swing?" he asked. "For the Lord's sake?"

"Don't blaspheme, young man," Lapham bellowed.

Sam walked half way to home plate.

"Out of respect to your age and your calling," he said, and he tossed the ball underhand.

Lapham followed the arc of its flight and then swung. He was rewarded by the solid thwack of bat against ball. He watched it soar high toward the hill at the edge of the outfield. The ball hit the ground two thirds the way up the hill and bounced into tall meadow grass. The outfielder trotted toward the spot where the ball had disappeared. The man from whom Lapham had taken the bat now strode to his side. He pointed toward first base.

"I can run it out for you," he said.

Lapham laid down the bat.

"I walk with the Lord," he said, and turned toward the path leading away from the field. The other man sprinted toward first base. By the time he was rounding third base, Lapham was reaching a point where the path curved. He did not look back as he disappeared around the curve. He heard the cheers as the runner crossed the plate before the throw. The umpire cried out "Safe," but Lapham just shook his head. "No, I don't think so," he muttered.

Later that afternoon, Sarah and Henry Cutter sat on the porch of their farmhouse. It was the house of a once prosperous farmer, with its drive lined with maples planted at even intervals and now reaching twenty five feet, its wraparound porch, and its diamond shaped woodwork separating the panes in the upper halves of the double hung windows. Margaret stepped through the front door and onto the porch. Henry looked at Sarah, and saw in her faded blue eyes the memory of the sparkle that now danced in his daughter's.

"I'm going berry picking with Sam," Margaret said. She swung her woven basket from side to side.

Sarah saw the flush on Margaret's cheek and frowned.

"Don't be late," she said.

"I won't. I'll be back in time for the cows."

"I brought her up sensible," Sarah said to her husband as Margaret fairly skipped away.

"I know you have. It's just that I've been thinking that maybe you never should have started doing their laundry when his wife took to her bed. That's when he started coming here."

"We needed the money, didn't we?"

He nodded.

"Well, there you have it," she said. "I can't do any more now. She's of age."

"Just barely."

"By a day, a week, or a year, she's of age." She shook her head. "I did what I could, and now it's in the hands of the Lord."

"I wonder about that," he replied, "after what happened to Benjamin. What's the good of all this church going?"

Her face darkened into something approaching rage.

"Do not blame the Lord for that, but thank him for what you still have."

He looked up toward the hill his daughter was approaching.

"That's what I'm thinking on."

"Think hard."

His expression was stone hard like the sun-baked soil beneath his feet. He sensed her anger, yes, but only as if it were reaching out like a hand stretching toward him from a great distance.

"I see you've brought your basket," Sam said. "We'd better put something in it so you can show what you and I were doing." Margaret blushed.

"It's all nonsense, isn't it? Just a show. My parents are not fooled."

His tone had been light and teasing. But now she saw his face darken, and his eyes narrow into sullen anger.

"As for them, they don't much care for me. I guess they have their reasons for believing what they need to believe."

She glanced at the ground. She had seen him in these moods before, but she insisted to herself that he was a man wronged, by family, and community, and that she alone understood him. She lifted her eyes to him, now, filled with her determination to soothe his hurt and prove her parents wrong.

"They will come around," she said.

"I don't think so."

"I know they will. And if they don't..."

"If they don't, what will you do? You're little more than a girl."

The remark was calculated to challenge her, and in so doing, make her even more his own. She seized his hands and held them to her breast, as though he could feel the strength of her heart beating.

"You know the answer to that."

She lay down on the grass and looked up at him. She reached behind her head and pulled out the comb that held her long, black hair up. It splayed down her back. She fluffed it and then shook her head until she felt it settle across her shoulders.

"The berries can wait," she said.

He lowered himself next to her.

"They can, but we won't."

The sun had begun to slide behind the hill. She stood up and smoothed her gown, checking it for grass stains on the back where they did not belong. She noted with satisfaction the traces of blueberry juice on the white trim of her sleeves and the basket overflowing with fruit. She offered him a particularly fat berry and smiled as he closed his front teeth on it so the juice dribbled down his chin. She caught it with her tongue.

"In the late afternoons," she said, "when it is hot, I sometimes go into the barn before dinner. It's cool in there. And the hay is comfortable."

"I remember," he said. "But ain't it also the place where that nigger sleeps?"

"He's got his place on the other side, doesn't he? And he generally doesn't come in until after supper." She took his hand. "It was nice for us that time," she insisted, "wasn't it?"

"The cows did get impatient," he smiled

"But you said they could wait. And they did."

"The barn," he said, "in the late afternoon. I do remember."

"I'll be thinking of you until then."

Her father was on the porch. He eyed the berries. She extended the basket toward him, and he took a handful.

"They're sweet," she said.

"No doubt not as sweet as him." He closed his hand into a fist and squeezed. He watched the juice flow between his fingers and then drip onto the plank flooring of the porch. The juice was blue like the berry, but it should have been red like blood, he thought, blood from his veins.

She walked into the house and through the kitchen to the backstairs, which led up to her room. Her mother was at the kitchen table, peeling potatoes. She placed her basket on the table. Her mother glanced at it.

"Could make a pie," she said. "Supper an hour."

24

"The cows," her father said as he entered the kitchen, "they're waiting on you."

The shadows had formed long and deep under the huge old oak where Isaiah had lain all day. Several times he had willed himself to stand, and even to take a step toward the house. All he had to do, he told himself, was steal his father's traveling case, pack it with his few clothes, a couple of shirts, socks, one clean set of underwear. But one step was all he could manage to take. He knew it was not fear of his father, or his own inability to find his way, that had him lie back down beneath the tree.

If only she had smiled at him, he would have the strength to stay on. Or if she had sneered at him, he could leave. But she had done neither, and so he waited as the sun slipped down. After a while his stomach demanded to be fed, but he ignored it and the ache went away. He closed his eyes, but sleep would not come. He would have to confront him, and when he did he would ask him the only question that mattered at this point.

It was an hour or so after dark when he heard his footsteps coming up the path to their house. The steps were irregular, and he could visualize his stumbling, shuffling gait. He would smell him before he saw him. He stood up and leaned against the tree. He heard his heavy breathing, and then the odor of beer, wafted toward him, and he stepped out to greet his father.

"Boy, what are you doing, coming at me like that?"

"I've been waiting for you."

"Just like I always said, who needs a dog when you got a son like you, just waiting for me to come home to be fed. Is that right, boy?"

"I ain't hungry."

His laugh deteriorated into a coughing fit.

"I'll bet you ain't."

"You been with her?"

"Now, you know what I was doing today." He stepped toward him and threw his arm around his son's shoulders. His voice turned gentle. "Come on into the house with me, and we'll talk about it while I fix us something to eat."

His father's strong arm urged him forward. He resisted for a moment and then yielded. Once inside, Sam lit the oil lamp in the kitchen. As its light filled the space around the table, Isaiah stared hard at his father's neck.

"What are you looking at?" Sam asked.

"A hair that didn't come from your head."

Sam reached up and grabbed a black hair eight or ten inches long. He laughed.

"Come on, eat up, boy. We've got work to do tomorrow."

"I said I ain't hungry."

"Then you can just watch me eat."

They sat on either end of the long oak table, which filled up almost their entire dining room. The house was a simple box, two floors, gables front and back and a sloping roof line that cut the walls of the two rooms upstairs. The father had the larger room, the son the smaller, an obvious distribution of living space that yet rankled the son as so many things did. Each irritation was like a pebble in his shoe, insignificant by itself, and yet collectively enough to cause him to hobble. The table was the only piece of furniture that survived the collapse of Sam's second marriage. He had made it for his new bride. Sam held his knife above his plate on which sat a half eaten steak and a baked potato. The plate in front of his son was empty.

"You know what that crazy bastard of a preacher did?" When Isaiah did not respond he continued. "He took the bat right out of Phil Jenkins' hand, stepped up to the plate. I threw him a lollipop and damned if he didn't hit it a mile. Then he just tossed the bat to the ground and walked away while Phil ran out his home run." He waited for Isaiah to say something, and when he didn't he turned his attention again to his food, sawing off a huge chunk of meat and bringing it to his mouth with the enthusiasm of a man whose appetites in all things governed his behavior. Isaiah stared at him while he chewed.

"You were with her later, weren't you?" Isaiah demanded.

"What of it?"

As Sam brought his knife down again to what was left of the steak, Isaiah gave voice to the question that had been turning over in his mind all day.

"Are you going to marry her?"

Sam cut a piece of coarse bread and smeared a gob of butter on it. It was warm and the oil in the butter dripped from the bread as he brought it to his mouth. He ran his tongue toward his chin but could not catch the oozing butter, which found a resting place in the cleft of his chin.

"No," he said. "But maybe you can." He lifted his napkin that was tied around his neck, and daubed at his chin.

Isaiah reddened, as though his father had somehow read the thoughts he permitted himself to enjoy each night as he lay beneath his thin cover on the lumpy mattress of his narrow bed, imagining Margaret next to him, her flesh warm against his.

"What are you talking about?" he demanded.

"Oh, nothing, just I see how you look at her. I'm not blind, you know."

"Then you are jealous."

Sam snorted.

"Of you, you pup. That's rich." He shoved his plate toward his son. "Take some food. A married man's got to work, and to work, he's got to eat."

Isaiah stretched his arm out so that his hand intercepted the plate half way between them. For a moment or two, they pushed against each other. It was apparent that Sam was stronger and that if he chose he could force the plate to his son's side of the table. But then he just shrugged and withdrew his hand.

"It's a sin to waste the Lord's good food," he said. "You can ask your grandfather about that, or maybe that preacher."

Isaiah pulled the plate toward him and sawed off a piece of meat. He put it in his mouth and chewed it with elaborate care. After he swallowed it, he pushed it back to the middle of the table.

"I wouldn't want to displease the Lord," he said.

"In this house," his father replied, "you're looking at him. Just you remember that." He drew the plate to him and again attacked the meat.

Isaiah rose and took a few steps away from the table. He could not get the thought out of his mind even though he knew it was out of the question. Still, he felt he had to give it voice.

"You didn't mean that, did you, about me and her, about getting married."

Sam stared at his son. His expression seemed unable to choose between scorn or amusement, and yet there was something else there, as well, something that bordered on the serious.

"It might just come to that," he said. Then he smiled. "I don't expect you'd mind getting damaged goods, anyway, would you? The way you look at her."

Isaiah started to frame a reply, but then he stomped out of the room. He could not say what he wanted, because he was ashamed to admit that his father was right. He would marry her. Damaged goods. He could save her.

That night sitting in the lobby of the Old Mission Inn, Frederick Gorschen turned the pages of the local weekly newspaper until he found an article that recommended cold baths for reducing fever. He always checked such medical advice columns in whatever newspaper he was reading, parsley and butter for wounds, lime water for burns, oil of cinnamon for hiccups, all these competitors for his bottles of laudanum, his opium based cure-all. He did not, of course, know if it cured a headache, or halted the ravages of tuberculosis, but he had seen it quiet bawling babies, and it was certainly preferable to all those remedies he read about in cases where calming the nerves was the desired result. He heard a thumping approach him, and he glanced over the newspaper, which he was holding within a few inches of his eyes.

"Sure is small print in those papers, isn't it?"

He laid the paper down and looked up into the blue eyes of the minister.

"Yes," he answered, "and my eyes are not what they used to be, I'm afraid. "

"Nor mine," Lapham said with a small laugh. The minister reached into his pocket and removed his reading glasses. "Try these," he said.

Frederick put on the glasses and saw the type magnified enough to read easily.

"These would suit me fine," he said. Lapham extended his hand, and Frederick handed him the glasses. "I had the pleasure, sir," Frederick said, "of hearing you in church today."

Lapham beamed.

"And what is it you do, if I might ask? I do not recall seeing you at service before."

"I'm a traveling man," Frederick replied. He laid the newspaper on the table and pointed to the column on remedies he had been scanning. "These sir, do not deliver what they promise. Old wives' tales, that's all, oil and butter, and parsley."

"You have something better, no doubt," Lapham said.

Frederick reached into his pocket and pulled out a small bottle of a clear liquid.

"Frederick's Elixir," he said, "product of the most up to date scientific knowledge." He leaned forward and lowered his voice. "I hope you will forgive my impudence, but I have been thinking that you might be interested in my product. To ease the discomfort of your..." he glanced in the direction of the minister's stump.

"Oh, that sir, there is no feeling in a piece of wood."

"But where it joins the flesh, does it not chafe sometimes."

"Chafe, why yes."

Frederick pushed the bottle across the table.

"I charge a dollar for this little bottle, and it is a bargain at that price. The young ladies particularly favor it. To settle their nerves."

"What is in your, uh, elixir?"

"Laudanum, and a couple of my own special ingredients to ease it on its way down."

"And what does it promise?"

"Relief," Frederick smiled, "relief."

"For that I have the good book. If I feel pain still, all these years later, it is but an affliction sent me by the Lord, to remind me of my mission." He pushed the bottle back.

"Ah the good book," Frederick said. "Of course". He scooped up the bottle and dropped it back into his pocket. "I will be certain to remember that."

2

———•———

argaret sat up in bed. She had not slept more than a few minutes waiting for it to come, and it had not. She lifted the thin blanket and lowered her eyes to see, but her white nightgown was as it had been when she put it on the night before. She rolled to one side and peeked at the place on the mattress where she had been lying, but again there was no sign. She pressed her hands to her belly and felt a twinge. Maybe everything would be all right after all.

She reached under her pillow for the page she had cut out of the *Montgomery Ward Catalog* just the night before. Smoothing the wrinkled paper, a shy smile formed on her lips, and she tucked it into her pocket, away from the prying eyes of her mother. If she met him today, she would show it to him.

She went to the chicken coop to gather eggs. She had never before thought of this activity as anything more than a chore. But today she handled each egg with a certain deference, and looked at the hens with new curiosity.

Putting the basket on the table in the corner of the kitchen, she took her seat at the breakfast table, feeling her mother's eyes on her, sure Sarah was reading her thoughts. Margaret lowered her eyes, and heard but did not see her father come in from milking the cows. She smelled the manure clinging to his boots, sensed an exchange of glances between her parents. Part of her wanted very much to unburden herself.

"Good morning, Margaret." Her father's voice was as it always was, quiet and yet infused with tension.

"Good morning," she replied and lifted her eyes to his. They held each other's gaze. She could read nothing in his face, and yet she was almost certain that her mother suspected the truth, and if she did, she would have shared it with her father. "Was Henrietta generous today?"

He almost smiled.

"You know she likes your hands better than mine. Always did."

"It's not just the cow that likes her hands." Her mother spoke in a dry monotone that exposed rather than hid her anger.

"There's nothing wrong with a woman having a gentle touch," Margaret said. Staring hard at her mother, she then glanced at her father, wondering whether they ever touched each other lovingly any more. She did not think so.

Sarah expelled her breath, but said nothing. Instead, she pointed toward the wood stove.

"There's coffee ready, if you want it." She scraped scrambled eggs from a skillet onto her husband's plate and her own. "You can cook up some eggs for yourself. I expect you know where to find them."

"I'll just have the coffee," Margaret replied. "I'm not feeling very hungry. I didn't sleep very well last night."

"No wonder," her mother replied and leaned toward her. She ran her hard fingers around the rings under her daughter's eyes. For a moment Margaret thought she might offer a word or two of comfort, of implicit recognition, but instead her mother sat back down, chopped off a piece of egg and brought it to her mouth.

Margaret poured herself a cup of coffee and sipped it. She enjoyed how it singed her lips and tongue.

"I'm going for a walk," she said.

"The garden needs hoeing," her mother said.

"I know," she replied. "At lunch time, I mean." She looked out of the window that faced the property behind the house. She saw one of the hired hands but because she was looking into the sun, she could not tell which one it was. Her mother followed her glance.

"Your father has other work for them to do, men's work. You can send them in for their breakfast."

"I see," she said. She took her sun bonnet off the hook next to the rear door and stepped out into onto the screened porch. She looked through the mesh of the screen at the hired hand. She still could not see who it was, but then she noted that the other was approaching. She glanced back at the kitchen table, but her father had made no move to get up. She tied the bonnet beneath her chin and pushed open the screen door that led down four steps to the garden. Her hoe rested against the house next to the stairs and she grasped it harder than was necessary and took a step toward the garden. In front of her stood the two hired hands, Edward Franklin, his fair skin reddened by the sun and Jim Waters, sweat already coating his black skin.

"You're wanted inside for breakfast, and then my father will tell you where he wants you to work."

"Yes'm," they muttered together.

"I need to hoe," she said.

Edward lifted his eyes.

"It would seem so," he said.

She blushed, ashamed at having felt obliged to say something so obviously silly.

"Well, go on then, you are waited for in the house."

They both looked at her. She thought for a moment that they had not understood, and she started to repeat herself when they nodded and shuffled off toward the house in that gait used by men accustomed to being told what to do. To walk with any speed would suggest more than a coerced acquiescence. She watched their backs, feeling she would not breathe freely until they were out of her sight and she was alone to work in the garden. She waited until the door closed behind them, and then she turned to the rows of beans. She knelt beside one plant burdened with blooms. She ran her finger over the nub where a flower had fallen off and a bean had begun to grow. She continued kneeling for a few minutes, feeling the mixture of excitement and sadness. She plucked the incipient bean and raised it to her mouth. She tasted it with her tongue, and then tossed it onto the ground. She picked up her hoe, and swung it with full force. The blade came down and lifted a weed next to the plant. She swung again, even a bit harder, and this time the blade cut the plant she had been examining. She paused, knowing how angry her father would be at the loss of even one plant. Then, she resumed her hoeing, taking better aim as she worked her way through the rows.

Isaiah lay in his bed and listened to the scraping of the chair in his father's room. His mind refused to move beyond the image created in it by the contemptuous "damaged goods," as though she were a garment besmirched with a stain. He was angry, of course, but also inflamed by the idea that she had been had. The fact that the man who had had her was his father only added to his confusion and anger.

"Get up, boy," his father stood in the doorway. The sun cast a pale, pink glow on Sam's white dress shirt. The slant of light coming in through the window on the east side of his room also softened his father's hard features. He looked almost kind. "I've got business that will take me some time," Sam said. "You will be on your own today, so find something useful to do. Maybe you can work on clearing that brush off the new road we started."

Isaiah swung his feet off the bed as though to rise, and watched his father's back start to descend the stairs. He stayed in bed listening for the front door to close. When it did, he lay back down and stared at the ceiling, following a crack in the plaster to the corner where it disappeared into a spider web. A fly, newly caught, struggled to free itself. Isaiah watched as it tried to move its wings, until exhausted it ceased its motions. He wondered what it was thinking, if it were capable of thought. Did it see the spider moving silently up a strand of the web toward it? Isaiah felt he understood the fly's plight, although the spider trapping him had just left him in the web, which was, in part, of his own construction.

Sam stretched his legs into a ground swallowing stride. Wilson, his neighbor, had borrowed Chester, his Percheron , so he had a long walk with an unpleasant task at its end. He approached the church, quiet now, and walked up the steps to the front door. He tried the handle, and it turned. Walking inside, he sat down in the front pew, lit by the sun coming in through the windows on the south end. The last time he had been in this building, sitting in this very seat, a different preacher, a young man, was in the pulpit. But it was not the sermon, he now recalled. Instead, he heard again the battered piano played with such grace that it almost sounded in tune, for at the keyboard was his wife. He smiled for a moment at the recollection until he saw again her tight lips pursed in disapproval, her nose twitching like a scared animal's, as though about to be attacked by the whiskey fumes on his breath. He tried to bring back the more pleasant memory of her sweet voice rising above the ragged tones of the congregation, but he could not.

He turned his attention to the interview he now faced. He did not know why he had been summoned, and that was the right word, as though he were a peasant being called to the court of the lord, never mind that he was the lord's son. He felt the need for divine intervention. His head bowed, he tried to formulate a prayer. He moved his lips but the words remained locked in his mind. It is not easy to pray for the death of your father.

Jim and Edward carried their scythes over their shoulders and walked toward the hay field. Edward increased his pace to move ahead of Jim.

"You be in a hurry?" Jim asked.

Edward did not answer, nor did he turn his head toward Jim.

"Whatcha runnin' away from, boy? I bet I know."

"You don't know nothin'," Edward muttered.

"I seen you, boy, I seen how you lookin' at her."

Edward stopped and waited. When Jim shuffled up to his side, Edward grabbed his shoulders and spun him so that they were facing in the same direction. Jim's shirt was hanging out of his trousers, and Edward lifted its back up until he could see the scars. He held the shirt up with one hand while he traced the angry ridges on the black skin with the other. Jim stood as patient as a child being examined for head lice.

"Just how did you get those?" Edward demanded.

"Why, boy, just doin' what you be doin'."

"I ain't nobody's boy, specially yours."

"That's a fact."

"Well?"

"What? Oh, that. I lookin' at a pretty young girl one day."

"You lucky then."

"You ever been whupped?"

"No."

"Then you don't know what you talkin' about."

"Whip better than a rope over a tree branch, I guess."

Jim turned to face Edward. As he did, he brought his right arm against Edward's left hand, which was still holding his shirt. Edward seized Jim's wrist, and for a moment the two men stood like two rams about to butt heads. Then, Jim opened his mouth and roared his laughter through the space where his front teeth should have been.

"Ain't we a pair," he demanded.

Edward permitted a grin to occupy his face for a second. Then, he pulled his hand away and stepped back.

"I ain't no part of a pair with you."

"No, you ain't. You just one man that's lookin' to get hisself into a piss pot of trouble. Damned good thing your skin is white."

They reached the hayfield. The bearded heads of rye grass stirred in a warm breeze. Edward turned to the southeast corner of the field, and brought his scythe down in a violent motion that almost left him corkscrewed into the ground. Jim watched, and then made his way to the northwest corner. He pulled the stub of a rolled cigarette out of his pocket, lit it, and for a moment considered the possibility of dropping the match into the dry grass, just to see how long it would take his fellow laborer to smell the smoke. But he shook the match until it went out and then ground it under the heel of his boot. He smoked his cigarette until he couldn't hold it any longer and then knelt to put it out in the hard dirt at the edge of the field. He stood, and began to swing his scythe with slow, powerful movements. He would not tire for a long time, for with every stroke he imagined the blade cutting through the neck of a white man who had struck him without cause, or who had humiliated him in one of a thousand ways. There were many such heads to take off, and he smiled as he worked.

Meanwhile, across the field, Edward leaned over panting, looking back over the section of the field he had already leveled.

"Damned nigger," he muttered. "What does he know about me?" The question calmed him, and he resumed work.

Sam turned the last bend and stopped. There before him was the house he had grown up in. He stared at the gabled roof on the southern end, at the double windows there on the second floor, and knew that behind those windows was once his spacious room. He recalled how it looked out over the wraparound, covered porch, and how he would hear the buzz of adult conversation float up to him on summer evenings when he lay awake in his bed.

He closed his eyes and he was once again in that room, beneath his blankets on a cold winter morning, feeling warm and secure. He snapped his eyes open, and all he felt was the cold. He looked at the path, lined with maples every thirty feet, and walked to where it ended at a white picket fence that enclosed the front yard. Beyond the fence gate another path began, which split into a horseshoe, each branch leading to steps up onto the porch. The entrance off the porch on the left opened into a hall that led to the dining room. The one on the right gave to another hall at the end of which was his father's study, where he was quite sure the old man was waiting behind his desk, either going over his books or finding an appropriate place in his Bible that offered just the right words with which to whip him. The path he had taken followed the fence around to the right to a farm gate. He swung this open and walked parallel to the south side of the house to a dirt track that led to the servant's and tradesman's entrance at the rear of the house. He went in through this door, and almost tripped over the servant woman who was on her knees washing the floor. She stared at his dusty shoes without looking up and a frown began to form on her face. Then, she lifted her eyes.

"I wasn't expecting to see you," she said.

"Why, Mary, is that how you greet me?"

She stood up. She was a woman in her sixties, her hair in a tight, gray bun.

"Well, how are you, young Mr. Logan?"

"I'm here to see my father."

"Did he send for you, then?"

"Yes."

"I think he's in his study."

"I thought so."

"Did you get the poor Cutter girl in trouble? Her father was here not long ago."

"No, but she did steal my heart, is all."

"It's a wonder she could find it."

"Ah, Mary, you're the one who found it, and you've kept it ever since."

"Pshaw. Go on with you."

"It's true. That's why I've gone from woman to woman since then, hoping to find another like you."

"Your father waits," she said. She knelt again to scrub the floor. She pointed to the area behind her, which glistened with water. "Be careful of my clean floor."

He found Charles Logan, as he expected, sitting behind his desk. What he had not anticipated was that his father would be holding not a pen, nor his Bible, but a baseball bat. Charles Logan looked up over his spectacles. He extended the bat toward Sam.

"Do you remember this one?"

Sam took the bat and ran his fingers over it. His fingers recalled the grain, and they searched for the one spot where he had not been able to smooth it around a knot. He found the imperfection, a very slight bump on the otherwise smooth surface.

"We still have that lathe on which you turned that out in the barn."

"I didn't know you were so sentimental," Sam replied, "particularly about something I made when I was no more than twelve, something used for pleasure rather than honest labor."

"You were eleven, and sentiment had little to do with it. Others know how to use a lathe, and it is a fine piece of equipment. Remember I bought it."

"You didn't call me here to remind me about making that bat."

"No, I didn't. But I thought it might be well to remind you that you have an honest trade, one even that our Lord practiced, though I fear the blasphemy of relating your carpentry to His."

"I'm sure I don't think of Jesus when I'm working a piece of wood."

"Or any other time, as far as I can tell."

Sam felt the usual exasperation rise.

"Well," he said.

"Yes, you want to know the occasion. Henry Cutter was here two weeks ago on the first of the month, asking for an extension on his loan payment, which I was happy to give him. He's a good man, working hard, but not wisely. But then he said you are involved with his daughter." He frowned and shook his head in disbelief as though he had just observed an extraordinary example of the frailty of fallen human nature.

Sam shrugged.

"What of it? She's of age."

"What of it!" Charles snapped. "You have had two children with two different wives and both times people were looking at the calendar when the babies were born. Now you are involved with a mere girl who used to wash your ex-wife's underwear."

"Crude, father. I didn't know you had it in you. But I think it was her mother who took in my laundry." He paused at the memory, how he and Isaiah would tote their dirty clothes to the Cutters, the pragmatic acceptance of the mother, the yearning in the eyes of the daughter. "Eustace would have her clothes clean. Was I to wash them?"

Charles nodded for a moment, and then the frown deepened. "I don't suppose you and Eustace will reconcile after what happened on the way to town that day."

"I was in a temper, over money. I would have her back. I said so."

"But she has no inclination. She attends service in town now, and leads the choir there as she used to here. She is happy."

Sam kept his face calm, even as anger rose in him. Eustace and her delicate condition, and her singing lessons, and her inability to cook properly or wash his clothes, and that medicine she was always drinking for her nerves.

"Do you ever see your new son?" his father asked.

"She does not permit it."

"You are making your payments."

"Yes."

Charles clasped his hands behind his back.

"Is the girl pregnant?"

"No, not that I know of."

"Do you intend to marry her?" He did not wait for an answer. "I tell you I won't have you again disgrace our family name. I will leave everything to Isaiah."

"You would do that?"

"Do it? I have already done so." He opened his desk drawer and pulled out a document. "This is my will. I drew this up after Mr. Cutter was here. It leaves you no more than that baseball bat. Then your mother came to me and pleaded your case. I thought long and hard, and I prayed for guidance."

Sam ran his hand up and down the barrel of the bat. He saw it crashing against his father's skull.

"And what," Sam asked, "did the Lord say to you?"

The old man's eyes stayed on the bat.

"I searched my heart, with the Lord's help, and at your mother's urging, I decided to give you one more chance." He pulled another document out of the drawer. "I drew up this version leaving my estate to you."

Sam walked to the double windows that looked out over the gently rolling hills of his father's home farm. Row upon row of cherry trees reached in lines straight as ruler drawn toward a last declivity leading to a beach and the blue waters of the bay he swam in summer mornings when he was young. He heard his father's step and then felt his hand on his shoulder. He knew that hand was roughened from years of farm work, but its touch today was gentle, as was his voice.

"Lovely, isn't it?" The hand tightened its grip and the tone hardened. "I haven't signed either will, and won't until this affair with Cutter's daughter is settled. If I am satisfied that you have decided to put your considerable energies into farming, rather than women, I will sign the second version. Even then I'm afraid I'd be making a mistake, but you are my only son. But if not, if you persist in letting your appetites guide you, I'll sign the first."

Sam shook off his father's hand.

"May I not marry who I choose?"

"To be sure. That is your choice." He pointed out the window. "That or the girl."

"So that's the way it is."

"Yes, you can thank your mother for this last opportunity."

"I didn't ask her."

"You didn't have to. She has a foolish heart where you are concerned. She does not want to see you in the state you deserve. Penniless. Two divorces, several drunken brawls, hitting your neighbor because he said your fence line was on his property, and nights spent in jail from which my hard coin had to release you." Charles sat down and put the two documents back into the desk drawer. He pulled out a ledger book.

"Your mother would like to see you," he said.

Sam sat on the porch in the wicker chair next to his mother. On the table between them was a pitcher of lemonade, beading. He lifted his glass to his lips.

"I must thank you," he said.

Livonia Logan began to shake her head, but then nodded. She was a thin, elegant woman with white hair that had turned when she was not forty, and green eyes that spoke of a passion that age had failed to diminish. Her face was lined but lightly, as though an artist had moved a pencil just over the surface of her skin. She reached for his hand. Her own was cool, in part because of the cold lemonade she had been sipping from the crystal glass, but most because of the discipline she exercised over her emotions. For now she was looking at the wayward son whom she continued to love with an unqualified affection.

"Yes," she said, "you must, once more."

"I don't suppose I should promise, in the way of appreciation..."

"No, you shouldn't."

He smiled, and her heart melted as it always did. She could not remember the last time her husband had smiled. On their wedding night, he had approached her with passion, yes, but it was the passion of a businessman closing a profitable deal, or perhaps closer to home, a farmer harvesting an abundant crop, with such emotion he had taken her until he grunted his satisfaction and rolled off her to stare at the ceiling for several moments. Then he had gotten down off their bed, a fine bed it was, all shiny brass and feather mattress, ordered right out of the *Sears Roebuck Catalog,* he had let her choose it, for he had told her the governance of the house was to be her responsibility, and he had beckoned her with a gesture of his arm to join her on his knees so he could offer a benediction of their union. She had refused, thinking the minister had already asked God's blessing and she did not feel obliged to consecrate the act he had just performed on her with no more feeling than if he had been poking a hole in the ground to plant one of his trees. She had waited for him to explode at her, to demand her obedience to him, but he did not. He simply shut his eyes and moved his lips in silent prayer while she lay watching him. Then he had risen, and straightened his clothes. He had not cared to undress more than was necessary while she had lain beneath the cover in her satin nightgown, which he, without ceremony, had lifted out of his way. He brushed his hair and indicated that it was too early for sleep, and he had his plans to attend to. Later, she had come down stairs to find him poring over the map of his new property, her dowry, drawing lines against a ruler, measured to scale, indicating where he would plant his trees.

He had not lifted his head to acknowledge her presence, and so she slept alone, even when his body slid into his side of the bed. Through the years of their marriage, she had from time to time seen signs of warmth in him, like a candle flickering on a cold night, but then the feeling would fade as soon as it showed itself, as though, she figured, he feared revealing in any way that he might need her for comfort or support or validation. For that, he had his ledger books, and the growing pile of maps, one for each of the farm lands he acquired.

But Sam, her only child, was a different matter. He was conceived in the dark of the winter as a result of one of their infrequent, and increasingly mechanical couplings, but born in the full sun of the summer, and as though the warmth of the season itself had informed the boy's blood he had all the love of life that his father lacked and his mother could barely remember herself having. So, she would forgive him almost anything as long as he beamed his smile on her, as he now did, and she did not want him to ruin the moment with a promise they both knew he could never keep. She wanted to say, darling, just smile, but she did not.

"I would not have you landless and penniless," she said instead.

"Ah, now, can I not live as tenant to my son the landlord?" he replied.

"You need not, if you tend to what I have obtained for you."

"And if I do not?"

She shrugged.

"I can do no more."

"He looks well."

"He is. He lives with his trees and the fruit they produce."

He downed his lemonade. As the liquid slid over his teeth he winced and turned his head to the side.

"What's the matter?" she asked.

He shrugged.

"Nothing much."

She placed her cool, elegant hand on his cheek.

"A tooth?"

He nodded.

"You should take care of it. Do you have something at home?"

"I think so. A bottle of laudanum Eustace left behind."

"I can get you something from the house, if you don't."

"Don't fuss, mother." He stood, and leaned over her to kiss her on the cheek. She rose and threw her arms about him.

"Oh, my Sam, try, just a little, for me."

"I will," he said. And until he walked out the door, he believed he would.

At the window above, her husband was staring toward the road where he watched Sam's figure recede. He had been unable to attend to the ledger with his usual concentration after his son left. He had not expected to be so troubled by his decision. Anyone would agree, surely, that it was based on sound business principles. He had never been one to throw good money after bad, and Sam simply was irredeemably bad. He had no faith that his son would manage to profit from the generosity that Livonia had squeezed out of him, and now he even scoffed at that word to describe an act so ill advised and so contrary to his customary practices. No, he hadn't believed his son's assurances concerning that girl. He had seen the almost invisible tightening of his jaw before he opened his mouth to lie. Not that he could claim to have provided his son much of a model concerning wedded bliss, no, he wouldn't say that. He and Livonia understood each other, but that was all. The love that should have grown between them had wilted before it could flower. He supposed, when he thought about it, that he must blame himself, for he could not in honesty find much to fault in her, but now as he looked out over his lands stretching almost as far as his eye could see he could say that at least he had given her that, and it was not his fault that the son on whom she doted was not worthy of succeeding to it.

He closed the ledger and took out the two drafts of his will. He read one, and then the other. He felt very weary, and laid his head down on the desk.

Margaret's uneaten lunch remained in the basket at her side, next to her hoe. She sat on the bank of the brook that sprang through the surface at the top of a hill overlooking her family's farm and then ran down toward the road before it curved back behind their barn. She was sitting in the shade of a willow on a slight elevation that gave her a view of the road that led north to Sam and Isaiah's farm. Perhaps he would come to see her today. She had taken off her shoes so that she could let the cold water run over her feet. Her heels dugs into the pebbled stream bed but the water was so shallow it barely reached her ankles. It would be very hard to drown here. But when the water slowed into its channel by the barn it deepened to more than a foot or so, almost waist high on a toddler such as her brother had been.

She looked at her reflection shimmering in the water, and she saw looking back her young girl's face. And when she stared harder to see if she could more clearly discern her own features, the shape in the water was now that of a little body lying face down in water deep enough to slide over it without being diverted. She pressed her fingers to her belly and thought she felt the life inside her afloat in its watery bed.

It was all too much. When her brother died, she had been in town visiting a girlfriend with whose family she boarded while attending school in the winter. She had overstayed her visit by half a day. She returned, filled with girlish enthusiasm, eager to share her gossip with her mother, only to find her father hard at work with a plane, smoothing the edges of the little coffin while her mother, her face wet from sweat and tears, sat and watched. Margaret had never heard her parents discuss the events leading up to the accident that made her, again, an only child. Nor had she asked for details. Just the simple fact that she lived and he did not made her guilty.

She had in her hand the advertisement for a baby carriage from the catalog but she felt her hopes of walking in town with her baby in such a carriage and with her husband at her side were as flimsy as the paper of the page she had ripped out. The thought of joining her little dead brother had its appeal, a symmetry that seemed right. Or maybe what pleased was the idea of revenge, let her mother now grieve for her as well. She looked hard at the water to see what it might tell her, and she did not hear the approaching horse and buggy.

Frederick reined in his mare to a walk. He could see the blue of the brook as it meandered down from the top of the hill to where a woman was sitting. He put on the brake and got down. He headed for the willow. She looked up at him as if in a dream.

"My little brother drowned in this stream," she said. "Not here, of course. There." She pointed down the hill. "The water runs right behind our barn. You can just see a little line of blue. That is it."

Frederick recognized her as the one he had seen at the cemetery.

"Drowned you say."

She nodded.

"That is a terrible thing."

She folded her hands over her belly. "I think it was only yesterday and that I should have been there. And now it's even harder."

"I can see how troubled you are." He reached into his pocket. "I can help you. With what's in this bottle."

"Can it bring back my brother?"

"No."

"Can it make my true love true?"

"No."

She shrugged.

"Then why should I be interested?"

He held out the bottle.

"I call it Frederick's Special Elixir. Take this as a sample. If you like what it does, I will come back with a full one, which I will sell to you at a reduced price of fifty cents."

"Frederick, is that your name, then?"

He bowed.

"At your service."

She took the bottle from him and held it up between her thumb and forefinger to the sunlight.

"Laudanum? I saw a bottle like this at a party once."

"Yes."

"How much should I take."

"Take just a teaspoon, no more, when you are thinking about your little brother, or your lover."

She clasped her fingers about the bottle.

"I'm not saying I'll try it."

"I will be back," he said. "You can tell me then."

After he left, she opened the bottle and wet her lips with the liquid it contained. She could not tell if the elixir had any effect. When she looked in the water it seemed to swirl, although there was no wind today. She put the cork back in the bottle and picked up her hoe. It would not do to have her mother or father come looking for her, wondering why she was taking her midday break at this spot and for so long a time. She removed the cloth from her basket and brought the drumstick to her mouth. She took one bite and then tossed it into the water, followed by the thick slab of bread. She put the bottle in her pocket, covered the basket again, picked up her hoe and headed down the hill.

Sam walked until he reached the crest of a ridge and could look back at his father's house. He had been covering the distance from the house in great strides. He was forty three years old and when he wanted to make love he had to find a spot outdoors, or sneak into her father's barn like he was again a teenager like his own son. If he married her he would have to live with her in his own, little house, not the grand one he had just left. His own house depressed him. It was poorly built, and he wanted to rip it down and start over again, if only he had the time and the money. He could still smell the chickens that the previous owner had permitted to share his living space. He had spent hours scraping the dried effluvia off the planked floor and finally, in despair, had bought a cheap broadloom and cut it to the size and less than square shape of the room. Still, the odors rose through it, and the dirt encrusted on the windows blocked the sun's light. He had brought her there one evening when Isaiah was visiting his grandfather. His bed had sagged beneath them in a manner that seemed to augur its imminent collapse.   He found himself leery of movement as he positioned himself between her thighs.

He started down the ridge, happy to lose sight of the house. His feet seemed to know where they were going. His tooth throbbed. That old bastard, he thought. What can I do? Not marry that girl, what is he thinking? If he knew anything about baseball he would know that you only get three strikes, and I've already had two.

As he walked his arms began to swing an imaginary bat, back and forth with growing intensity as the rage and despair rose in him. The problem is, he thought, she has gone and fallen in love with me. I may not know much about farming, or making or holding onto money, but I do know women, and I see how she looks at me. Well, what the hell was I to do, live like a monk, and she right there. She used to follow me around like a little puppy dog when I brought Eustace's laundry over. I knew what was in her head. Was I supposed to refuse a gift so freely, so warmly offered? And now Isaiah is mooning over her, and the old man knows just how to twist the knife.   I should have let that boy have her, one puppy dog for another.

3

———

Margaret continued to swing the hoe. The calluses on her hands dribbled blood. She squeezed the handle and lifted it high over her head yet again, and she brought it down even though her back and shoulder muscles screamed their protest. She had already cleared the bean field but she was retracing her steps and hacking down the stray weeds she had missed. In one pocket she had the page of the catalog; in the other was the bottle of laudanum. If she did not have the opportunity to see him and show him the one, she would perhaps take comfort in the other. In the meantime, she continued to swing her hoe. The sweat gathered around her eyes so that she saw the plants as though they were underwater, and yet she did not stop. In the back of her mind, where she had forced it, was the thought that she might be able to work herself out of her problem, induce an end to it simply by pushing her body past its limit.

She put down her hoe and walked over to the stream in the shadow of the barn. She splashed water onto her sweat streaked face. The water was cool, but it still stung the places on her palms where her calluses had opened up. She placed her aching hands into the water and moved them about until she found soft mud between the rocks on the stream bed. Then she leaned forward and put her whole head into the water. As she lifted her face out of the water she took a long gulp.

She walked back into the bean field and picked up her hoe. Halfway through the field she noticed one milkweed vine near a bean plant. With weary determination she lifted her hoe one more time and was about to bring it down when she saw something move on the vine. She peered more closely and saw the orange wings framed in dark blue lines with contrasting white spots of the monarch butterfly. It was newly emerged from its chrysalis and seemed to be drying its wings in the sun. As she watched, the butterfly flapped its wings several times, and then fluttered away. She knelt and snapped the stalk of the milk-weed vine until its white fluid oozed onto her open palms. She rubbed it onto the raw skin and then onto her fingers.

At the edge of the potato field, some distance away, Edward watched. He sank to the ground and pulled off a beetle. He sliced through its shell with his thumbnail. The beetle emitted its life's fluid and Edward brought his finger to his lips, and he drank. He was still on his knees when she approached. He looked up and wiped his lips with the back of his hand.

"Your father is looking for you," he muttered. "He says he came out to this field expecting to find you."

"I was getting a drink from the stream. Tell him I'm going to take a rest in the barn where it is cool. He must have seen that the field is done."

"He did. He said so."

"Do you have anything else to tell me?"

"No." His eyes moved from her face, still damp with perspi-ration and then down to her waist where her bloodstained hands were clasped on the handle of the hoe.

"Then be on your way."

"Yes'm, but you ought to tend to your hands."

She did not reply. She wanted very much for him to leave.

"Next time, ask me and I'll do the weeding for you." He held out his rough, dirt stained hands. His fingers were short and powerful. "See, work can't do no harm to these hands."

"I see. Now on your way."

He dropped his hands to his side, and ambled off toward the house.

She made her way to the barn. She was sure that the child had been conceived on a bed of hay while the cows below had mooed their impatience waiting for their swollen udders to be relieved. She heard the animals shuffling about below. It was not yet time for them. It was time for him. There were two lofts in the barn, one on each side, both heavy with hay. But on the loft on the north side the hay had been hollowed out in the middle to create a sleeping nook for Jim. She leaned the ladder against the hay on the south side loft and climbed to the top. She lay down and closed her eyes. Perhaps he would come if she thought about him hard enough. She tried but soon the exhaustion of the day softened her resolve and too weary to think another thought, she fell asleep.

Isaiah laid down his ax and looked behind him at the brush he had cleared. It was slow, tedious work, but he enjoyed the physical exertion. He focused on bringing the ax head down on the stalks as close to the ground as he could manage. Often the force of his blow sank the ax into the earth, and then he yanked it out. The road he and his father were clearing ran from their property toward her family's before angling off to the shore of West Bay where the new resort was being built. The road would bring in income. It also led almost to her door.

He took one more swing at the brush in front of a grand old white birch. Then he shouldered his ax and walked southwestward over the uncleared ground toward her farm. He pulled his ankles free from vines, and he swatted at the mosquitos that buzzed about his head. He walked with a sense of urgency. He was sure that his father was on his way to visit her, and he felt he must intercept him. If he did not, something terrible would happen, although he could not say what he feared.

He veered into the woods as he crossed onto Cutter property and made his way between the trees until they thinned as the ground ascended to the hill overlooking the farm. He paused just for a second by the stream to wash his face and slake his thirst. He focused on the narrow footpath that circled back to the east where it joined the north south road. A speck was approaching, and he knew it was his father. He watched the speck get larger, and soon recognized Sam's familiar, loose jointed stride.

He started down the hill in a trot and then into a stumbling run. He extended the ax like a tightrope walker sweeping the air with his long pole. He reached the foot of the hill and bent over to catch his breath. He jabbed the head of the ax into the ground in front of him and pushed himself upright. He had came to a stop with his back to the oncoming figure. When he turned around, his father was upon him. Sam looked at the ax, at his son's sweat streaked face and startled expression. Sam shifted his gaze first toward the Cutter farm and then the woods leading to his.

"Did you get lost?" he asked. "Or did you have some other idea in mind for that ax?"

"Neither," Isaiah said. "I just forgot I was carrying it."

"Were you surveying where our road should go?"

"No."

"I didn't think so."

"I was coming to find you."

"With an ax in your hand and Lord knows what in your brain."

"Before you could get to her, I thought I could stop you."

Sam seized the ax handle. Isaiah held it for a moment, and then relented.

"From doing what?"

Isaiah remembered her long black hair on Sam's shirt.

"I don't know. Maybe you can tell me."

"Maybe it's something you want to do yourself."

An image of Margaret, her arms open for him, flashed into Isaiah's mind. Of course, that was in his mind now. It always was. But he shook his head.

"It's you I'm thinking about," he said.

"Better go back to work on that road."

"While you're with her? First my mother, then Eustace, and now her. She's only a girl and you're a..."

"Man," Sam interrupted, "which you ain't. But I'll tell you what. Why don't you just come along with me. To make sure I don't do something awful."

He handed the ax back to Isaiah, and then he started walking toward the Cutter barn   Isaiah followed, feeling like a dog that had been whipped before he even had a chance to bare his fangs or give out a good growl. He couldn't just turn and go home, and he couldn't let his father win so absolutely, and yet with every step he took, matching his pace to Sam's, he felt frustrated and ridiculous.

Margaret dreamed she was holding her baby to her breast. She was sitting at the table and there was another figure across from her. Although she was in the light, shadows obscured her companion. She strained to see through the gloom. She opened her mouth to inquire but when she moved her lips no words came out. There was a candle on the table and she shoved it toward the other. She knew it must be him, just having come up from the shop. They were living in town, now, for after all he was not a farmer, and he should never have pretended he was, no, he had opened a cabinet making shop on the street that fronted the river, and he was prospering. They were living upstairs, over the shop, and the pungent aroma of freshly cut wood rose through the floor boards as she heard the rasp of his plane and the stroke of his saw. At dinner, he would tell her his day's activities, and she would offer little stories about their child's progress. Perhaps this was the day he took his first step, she was sure the child must be a boy, or maybe he had made a sound that she could believe was a word. He held the baby while she cleared the dishes, and then they walked in the evening. The baby looked so fine in his carriage as they greeted their neighbors strolling near the water's edge.

But the figure across from the table now picked up the candle and held it against a face, and she saw the disapproving and pained expression not of Sam but of her father. He did not talk, but instead just shook his head from side to side. She held out the baby, his grandson to him, but her father sat with his arms against his side, and then began to shrink until he was gone, replaced by her dead baby brother, Benjamin, his face bloated. She tried to tell Benjamin that she was sorry he was dead, but he opened his mouth in a silent howl. She scooped up the baby and ran out the door. She heard someone calling her name, a familiar voice. Shaking herself awake she found herself in the barn. There below her Sam stood. She was about to jump down and into his arms when she noticed the other figure slumping against the door, and why on earth was Isaiah here?

Starting down the wooden ladder that leaned against the loft of hay, she caught her dress on a stalk that protruded from the pile and reached between her legs. She lowered her foot to the next rung and her dress rose above her knee. She became aware of what she must look like from below. If he were there alone, she would not mind, she would even, perhaps, let her hem ride a little higher to show him a flash of her thigh before brushing it down with one hand while holding on to the ladder upright with the other. But Isaiah lurking in the corner with his sad, angry eyes, was another matter. She leaned back and away from the pile and grabbed at the stalk. Her dress, though, was of a loose weave, well worn, and the stalk had found a space between the fibers. She swung further back and yanked the stalk. Her motion caused the ladder to move toward the vertical. The stalk came free, and her dress settled back to her ankles, but the ladder now began a slow movement back. She threw her weight forward, and for a moment the ladder hovered. She heard him yell "Hold on," and then the ladder fell back against the hay pile. She looked down to see him standing right below her with a big grin on his face. His boy, too, had taken a few steps toward her, and now stood staring at both of them.

"Alright, now," he said. "Come on down, and take your time."

She knew she was flushed and took a deep breath. She didn't want him to see her looking like a red faced schoolgirl when she told him. After all, she was certainly a woman now, the proof was growing in her belly, and he would see that. How could he not? She lowered herself, one careful rung on the ladder after another, and with each step she held her breath and then exhaled through clenched teeth until her feet found the plank floor of the barn. She relaxed her mouth into a bright smile.

"You remembered where I would be, didn't you?" She positioned herself so that his large frame was directly in front of her. She could see him and only him, not the sullen young man still standing in the shadow of the doorway. She held his eyes, searching for assurance. He offered none. He shifted his glance from her back to the ladder, which he still held with one hand. She knew then, before he spoke, that he would not listen, or worse that he would be angry, and yet she must tell him.

"Yes," he said, simply, "I remembered. And I wanted very much to talk with you." He looked back over his shoulder at his son. "Isaiah has come, too," he added.

"I can see that," she replied. "But why?"

"He wants to protect you. From me." His voice regained some of its usual mocking confidence. "Isn't that so, boy?"

Isaiah wanted to step forward, to erase that contemptuous smile from his father's face, to tell her she was just another in a line of conquests that stretched back to his own mother and before, and would, if unchecked, continue into the indefinite future with or without her. But no, even if she recognized the beginning of the line, and all the women leading to her, she would somehow believe it would stop with her. He strained to lift his foot, but it felt anchored to the barn floor. He pulled it up and then the other until he was within a few feet of them.

He kept his eyes on his father's hand. He had once felt its force in a brutal, short backhanded blow that sent him sprawling into a corner, his eyes stinging with humiliation, his face throbbing with dull pain. He was still holding the ax, and his fingers tightened around the wood of its handle. He imagined its sharp blade cleaving his father's head. But it felt so very heavy that he realized he could not lift it far enough.

"Isaiah, you must go home," Margaret said. "I need to talk with your father. In private."

"No, you mustn't," Isaiah replied.

Sam spun around to face his son. Isaiah stumbled back, his eyes on Sam's hands, but they remained at his sides. When they did move, they were gentle. Almost like the parody of a bird taking wing, they settled on Isaiah's shoulders and pulled the boy into an embrace. He whispered in his ear.

"It's alright, boy. You just go and bide outside while I take care of some business here."

"Business is it?" Isaiah muttered.

"As a matter of fact, it is. And when it's done I think I may have something to tell you that you'll want to hear. Now, go on out and wait." His hands slid down to Isaiah's biceps, and then pushed him toward the door, not with violence, but with implacable purpose. Isaiah permitted himself to be pushed, soothed perhaps by the voice he could neither trust nor deny.

"I *will* be waiting for you," he said, "as long as it takes." He turned and hoisted the ax to his shoulder. Now, with his back to his father, it felt light.

Sam watched his son retreat through the open barn door. Once Isaiah was outside, Sam strolled over to the door and slid it shut. As the heavy door met its stop, there was a loud thud and then it shuddered. Sam reached up and ran his thumb over the sharp blade of the ax. He shook his head.

"Don't know what to do with that boy," he said.

"Forget him," Margaret said, "and come here."

He took a step forward and hesitated. Her invitation was clear, but so was the purpose with which he had sought her this afternoon. She reached out her arms.

"There," she said, as he walked into her embrace. "That is much better." She pulled him toward her in a way that was not exactly loving. She wanted him to feel her swelling belly against his. Then he would understand, and she would not have to explain. She held him against her for a few moments, and when she stepped back she took his hand and pressed it against her stomach. He was happy to oblige her, and then slid his hand lower.

She began to protest that was not what she had in mind, but, in fact, that was what was on her mind whenever she saw him, even more so since she realized that part of him was inside of her. The motion of his hand caused her dress to slide up, and in so doing she sensed more than she heard the wrinkling of the paper of the advertisement she had in her pocket. She pulled back.

"We need to talk," she said.

He shook his head. The feel of her body against him had driven his plans out of his head. The fact that Isaiah waited in helpless rage outside, with his ax stuck in the barn door, only made the prospect of lying with her the sweeter.

"Later," he said. "We will talk after."

The mooing of the cows roused them. Margaret was lying with her head on his chest, listening, half awake, half dreaming, to his heartbeat. She sat up with a start and began straightening her clothes. He lay still with his hands clasped behind his head watching her. He could almost imagine what it would be like to wake up so every morning. He would linger in bed while she dressed, and then when the aroma of coffee reached him he would find the clothes he had tossed aside in the hurry of the night before and get up. It was a pleasing picture. It was, however, not to be.

She leaned over him, her breasts still uncovered as his fingers had left them. She let them brush his lips. He bestowed a languorous kiss on first one, and then the other. She permitted herself a few more moments of pleasure but then pulled away. She reached into her pocket and removed the carefully folded advertisement. She placed it on his bare chest, and then lifted his hand to feel it.

"The cows," she said.

He nodded and lifted the piece of paper. She did not have the courage to wait to see what his expression would be. She climbed down off the hay and finished buttoning her dress. She moved the first cow into the milking stanchion. It turned its large head to look at her for a moment, and then started munching the hay from the feeding trough it could just reach by straining its neck. She pulled the milking stool close, positioned the pail, and reached for the swollen udders. Her own breasts seemed to ache in sympathy as she squeezed. She imagined him above her now, on the hay, examining the picture of the carriage, looking down at her with tenderness as her hands worked the udders and the milk splashed warmly into the pail.

He did glance down at her and was filled for the moment with the allure of the idyll, imagining her the milkmaid and he the prosperous landowner. When his thoughts drifted, however, toward picturing her as his wife he heard his father's words and saw the sadness in his mother's face as she bade him farewell, and he closed his eyes until he was sure that when he opened them again and stared at Margaret he would be reminded of what he must do. His breath stirred the paper on his chest and it slid into the hay next to him. He felt too lazy to pick it up, but then he saw her look at him out of the corner of her eye. She turned away and continued to squeeze the udder until the only sound in the barn was the splash of milk into the pail. He reached for the paper without taking his eyes from her. His fingers groped through the hay, feeling its prickly texture until they landed on the paper. Bringing it up, he positioned it so that sunlight coming through cracks in the barn wall fell on it. He studied the image on the paper. His stomach clenched. He looked again at the paper and crumpled it, dropping it on the hay next to him, as though to dismiss the idea it represented. She kept her eyes on the cow's udders and continued to milk.

"What do you think?" she asked.

"What about?"

"What you were just looking at."

"I'm thinking that you took an awful roundabout way to tell me."

"I was afraid of what you might think."

He didn't respond, then realized with a start that the thought of fathering a baby with her appealed to him. She seemed to see something in his expression that revealed this feeling, which he could not suppress. Rising from the milking stool she beckoned him, and he climbed down the ladder and stood next to her.

She took his hand and pressed it against her belly.

"Feel," she said.

He nodded.

"We will be fine," she said.

"My father..." he began. She pressed her fingers to his lips.

"Hush," she said. "Do not think about him. He will come around when he sees our baby, when he holds it in his arms."

"Sure, he will," he said, his voice filled with a specious conviction that he knew she would take for genuine. He had wanted to tell her. He had made up his mind to play this one straight, and yet his will had deserted him with unexpected alacrity the moment she looked at him with such determination to make things right. He knew that he

54

was trapped between her undeserved love for him and the equally un-merited cold wrath of his own father whose approval he still sought even now. He wanted to hurl his frustration to the heavens to see if God were listening and watching. Instead, he took her into his arms, and murmured in her ear, again, "Sure he will."

The cow she had been milking turned its large head toward her and mooed.

"You had better finish what you started," he said, happy for the interruption, so banal and yet so necessary to snap his feet back to the ground. "I'd better go fetch Isaiah and take him on home."

"You did mean what you said."

"I did."

She sat down again on the stool. She radiated joy.

"When will you speak to my father? We should not wait long."

"Soon," he said, with his hand on the door. He pushed it open and stepped outside. He breathed in the air that had a touch of a chill. Isaiah was sitting with his back against the barn wall. Her father was approaching from the house. He glanced from one to the other. Then, he saw the ax still embedded in the door. He pulled once, and when it did not give, he yanked harder. It came free, and he held it out to Isaiah. With a sudden clarity he knew what he must do. He felt that perhaps God had been listening after all.

"Take the ax, son," he said. "We need to make things right with Mr. Cutter."

Isaiah held out his hand, palm up, and accepted the ax. He closed his fingers around it and glanced back over his shoulder at the gash in the barn door.

"That's right," Sam said, "you did that. And what we're going to say is that you did it in an exuberance of love."

"I heard you in there," Isaiah said. He let the ax swing to his side and then using just his wrist and forearm muscles, he flipped it up so that its shaft rested against his shoulder. He appeared ready to strike.

"You'd like to, wouldn't you boy," his father said. "But you won't. Because I'm the one that always helps you, ever since your mother abandoned you when you were little, and I don't mean about that door, but what's on the other side of it, right now, all ready for you as soon as you can show you're man enough."

Isaiah tightened his hands on the ax handle.

"I could show that right now."

"But then all you'd get is a jail cell."

They both stood silent as Henry Cutter approached. Sam leaned toward Isaiah.

"You just follow my lead. You'll do it, now, if you ever want to have her," he said in a harsh whisper. Then he turned toward Henry, and extended his hand.

"Well, hello, Henry."

Henry grasped Sam's hand in his own, and he squeezed so that the other could feel the strength of his grip, understand the honest work that had hardened his flesh.

"I spoke to your father about my payment," Henry said.

Sam shook his head and smiled.

"Why I wouldn't know anything about that Henry. That business is between you and my father. I've come on another errand." His eyes shifted toward the closed barn door.

Henry followed his glance and clenched his jaws. So he was here about Margaret. He would not give his permission. He would not suffer that indignity. His eyes still held the barn door, imagining he saw through it to his daughter sitting on her milk stool, her hands on Henrietta, and the cow responding as she never did for him, or anybody else. There was a gentleness in his daughter, he knew, and the thought of her with this man in front of him was simply not tolerable. As he stared at the barn door, he noticed the gash and took a step or two toward it. Sam placed his hand on Henry's shoulder.

"That's part of what I want to talk to you about. Well, not exactly, see, but as a matter of coincidence."

Henry took Sam's hand off of his shoulder.

"You're not making any sense," he said.

"I know," Sam replied. "But I will. See, that's my boy Isaiah over there, holding onto the ax that until a little while ago was in your barn door. He didn't mean any harm, and I'll be happy to pay you for the damage. Or we can include it in the details we got to negotiate."

"Sam, what are you talking about?"

"Marriage, I'm talking about your daughter and my son."

"The ax?"

"Just excitement."

"You taking me for a fool, Sam Logan." He pointed to his eyes. "I've seen you. And my daughter."

"I won't lie to you. Not when you have seen what you have. But there are reasons I can't marry her. And now that she needs to get married..."

"You don't mean..."

Sam nodded with a slow deliberate motion as though the effort to lift his chin off his chest against the weight of what he had to say exceeded his strength.

"Yes."

"You've brought disgrace down on my family. Just like you did those others, twice before." Henry's voice trembled.

"I don't deny it. But I've come to offer you a solution, not the best, I grant you, but in this imperfect world, not the worst. My son loves her."

"And she?"

"Pshaw. She's a girl. She thinks she loves me." He stepped closer to Henry. "And my father has a soft spot in his heart for Isaiah, his only grandson, if you know what I mean."

"I see," Henry replied. "But Margaret is strong willed. She will want to marry you."

"But do you want her to marry me?"

Henry shook his head.

"I didn't think so," Sam smiled. "You'll have to talk sense to her." Sam beckoned to Isaiah. "Come here son, and tell Mr. Cutter your intentions."

Isaiah, who had been listening as though to a text written in some exotic language tried to collect his thoughts enough to say something intelligible. He still had the ax on his shoulder.

"I'm sorry about your door," he managed to say. He glanced at his father who was offering him the opportunity to have what he most craved, and yet he wanted to kill him for the manner in which he was bestowing this gift upon him. He stood, his tongue unable to move, paralyzed between lust and rage. "I do love your daughter," he said.

The barn door opened and Margaret strolled out blinking in the rays of the setting sun. She shielded her eyes, and then trotted toward the three men. She seized Sam's arm, her eyes bright.

"Did you tell him?" she asked.

He saw the hope in her eyes, and for a moment he weakened, but then he said, "Your father needs to talk with you. Come Isaiah." He took a step, but she held his arm. He unwrapped her fingers. "Talk to your father," he said.

"When will..." she began, and reached for him again.

"Soon," he said. "Talk to your father." Isaiah hadn't moved. His eyes were fastened on her. He thought he could feel her heat, the still warm embers from her embrace of his father. He imagined that the two fathers would walk off together, negotiate whatever they had to, and then he would have her. He had thought he would be too proud to have the leftovers from his father's feast, but now he knew how wrong he had been.

She felt Isaiah's eyes on her, and remembered how he had gazed at her each time they had met in the past, even on those long ago days when he trailed behind his father carrying the soiled linens that she and her mother would wash. She had thought only of Sam, and Isaiah only of her, and here they were now in this most ridiculous situation. She could only wonder what her lover had been talking about with her father. The look in his eyes, though, told her that they had not been discussing her marriage to Sam. She felt the yearning of Isaiah as a physical force reaching toward her, and now she saw something new in his glance, something approaching hope. She shuddered with the realization.

Sam took his son's arm. With gentle but irresistible force he turned Isaiah toward the road that would lead them home.

They sat around the table, mother, father, and daughter, each looking past the others, their supper untouched on the plates in front of them. Henry held his fork suspended over the stew meat. Sarah's fingers clenched and unclenched around the empty air. Margaret held her arms rigid by her sides, fighting the impulse to stand and walk through the door and into the darkness. The only sound was the steady tick tock of the mantle clock. It chimed the hour, seven o'clock. It had been half past six when they sat down, and nobody had yet completed a sentence. Henry tried again.

"Do you have no feelings for the boy?" he asked.

Margaret shook her head.

"She only thinks about him who put a baby into her belly," Sarah said. "Isn't that so?"

"Yes."

"Good. That is said," Sarah replied. The sun was just about down, its rays coming level through the window and onto her hard face, reddening her cheeks and seeming to drive her eyes back into her head. She turned away from the light, and her eyes now flashed hard and cold. "Natural enough," she said. "My daughter is just a natural woman who hasn't ever, and won't ever, feel the Lord touch her soul. No, not like that man has touched something inside her."

Margaret lowered her head, resigned to endure the verbal whipping, which stung as hard as any cut of a whip. She waited, eyes closed, for her mother to continue.

58

"I've done," Sarah said. "You can lift your head, if it is not too heavy."

The memory of her mother, softer and kinder, before her brother died, floated up in her mind like a distant lullaby. She raised her head, and lifted her hands, palms up, towards her mother.

"What would you have me do?" she asked.

"Have you do?" Sarah asked. "It's what you have already done."

"Now, mother," Henry tried. "What's past is past. We need to consider what to do now."

Sarah stiffened.

"I washed that man's linen. And his wife's. I cleansed the stains left by their unclean bodies."

"Yes, you did," Henry agreed. "But that is not what we must talk about. Our grandchild will be a bastard."

"That he will," Sarah agreed.

"Unless we act now."

"What we do now changes nothing."

"I won't marry that boy," Margaret said. "I'm sure you did not understand what Sam was saying." She rose.

"Sit back down," Henry said.

"Never mind her," his wife replied. "Leave her to me. Now you tell me again what that man is offering."

"I won't listen," Margaret said.

"You needn't. It doesn't concern you," Sarah said.

"Doesn't concern me?"

Sarah pressed her hand against Margaret's belly.

"All that concerns you is in there. You took care of that, well enough, and now your father and I have to fix things up as best we can." She stood and walked to the shelf and picked up an oil lamp. She pulled out the wick, lit it, and set it on the table. She sat down.

Margaret swiped at the tears as they began to trickle down her face.

"You two can talk all you want. I'm old enough to have this baby, I'm old enough to decide my own life."

She walked out of the house and toward the barn, her feet finding the path in the darkness. She looked back over her shoulder and saw in the pale glow of the lamp her mother and father leaning toward each other in earnest conversation. She realized they hadn't talked that way since Benjamin drowned. She felt as alone as a single star in a black sky. Inside the barn, she found her way in the dark to the ladder and up to the loft where they had lain. She climbed the ladder and lay down on their spot. She fancied she still could feel his body's heat on the hay. She ran her fingers through the hay as though it were his hair, first brushing it from his forehead and then running down across the stubble on his cheek to his chest and still lower over his belly and then stopped. Beneath her outstretched fingers lay a crumpled piece of paper, torn from the pages of a catalog. She seized it and squeezed, and as she did his imagined warmth dissipated as though before a cold wind.

At this moment, he was sitting at his own dinner table, chewing his meat, and using his knife to roll the peas on his plate in a line. He swallowed the meat and brought his fork next to the peas. His son watched.

"Imagine these peas are your chances at happiness. They all look pretty much the same, but let's suppose this one here," he pointed to one at the end of the line, "is actually the sweetest." He stabbed a pea at the other end of the line and ate it. "You get a chance at each one of these, one at a time, and nobody ever gets to try them all." Then he brought his knife through the line and dispersed the peas. "Now, you don't know which one is that special one. Maybe it's this one, or that one. You can eat them one by one, but maybe you will die before you ever find that special one."

"And you. Did you ever find that one?"

He pushed the remaining peas onto his fork and swallowed them

"That's my problem. They all tasted sweet to me."

"That's why you can leave her. So you just wait for the next one."

"Exactly," Sam said. "For me, there's always another sweet pea in the garden."

Isaiah had been working things over in his mind all the way home. There were a couple of pieces of the puzzle missing. To be sure, he had witnessed his father's inability to remain satisfied with one woman, starting with his own mother. It was not surprising, then, that he would tire of Margaret.

"Why now?" he asked.

Sam shrugged.

"I suppose you will need to know. I was hoping we could get this deal done soon enough so you would think you were the father of your new brother or sister."

Isaiah leaned back in his chair. So, there was one of the pieces. He had the puzzle almost in place. There was one more.

"You would have let me think that?"

"What's the harm?"

Isaiah shook his head.

"I don't suppose you would see any." He rolled the peas on his plate onto his fork and ate them, one fork fill after another, sucking them down more than he chewed them. When he had finished, he began to think he knew what the last piece was.

"That morning, the other day, when you were dressed in your good suit, where were you going?"

"It wasn't to church, although I did stop there on the way."

Isaiah saw the dusty road leading past the church, saw his father stepping into the deserted building, and knew that he would do so in preparation for meeting only one person.

"What did grandfather have to say?" he asked.

"He inquired about my affection for the girl, my dedication to his empire, my thoughts about you. Now do you see?"

Isaiah rose.

"Yes."

"Will you do it?" Sam asked.

Isaiah felt the rush of power. For the first time he was in control. His father needed his cooperation.

"I do not know," he said.

Sam sawed off another piece of meat and chewed it deliberately. When he finished, he reached across the table and pulled Isaiah's plate toward him. He sliced the meat Isaiah had left untouched.

"Don't take too long, thinking about it," he said. "There are always other candidates for the job, if you don't want it."

Isaiah lay in his bed. He heard the front door slam behind his father. The quick rush of power had dissipated with that last comment, hurled at him with seeming indifference from a mouth full of the food he had chosen not to eat.

Edward and Jim trudged back toward the barn.

"I'm too tired to eat anything," Jim said. "I'll just turn in."

"Don't you ever want to have a proper bed?" Edward asked.

"Hay's good enough for me. 'Sides the boss don't give me no nice little room in his house like he give you, so where that bed supposed to be?"

Edward shrugged.

"I was just asking."

"Don't make no sense askin' about stuff like that," Jim muttered and received a hunch shouldered shrug for the start of a reply and a stream of saliva spat into the dust for its end. Edward watched as Jim walked to the door and ran his fingers over the gash left by Isaiah's ax. He slid the heavy door open and took a tentative step in. He imagined he saw a shape, ax in hand, in the shadows inside and he froze.

"Who's there?" he cried out.

Something stirred in the hay. Jim took a step back and motioned to Edward.

"You hear that?" he asked.

Edward shook his head, and then came up beside Jim. Again, something seemed to be moving in the hay.

"Probably a cat," Edward said. "You ain't afraid of a cat, are you?"

"Haven't I been sleepin' in this barn and wouldn't I know what lives in here with me? That old barn cat don't make noise like that. How's he supposed to be catching mice if he be makin' all that fuss?"

They both stood and listened for a few moments.

"Whatever it is ain't there no more," Edward said. "You goin' in?"

"Sure thing," Jim said, but he did not move.

"I'm beat," Edward replied. He looked toward the path that led to the farmhouse.

"Pleasant dreams," he said.

Jim nodded but did not turn around. He focused on that spot in the hay loft where he had heard the noise. He felt sure he had also seen something there. He took one cautious step in that direction and then another. He stood still. Something rubbed against his leg. He looked down and saw the cat.

"I told you so," Edward called to him.

Jim shrugged.

"Shut the door, will ya?"

The door slid shut and the interior of the barn darkened. Just enough light came through the gash in the door and the small windows to either side of it to enable him to see the shape on the loft. He walked across to the wall where tools were hung. His hand found a pick ax.

"You can come on down, whoever you is," he said.

Up in the loft, Margaret sat up.

"It's only me," she said.

"What you doin' up there? You tryin' to get me killed? Somebody see you in here with me, what they gonna think?"

"I'd tell anybody I just forgot and fell asleep."

"Just get on out."

She came down the ladder.

"I needed to be in here," she said, when she was standing before him. "I can't explain why."

"Don't you think I know?" he asked. "I smell you two when I come in here."

He saw her hand coming but stood still as her open palm smacked against his cheek. She pulled it down as though she had touched something scalding hot.

"I'm sorry..." she began, and then turned. "You shouldn't have said that. About us." She strode to the door and started to slide it open, but it would not move. He was at her side and put his weight against the door and it moved. He sensed the warmth of her body. He remembered that other woman so long ago and recalled the stripes on his back. Still, he took her arm.

She pulled her arm away, and then touched his cheek where she had slapped him.

"I"m sorry," she said.

She walked out and took the path toward her house.

In the shadow of a tree some twenty yards away, Edward watched. His face formed a black scowl. He watched her until he could no longer see her, and still he stood.

4

———

With each passing day, spring asserted its presence. The warming air muscled aside the remnants of winter's chill. The crops yearned toward the sun and grew with increasing vigor. Strawberries reddened on their vines, and the farmers spread netting over them to protect them from the birds seeking an easy meal. It was still too early for corn, and blossoms were just beginning to show on the cherry trees. People's faces wore smiles as they felt the promise of the season, the affirmation of new life after the annihilation of winter's frigid white blanket.

Margaret's mother stood at the stove frying eggs. Her father held the back door open while he talked to Edward and Jim.

"They've eaten," her mother said, with a gesture toward the hands. "You can clean up after them."

Margaret picked up their plates and scraped off bits of eggs and bread into a bucket.

"I'll feed this to the chickens," she said.

Her father returned to the table.

Each looked at the other but nobody spoke. Sarah served a plate to Margaret and Henry. She stood by the stove with her skillet in one hand, and a cup of coffee in the other. She took a sip. Margaret scooped up a fork full of egg. Henry held his fork over his plate.

"We should make plans," Sarah said in a flat, cold tone. "We do not have time. People will know anyway, but we don't have to show them your belly sticking out."

"Mother's right," Henry added, his voice a little warmer. "I can speak to Minister Lapham this week."

"No, don't," Margaret replied. "I will look for him today at the church."

Henry clasped his hands in front of him next to his plate.

"You don't mean you've changed your mind," he said.

"Look at her," Sarah said. "Fire in her eyes and her chin jutting out, just like when she was a child and she set her mind to do something we told her not to do."

"Well, what is it?" Henry said. His eyes betrayed his hope.

"I will talk to him about my wedding to Isaiah."

Henry looked at Sarah.

"See, Mother, she's coming around."

"I'm going to tell him," Margaret continued, "that I will not need him to perform that ceremony because there won't be any such wedding."

Henry unclasped his hands and gripped the edge of the table hard enough to cause the veins in his forearms to bulge.

"You're going to have his bastard, are you?"

"No," Margaret replied. "I'm going to have his baby."

"Without the sanction of marriage? Without a proper ceremony before God?" Sarah demanded. She lifted up the skillet and then put it down with a clang on the side of the cast iron stove.

Margaret got up.

"I've no need for breakfast today."

"The cows," Sarah said. "They're waiting on you."

"I can tend to them this morning," Henry said.

"I'll do my chores," Margaret replied. "Like I always do."

"Yes," Sarah said, "just like you always do."

"We need to finish clearing that road to the resort," Sam said.

Isaiah nodded. He had just about lost the power of speech in his father's presence, so consumed was he with a potent mixture, equal parts of rage, humiliation, and jealousy. Of course, he could rid himself of all of it, if only he would give up the idea of having her, but that was as likely as would be his deciding that he no longer required air to breathe. Now, sitting on the wooden step leading up to their porch, he just looked at his father without responding.

"What's the matter, boy? You know what I'm talking about. I saw Mr. Ferguson in town, the other day, and he wants to know when he can start telling his visitors that they can cut across our place to get to his resort. Once the road is open, we're going to get some income for the right of way."

Isaiah found his voice.

"When's the last time I saw any income out of what work I do for you?"

Sam looked up at the roof.

"Over your head, boy, and on your table, that's where you see it." He rose. "I'm going to take a walk to see what's left to do. Care to come along?"

"No."

"Well, I don't need no sick looking puppy moping after me. You just sit here and think of what might be in store for you if you do like I told you   And when you choose to get up, there's that field to prepare."

Isaiah continued sitting after Sam left.   Ordinarily, he would welcome the opportunity to feel warming earth between his fingers after the long, cold northern winter. But today he could not rouse himself to get up. Anyway, he needed a plow for the work. Perhaps tomorrow his father would send him to borrow one, either from Wilson to the north or her father. He paused on that thought, savoring its irony, that his father should have to borrow a farming implement from the family who was knee deep or higher in debt to old man Logan, whose women, not so long ago, were doing Sam Logan's wife's laundry while Sam commenced his seduction of their daughter. It was all too much, too bizarre. It forced a grim smile to crease skin now habitually stretched tight over bones beneath his long, narrow face.

The sun was bright in a blue sky and there was a gentle breeze. Margaret paused at the farm road that led to Sam's house. Perhaps she should confront him right now, ask him just what he was thinking. But her courage failed her. She was afraid she knew what his answer would be. She continued walking north. She passed potato and strawberry fields between the orchards of fruit trees. Some of the cherry trees showed green fruit between their white blossoms. The apple and peach trees were fully leafed out but not yet bearing flowers. At one farm, a dozen girls recruited from town were on their knees picking strawberries. One of them got up and waved to Margaret. She held out a handful of strawberries.

"Take some. He'll never know the difference," she said with a gesture toward the farmhouse behind her. "Anyway, he don't mind if we have a few. There's so many."

Margaret held out her hands to receive the berries. They were bright red, the color she had been hoping to find on her sheet one morning.

"Thank you," Margaret said. She took one of the berries into her mouth.

"Sweet, ain't they," the girl said. "Just like my beau." The girls nearby giggled. Margaret smiled her assent. She looked at the blush on their smooth skin. She brought her hand to her face and thought she felt the dry wrinkles of an old woman.

As she passed other workers in the fields and orchards she waved at them and acknowledged their greetings. And yet it seemed as though she no longer belonged to these people, especially those whom she had known her whole life. It was as though she had awakened in a country a thousand miles from her home.

Up ahead, through a break in the maples that lined the road at this place she saw the white bell tower of the church. She was overheated from her walk and recalled how the trees kept the interior of the building cool even on hot summer days. And then there was the shade behind the building. She stood outside the front entrance where the sun beat down on her. Feeling dizzy, she sat down on the top step before the door. Unbidden images flooded her mind. She saw herself dressed in white, going through that door, a bouquet in her hand, the piano playing the wedding march. As she walked down the aisle on the arm of her father, her mother looked back at her from the front pew. She wore a grim smile on her face. The minister waited, holding a small book in his large hands.

She shut her eyes and concentrated. There were two men standing with theirs back toward her, facing the minister. One was wider and taller than the other. Sam. The other Isaiah. She wondered which one would turn around to greet her as his bride. She looked at the person playing the piano. It was Eustace, whose clothes she and her mother had washed. As the music got louder, people in their seats turned to watch her, nodding their heads in a knowing way and gesturing at her belly pushing through her gown. One of the men swiveled his head around, smiling.

Closing her eyes, she dropped her head into her lap.

"Are you waiting for someone?" The voice belonged to an old woman.

Margaret raised her head, and felt the door behind her.

"I must have been asleep," she said. "The minister, I need to speak to him."

"Oh, he won't be here today. I live right over there across the road." She pointed to a neat, little frame house. "I expect I know his comings and goings. You looked flushed. Would you like to come in for a little while? My house is nice and cool."

"No thank you."

"Come back Sunday," the woman said.

Margaret watched her walk to her house. A dog barked from inside, and then she opened the door. She scratched the dog's head, and closed the door behind her. Margaret looked up and down the road. A crow swooped over a corn field behind the woman's head, cawing loudly. It landed in the field, and then all was quiet again.

After a while, she got up and walked around to the back of the church into the little cemetery. She found her brother's grave. It was cool there, in the shade of the trees. She sat in the grass next to the grave, with her palms resting against her belly. It felt as though it were beginning to push out, just a little.

I must talk to Sam, she thought.

With the afternoon sun full on his face, Isaiah dozed. Her features formed in his mind, and his smile broadened. She was standing in the pasture between their farms, her black hair loose and tumbling to her shoulders. She was wearing a summer dress of a thin material, and there was a light breeze that molded the fabric to her body. The golden heads of daffodils punctuated the dark green of the grass. She began to walk toward him and he could see that she was barefoot. She was carrying a woven basket and a blanket. She reached a tree at the edge of the pasture and spread out the blanket and uncovered the basket. She crooked a finger toward him, and he started to trot toward her. But then she disappeared into a black shadow. Something had come between him, her, and the sun. He looked about, sure that it was his father. His jaw set in anger and frustration. He concentrated, trying to will the shadow away, but it remained. He snapped open his eyes before he would see his father's face replace hers. She was standing in front of him.

"I didn't mean to wake you," she said. "But I must see your father. You know why. What was said yesterday."

Isaiah's jaws had begun to relax into a grin, the pleasure of seeing her as though she had just walked out of his dream being almost too intense to bear. But he felt his features form into a scowl.

"He's not here," he said. "About what was said..." He saw her cheek muscles tighten and then she gnawed her lower lip until he thought blood must soon flow. He wanted to embrace her, to comfort her, to tell her that he really did love her, she didn't need his father.

"Don't, Isaiah," she said. "That's what I must speak to your father about. When will he be back?"

He felt as though he had just been hit in the midsection.

"He's out surveying the new road to the resort." His voice sounded distant to his own ear. He glanced in the direction his father had taken. "I could take you there. I was going to join him." He added the lie without reflection, and saw by the confused look in her eyes that he had made a mistake. Of course, she wanted to see his father alone.

"Do you have a piece of paper and a pencil?"

"In the house."

"Could you?"

"Sure."

He returned to find her sitting on the porch step, her face furrowed in concentration. Apparently, she was composing her note in her head. He handed her the paper and pencil, and watched her write. She paused two or three times, her lips compressed into a single line. Her fingers were long and thin, but strong. No doubt they had been well accustomed to work, as well as the softer motions of love, and he imagined them on his own flesh. She held out the paper.

"Could you give this to him as soon as you see him?"

He held out his hand, and she pressed the paper against his palm. Her skin was warm and moist. She leaned forward and brushed her lips across his cheek. She stepped back with a girlish smile on her face. She turned her back to him, and seemed to be gazing toward East Bay, which appeared as a thin sliver of blue above the green of the trees. He stood next to her and looked in the same direction.

"It's pretty, isn't it?" he asked.

She started to shake her head no, but then nodded.

"It's the water, I suppose. Ever since my little brother...but you must have heard that dreadful story."

Isaiah had, of course. Everybody had. He sought the right words.

She put her finger to his lips. "There's nothing you can say. Or do." She brightened. "Except make sure your father gets my note right away. That'll make everything right." And a moment later she was gone. He wondered if she had actually been there, but then he felt the note still clutched between his fingers. He hesitated to touch it with his whole hand as if it might disappear, and then he would know that he had imagined her visit. Dropping the note into the palm of his other hand, he picked it up again. It was real. She had been there. She had kissed his cheek. He could still feel the pressure of her lips, and her fingers against his own lips, as well. He wanted to keep the note as long as he could, to wait for his father to come back before yielding it. But then he would fail her wouldn't he? Sitting down he very carefully opened the note. Her hand was childish, with large circles and loops, and carefully drawn lines. He read her words with, at first, a guilty pleasure, then with growing despair. He folded the note again, and put it in his pocket.

He found his father a short distance beyond the white birch, sitting on a boulder he had rolled to the side. He was staring without much enthusiasm in the direction the road would take. The terrain was rough, with several sharp drops and rises, covered by low growing shrubs intertwined with each other and, snaking through it all, thick vines.

"She stopped by to see you today," Isaiah said.

Sam got up off the boulder. Isaiah felt in his pocket for the note but then dropped his hand. It was written in her hand, and even though it was directed to his father he felt he now owned it. It might be as close as he ever got to her. He recalled how her graceful, strong fingers had moved the pencil in its childish strokes, her lips pursed as she composed her simple request.

"What'd she want?" Sam said. "Did you tell her where I was?"

"I did, but she just wanted to leave you a message."

"Did she write it down?"

Isaiah was about to yield the paper when he was stopped by the grin spreading on his father's face.

"No," Isaiah replied, sure now that he would not permit the paper to fall into his father's hands. "She told me to tell you to meet her in the usual place, in the hemlock swamp near the shore. The usual place," he repeated, and permitted his contempt to flavor the words. "Tomorrow at noon."

"Is that all?"

"Yes."

"I don't have time for such foolishness," Sam said.

"She'll be waiting for you."

"Maybe you should go instead." Sam smiled in a way Isaiah imagined the devil would smile when he closed the deal for someone's soul. "Why she's almost your intended, isn't she?"

"No," Isaiah replied. He remembered her expression as she asked after his father, like a dying traveler in the desert in sight of water. "She's your problem."

Margaret looked down the dusty road that led to her house, and then at the hill that rose beyond the barn. She strained to see the dark blue water of the creek and found it in one spot where the sun had gilded it. She had not expected to have to face Isaiah alone, after all that nonsense spoken between their fathers yesterday. He must have understood how unreasonable the whole idea was; at least he didn't insist on talking about it. Once she saw Sam she would be able to explain what she had worked out during her sleepless night. She wrapped her fingers around the bottle in her pocket. Not now, but perhaps later.

She could not make up her mind where to go. Her home where she had lived her whole life, which until recently had felt so safe, now offered her no sanctuary, nor did the barn where they had lain, nor the stream where her brother had drowned, and not the farmhouse itself where she would encounter the stern, disapproving gaze of her mother, and even worse the tortured stare of her father who seemed willing to have her marry that boy, perhaps as part of some business deal.

Town was only a couple of miles further. She had nothing but time to fill before she would meet Sam tomorrow. For a moment, panic gripped her as she recalled the strange look in Isaiah's eyes as he had taken the note from her. What if he didn't deliver it? What if he threw it away? Or showed up himself? But what other choice had she had?

She turned away from her home and continued on the road to town. As she did, she saw Edward trotting toward her. She did not stop. Before long he was at her side.

"Your mother's been lookin' for you," he said.

"Tell her I have to go to town. To see somebody."

"Who?"

She heard his voice as though coming from under a deep pool of water. It vibrated in bass tones. She wondered at his insolence. She had no time for foolish questions from hired help.

"Just tell her," she said.

"The cows..." he began.

"You can milk them, or she can. I don't care."

"But Miss..." Edward tried.

She started walking again. He followed a few feet behind.

"What should I tell her?" he called out. "She'll think I'm lyin' that I didn't find you. That's what. I can't afford to lose this job."

She gave her shoulders a little shrug and quickened her pace. Let him drown, she thought, just like her little brother had. After a few moments, she heard his voice again, this time seeming as though it were coming from an even greater distance. On some level she realized that she was not thinking clearly, perhaps even imagining the conversation she had just had with Edward. But she did not care. She only knew that she could not go home, she could not go back to Sam's farm, there perhaps to again face Isaiah, whose intensity frightened her so, nor to the barn, no longer safe for her after the last time she was there. She knew hardly anybody in town, and anonymity was exactly what she sought.

She followed the road until it reached the foot of the Peninsula. Before her the road continued into town, but to the right another street led along the bank of the Boardman River, which emptied into the bay. She chose that way. Grand houses faced the river along this street. The grandest was a huge mansion with its aspiring towers on the corners flanking a gable roof, and its generous wrap around porch. She seemed to remember that it had been built by the local lumber baron.

A brougham pulled by a team of matched brown and white Appaloosas raised dust as it rolled to a stop in front of the mansion. The driver hopped down and opened the door that faced the house. On the porch appeared an elegantly dressed young woman, in yellow gown, with matching gloves and hat, carrying a parasol. She turned to say good-bye to somebody within the house, and then descended from the porch and disappeared into the carriage. The driver closed the carriage door behind her, and climbed back onto his seat. He released the brake, and snapped his whip over the horses' heads. The dust rose again behind the carriage as it turned onto the street. Margaret stopped to watch the carriage ride by. Through its window, she saw the profile of the young woman. She wondered with pointless curiosity where she might be going.

It was late afternoon, and the street was quiet. Two boys and a girl were fishing in the river. The tall one wearing an engineer's cap held the pole while the other two stared at the water. They shifted their gaze toward her. A young man was lying on the grass of the river bank, holding a book. She watched the children to see if they were having any luck. The pole dipped toward the water, and they turned away from her. She watched as the boy pulled in a fish. She continued walking.

Daniel McConnell stared for a moment at the flash of yellow gloves in the window of the carriage, and then returned his attention to the book in which he was writing. He sensed somebody approaching. He looked up at Margaret. She was close enough for him to see that her face was streaked with perspiration. Strands of her long hair hung damply across her forehead. Her shoes and the lower portion of her summer dress were covered with the dust of the road. She walked favoring her left leg, as though there was something wrong with her foot, or perhaps her shoe. It was her eyes, however, that drew his attention. The pupils seemed enlarged and it appeared as though she were looking toward something very far away that she could not see. But then every few steps she would turn her gaze onto the water, and then her eyes focused on the slowly moving river. She had something clutched in her right hand. It was small enough to be hidden by her fingers. He rose to his feet and offered a little bow.

"It's very pleasant here, don't you think?" he asked.

"It's the water," she said. "I am drawn to it."

"Did you see that carriage that went by?" he asked. He held out his leather bound journal book. "I was just sketching that house."

"Are you an artist?"

"No. A writer. For the newspaper. I'm working on a story about how the other half lives." He turned the book so she could see his sketch. "You can see," he continued, "that I'd better stick to words."

She glanced at the sketch.

"I'd like to keep walking," she said.

"May I accompany you?" he asked.

"If you like," she replied.

She looked back in the direction from which she had just come. The boy with the pole was baiting his hook. Then she gazed the other way where the Boardman disappeared around a bend before emptying into the bay. She started walking that way, and he followed. She seemed sure of her purpose.

She was only dimly aware that she now had a companion. With each step she had taken toward town her mind had wandered further from her feet along the dusty road. A gnawing discomfort in her stomach, however, brought her body back in contact with her mind. She stopped walking and turned to Daniel as though seeing him for the first time. She opened her mouth to speak to him, but he was moving in circles around her. She reached out to grab hold of him, to stop his motion so she could tell him something that was very important, but he would not stop moving. She snatched at his sleeve as he whirled by. And then the ground rushed up to meet her.

"When was the last time you had something to eat?"

Daniel's voice reached her from a great distance. It was gentle. She thought for a moment that it must be him, but when she opened her eyes, she looked up into a stranger's face. It was a pale, narrow face, with brown, intelligent eyes beneath a high forehead. He was young, she thought, maybe her age. She did not know where she was, or why he was talking to her.

"You fainted," the voice said.

She started to sit up, and realized that she was lying in grass that prickled against the bare skin of her hands and wrists. His eyes, searching hers, looked kind, but his face was spinning. She closed her eyes. She put her hands to her forehead. It was damp and clammy.

"Here," he said. He handed her his handkerchief. She took it and wiped away the perspiration. She lay back down. He felt the coins in his pocket. He had hoped to stretch these slim resources for two or three days.

"I'll get you something to eat, as soon as you can walk," he said.

She nodded and held out her hand.

"Are you sure?" he asked.

"Yes."

He took her hand and lifted. Under the best of circumstances, he was not very strong, and as he pulled, his lungs betrayed him. He eased her down and then bent over in a prolonged coughing fit. He held his handkerchief in front of his mouth and felt the warm blood mixed with the fluids rising up from his diseased lungs. When the coughing stopped, he stood up straight. He examined the handkerchief, checking the spots of bright red blood, doing the usual calculus to determine how bad the fit had been, and figured this was at a medium level. He felt her eyes upon him.

"Consumption?" she asked.

He nodded.

"You need not fear," he said. "I have not managed to give it to anyone else, even my closest and dearest friends."

"If you did," she replied, "you might well be doing me a favor."

He studied her eyes, now bright as though in a fever. She held out her hand again, and her flesh was cool. The fever of life, he decided, like a candle consuming even one so young and beautiful as she. He began to move his lips to give voice to this thought, but his courage failed. Or perhaps it was the realization that for one such as she to be both free of obvious disease and yet holding out her arms to welcome, even beckon, death, she must have given her heart so fully to another that it would be impervious to any assault he might make on it.

"There's a restaurant not far from here," he said. "I hear it has swell food. We can have our last meals there together."

A smile came unbidden to her face, and she strove without success to drive it away. She took his hand, and this time he pulled her up.

"This way," he said.

Sam's tooth ached without pause. Searching among the bottles on the shelf in the kitchen, he found the little bottle behind two larger ones. He thought it was the right one, but the writing, in pencil, on its label was too faint to be read. He unstopped it and brought it to his nose. He thought he heard somebody pounding on the door. He took a sip and then another. He sat down on the chair next to the kitchen table. The pounding continued. But the pain began to recede.

"So, Eustace," he muttered, "this is what you took when things got too tough."

The pounding seemed to have stopped. He walked on unsteady legs to the door and opened it. There was nobody there. But the pounding began anew. It was in his head. He sat down and laid his head on the table.

After a while both the pounding and the pain receded.

The laudanum bottle was on the table next to her water glass, and her hand moved from one to the other. She settled on the bottle and curled her fingers around it. Daniel reached across the table and put his hand on top of hers. He did not try to unwrap her fingers. He just gave them a gentle squeeze. She suffered his touch, which felt very warm, warmer than the temperature would have suggested.

"Do you know what you have there?" he asked.

"Laudanum. Some of the girls I know like to sip it," Margaret said.

"And do you know what happens if you drink too much of it?"

"I hope so," she replied. "A man gave it to me, and said I should try it. He didn't want any money. He said if I liked it he would sell me more."

"If I were a religious man, I'd say he was the devil."

"Tempting me?"

"Yes."

"But you don't believe that."

"No. He's just a drummer."

"Maybe he's an angel."

The waitress arrived with two plates of steaming stew. She stood waiting. He let go of Margaret's hand, and the waitress placed his dish in front of him. Margaret's arm was still on the table in front of her, holding the little bottle. Daniel motioned for the waitress to put Margaret's plate on the side of the water glass where there was just enough room. She did so, with a frown.

"When that goes crashing to the floor," the waitress said, "I hope you'll do the right thing."

"I will. I'll make it right with your boss," he said. The waitress walked away, shaking her head. Daniel took a fork full of the stew.

"It's as good as advertised," he said.

The aroma of the meat and vegetables reached her nose and reminded her how hungry she was. She moved the plate in front of her and began to eat. They had pie for dessert, and Daniel paid the bill, leaving himself less than a dollar for the next week.

"You know," he said, "I was thinking that if you didn't have any immediate use for that laudanum I could use it. Maybe I could borrow it just until tomorrow, or the day after at the latest, until I find that drummer again and get my own." He extended his hand, palm up toward her.

"No," she said, "I cannot do that. But I thank you for your kindness."

"I'll walk home with you then," he replied.

"Home," she said.

"Yes."

"But first I must find Mr. Logan. I left him a note."

"Oh," Daniel began, surprised at how his heart had dropped at the mention of another man's name. "He is..."

"We are to be married," she said. She stood up. "Would you be so kind as to walk me home, as you said you would. I must get ready."

"Of course," he said.

"She's not home yet," Sarah said in the flat tones that Henry long ago recognized she used when she had to mouth words she found unpleasant. It was her way, he figured, of denying her deeply buried feelings. Her face, too, wore that stony mask behind which she walled herself at times like these. Sadness fell on him like the gloom of the falling night outside.

"Have you asked the hands if they saw her?"

"I sent Edward to look for her. He saw her heading to town."

"Why didn't he stop her?"

"Now isn't that a fool thing to say," Sarah said, and her voice betrayed just a glimpse of the concern that he knew was hidden behind her seeming indifference.

Neither of them stirred from the table. The supper she had served remained on their plates untouched. He made a half hearted effort to bring his fork to his mouth, but the thought of food was repugnant. It was like the night they had sat in stunned silence after the dead body of their son had been pulled from their creek. Only then they could comfort themselves in the knowledge that their daughter was safe. But now, as they peered through the window toward the road from town, its contours fading in the growing darkness, they felt bereft of all hope. He wanted to confess that he had pushed Margaret too hard to accept marriage to a boy she did not love. His wife knew that her grief for her lost son had hardened her heart against her daughter. They sat in their separate pain, unable or unwilling to reach a hand to the other.

Finally, just as she rose, determined to take her isolation with her to her side of their bed, they heard the murmur of voices outside the front door. It swung open. Margaret offered a quick, nervous smile. At her side, and a step or two back in the darkness, was Daniel. She motioned him to step forward.

"This is Daniel," she said. "I met him in town."

"She was unwell," Daniel said. "I got her something to eat and walked her home."

She linked her arm in his.

"He was so very kind to me," she said.

Henry bestirred himself with a tremendous effort of his will. His emotions tugged in opposite directions, relief that she was safe and had come back, distressed that too late she seemed to have found a respectable young man. Sarah gave voice to his frustration.

"Too late," she muttered. She got up and started to walk out of the room.

"Mother," Margaret said.

Sarah stopped. Margaret approached her and threw her arms around her. Sarah returned the embrace, but her eyes were filled with tears. "Too late," she said in a harsh whisper.

Daniel watched the scene, aware that he had walked into the domestic crisis that had led Margaret to wander confused into town. He had not been able to plumb her despair to uncover its source. He looked at the stern-faced mother, tears running down her cheeks, and at the father whose face revealed his agony, and he saw that neither could, or would, express their relief at their daughter's safe return. He wanted very much to stay with Margaret, to make sure she did not turn to that bottle he knew she still had in her pocket. But Henry rose from the table and walked toward him, with his hand extended. Daniel took it.

"Thank you," Henry said. "Were you put to any expense?"

"No," Daniel said, "none worth talking about."

"Then I'll bid you good-night," Henry said.

The door closed behind him.

"He's a nice young man," Margaret said.

"But," Sarah replied, "he's not the one whose baby you are carrying."

Edward lay on his bed in the attic, directly above Margaret's room. He had the dormer window propped open with a stick, and the cool night air washed over him. He was not refreshed. He had been feeling feverish all day since he had chased after her down the road toward town. He did not think he was sick. This was a different kind of heat he was suffering from.

He heard their conversation rising up two levels through the cracks in the floorboards. He strained to make out their words, but they never spoke loudly or raised their voices, no matter how provoked they might be with him, or Jim, or an animal, or each other, or God for not providing rain, or the soil for refusing to yield a decent crop no matter the extent of their sweat, no these people simply did not yell, or laugh, or cry. Their control was unnatural, frightening, suggesting a discipline that drove passion into a corner until it lay subdued. Of course, he had to restrain his emotion, the dull ache of resentment he carried inside of him. Hired hands were not permitted to display their feelings to their betters, and he would be damned if he would reveal himself to that nigger either. So he lay there seething, wondering when he would find the opportunity for payback.

She climbed the stairs. He imagined her disrobing and lying in her bed. He imagined her waiting for him to join her.

Sam sat at the table as the laudanum began to wear off. He looked up the stairs toward Isaiah's closed door. I've done too good a job with her, getting her to thinks she loves me, he muttered. And not a good enough job with him, so he would understand how I'm looking out for him.

5

───•───

The next morning, Margaret awoke late. She remembered that she had been dreaming, but could not recall about what. Whatever her dreams had been, however, they had lifted her spirits and she came down to the kitchen with a bright smile. Her mother was rolling dough for a pie.

"Your blueberries," Sarah snapped. "They'd spoil waiting for you to do something with them."

Margaret threw her arms about her.

"Some flowers for the table would be nice," she said.

"We certainly don't need that, unless you're expecting company."

"Maybe I am," Margaret replied, without thinking, and then she realized that Daniel's face had flashed up from her memory.

"And who would that be? Your nice young man from last night?"

"He think's he's dying," she replied, her tone too bright by far for the morbid message. "He has consumption."

Her mother did not reply, but she seemed to be wielding her rolling pin with greater force. Margaret could not explain why she felt so much more positive. Perhaps it had something to do with Daniel, but that didn't make any sense. She just knew that Sam must have come to his senses, realized how much he loved her, and would abandon his crazy scheme of having her marry his son. Why, the whole idea was just so ridiculous. Maybe that was what her dream had told her. She had felt warm when she awakened, as though he had been pressed against her the whole night. She would meet him with her basket on her arm, just as she had the last time, and they would lie down in the tall meadow grass, listening to the chickadees and the cardinals in the trees above them. And this time, maybe, he would come home with her and they would have a piece of her mother's freshly baked pie. And there would be fresh cut flowers on the table.

"Your chores," her mother said after a while, "the cows and the chickens are waiting for you."

Sam lay in his bed unable to rise. The shape of yesterday's conviction, which had seemed so clear, now appeared as though it lurked in a thick fog, moving in and out of his sight with winds blowing from opposite directions. Sometimes he thought he could make it out, but then the breeze would rise and the fog would thicken and he would be unable to find it until it emerged again in a different place.

Perhaps the problem was that he had never been much of a planner, more a creature who responded to stimuli, relying on his quick wits and smooth tongue, or when these failed his fists, to navigate whatever troubled waters he might find himself in. But this time, the waters were more treacherous and he was well out of sight of any shore, facing precipitous rapids in front of him, and a sucking whirlpool behind him. He felt, for the first time in his life, out of his usual depth.

He had thought about their meeting, how she would no doubt reiterate her undying love, her determination to make things right with him. He was certain that he must keep the appointment. They would simply have to come to some kind of decision today. He heard Isaiah stomping about downstairs, and he swung his feet onto the floor. How irritating it was to have his son know his business. That thought bothered him almost more than any other circumstance this difficult day.

"I'm going to work on that road this morning," he said.

Isaiah nodded.

"Take Chester over to Wilson's place and see about hitching him to that plow, which we need to turn that sorghum field over. Then find your ax and join me about one o'clock."

Isaiah remembered the noon meeting in her note.

"Talkative this morning, ain't you?" Sam said.

"Ain't got much to say," Isaiah replied.

"Well, then, just do as I say."

"Don't I always."

"Mostly," Sam said as he walked out the door.

Margaret took her time milking. She talked to each of the half dozen cows by name, Daisy, Flo, Hortense, Ruth, Bernice, and most especially Henrietta, whom she did last, for she was the most difficult. She worked with a gentle rhythm. The splash of the warm milk into the bucket seemed to soothe the jagged edges of her nerves, so sensitive these past few days that every sound no matter how soft thundered in her ears, every image no matter how faint blistered her retina. But not today. It was as though she had been ill with a high fever that had broken during her unremembered dreams of the night before, leaving her weaker, to be sure, but with a growing strength that would prepare her for her meeting with him later that afternoon. Why, she was even confident that she had thought of just the right way he could make amends with his father, and once that was done, there'd be no more ridiculous talk of her marrying that boy, with his moonstruck eyes and tongue that seemingly could not form the simplest words.

Her hands worked Henrietta's udder. The cow turned her head, shifted her weight, and swished her tail, but stood still enough. Her father had said on more than one occasion that the only thing that stood between Henrietta and a trip to the market for whatever an ill-tempered old cow could bring was his daughter's calming touch.

Margaret stood up from the milking stool, bucket in hand, and found herself face to face with Edward.

"Can I carry that for you, miss?" he asked.

She handed him the bucket, and took a basket down off its hook on the wall.

"We need flowers for the table," she said.

He watched her swing the basket as she followed the creek up the hill. He heard footsteps in the hard dirt outside of the barn.

"Have you seen my daughter this morning?" Henry asked.

Edward understood. Of course, Cutter had observed him watching as Margaret walked away. The question was intended only to indicate what they both understood.

"I offered to help her," he replied, and held up the bucket. It swung in his hand, and milk sloshed over its top. Henry took the bucket from him.

"She usually don't want any help," he said.

"Maybe because I asked."

"Maybe," Henry replied. He looked out of the barn toward the north. "That new fence on my property line. I'm thinking I want that fence up between me and Logan. I'll send Jim after you to help."

It's a little late for that, Edward thought, but he said, "I don't welcome Jim's company all that much."

"Nor him yours," Henry muttered. "You both work better alone, but the point is, I guess, you both work hard enough. If you didn't..."

But Edward had already lifted the post digger to his shoulder and stalked out of the barn

"There's plenty as would," Edward completed Henry's thought. "As if I don't know that full well."

Isaiah waited while John Wilson finished hitching his sulky plow to Chester, their large Percheron. Wilson was in his sixties, his body bent from years of hard labor, his hands moving without wasted motion, tightening the straps, giving them a tug here, and a pull there, to be sure the tension was correct. Finishing he stepped back to look at the rig, as a painter might examine his newly completed canvas. Beside him Isaiah had been shifting on one foot to the other.

"Can't wait to get to work, can you?" the old farmer asked. "Or do you need to pee?"

"I guess I'm just antsy today," Isaiah replied.

"Two days, you say?" Wilson asked.

"No more, maybe less," Isaiah replied.

"Well, your father said you'd do my field when you came back. Is that right?"

"That's right," Isaiah said. "But I might be back tomorrow."

"Suit yourself," Wilson said. "As long as you do my field."

"I said I would, just like my father promised you."

Wilson handed the reins to Isaiah.

"Off with you, then."

Isaiah slid into onto the seat.

"Gittup, Chester."

The huge work horse stepped forward, and the plow lurched after it.

"Make sure you keep that bottom lifted," Wilson called after him.

Isaiah guided the rig back to the town road and followed it to the turnoff to their farm. He hesitated. She had written in her note that she would meet his father at noon. What if he unhitched the plow and continued on horseback to find her? He could tell her the truth about his father, tell her how he himself was the one who loved her, would treat her the way she deserved, even raise the child in her belly as his own. He would forget who planted that seed in her, what more would she need to know to measure his sincerity?

But even as these thoughts raced through his mind, he knew what a ridiculous figure he would be riding up to her, his legs splayed across the broad back of the work horse, his heels drumming without stirrups the animal's flanks, the whole picture as far removed from a knight coming to the rescue of the fair maiden as he could imagine. She would not take him seriously, and he would bide for a better opportunity.

He hauled on the right rein, pulled the horse's head around, and turned the animal again into the field on the southeast corner of their land. Diagonally across from him, his father was clearing brush for the new road on the northwest corner. At least, he was as far apart as that. He lowered the bottom and watched the soil separate beneath it as he started the first furrow.

The blade dug into the soil, turning over a sand and clay mixture. Looking behind him at the furrow, he saw it was straight and true. He raised his eyes to the east, there where she had said she would be.

Sam had taken his time to begin his work today. His tooth raged, and he thought about returning to the house for the laudanum, but he chose instead to just sit beneath a tree, with his chin propped on his knees, waiting for the throbbing to subside. It was as though all of the stress he was experiencing, his father's decision to essentially disinherit him, his son's surly indifference to every common interest, and mostly Margaret's starry eyed innocence, now anchored to the reality of his baby in her belly, all of this combined itself into the massive ache in his jaw, so intense that he found it just about impossible to connect one thought to another. He pressed against the spot as hard as he could in an attempt to replace one pain with another. Then he clamped his teeth shut and ground them back and forth. This combination of assaults somehow had the effect of dulling the throbbing, and he rose to his feet.

He held his long handled ax on his shoulder as he reached the white birch. He ran his fingers up and down the tool's handle, feeling how the wood had been turned, and remembering the lathe on which he had fashioned that first baseball bat so many years ago. That was what he should have been doing all these years, working wood into useful shapes, not breaking his nails and straining his back cultivating the soil. But his father had given him the money for this farm when he had asked him to finance a carpentry shop in town. Now, the old man remembers fondly that bat, fondles it in front of him, forgetting how scornful he had been years ago of his son's obvious talent, insisting instead that he, too, farm. That was where it all began, Sam concluded, the day he set foot on this accursed land with his new bride in the farmhouse, as ill-suited to her role as farmer's wife, as he to being a farmer. Isaiah was all that remained from that misguided and ill-fated union. As for his second marriage, it was to him very like the aching tooth he now suffered, as though he had tasted a sweet that inevitably led to decay.

He hadn't intended to get involved with another woman, but Margaret had looked at him with an awakening passion that he found irresistible, the idea of being her first too tantalizing to turn down. He was seeing himself closer to the grave than his chronology would dictate. Although still robust, he felt as though his life had run its course, that he was like a train shuttled off to a siding in the yard, disconnected from any engine that might move him back onto a track leading toward a future worth contemplating. The pride he had once felt in the strength and competence of his hands had disappeared as he scratched the stubborn earth. In his son, he saw the youth forever lost to him, and in his father, the nemesis that like a dark cloud hovered over him. Only his mother provided any comfort, and there was little she could do for him except to encourage him to go on.

So, it was no wonder, at least to him, that he had so readily availed himself of the one medicine that could serve as an antidote to his malaise. When he was with her, he again felt he was worth loving, for she so clearly did love him. He was emboldened to think he could still win a competition with both his son and his father, his success with her demonstrating his superiority to the one and his independence from the other.

But today, as his tooth raged, he again felt his world narrowing to these forty acres in a corner of which he would be buried. Rather than clearing brush for a road to the bay to accommodate travelers to the new resort, he should be finding a dank plot of earth to mark his grave. He now saw the sheer lunacy of his wild plan to solve his problems by compelling her to marry his son. True, there would be a tinge of vicarious thrill to think that the flesh of his flesh was now united to her, but that would be bittersweet at best.

If he had the money, he would consider suggesting that they run off together, to start again further west, or even try an east coast city, far from any stench of manured fields. But he did not have the funds for such a venture, there was no bank ready to float him a loan, and the very thought of starting over again for the third or fourth or fifth time, was simply too exhausting.

He swung the ax back and forth, and then he brought it down on the brush in front of him, until swinging the ax in an increasing rhythm, the sweat gathered on his neck and ran down his back. He made steady, slow progress for half an hour until the ax began to feel like it weighed first ten, then twenty pounds, and finally when he could barely lift it over his shoulder, he knelt down in the shade of a maple and let it drop. He was just about at the top of a ridge, and as he swiped the perspiration from his eyes, he could see the blue of the west bay. He looked up through the trees at the sun straight overhead. He pulled out his pocket watch, given to him on his eighteenth birthday by his father. Its gold case was tarnished and scratched from years of residence in the rough pockets of his work clothes. He snapped it open. It was a little after noon. She would be waiting for him.

Edward turned the post digger into the ground. The calluses on his hand felt as though they would explode as he twisted the handle to drive the auger. He was at the edge of a field right before the tree line that marked the end of the Cutter property. He remembered how he had seen her pass by heading toward Sam's farm, and he recalled the tone of voice in which Henry Cutter had inquired about *his* daughter. She might just as well be living on the other side of the earth instead of sleeping in a room beneath him, separated only by a few inches of board lumber.

He finished the hole, set the post into it, and walked into the shade of the woods. He thought he heard a rhythmical, swishing sound and he followed his ears. He made his way through the trees. With each step, he realized he was leaving his job responsibility behind, and he felt a mixture of fear and liberation. He walked down a declivity and then up the side of a ridge. When he crested it, he realized the sound had stopped. He looked around, and there some forty or fifty yards away in the shadows at the edge of the woods was a man. He thought he recognized him and called out.

"Is that you, Mr. Logan?"

The man waved and continued walking. He was heading east.

"I thought I heard something," Edward continued. "That's why I come here."

The figure did not respond. If anything he seemed to increase his pace. Edward made his way to the spot where the man had been. With the unthinking curiosity of a man who works with his hands for his bread, he looked at the freshly cut brush, and calculated how long it must have taken. Then he made his way back to the fence line, picked up his post digger and returned to his own labor.

Margaret swung her basket like a young girl going out to play. She thought of herself as Jill, carrying her bucket. Only she was walking down a slope toward East Bay where she would meet her Jack. She recited the silly rhyme in her head as she walked. The sun was warm against her cheeks. Her feet felt so light that they scarcely touched the ground. She almost felt like skipping. In her pocket, she had her egg money, five dollars. The carriage only cost three dollars and sixty five cents. Of course, there were fancier ones, upholstered in silk, for twice that much. But this one was more than good enough. Why, it even had a little parasol attached and a sturdy maple wood body. It would all make perfectly good sense. He would have to agree. It was spring, after all, the time of new life.

At the bottom of the slope, she entered a cherry orchard. Some of the trees had dropped their white blossoms and in their place were the small, green balls that would become the fruit. The other trees were still dressed in white, just like, she thought, wedding gowns. The combination of the white clad trees on one side, and those displaying new fruit on the other made her giddy. As she got closer to the hemlock swamp, she remembered to keep her eyes focused on the ground, looking for the low growing arbutus vines, with their tiny pink and white flowers. She would bring back flowers for the table. She must come back with her basket full. When she was in town a few days ago delivering her eggs to the market, she heard the servant girl from the Wilson farm say she had picked bunches of the new blossoms just in the area near the swamp.

Crossing the road to town, her feet more than her eyes found the path that led through the hemlocks. It was here the girl at the market had said she found the flowers, and there they were. It was going to be a good day, the best day of her life. Kneeling, she started to pull the blossoms off their vines, but they did not come free, and her fingers slid up the stalk and crushed the flowers. She looked down at her hand as though it belonged to somebody else, and she should chastise it. Instead, she brought the offending fingers to her mouth and licked the plant juice from them. The taste was bitter. Reaching to another cluster of blossoms, this time she dug her fingernail into the vine and snapped the flowers off and put them into her basket.

She became aware that her knees were wet, and feeling the ground about her she realized that she was kneeling in a marshy area where the waters of the melting snows and spring rains sought their way down toward the bay. She stood up and walked in a semi circle until she found a place where the water flowed a couple of inches deep through the grass. Taking off her shoes, she walked into the water. It was warmer than she had anticipated. She thought it would be like the water that ran over the stone creek bed above her farm on that day years ago. That water never seemed to warm up, even when the summer sun beat down on it.

Although the day was quite warm, she felt chilled and wanted to follow the moving water to the bay and lie down in it. With an effort, she recalled that he would be meeting her very soon, that perhaps he was already there, and forcing a smile to her face, she reached into her basket and took out blossoms still attached to the vine where her fingernail had sliced it and wove the flowers into her hair behind her right ear, and put her shoes in the basket next to the flowers. Her feet found the path again and she picked up her pace. There were only a few flowers in her basket, and she knew that she would need more, but for now the most important thing was to see him, to talk to him, to assure herself that everything would be all right.

He knew the place, a small rise at the edge of the swamp with a view of East Bay, and the time, noon. He looked up at the sun. It was a couple of degrees down from its straight overhead position. He was unaccustomed to panic, and yet that is what he now felt gripping him. It was terribly important that he not keep her waiting. She was so fragile she might crack into a thousand pieces. What would she do then? He broke into a trot until his breath got short and perspiration filled his eyes. Still he urged his legs on. Isaiah would be looking for him soon to help clear the new road. He should be there. He should be with her. She might go to talk to his father. She was just young enough, innocent enough, and strong willed enough for such foolishness. He must not let her do that. He would convince her that the best thing to do was marry Isaiah. If she refused, he would have to tell her that *he* simply could not marry her. He would not live like a pauper, only to watch his own son inherit what was properly his. If she agreed, they could form a little family. Why, it would almost be like they had married. Maybe after a while he would forget that she was now his daughter. What did the Bible say about that? He recalled something about Noah's daughters and their father's nakedness. Well, he was not Noah, and she wouldn't really be his daughter.

With each step over the rough terrain his tooth throbbed with greater intensity until he thought that he must stop and find a way to remove it. He saw the ridge where she would be waiting, and he slowed to a walk. He did not want her to know how hard he had been running to get to their meeting place on time, not wanting to cede that much power to her before they had even started to negotiate, for that was what they must do, he suddenly realized, they must each put cards on the table and see who had the stronger hand. What did she have that could trump him? Nothing more nor less than the ability to ruin his life by the simple act of revealing his paternity to his father. He did not care if she shouted it to the community at large, who despised him anyway, and would be titillated at this most recent evidence of his depravity. Nobody in that community could do any more harm than wag a tongue in his direction.But his father was a different matter.

He saw her sitting in a low spot before a small ridge that rose beyond a grassy area. In front of her, the grass gave way to damp earth through which trickled threads of water making their way toward the bay. Her footprints were visible in the wet ground. Her shoes were off, and he could see mud on the soles of her feet, and two or three pink and white flowers in her disheveled hair, which cascaded down her back. At other times, he would have thought how lovely she looked. The wildness of her hair, adorned with flowers, the natural carelessness of her soiled feet would have excited him. But today that same lack of control disturbed him. He needed her to listen to reason.

For her part, she felt the familiar excitement his nearing presence always stirred, and ran her fingers through her hair, not so much to straighten it as to draw his eyes to it. She knew how much he loved its unburdened fullness, freed from the restraint of comb or clip. She rose to her feet and realized with a start that she was dizzy and light-headed. She leaned her head down until the ground stopped spinning, and when it did she picked up her basket and waved to him.

"Do you not feel well?" he asked, his hand on her cheek. "You are pale as a ghost."

She thought for a moment.

"I do believe I forgot to eat today. All I was thinking about was seeing you this afternoon." She pulled out a wrinkled piece of paper.

"Why what's that?"

"The picture from the catalog." She again reached into her pocket. "And here is the money to pay for it."

"We need to talk about that. In another way."

"Why what other way is there? Surely, our child must have a carriage." She held out her fistful of coins. "You needn't worry about the expense. I've got my egg money." The sun sparkled off the one coin that was new, but seemed to ignore the others whose surface had been dimmed through the passage of work thickened fingers.

"You don't seem to understand..." he began.

This was coming out all wrong. It seemed as though he were on top of a mountain looking down at a little girl in a valley below. His heart softened toward her, unexpectedly so, and began to win the argument with his head, which demanded that he pay attention to his own best interests, insisting she would somehow get past this, she was young, while he had no more rolls of the dice if he crapped out this time.

"Isaiah, you must have seen how he looks at you," he said.

"Indeed I have," she replied. "He makes a sad spectacle of himself. He's but a boy."

"And you..." he began, but stopped himself as he saw the thrust of her jaw and the flash in her eyes.

She had been feeling weak in his presence but now her anger rose. Who was he to treat her so? He had bullied her father into agreeing to his absurd proposition, but that was because of the money, always the money, when these men dealt with each other. But she had a much more compelling claim on him than a few dollars.

"Yes," she said, "I am the young woman who is carrying your child."

He stepped back, stunned for the moment at her strength. She had always been so malleable in his hands, so eager to please. Now, when he needed more than ever before to mold her to his wishes she seemed on the verge of utter rebellion. As if in answer to his growing frustration at her obstinacy, his tooth, which had quieted, began again to throb. He pressed his fingers against his jaw at that troubled spot, and his skin there seemed to his touch to be inflamed. The pain shot up across his cheek, behind his ear and into his skull. He could not see. A bright light danced in his eyes. He pressed his eyes shut with the palms of his hands. He knelt onto one knee, and let his head come to rest, ever so gently, onto his chest. He remained motionless until he felt her cool fingers touch his cheek where he had been pressing his fingers.

"What is it?" she said, and her voice had lost its tough edge.

"My tooth. I can't tell you how it hurts. I would yank it out if I could."

She pressed her soft finger tips in a small circle over the troubled area and then moved them to his lips.

"Hush," she said. "I think I have something to help you."

She reached into her pocket and withdrew the bottle of laudanum.

"Look."

He opened his eyes, blinked, and waited for them to focus. He reached into his pocket, convinced that somehow she had picked it.

"But how..." he began, and then he remembered that he had left his bottle at home.

"A man gave it to me when he saw how unhappy I was."

"My wife used to take it," he replied. "And she was pretty damned unhappy. She said it was for her nerves though." He took the bottle from her. It was almost full.

"I was afraid," she said.

He pulled out the stopper and brought the bottle to his lips. The liquid tasted bitter, but he swallowed, and then took another good sized sip. He looked at the bottle and saw that a third of its contents were gone. He lay down. He felt himself begin to smile. She leaned over him and kissed him. He held her to him. She lifted her head and studied his face.

"Does it make you happy?"

He nodded.

"The pain is going away."

He sat up and narrowed his eyes. It was hard to focus on her, but he knew he must. He got to his feet and walked back into the grassy area. He started to sit down, and lost his balance, landing on his back. He lifted himself to sit cross legged in front of a lone maple that towered above the surrounding hemlocks. He patted the ground next to him. When she had settled herself next to him, he took her hand.

"We cannot marry," he said.

"You are worried about the money. We must talk with your father."

"It is not about money," he said.

"Of course it is," she insisted. "It always is. What else could it be? You have told me often how you love me, and I you."

"Love..." he began, and then shut his mouth hard against what he was about to say. His teeth jarred together, and sent a muted wave of pain up the side of his face.

"Yes, love," she said, in a most gentle voice. "I think you don't know what it is. I am not at all like Eustace."

He felt himself smiling. His fears and concerns were receding, just as the pain from his tooth.

"You are smiling," she said. "What are you thinking?"

He shrugged.

"I do not know."

There seemed to be a glow about her face. She looked insufferably beautiful.

She reached for the bottle. "Then let me drink. I want to feel what you are feeling."

He handed her the bottle and watched as she first took a delicate sip, and then took two big mouthfuls. She paused and then started to lift the bottle to her lips. He had been watching her with a grin on his face, thinking it would be wonderful if she could float up to where he was. Then, the recognition hit. He reached for her hand.

"Don't," he said. "Too much..." But he found himself laughing, and he could not control the movement of his arm. He watched as she tilted the bottle and swallowed its contents.

She let the bottle roll out of her hand. She lay down on the grass and gazed up at the blue sky. The sun seemed to float away until it was only a tiny yellow speck. The moisture on the grass seeped through the thin material of her gown. She felt his breath on her face, his lips on hers. She closed his eyes while he held the kiss.

Her hands were clasped over her belly. They lay together for a period of time. He did not know how long. It could have been minutes or an hour. He felt her breath on his cheek. He heard the wind rustle the leaves in the tree. It got louder. He realized it wasn't the wind but her breathing, which had become labored as though she could not inhale.

"What is it?" he asked. He lifted himself onto an elbow and looked at her.

"I can't," she said in a whisper. "Help me."

He looked at the bottle. He realized she might die if he did not get her help. He thought about lifting her onto his shoulder and carrying her. But to where? How explain? And if she died, why, would that be his fault, after all? He would be free. But she would be dead. These opposing thoughts spun in his mind. He heard a tree branch snap beneath somebody's, or something's feet, in the woods behind them. He paused to listen, then staggered up. Maybe whoever it was could help them. He took a step in the direction of the sound and lost his balance.

Her right hand reached up and into the bark of the tree. The water was cold and she felt it fill her lungs. Her nails scratched against the bark. She opened her mouth to gasp for air but the water rushed in. She pressed her lips shut. She was on the bottom of the stream. The cold water slid over her. She came to rest next to a small figure. She put her arm around it.

He lifted himself. His right knee and elbow ached. He must have fallen. He saw her arm drop from the tree, and then she was still.

"No," he said. "You mustn't."

He crawled toward her and grabbed her shoulders. He lifted her. She was not breathing. He shook her, harder and harder, his hands tightening on her neck. Her eyes bulged, but he did not stop. "No," he muttered again and again. He eased her down. And then the ground rose up to him.

He opened his eyes. She was lying so still. Maybe she was asleep. He leaned over her and it seemed that she was looking up at him. He pressed his ear to her chest, but he could hear nothing. He felt for a pulse on her wrist, on her neck, saw a slight discoloration of her flesh where his fingers had seized her. What had he intended at that moment? The question buzzed in his brain. He could not remember. He must have been trying to revive her. But what if he hadn't, what if that darker angel that had caused him to raise his fists so often before had sat on his shoulder and screamed in his ear, "Be free, you fool, be free!" What had he done?

He pulled her hands across her chest and placed the basket next to her. She looked so beautiful, so innocent, so pure, so lovely. The flowers in her hair, even her mud coated and bare feet. He felt a sorrow more than he had ever experienced before begin to settle as a hard, empty space in his gut.

He stood up and started to walk away. He was breathing hard, and his shirt was soaked through with perspiration. He stopped. What was he to do? She was dead. He could not change that. It was an accident, wasn't it? Or had he strangled her while she was still alive? He looked down at his hands as if they no longer belonged to him. Should he just leave her there? Hide her? Yes, he could cover her with the decaying brown leaves on the ground between the trees. No, he shook his head. When she was found people would think that some-body had hidden her, and there would be only one explanation for that. But if she were lying peacefully, depressed and unstable as everyone knew she had become, then that might lead to a different conclusion. He examined her neck. No doubt there were marks, but they were faint, and closer to her shoulders than her throat. Maybe he hadn't caused her to die. That must be it. And he would leave her so people would understand. Then he would meet Isaiah. He saw the bottle of laudanum a few feet away. He placed it next to her.

He was feeling calmer. He rode a cloud. He looked down and saw her, looking so peaceful. He must be mistaken. She was not dead. She was sleeping. He would rouse her and they would go their separate ways. All would be well. He struggled to walk away from her. His leg muscles did not want to obey. They wanted to bend his knees in contrary directions. For a moment, he thought he saw her chest move up and down. He considered going over to her, sitting down next to her, and saying how sorry he was, and yes they could talk about baby carriages, and even marriage. He stared at her chest. It was motionless.

He heard a sound, something rustling the leaves on the ground. He peered at the trees and the brush between them.

"You can come out," he said. He walked toward the sound and a little red squirrel dashed by. He looked behind him at the ground he and she had covered to reach the maple tree. He saw their footprints in the mud. He walked into the woods.

After a short while, the woods gave way to a flat open stretch of low growing vines. He continued until he reached a rise on the far side. He climbed to its top. He looked back across the tops of trees to the blue waters of the bay. He remembered something about a lake of fire that he had heard in a sermon once when he was a little boy. It was in a church in town, and he had been very frightened. His father had comforted him and said that they wouldn't go to that church again, they would only attend the one near their house. But now he was sure that the blue waters of the bay were tinged with the red of flames rising from their depths.

Edward looked up as a man came toward him from the direction of the woods. He thought at first it was Sam again.

"Boss said I should lend you a hand," Jim said.

Edward looked past him into the woods from which he had emerged.

"I took the long way around," Jim said. "I wasn't in no hurry."

"I thought I heard something," Edward said again. He regretted having said it as soon as the words were out of his mouth. He didn't have to explain himself to this nigger, did he? Maybe he had just wanted a little privacy to answer a call of nature. He looked down as though to see if his buttons were in place. Jim glanced in that direction, and then trudged back toward the new fence line. Edward waited before he followed. It was going to be a long day. And as he walked after Jim, he wondered where Sam was going, if that was, in fact, Sam. He hadn't seen clearly, and he knew that Jim was not above stealing the odd half hour when he was supposed to be moving to a work site. Maybe it was Jim he had seen and called out to.

"You did take the long way around, didn't you?" he asked when he caught up to Jim who had already started on a new hole.

"Not so long as anybody would notice," Jim replied. Then he gave the post digger's handle a violent twist. "I'll dig," he said. "You plant the posts."

"Suits me. Work is work, don't make no difference."

"You got that right," Jim said.

Isaiah unhitched Chester. He looked over the furrows he had dug in the last hour. Unlike the first few that were straight and true, these zigged and zagged across the field. In a couple of places, one furrow veered across its neighbor. He did not care. He led the horse into the barn, found the second ax, and trudged off toward the new road.

Sam swung his ax at the low growing vines. His head was beginning to clear. Isaiah would be coming soon. Should he tell him? Tell him that the woman he loved, the woman he hoped to marry was lying cold and stiffening beneath a maple tree within sight of East Bay? He took another short, violent swing. He looked back in the direction from which Isaiah would be coming and saw the glint of the sun off the blade of the new ax. He brought his ax down another time. He walked back to the beginning of the new road just as Isaiah arrived. For a moment he thought how wonderful it would be if he could explain to Isaiah what happened. But as soon as he saw the fierce unhappiness in his son's eyes, he changed his mind.

"You are a little late," Sam said.

"Yes."

"Come, on then."

Isaiah strode ahead over the cleared section of the new road, just ten or fifteen feet past the white birch where the way disappeared again beneath vines and tall, spindly weeds.

"It's harder to clear than it looks," Sam said.

"I guess it must be," Isaiah replied. "Did you..." he began but stopped in the realization that he did not want to hear the answer.

"Did I what?" Sam demanded.

"Nothing," Isaiah said in the voice of a sullen child.

"You should ask what's on your mind," Sam said.

Isaiah did not respond. Instead, he started swinging his ax. They worked side by side until the sun set and never exchanged another word.

6

———

Daniel sat at the table at Mrs. Svensen's boarding house, nestled between the Boardman and the railroad tracks. A train rumbled by and the platters on the table, heaped with eggs, sausage and thick slices of bread, rattled. His mind was elsewhere. He must see that young woman again. Something was squeezing the desire to live out of her, and he would seek it out, help her if he could. And if he could not, he would add her troubled heart to those already waiting his study on the desk in his small room, there to be made to yield their truth, which he would report, without bias, to the waiting world.

He took a swallow of his coffee, looked at the food on his plate, but stood up with a nod to Mrs. Svensen.

"I guess I'm not hungry today," he said.

She reached across the table and scooped the eggs and sausages back onto their serving dishes.

"Somebody else no doubt is. It is a sin to waste the Lord's bounty."

Sam lay in his bed, feeling the first rays of the sun creep in through the window. His body ached. He and Isaiah attacked the brush the day before as though each of them saw in the vegetation a mortal enemy, or perhaps it was just each other that they imagined felling before their hacking blades. He stretched to relieve the stiffness in his arms and back. Bringing his hand to his cheek and pressing against the tooth that had been tormenting him, he managed to mute the pain. He recalled now that he had been unaware of the tooth's throbbing since yesterday.

He heard his son's irregular breathing in the next room, and thought he probably had not slept either. For a brief moment, Sam remembered his wonder as he stood over the cradle in which his infant son lay, watching the tiny chest rise and fall, the puckered expression of the small face as though he had just had a perplexing thought, the utter and absolute innocence of the sleeping child. The memory was vivid, but brief, evaporating into the confusion of the present moment.

The sun was shining through his window, and he knew he should get up and go about his business just as he would any other day. But each time he began to rise from his bed, he saw her again lying among the arbutus vines so peaceful, so lovely, and he feared that if he rose, so would she, and he would find her waiting for him outside his door, so he closed his eyes, craving sleep, but his imagination insisted on flashing her face with her mouth forming words that he strained, without success, to hear. Snapping his eyes open, he stared at the cracked plaster of the ceiling, fixing his gaze at the corner where a spider was dangling on its invisible thread. As long as he stared at this busy little creature, he did not see her. His lids, though, felt as though each weighed a hundred pounds and they started to slide shut in spite of his best effort to keep them open. He jammed his thumbs onto them and pressed up until his eyes teared and he could no longer see the spider.

He had just resigned himself to a silent conversation with her, when he heard a loud thumping coming from the front door. He waited for Isaiah to see who was there, but when no sound came from his room, he willed his feet onto the floor. He realized, with a start, that he was still wearing his work clothes from yesterday. He looked down at his shirt. He expected to see her blood on it. He thought about pulling on his work boots. They were caked with mud from the wet ground where he had left her so instead he clambered down the stairs in his stocking feet and waited by the door, hoping that whoever knocked would have gone away, discouraged. Questions. He was not ready for them.

When the thumping resumed, he grasped the door handle and turned it ever so slowly until it swung open. There stood Henry Cutter, his eyes red and his lower lip specked with blood.

"I don't suppose you might know where she is," Henry said, the words forced out, and when they were his teeth gnawed on his lip.

"Who?" Sam replied.

"My daughter."

"Oh."

"She's been gone since yesterday. We thought you might have an idea where she is." Henry raised himself on his toes as though to look past Sam into the interior of the house. A shuffling of feet across a wood plank floor drifted down the stairs. The shuffling stopped on the landing where the stairs turned. Henry peered in that direction. Sam stiffened. He expected to see her fingers, bloody from clawing at the tree, pointing at him.

"Is that...?" Henry began.

"No, of course not," Sam managed to reply without much conviction.

Isaiah's large foot came into view on the landing. He looked down at the two men. He saw the angry concern in Henry's face, and the unusual lack of confidence in his father's eyes. He took the remaining steps two at a time, almost losing his balance as he came off the stairs. He righted himself and stood beside his father.

"He's looking for Margaret," Sam said. "He thought she might be here, or we might know where she's at."

Isaiah heard the uncertainty beneath his father's words.

"She's not here," he said.

"Do you have any idea?" Henry asked. His eyes were still angry, but his voice betrayed his fear. "It's not like her to stay out all night. Her mother and I, well, we thought she might have come over here, seeing how there has been an arrangement, and all."

"No," Isaiah replied. "And I don't know anything about no arrangement. As for that, you can talk to him." He nodded toward his father, and turned back to the stairs. "She sure as hell's not in my bed. Maybe you'd better look in his."

"Sam," Henry began, "what's he talking about?"

"Don't mind him. He'll come around."

"No need to bother about that," Henry replied. "I've been thinking it over, and changed my mind."

"You're upset."

"Of course I am. Look. She's not here. You and your boy don't know where she's at. We're forming a search party to look for her."

"Do you know where she was going?" Sam asked.

"Don't you?"

"No."

"To pick flowers."

"Whereabouts?"

Henry shrugged.

"I was working on that new road," Sam said, pointing to the west. "I didn't see her, but there's flowers thereabouts."

"Thereabouts, and all about," Henry muttered. "Say, you don't think she was looking for you?"

"No. I told her I'd be working all day. Isaiah was with me in the afternoon." A story was forming in his mind, and he would soon believe it was true. He always did come to believe his fabrications. "But then again, she might have. I'll get dressed and maybe we should start looking there."

"As good a place as any, seeing how fixated she was on you."

Isaiah had stopped on the landing to listen in to the end of the conversation. A terrible thought began to form in his mind. He tried to push it away. He contemplated rushing down the stairs to tell Henry Cutter about the note. But then the door slammed, and like the air flowing out of a punctured balloon, his energy to contest his father left him and he made his way up the stairs, with each step seeming to be immensely distant from the one below it.

"I'll join you in a moment," Sam said. "Got to put my shoes on."

Henry glanced down at Sam's feet and nodded.

"I'll wait on you," he said.

Sam felt his tooth begin to throb. He walked into the kitchen and found the bottle of laudanum. He took a swallow, put the bottle in his pocket. He felt Henry's eyes on him.

"Toothache," he said.

A dozen men had gathered at the Cutter farm. More would be coming from town as the word spread. Edward stood at the fringe of the group, and Henry motioned for him to come forward.

"My man here says he saw her leaving with a basket to gather flowers," Henry said.

"What direction was she going?" asked one of the men.

Edward shook his head.

"I just seen her walking away from the barn. I had my work to do, and she didn't make a habit of telling me where she was going."

"That's all right," Henry said. "You can't say what you don't know."

"Say," said another voice from the crowd. "Ain't it true, Henry, that your man, there spent some time in the Antrim County jail. What was that for?"

"Yeah, I heard," said another, "that he raped his boss's daughter."

"It's a wonder," came a voice of an old man at the rear, "how some people don't mind who they let in their house."

"I heard your nigger had that kind a problem," said still another.

"Now that's just about enough," Henry exploded. "I don't know anything about these rumors. These men work hard for me. And you're here to help me find my daughter. If you got other ideas in your heads, you can just go back home. Now, anybody else got something dumb to say or can we get on with finding Margaret?" He waited, and the men stood, moving their feet in the dust, their eyes lowered. "Well, let's get to it," Henry continued. "Since we don't know anything better, Sam here says she may have been walking across his place toward his new road."

There was a murmur and a shaking of heads.

"Did he see her?"

"No," Sam said. "I'm just supposing."

"I saw you in the woods that day," Edward said. "And I think you was heading east."

Sam felt the panic rise but he stiffened against it.

"You must be mistaken. Unless you mean when I was coming back to meet Isaiah."

"It was a little after noon. I know because the sun was straight up and we were planting a new fence, and it was hot."

Sam shrugged, and forced a condescending smile to form on his face.

"You must be mistaken."

Henry shifted his glance from Sam to Edward.

"I could be," Edward said.

"It don't matter," Henry said. "We'll start looking from here to Sam's place, and heading on toward the new road he's clearing. Unless somebody's got a better idea."

Standing some twenty feet away was Sarah, her eyes filled with hateful suspicion and fixed on Sam. He felt her gaze as though it were a tangible force and he knew he could not deflect it. He formed his face into what he imagined was a sympathetic expression, and nodded toward her.

"We'll find her, Mrs. Cutter," he said.

"I am sure of that," she replied. "But how will she be when you do? That is what I would like to know."

"Are you coming?" Henry asked.

"The cows," she replied. "Someone has to tend to the cows."

The search party numbered over thirty, as more men drifted to it both from town and the northern end of the Peninsula. They started from the hill behind the Cutter house, crossing over the narrow stream, now no more than a trickle of water across the muddy bottom as the sun beat down on it. They fanned out in an uneven line, working their way downhill to the meadow where Edward and Jim had planted the new fence, strung with barbed wire to contain the cows that Henry intended to move from the pasture they had exhausted on the other end of his land. Henry had brought a pair of wire cutters, and he snipped open the newly strung wire, and the men, their faces grim and glistening with perspiration filed through, gathering at the edge of the woods beyond.

Edward looked at Sam.

"Ain't this where you was yesterday, heading that way?" He pointed to the east.

"No, friend," Sam replied. Nobody was going to believe this hired hand whose past was blacker than his own.

Edward shrugged. His mind raced. He would sell what he saw, or thought he saw, it didn't matter which, for he would swear to whatever was necessary.

"There aren't many arbutus vines over this way," said the youngest member of the party, a boy of sixteen. He had red hair, freckles, and a space between his buck teeth, altogether an appearance that people found hard to take seriously. But his neck was thick and red from the sun, and his fingers powerful. "My sister was picking them over that way." He indicated the east.

"Maybe we should split up," the boy's father said, with his arm about his son's shoulder.

Henry considered for a moment and then shook his head.

"No. We'll all go this way, spread out in the same direction. There's too much ground to cover. We can go the other way later."

Sam took a deep breath. His nerves were drawn tight. The pain in his tooth was beginning to work its way through the laudanum. One moment he wanted to step forward and explain what had happened, how he had passed out from the drug and had awakened too late, and how he had tried to revive her, for this was the narrative he now had convinced himself was the truth. But the next second, he rejoiced that the search party was headed in the wrong direction, allowing him to contemplate returning alone at night to move the body to someplace they would never find it. But as soon as he entertained that idea, he shuddered at the prospect of seeing her as he had left her, imagining she would sit up and open her mouth through which would slither white maggots, her lips moving in silent imprecation. He felt himself shivering, and was convinced that all eyes were on him. He turned and started walking toward his land. When he dared to look back, he was surprised to see the others following. At first, he thought they were pursuing him, convinced that he had evidenced his guilt, but then he saw how they had spread out once again, their eyes on the ground in front of them. Henry caught up to him and walked with him stride for stride.

The red headed boy and his father, though, had not joined the others. Instead, with the boy in the lead, they headed toward the east. Sam saw them and forced his nerves to settle. He gestured toward them.

"Stubborn, ain't they?" he asked.

"We don't need them," Henry replied, "and if they do find something, there will be time to thank them."

As they walked, Henry did not stray more than a few feet from Sam, although the other searchers separated by ten or fifteen yards from each other. For his part, Sam began to doubt where he had been with her yesterday. He believed at every step her hand might reach up to seize him and pull him down next to her. A cooling breeze stirred through the trees, but the sweat continued to gather in the creases of his skin.

Daniel's lungs ached but he willed his legs to keep moving as he walked up the road from town onto the spine of the Peninsula. He noted fields of corn, stalks thigh high, acres of potatoes with their bushy tops, orchards showing the first bright red flash of cherries. Life coursed up from the earth and into the plants, and yet there seemed to be a pall over the land, which he could not at first explain until he realized that he had not seen a single worker. Nature provided its bounty on this day without an assist from human hands. Turning on the path to the Cutter farmhouse perched on the hill, he heard the loud mooing of cows whose udders had not been emptied, and then he saw Mrs. Cutter sitting on her front porch, rocking very slowly. When he got even closer he could discern the movement of her lips as, with eyes closed, she engaged in a fierce but silent monologue. He concluded she must be talking to the deity, and wondered, almost idly, if an answer was returned.

"Good morning," he said.

Her lips continued to move, although her eyes remained closed.

"Morning, ma'am," he tried again, in a louder voice.

Rocking and mouthing her silent words, her eyes remained shut. He waited, and with a sudden start, as though waking, or coming back from some distant land, her eyes snapped open and stared hard at him. She pointed toward the barn.

"He drowned in that creek behind the barn," she said, "though you wouldn't think so today. The water's not deep enough to drown a mouse."

"I've come to talk with your daughter, ma'am," he said. "I brought her back from town the other night. Perhaps you remember."

"That creek is all dried now, so she could not have drowned."

"Is she at home?"

Sarah shook her head ever so slowly from side to side, as though the effort to move it drained her remaining strength. She collapsed against the back of her rocking chair.

"No," she said.

"Where...?" he began, but she had shut her eyes again. After a few moments, she lifted her arm and pointed in the direction the others had taken.

"They are looking for her. They will not find her there. She is near the water. Where her brother waits."

"Yes, ma'am. I understand," he said. And he did. "Which bay?" he asked.

She looked, eyes closed, east and west.

"To the water," she said again. The mooing was becoming increasingly loud. She turned her head in that direction. "She ought to have taken care of them this morning. I am too tired."

He waited to see if she would say anything more. She seemed to be looking past him toward the barn.

"I'll just catch up with the others, then," he said, "and I will be sure to tell them what you have said. 'Bout the water."

"I must tend them," she said, and rose from her seat. He watched as she walked, ever so slowly, toward the barn.

The searchers were hungry and irritable. Heading north and west, they tramped up and down the hills, through woods where low growing vines caught at their boots and onto flat meadows where high grass hid the uneven ground. At noon, they gathered at the new road Sam was clearing. He showed them where he had been working the previous day. They did not seem interested. What did occupy them was the obvious absence anywhere they had walked of arbutus flowers.

"Maybe that Henderson boy was right," someone said. "Why would she be coming here to pick flowers which ain't to be found?"

"Maybe she didn't know."

"Oh, she would have known alright," Henry replied. "My Margaret would have known." He turned to Sam. "Wouldn't she?"

"I imagine so," Sam replied. There was something in Henry's tone, not quite accusatory yet, but not friendly either. "Let's just go on. Maybe what she was looking for is up ahead, and there's where she'll be, with a basket full of flowers wondering what all the fuss is about."

"You'll recall she did not come home last night," Henry said. "Was she with you?"

"I already told you about that this morning," Sam answered. He felt eyes on him, probing. "And the answer is no."

Daniel caught up to the search party, and he saw how Isaiah was hanging back from the rest. Forcing himself to draw in a deep breath, which turned into the familiar hacking cough, he winced at the pain in his chest. Isaiah, who had been staring at his father and Henry, turned to the reporter.

"Are you all right?"

Daniel daubed at his lips with his handkerchief. He knew there was blood on it, and he kept it hidden in his hand.

"I'm fine. A little out of breath."

"I don't think I know you."

"Daniel McConnell."

"Isaiah Logan."

Daniel extended his hand. He knew he had heard the name before. As he felt Isaiah's rough palm, he remembered.

"You were to be married," Daniel said.

Isaiah pulled his mouth back into a wide, mocking grin.

"I think you are mistaken," he replied. "Where did you hear such a thing?"

"She told me herself, the other day, in town."

Isaiah seized Daniel's shoulders. He wanted to shake the truth out of this frail young man.

"Do not trifle with me," he said.

"I would not," Daniel shrugged himself free.

"Why would she tell you such a thing?" Isaiah demanded.

"She was distraught about something," Daniel replied. "I met her wandering by the river in town. I took her to get something to eat, and the last thing she said is what I have just told you."

"I cannot believe it," Isaiah said.

"When we find her, you can ask her yourself."

"I don't think so," Isaiah replied.

Daniel knew why he said that, so he didn't ask. The whole day had the aura of a funeral. All that was missing was the dead body.

As dusk approached, some of the searchers began to fashion crude torches out of branches. Sam stumbled ahead, and Henry followed close behind. Low hanging branches now snapped across Sam's face, and he felt the blood trickle down his cheeks to merge with the sweat that coated his skin. Still, he crashed on through the woods until he came to a clearing that he thought he recognized, but in the failing light he was not sure. It might have been one of the places they had met. He had the sudden thought that it was where they had been yesterday, and he slowed his pace, his eyes glued to the ground step by step in front of him. His tooth throbbed with each step.

"Do you see something?" Henry demanded.

Sam waved his torch.

"No."

"You looked as though you did."

"No," Sam replied. He stared at the darkening sky. A little longer, he thought, and they would have to quit for the night. And when they did, he would go home for a while. Then, he and Isaiah, yes Isaiah must be complicit in the deed, together they would find her and remove her to where she would not be found for days, if ever. He began to breathe more easily. He might yet find a way out. But it was not to be. A shout rose to them from the easternmost fringe of the line of searchers. He knew what it portended, and his shoulders slumped.

With his red hair the same color as the sun now sliding behind the hills that blocked the view of West Bay, the Henderson boy led the searchers to the south and east. Sam, though, lagged behind.

"Come along," Henry said. "Or is there a reason you don't want to?"

The bastard knows. The thought came to Sam with the suddenness of lightning across a black sky when the thunder has not yet been heard. He took a deep breath as though he were struggling to get his wind back.

"You go on ahead Henry. I'll be along shortly."

"I think I'll wait on you," Henry replied.

"Please yourself." Sam felt despair descend on him and he thought for a moment of simply starting to run, but in what direction? He tried to will his feet to move, but they refused. He stood, and Henry waited.

"What is it?" Henry asked. "Are you hurt?"

Sam thought he detected mockery in his tone, and what remained of his pride surged to muscle aside the gloom that had settled over him.

"Not at all. Let's go."

They caught up with the others, joining the straggling human line walking across the soft ground of the swamp.

"Here," the Henderson boy said, "I found tracks going up to that rise."

Sam strode to a position next to the boy. Isaiah and Daniel flanked him on the other side.

"Whereabouts do you think?" Sam asked. He lowered the torch so that he could see the ground. His prints must still be there, he thought, but the flickering light of the torch did not provide enough light to be sure. Still, he lifted his torch.

The boy gestured toward the maple tree rising above the hemlocks. Sam nodded, and began walking in that direction, through the tall meadow grass and then onto the muddy area in front of the tree. Isaiah took his father's arm.

"You don't have to," Isaiah said, "I'll go on ahead." He looked hard into his father's face, seeing how his father's eyes seemed to have rolled back into their sockets, so that the whites reflected the red glow of the smouldering branch he held in front of him. Looking around, he saw that nobody else had taken a step in the direction the Henderson boy had indicated. All eyes seemed to be on his father.

"Come on, then," said Sam, and he shook himself free from Isaiah's grasp. He now felt, almost with joy, that he would soon be delivered from his torment. He wanted to rush ahead, but his legs would not cooperate. Instead, he watched as Henry trotted forward, his torch bobbing against the shadows. Isaiah and Daniel followed. The others looked from Sam to Henry and waited. Sam took a deliberate step forward, and then another while Henry's torch bent down beneath the shadowed form of a maple tree.

And from Henry came a howl of despair.

He was kneeling next to a shape on the ground. Sam stopped fifteen or twenty feet away, knowing what Henry was looking at, feeling the breath of the others on his back. Isaiah held his torch next to Henry's. Their garish glare turned her pale skin red. She was lying as though asleep, her arms crossed on her chest. One crushed pink arbutus blossom poked out of her hair near her right ear. Isaiah moved his torch down her body pausing at her hands. Clotted blood stained the middle three fingers of her right hand. He looked a little closer and noted what appeared to be a sliver of wood beneath the nail of her index finger. Sweeping his torch light up the trunk of the tree, he found a place where bark seemed to have been peeled off. On the ground next to her was a bottle. A little further away was a basket with its wilted blossoms. Henry leaned across the girl who used to be his daughter and looked at the bottle.

"Laudanum," he muttered. "Where'd she get that?" He looked first at Isaiah, and then past him to Sam. A tear formed in the corner of his eye, and he swiped at it as though it were a noisome insect.

Daniel began to open his mouth, and then thought better of it. Nobody else had heard the question except Isaiah, who did not seem to have processed it, and this other man, who must be Isaiah's father, and he, too, did not seem to have paid any attention to what Henry asked. No, he would bide his time and tell what he knew to somebody in authority. This young woman's death had to be explained, and when the explanation came, he did not want to be more involved as a participant than he had to. He felt the reporter's urge to seek and share the truth. To do his job, he must remain outside the circle of the action.

"Didn't you have a bottle in your house? For your tooth?" Henry called to Sam.

Sam felt panic tighten his throat. His tooth still throbbed. He took a couple of steps closer.

"That was my wife's, you know." He felt something press against his thigh from inside his pocket and remembered. He pulled out the bottle.

"Here's mine," Sam said.

Henry strode back to Sam and held up the other bottle.

"So you know nothing about this one?"

"No, I don't."

Henry looked back toward his dead daughter.

"Don't you want to take a closer look?" Henry asked, and his voice dripped his contempt.

"No," Sam murmured.

The others had now gathered about them. At the back of the crowd Edward studied Sam's face. He could almost see the perspiration pooling at the base of his spine. Oh, yes, he knew how sweat did that when panic begins to hold you in its clench. That man, he concluded, had reason to sweat, and that sweat was going to buy himself a ticket out of here and a new life in California.

Jim lay on the hay in the barn, his eyes searching the shadows in the rafters where he had heard a rustle of wings. Some dumb owl, he thought, how do they see in the dark like that, and why? The good Lord made them creatures of the night, just like he was, for when darkness fell he could blend into it, his skin no longer standing out in stark contrast to his surroundings as it did in daylight. Unlike the snake, he couldn't shed his skin, and even if he could it probably would grow back blacker than it was now.

He had seen the look in their eyes when they left searching for her. He had followed from a discrete distance for a while until he saw them light their torches. That combination of concern and fear in white men's eyes illuminated by the glow of torches was his signal to melt back into the night. He had a few belongings rolled up into an extra shirt, and he was ready to run, if he had to. But a fool he wouldn't be. If he took off before their suspicions landed on him, he would draw suspicion to him. Better then to wait, and watch and be patient.

"You do remember," Sam insisted, "we were working on the road yesterday afternoon."

"I remember," Isaiah said.

"And if they ask you, you'll tell them, won't you?"

"I'll tell them exactly what I know about yesterday."

Sam remembered the noise he heard in the woods.

"And what is that?"

"Just what I said."

Isaiah got up from the table and climbed the stairs to his room. He shut the door behind him. He listened for his father's footsteps, leaned his body against the door, but he heard nothing. Dragging the clumsy, high backed chair from next to his bed to the door, he jammed it under the knob. Then he lay down. He shut his eyes and opened his mind to the image of her on the ground. He needed to study it, to make love to it.

He started with the pink blossom braided into her hair, as though she were dressed for her wedding. Henry had closed her eyes, and so now Isaiah willed them open to stare into and through their deep blue color. He imagined they returned his look. Her hair in wild disorder framed her face. Her lips opened to speak words he could not hear.

The effort of recalling her image exhausted him, and he lay back on his bed. He had begun to feel aroused as his mental fingers traced her face, and now he was nauseated at the very thought of touching her. His mind moved against his will to the exchange he had just had with his father. They both knew that Sam would be an obvious suspect if it were determined that her death had been a murder, and not the suicide that the empty bottle of laudanum might suggest. He sat up as though somebody had just slapped him. Of course, how could he have forgotten? It was not only she who was dead, but the life growing within her. His new brother, his father had mockingly said. He could raise him as his own. He remembered now with a bitterness that seemed corrosive enough to eat through his heart. He was to marry her as a surrogate for his father, to enter her where his father had already been. But the thought was just too horrible. He must gag on it. He staggered to his feet and knelt next to the chamber pot in the corner. It had not been emptied, and its acrid aroma caused his head to jerk back. Still he lowered his face, trying to will up the bile that had climbed to his throat. But there it stopped, and he was left with its bitter taste in his mouth. And that seemed right. He could not imagine ever again enjoying the taste of anything sweet, not chocolate, or honey, or ripe strawberry juice against his palate.

In the confusion of his thoughts he had forgotten, how could he have, what his new friend, that consumptive reporter, had said. She was going to marry him, Isaiah, after all. Was it possible she loved him, even a little? Or was her love for his father so strong that she would go along with his bizarre proposal? If that were the case why would she take her own life with the laudanum? Or why would his father have killed her? The alternatives raced around his mind, her hand bringing the bottle to her lips, his father's hands upon her, faster and faster the images spun until he could do no more than clutch the chamber pot to his breast until cold sweat bathed him.

Later, when the spasms had stopped, he lay in his bed. His head cleared and he realized that he would be asked where his father had been on the day she died. What would he say? He thought he knew his father's many sides, his careless cruelty, his sudden gestures of warmth and affection, now only rare but still fixed in memory. But he could not wrap his mind around the concept of his father as a murderer.

Still, there was the note he had never given to his father. It was still in his pocket. What if he had never delivered its contents to his father? Would she still be alive?

He took it out and stared at it. It felt warm in his hands, and then he realized that his face was flushed. He thought he should burn it. But then he decided that he must keep it against some circumstance he could only dimly imagine. He would secrete it someplace where he would be able to put his hands on it, but somewhere it would be most unlikely that his father would stumble upon it. He smiled as the idea of such a place occurred to him.

Sam sat at the table stretching and clenching his fingers. They insisted on feeling again her warm flesh. He dug his fingernail of one hand into the finger tips of the other and pressed as hard as he could. Then he reversed the procedure and pressed into the flesh of the fingers on his other hand. He wanted to feel pain, but all he experienced was her soft skin. His tooth had stopped throbbing. He would be happy if it would begin again. He dipped his finger into a jar of honey. He licked it clean, and then dipped it again. Then he ran his finger, coated with the thick honey, over the inflamed tooth. He braced for the head splitting pain he knew would come. But it didn't. His tooth had gone dead. His whole body seemed without sensation, all that is, except his fingers, which reminded him of how her skin had felt beneath them.

He looked up the stairs toward his son's room. He didn't know if he could trust him to do the right thing. He thought of going to bed, but the idea of lying in his small room staring at the ceiling depressed him. Instead, he walked outside. The night was clear and the sky was filled with stars. He looked up at them, and in the immense void between them, he felt strangely comforted.

Henry sat across from Sarah. He was groping for words to tell her what he had seen.

"You needn't bother," his wife said. "She's dead, isn't she?"

"Yes."

"Then there is no more to be said. We will bury her next to her brother."

He got up and walked to her side of the table. He stood behind her and put his arms around her shoulders. She did not shrug him off, nor did she accept his embrace. It was as though she did not acknowledge his presence.

"I milked the cows," she said. "I guess that's my job now."

It was late by the time Daniel opened the door to his tiny room. Throwing open the window, he sat in a chair next to it, breathing as deep as his lungs would permit. He remembered Isaiah had withdrawn into himself once he looked at the body. Then, he had walked into the woods at a pace that Daniel knew he could not match. He had no desire to go crashing about unfamiliar woods in the dark, and so he had let him go. On his way back to town, he had passed the Cutter farm, heard the cows mooing, and continued on.

Recalling the innocence of her face, he looked up into the star filled night and saw only black between the bright spots of light. If there was a deity up there, He most certainly must have had His back turned when that precious life had been snuffed out between cruel fingers.

7

—◆—

S am lay in his bed, his body numb except for his tooth, which had begun again to ache. The first rays of the sun shone through his window, and he shuddered as though the rays were fingers of ice on his face. He had not been able to figure a way out of what he had to do this day. He simply rose and dressed in his suit. He knocked on the door to Isaiah's room, but heard no response. He opened the door, and saw the bed was made. Feeling the pillow and underneath the thin summer blanket, he found both were cool. Downstairs, he found Isaiah sitting at the table in the kitchen.

"Is that how you're going to church?" Sam asked. "In your work clothes?"

"I'm not going," Isaiah replied.

"I'd rather you did."

"I don't want to see her put in the ground."

"Your grandfather will be expecting you."

"I know."

"And so will..." Sam paused.

"You don't have to say it. So will the others. But they won't expect to see you, and if you do show up, they'll wonder where I am."

"That's right."

"You could stay home yourself."

"No, I can't."

"You go on ahead. Maybe I'll change my mind."

"Suit yourself, then," Sam replied. He walked out the door and took a few steps toward the barn.

"No, I think I'll walk," he muttered. "Damn that boy."

Although it was a Sunday morning, and he was expected in church, County Prosecutor Bill Heller was settled into the chair behind his desk in his office on Union Street, close by the county courthouse. He was a tall, powerfully built man, who had worked in the lumbering camps as a young man. Reading over the notes prepared by Sheriff Clarence Billingham, he saw the autopsy report was not yet available, and although some people insisted that the young woman had committed suicide, a theory supported by the presence of an empty bottle of laudanum at the scene, as well as statements from a waitress and two boys and a girl fishing in the river of a distraught woman who bore a striking resemblance to the victim, in spite of these suggestions Heller had convinced himself that the young woman had been murdered. His bones told him that. He always listened to his bones, especially when their advice agreed with his ambition. And if she had been murdered, no doubt her killer had known her. How else explain the sleep like attitude of the body? She did not seem to have struggled. Her lover, whoever he was, seemed the most logical candidate. And it should not take very long, in a small community such as this, to find out who he was.

Sarah Cutter knelt before Benjamin's grave as she had done every Sunday since his death, and then she moved to her left and looked at the new wound in the ground, the freshly dug earth piled onto the grass next to the hole in which her daughter would be lowered next to her brother. Her head swung like a pendulum from the old grave to the new. Henry walked to her side and touched her shoulder. She did not acknowledge the pressure, and eventually he turned away, his eyes traveling up the bell tower at the front of the church, to the pointed arches of the window that paralleled the sharp angle of the gabled roof behind the tower, the whole architecture of the building expressing an upward aspiration in sad contrast to the dark earth behind him that had swallowed the son he thought would grow up to work side by side with him on his farm, and would receive later this day the daughter whose life, in a sense, had ended with her brother's, although she had lived on to a conclusion beneath a maple tree in the hemlock swamp overlooking East Bay. When he sensed Sarah getting up, he took a step toward the path that led to the front of the church. In a moment, she took his arm, as she always did, and everything then was the same. Yet everything was totally different. For in his mind's eye, he envisioned the earth being closed over his daughter. He could not imagine how he would endure an endless stream of Sundays with his wife kneeling at the graves of their children while he wanted only to hurl his curses heavenward to ask God just why He had decided to afflict them with these terrible losses.

Arm in arm through the front door of the church, they looked for all the world like any other pious couple. Only someone looking more closely, someone like Daniel who nodded to them as they passed him sitting near the rear of the sanctuary, only such a sharp eyed observer paying particularly close attention, would have noted the rigidity of her expression, or the slight quiver of his lip, evidencing their tension as they made their way toward their seats.

In front of the pulpit, on a support crudely fashioned out of raw lumber lay the simple pine coffin that Henry had made. On top of it was a bouquet of pink and white arbutus blossoms.

Sam walked up the path toward the front door. His shiny leather shoes, now covered with the dust of the road, pinched his toes, in counterpoint to the throbbing ache in his jaw. He welcomed the pain, however, as it made it hard for him to think, and thinking was the last thing he wanted to do this morning.

He heard the bell toll while he was still a short distance away. On arrival, he opened the door as gently as he could though still it complained. Walking into the vestibule, he stood by the bell tower rope and had the sudden thought that it would most certainly hold his weight. He wondered how the congregation would react to seeing his body swinging at the end of the rope as they made their way out after the service. The idea intrigued him and he remained next to the rope, his right hand clutched about it while he contemplated the image. But then he saw his father staring back at him through the opened door that led into the interior, and making his way ever so slowly down the aisle, he remembered watching two brides walk down it, each flanked by a man who looked very much like his own father, on their faces an expression of feigned joy as they passed their precious daughters to him, a man they had every reason to fear. He knew then, each time, that it was his father's money that had persuaded those men to commit their girl children into his care.

Halfway down the aisle, he paused and stared at the coffin. He studied it as an artifact of woodworking. He noted where the edges could have been more exactly joined, the nails driven in with more care. Then he raised his gaze to the flowers and it was as though he had been struck a blow to his sternum. Nausea welled up, and the coffin seemed to rise and spin about. Shutting his eyes, and opening them again to find the coffin remained as it was, he resumed walking. As he did, he felt eyes shredding his fine Sunday suit until he was naked and bleeding. He imagined fingers pointing at his back as he walked by. When he reached the front pews he stopped. To his right were Henry and Sarah Cutter. To his left his were his father and space for three people. The last time he had attended services some time ago, his mother and son flanked his father, and he had sat on the aisle, as if to emphasize his marginal presence in that family grouping. Today, his father sat alone. Charles turned to him and gestured to the aisle seat that Sam knew would remain reserved for him if he never again attended a church service. He gathered what strength remained, and nodded toward the Cutters. He waited for her to return a greeting. They were, after all, neighbors, but her head did not move. Henry glanced at Sam, and then turned his attention to the hymnal, which he had already opened. Sam slid into the seat next to his father.

"I did not expect to see you here. I never expect to see you here, but most especially today." His father's voice was a harsh whisper.

Sam sought the lie that so often came to his lips, almost unbidden, but not today. He sat mute.

"Do you need money?" his father asked.

He shook his head.

"For a lawyer, I mean," his father insisted.

Sam did not answer.

"I suppose I'll have to clean up your mess," Charles continued. "Just like I have done since you were old enough to get into trouble."

"I..." Sam began.

"Don't bother," his father replied. "Just calm yourself down, and sit here in a manner befitting your position as my son, heir to my wealth and lands. Beyond that, say nothing to anybody until you hear from me, or the attorney I will hire to defend you."

"Yes," Sam replied.

"Your son," Charles said, "where is he?"

"Home. He said he did not want to see her put into the ground."

Charles let out an audible sigh.

"I suppose I will have to have a talk with him as well."

The door to the side of the raised platform opened. The thump of wood against wood announced the arrival of the preacher. Lapham walked with deliberate step to the platform. He looked out at the expectant faces of his congregation. He paused on the unfamiliar face in the front row, and then remembered those same features beneath a baseball cap. He swept his eyes to the left of Sam and stopped at Henry and Sarah. The pain in their eyes was palpable. Their daughter, he thought. He had seen her in distress in the cemetery, and he had offered her only a platitude. And by failing their daughter he had failed them.

He stared at the flower bedecked coffin and began.

"My dear friends, I am unworthy of your respect. You look upon me as one who has escaped Satan's snares. But I have not, any more than the worst sinner among you. I recall that day when the Lord stung me with His displeasure, and smote my leg from my body. I was then, as I am now, as we all are now, a sinner before God's purity. But, you ask, what about Margaret Cutter, there in her coffin?

"Her death, as terrible a blow as it is to all those who knew and loved her, is just like the Lord's lightning that struck me. She did not die from disease, for all reports are testimony to her vibrant good health. She died from the common human weakness, whether by her own hand, or more probably the hand of one who had been her intimate, for the manner in which she was found does not argue for the violence of a stranger. God has chosen to use the unfortunate woman as a sign of His general displeasure with His people. No doubt," he lifted his eyes, "God has swept the poor young woman up to heaven where she can weep at the feet of Her Savior."

Sarah listened. She wanted very much to believe that her daughter had been chosen for a divine mission. But she remembered seeing Margaret standing with Sam on the hill across from their house only a few days before. The sun was just setting, but their figures were still illuminated. He had his hand on her hip. She was quite sure of that. And then their heads had moved toward each other, and she had walked back into the house. When Margaret came in some time later, her face was flushed although the night air was chilly.

How then, she thought as the minister spoke, could this young woman, so obviously in a carnal relationship, have been chosen as a vessel for a divine message? It was much more likely that God had struck her down simply because she deserved His wrath. Since she herself could not forgive her, she could not imagine that her God would. Just as Lapham was riding his last majestic period, she plucked Henry's sleeve.

"Now," she whispered. "I have heard enough. This man does not speak God's truth. I will wait by the grave for them to come out."

Henry remained sitting. Each word of the minister's sermon pierced his heart. Unlike his wife he had not come to any judgment concerning Margaret's death. The wound was still too raw. The preacher's words opened the wound wider. Since he had seen her lying there with her arms crossed across her chest, he could not rid himself of the image of those hands working the udders of the complacent cows, who stood for her as they stood for no-one else.

Later, he would begin to think about how she came to be dead. He would conclude that she had been murdered. His anger, then, would replace the pain of his grief. He would come to a sure conviction as to who the killer was. But that was later.

The congregation watched Sarah leave. Their heads nodded in sympathy. One woman reached her hand out as Sarah came abreast of her. Sarah, who seemed not to be looking where she was walking, still sensed the gesture. She stopped and looked at the woman, who had her arm around her own daughter, a child of about ten, her face still informed by the innocence she would lose within a very few years. It was as though that mother understood only too well what Sarah was thinking about Margaret. She would shelter her daughter for as long as she could, but in the end she would have to step back and watch and hope that she did not make the same mistake that Margaret had. Sarah squeezed the hand in silent communion and then continued out the door.

As Sam listened to the sermon, he relaxed into the flow of words. He wanted to follow where the words led, to a beatific image of Margaret being blessed by Her Savior. But his mind, unused to such celestial heights, returned instead to memories from his teen years when another preacher painted a picture of hell fires ready to consume those who, like himself, found it impossible to resist the emerging lusts of adolescence.

By the time Lapham was finished, Sam was drenched in per-spiration. The minister nodded toward Henry. Henry rose and walked to the coffin. He was joined there by two others. He turned toward the congregation, looking for someone who did not appear. A woman stood up.

"I'm sorry, Henry, but Silas is home abed and sick."

Henry nodded and seemed lost in thought. Then he focused his gaze on Sam. He motioned him up.

"It's only right," he said.

Sam shook his head.

"Surely, you won't refuse," Henry said.

"Go on up there, you damned fool," Charles whispered into his ear. He seized his son's arm and pushed him up. Sam rose on unsteady legs. He nodded at Henry and wiped the sweat from his hands on his trousers. He took the front corner of the coffin, across from Henry. All four lifted and began the slow walk toward a door behind the pulpit that led directly to the cemetery. The minister preceded them. Sam felt lightheaded. He did not think that he could continue. He wanted to pull open the lid and climb in, he wanted to drop his end of the coffin and run. Instead, he struggled on with the others until they reached the grave side. Sam and the other pall bearers were acutely aware of the flowers still balanced on the coffin. They kept shifting their hold to make sure the bouquet stayed put. The sexton, a broad shouldered man in his fifties, with stubborn dirt beneath his finger-nails, had also gone on ahead and stood off to a side with a shovel. Sarah got up when they arrived. They put the coffin down, and Henry took his wife's hand. She picked up the flowers and then let herself be led a few feet away.

The congregants joined them. Lapham, having delivered his remarks inside, confined himself to a simple prayer consigning the body to the care and mercy of the Lord. With the sexton's assistance, they lowered the coffin and Lapham tossed dirt on it as he finished the prayer. Sarah dropped the flowers in, one bloom at a time, picking off each tiny blossom as though it were a piece of her heart. Sam thought at any moment he must collapse, and yet he remained standing. Understand-ing not one word that the minister said, he realized that Lapham had stopped talking and people were coming up to Henry and Sarah to offer their condolences. He felt pressure on his arm, and turned to see his father.

"Come," Charles said, "my buggy is out front."

He put his hands on Sam's shoulders and guided him away from the grave. The sexton began shoveling the dirt with muscular motions, and Sam shuddered. Charles and Sam found the minister in their path.

"Wonderful sermon," Charles said, as he took Lapham's hand. "I don't know if you have made my son's acquaintance. He usually worships in town, nearer to his house."

Lapham took Sam's hand, and felt the moisture on his skin.

"I believe we have met. At a baseball game."

"I see," Charles said. "Very like, very like."

Sam gathered himself.

"I do recall," he said, "that you took to the game."

Lapham smiled.

"I trust you do not misunderstand me. Now or then."

"Come," Charles said.

Sam followed his father through the door back into the church and through the sanctuary. They emerged into the front entrance. He paused by the bell rope and ran his finger up it as far as he could reach. Then he looked at the door at the side of the entrance. He remembered going through it the day of his second wedding, when the building was new, and he needed a private space for conversation with Isaiah, who did not want to be an usher at the ceremony. The door led to stairs down to the basement where it was dark, where he could hide.

But his father tugged at his sleeve, and they walked out into the bright sunshine.

Heller hurried along Washington Avenue toward the First Baptist Church, which was housed in an impressive brick building, featuring a cone topped tower on one corner in the same Queen Anne style as the mansion of the lumber baron on Sixth Street. The rear of the church offered a view of the Boardman, and if the building had not been built for worship, the site could have been used for a residence for one of the booming town's growing population of wealthy citizens. The building gave off a palpable aura of affluence.

Right up the block was the county courthouse where Heller tried his cases. He looked at that red brick and sandstone building, with its symmetrical Romanesque style, a square base surmounted by a clock tower, which showed the same time on each side. Heller paused for a moment, experiencing one of those distracting, metaphysical thoughts he had from time to time. He had studied philosophy at the university after all, and had even considered the ministry before deciding that he wanted his feet planted more firmly in the here and now. But for the moment he was struck by the contrast between the clock tower's insistence on the temporal and the eternal orientation of the church he was about to enter.

He took his seat next to his wife, Hatty. She had her eyes on the collection plate, which was moving in the pew in front of them. He took her hand and squeezed, but she did not return the pressure. The plate at the end of its long pole was now in front of him. He looked up at the smiling face, missing the lower front teeth, of the elderly deacon holding the pole. Reaching into his pocket for coins, his fingers closed only on one, and it was large and heavy. Hatty nudged him, and he dropped the dollar into the plate. The deacon nodded his approval. Hatty took his arm as they walked out after the service, but he felt the formality of her grasp rather than the warm squeeze she usually offered.

"Wonderful service," he said to the minister, a young man with fuzz on his lips.

"You are well known for your powers of deduction," the minister said.

"How's that?"

"To be able to infer so much from so little," the minister smiled.

"A case," Bill said. "A very important one. I'm afraid I permitted myself to become immersed in it at my office this morning."

"And on the Sabbath," the minister replied. He glanced in the direction of the courthouse. "May the Lord help you wield the sword of justice."

"My husband does work too hard," Hatty said. "I'll take him home now for a good Sunday dinner."

"You do that," the minister said.

Heller was aware that those around them had been listening to this exchange. He nodded in their direction.

"I can't tell you anything yet, folks," he said and led the way down the steps.

"You enjoyed the attention, didn't you?" Hatty said when they had walked a little distance.

"Just doing the Lord's work," he replied. "In my own way."

Edward Franklin did not go to church this Sunday. He sat alone in his attic room. Usually, Sarah would insist that he attend service, but today she did not call him down as she usually did, so he peered through the little window in the gable end of the attic and watched them walk off, then sat back down on his bed.

No, he did not want to listen to some preacher go on about Margaret's death, envisioning her up in heaven floating around with the angels. For all he knew, she was in hell this moment, thrown there as a consequence of her fornicating habits. In his mind, though, her death was now the basis for a business transaction because he had information to sell to whoever wanted it. If he went to church, he might start thinking about how he looked at her, how he wanted her. He could not afford to have such thoughts cloud the hard cash basis he hoped to present to his buyer.

He had looked down at her dead body with a moment's intense pain at the great waste and anger at the man who had first had her and then killed her. But the anger faded into his usual recognition of his place in the world, like a poor man with his face pressed against the window of the store whose merchandise he would never be able to afford. That thought led him to the think that if he could not have her in life, he could profit from her death.

He lay down and closed his eyes, needing to decide whom to approach first because he might not get a second chance. But as he lay there his mind filled with images of the dead woman. She walked out of the barn that morning. He could have stopped her. He knew where she was going, where she always went, to meet Sam Logan. If he had, she would still be alive.

He got up and paced back and forth along the center of the room where the rafters were high enough for him to walk under without stooping. It was hot there as it always was in the summer, and yet it was the coldest spot in the house in the winter. Just like his life, he thought, always getting the opposite of what he needed. But this time he was going to change things. He paused by the window. As he did, he saw a figure emerge from the barn. He was carrying a sack on the end of a pole over his shoulder.

"I'll be," he muttered. "He's leaving. Maybe it was him I saw that day."

Jim looked once back over his shoulder. He had not hesitated. Times like these were trouble, and he was not going to wait around for it to land on his head as it had done so many times before. He sensed somebody watching him and turning to see who it was he caught a movement in the attic window. He waved for Edward to come down, then waited, but there was no response. He trotted back toward the house and stood beneath the window.

"You're Irish trash, a white nigger, so you might as well come down and join with me," he called up to the window.

There was no reply. Jim shrugged and headed away from the house.

Standing beside the window, Edward uttered a curse.

Isaiah sat at the table stirring a spoon through his cold coffee. He brought it to his lips and sipped. Somehow the cold, bitter taste suited his mood. He knew he was expected to stand at his father's side to deflect some of the finger pointing that would be aimed at Sam.

But that was the problem. A little voice growing louder and more insistent in his mind demanded that he point his own finger at the man whose blood flowed through his own veins. He struggled to quell that voice because he was sure it was unnatural. But it would not be still.

He swallowed the rest of his coffee. He needed advice, and he knew the one person he could trust to guide him through the morass he now found himself in.

8

―――――

The baseball bat was still propped in the corner of the office. Father and son looked at each other across the desk. Charles Logan opened a drawer of his desk and pulled out a leather bound volume containing blank drafts on his bank in town.

"This is going to be expensive," he said.

"What exactly do you think you can buy?"

"The best lawyer I can find."

"I haven't said anything."

"You didn't have to. Didn't you see how everybody was looking at you? It won't be long now before you hear a knock at the door."

Sam stood up and walked to the corner. He picked up the baseball bat. He ran his fingers over the smooth grain, remembering the hours he had spent at the lathe, the blade hot and the air rich with the aroma of wood. He felt an overwhelming sadness. Taking two long strides, he reached his father's desk and raised the bat over his head. He stared hard at Charles, and lifted the bat a bit higher. Arm and shoulder muscles tensed, and then he started to bring it down. Charles followed the motion, but did not flinch. Sam let the bat thud down on the desk surface.

"A carpenter, I should have opened a shop. Why didn't you let me do what I was good at?" Sam said, his voice between a snarl and a cry.

Charles pushed at the bat, and with a flick of his wrists Sam swung it to his shoulder.

"Maybe you should have," Charles said. "But you are my son, my only son, and I have acres of farmland I'm too old to work."

"There's Isaiah, as you have reminded me."

"Yes."

Sam sat back down, his hands still wrapped around the baseball bat.

"You think of him as the one who will save your land for you and provide you heirs. But he is also mine."

Charles leaned forward over the desk.

"You mean he will stand up for you?"

"He's my son."

"But will he?"

Sam shrugged and stood up.

"If he doesn't, I'll be gone, he'll be your heir, just like you want."

"Whatever my private thoughts," Charles said, "I'm not ready to see you in jail." He opened the draft book and with vigorous strokes signed one.

"I will see what I can buy with this."

"You could give it to me," Sam said.

"I could. But I won't. If you run, you will prove that all those people looking at you with suspicion are right. I can't have it."

"I'm touched. That you care so much for my well being."

Charles permitted himself a mocking laugh that started in high spirits in his belly but turned to contempt when it reached his mouth.

"You know better than that."

"I certainly do," Sam replied.

"Your mother didn't attend church today," his father said. "It's the first time she has not gone since you were born. Fitting, don't you think?"

"I wouldn't know about that," Sam said.

"No, you wouldn't."

Sam got up and looked out of the window at the buggy that had taken them from church. He leaned the bat back against the wall.

"It's a long walk home," he said.

"The horse is tired," his father replied. "And you know I don't ever abuse an animal."

"I'd better get started then," he said.

His mother was waiting in the hall outside the study. She embraced him. He could smell the lilac water he remembered she splashed on herself every Sunday, to make herself fresh for the Lord, she used to say with a girlish giggle. She stepped back and he, seeing the tears in her eyes, began to open his mouth, to find, as he always did, the words that would make her smile at his foibles. She pressed her fingers to her his lips.

"Don't," she said, "not this time. I don't want to hear you say anything about this awful matter. In my heart I know you could not have done anything terrible."

The truth welled up in him, pushing against the dike of his restraint. He needed so much to let it out, and the only person in the world to whom he could was standing in front of him.

"I know," she said. "But don't."

"Don't think bad thoughts," he said, fixing his lips into their usual knowing grin, "why I was only going to compliment you for smelling like a lilac bush in spring."

She shook her head and her eyes glistened even more.

"Your father," she said, "he will do what needs to be done. You know that, don't you?"

"Yes, as always," he replied.

"Then, go home to your son. He must need you at this time."

As I need him, he wanted to say, but he squeezed her hand, and then turned down the hall. As he reached the door, he found Mary polishing the knob. She looked up at him, but then turned back to her task.

He put his hand on her arm, but she shook it free.

"I've heard," she said.

"I see."

She opened the door.

"I do wish you well," she said.

Isaiah sat astride the broad back of the workhorse so that with each step the animal took, he jogged his mind to frame the question he must ask. His conflict was simple, he thought, should he protect his father or should he serve truth, at least that sliver of it contained in her note. Three sleepless nights since he had looked down at her still body, and how far had he come in his thinking? He had arrived at the awful conclusion, buttressed by the note he had now hidden, that only his father could be responsible for her death. That was the truth.

If he served that truth he would remove his support of his father's alibi. If he supported that alibi, he would desert truth. With each jolt of the lumbering animal's stride he bounced between these two poles. His one hope was that his father's father could remove him from the horns of this dilemma.

The horse climbed the hill just south of the harbor at the tip of the Peninsula where the big steamers coming up from Chicago dis-gorged their white linen-clad gentlemen with their ladies in bright col-ored gowns onto the dock where carriages waited to take them either to their summer cottages or to the Old Mission Inn. He reined in the horse and looked to his right at the blue waters of the bay. There, almost on the horizon, he saw white puffs that looked like low floating clouds but beneath them he could make out the bulky shape of the ship, one of the hundreds of freighters that plied the lakes, sending billows up through its smokestack. He felt drawn to the water and that ship as he had never been before. It suddenly came clear to him that he would never be happy with the ground beneath his feet: it was too solid, too unyielding. He preferred the soft cushion of the lake's surface, the ambiguity of its motion.

He dug his heels into the horse's flanks and the animal lurched forward once again, following the road that took him along the beach at the edge of the harbor. Passing the fringe of the village, he turned onto a narrow way that wound and rose through the woods to the ridge on which sat his grandfather's house. As he entered the shade of the trees, whose leaves brightened in the sun reaching through the dense branches, he detected movement a short distance ahead, just coming around a curve. Before the figure was fully visible, he knew who it was.

His father's face was grim. Isaiah reined in the horse and waited. Sam strode toward him but did not appear to see him. His lips were moving as though he were muttering to himself. At the last mo-ment, just before he walked into the horse, he stopped and looked up at Isaiah. He seized the reins.

"Get down, boy," he said.

Isaiah did not move. Sam yanked the reins but Isaiah held his end fast and then wrapped them around his wrist.

"I need to speak with Grandfather," he said.

Sam looked up at his son, who sat motionless on the horse's bare back. His tooth ached as it had that other day, and he felt his forehead begin to throb. He wanted nothing more than to get home where he could draw the curtains and lie down in the darkness of his room while he puzzled out what to do next.

"Step aside father," Isaiah said. His voice was preternaturally calm. He felt, for the first time in his life, in control.

Sam sensed something snap in his forehead. He clamped his lower jaw against his tooth. With a sudden yank on the reins he hauled Isaiah off the horse. The boy tumbled to the ground, but was immediately on his feet, his fists balled.

"Go ahead, then," Sam said. "If you think you're ready."

Isaiah launched a roundhouse right at his father's jaw. Even as he did, he feared that it would connect, while at the same time the explosion of energy was wonderful. Sam raised his left arm and blocked the punch. For a moment they closed, felt the other's breath until Isaiah stepped back.

"Take the damned horse, old man," he said.

Sam rubbed the place on his forearm where Isaiah's angry fist had landed. Isaiah spun around and was on his way down the road.

"He'll be happy to see you," Sam shouted after his son, and the words, true as they were, felt as though wrenched from his gut. He swung himself onto the horse and headed home.

"You must," Charles said. He took his grandson's hand between his and squeezed it.

"I don't know if I can," Isaiah replied. They were in the old man's office, looking out the window at the acres of orchards, and at the road Isaiah had just traveled to reach the house, and which led back to the highway to town and his father's place. If he strained his eyes to the east he could see the blue waters of the bay.

"I must leave here," he said.

Charles shook his head.

"Not now. Perhaps later. After this is all over. I need you to do what is right."

"Right?"

"Of course. And when you do, I will remember."

Isaiah didn't know if it were anger or disgust that now caused nausea to roil up from his stomach.

"Do not be hasty," his grandfather was saying. "Think what you will be giving up."

"Did you make a deal with him?"

Charles dropped his grandson's hand as though suddenly realizing that it was coated with something horrible.

"What do you take me for?" he asked.

"I thought I knew," Isaiah replied, "but now I don't."

"What is your surname?"

"Logan, of course."

"And mine?"

"The same."

"Then, there is nothing more to say."

"So we share the name..." Isaiah sputtered.

"And the blood. Don't forget the blood."

"I don't," Isaiah snapped. "But I think you do. It's just the name you're thinking about, isn't it?"

Charles leveled a steady gaze at his grandson.

"That's unfair," he said. He grasped Isaiah's shoulders and stepped a little closer. "Then you will, you must."

Isaiah freed himself with a shrug.

"Think about it," he said, "that is all I can promise."

"Think very carefully, then." Charles sat back at his desk and opened a huge account book

Isaiah peered over the old man's shoulders at the lines of neatly entered figures.

"Is my soul in there, do you think? How do you value it Grandfather?"

"Silly boy," Charles replied. "It is priceless."

It was near dusk when Isaiah opened the door to his house. The room, he saw, was in shadow, and he found his father sitting at the table. In front of him was a bowl of soup, a spoon in one hand, and a wooden match in the other. Next to the bowl was an unlit lamp. A ray of sunlight was shining through the window onto the dull surface of the spoon. When the door swung open, Sam looked up.

"What did he have to say?" he asked.

"He said I should think of the family's honor."

"I expect he would."

"I told him I'm thinking about it."

Sam nodded. He flicked the head of the match with the nail of his thumb. It flashed into flame. He held it to the wick until the wick ignited, then stared at the two flames the larger one on the lamp wick, and the smaller, fading one on the match.

"One of these is me," he said, "and the other is you. You got to figure out which is which." When the match burned down to his thumb, he shook it until its flame went out, and looked over his shoulder toward the stove. "There's soup if you want some." He got up and walked to the stairs. "About the horse..." he started, but then he just shrugged and went up.

Sarah and Henry stood in front of the open door to Margaret's room. They peered in at the unmade bed.

"Not like her at all," Sarah said.

"No," her husband replied. "She must have been in quite a hurry to leave."

"To meet him."

"We don't know that."

"We do."

"If we did..." he left the sentence unfinished, for a moment, and then resumed. "If we did, I still have my pistol."

"Do you have what goes with it?"

He nodded.

"In a box beneath a loose board. I hid it, so he wouldn't fool with it when he got bigger."

"No worry about that, now, is there?"

"There would have been. You know how it is with boys and guns."

"Do you remember how to use it?"

Henry closed his eyes. He saw the smoke of thousands of gun powder explosions, heard the continuous explosions, and the startled moans of those hit. He felt again the heft of the Army Colt revolver, the jolt of the recoil, the heat thrown back from the cylinders.

"You don't ever forget," he said.

"We don't need to wait for the law, Henry."

"No. But I want to be just a little more sure."

"You always were that cautious." She walked into the room and began making the bed. Lifting the pillow to straighten it, she pulled the blanket smooth except for the foot of the bed where there was a lump. She lifted the blanket, and finding the bulky shape of a Montgomery Ward Catalogue, she opened it to a dog-eared page. One illustration was ripped out. She showed the page to her husband.

"She was planning to be married," she said, "To him." She swiped at the moisture in her eyes. Her face hardened. "Foolish girl."

"He took advantage," he said.

"What are you going to do?" she asked.

"If the law fails us," he said. "And if we're sure." He handed the book back to her. "I just had a thought," he said.

"If it points anywhere else, it's wrong."

"It does. I haven't seen Jim all day. And she used to go to that barn by herself with him in there all the time. I never was comfortable with that."

"Pshaw!" She uttered the word with an explosion of contempt. "She wouldn't be looking at this page in this book if that's what happened, do you think?"

"I don't know. It don't seem likely."

"Impossible, that's what it is."

"But still, I ain't seen Jim since she disappeared."

"Well, then, I suppose you'd better go look for him. To satisfy yourself." She sat down on the bed and studied the torn page. "It was not meant to be," she said. Then, she looked up at her husband and waved him out. "Go on, then. See if he's there."

Henry slid the barn door open. He held a lantern in front of him as he walked in.

"Jim," he called. He realized he had kept his voice low as though afraid to wake his hired hand. "Jim," he called out louder. He stepped further into the barn. Swinging the lantern about in a wide sweeping arc, he remembered how she liked to come in here on a hot afternoon. Maybe one day Jim was there. It could have happened.

He saw the ladder beneath the place where Jim slept, and had often enough seen how he constructed a little shelter for himself out of bales of hay. He climbed the ladder, recalling the thin blanket that Jim had spread there, but it was gone. Placing his hand on the hay he sought the traces of his body's warmth.

He clambered down the ladder. He made his way to the side wall and then walked exactly six strides toward the center. Kneeling down, he ran his fingers along the rough planks of the floor until he found the notch in a plank, just big enough for him to get his thumb into. He lifted the plank and felt beneath it until his fingers found a box. Bringing it up, he sat back on his heels. Reaching further beneath the plank, he pulled out the revolver itself, wrapped in an old, oiled cloth. He moved the lantern closer and opened the box. Inside were the paper cartridges and percussion caps, just as he had left them there so many years before. He picked up a cap in one hand, and a cartridge in the other. Did his hands remember the loading process? He shoved a cartridge into a chamber, turned the cylinder to align the chamber with the loading lever and rammed the cartridge home. Rotating the cylinder, he repeated the process until each cylinder but one had received a cartridge. He took a cap out of the box and held it between his thumb and forefinger, then brought it to the first cylinder and sought the nipple on which it would sit. The cap fell to the floor. He searched for it and found it next to the toe of his boot and tried it again, managing to place the cap properly. In a couple of minutes, he had the weapon loaded, leaving the chamber on which the hammer rested empty.

"Johnny Reb would have had me if I had been this slow then," he muttered. "But I guess I'm not in such a hurry now."

He stood up and put the revolver in his belt. When he walked past Margaret's room back in the house, Sarah was lying in the bed, her eyes closed. He moved on and paused in front of the closed door that by tacit consent they never opened now. This evening, though, he paused and did not avert his eyes as he usually did. He placed his hand on the knob and steeled himself. He knew well enough what he would find inside that room if he dared enter.

He dropped his hand from the knob and walked past the room of ancient sorrows into the one he shared with Sarah. Feeling the pervasive sadness now in the house, spreading from his dead daughter's room through his dead son's, and extending its gloom over the marital bed on which he now sat, he undressed and placed the revolver on the table next to the bed, and waited for her to join him. When she did not, he closed his eyes and tried to force himself to sleep by taking deep and regular breaths. When that failed to relax him, he took the gun into his right hand and stared at the ceiling where his imagination drew the faces of Jim and Sam. He alternated aiming the heavy weapon at each one.

In Margaret's room, Sarah lay with her eyes fixed on the wall that separated her from Benjamin's empty bed, which remained unmade as it was on that day when the press of the farm's chores delayed her getting to it until it no longer mattered. She began to shiver at that memory even though the air was warm. Pulling Margaret's blanket over her, she lay very still.

In the attic above them, Edward stretched on his bed, his hands clasped behind his neck. Thinking carefully, he knew he might never get another chance like this to sell a bit of information and with the money he could buy his freedom. He had turned the matter over in his mind so often that he no longer knew for sure what he had seen on that day, and he did not care. He would find out what statement would draw the highest price, and then he would say it with all the conviction he could muster.

The first thing next morning, he headed into town to seek somebody to talk to, someone from whom he could begin to gauge the market value of his information.

Jim sat in low growing shrubbery a few feet from the railroad tracks. He had seen a train in the station here in town, three or four boxcars and half a dozen flatbed cars stacked high with timber. This train would be heading south in the morning, he figured. He would be on it. A white woman was dead, and he was in the neighborhood when she met her fate. That was all he needed to know to convince him that it was time to move on. He would change his name and try to reach Detroit or Chicago where he would be a lot less conspicuous than he was here, a place where he could blend into a crowd whose skin matched his.

9

Nobody had said anything, but Sam felt that he stood accused. He sat at the bare breakfast table, where he had been since abandoning his bed in the middle of the night, and lifted his head. His bad tooth throbbed. He remembered how the touch of her fingers had been a balm. There was a dentist in town who could take out the tooth, but could he remove the memory of the touch of her hand?

The glaring sun through the window assaulted his eyes. He saw a head floating before him with an aura glowing around it. His pupils contracted against the glare until he could make out a body beneath the head. For a moment he thought the figure would extend its arms and beckon to him, but it did not move. Then he saw the quizzical smile on his son's face.

"Is there something wrong with your bed?" Isaiah asked.

"I don't find it much comfort these days," Sam replied.

"I don't wonder."

Sam got up and walked over to the stove, which was cold.

"I was going to make some coffee," Isaiah said. "But we don't have any. I could go into town."

Sam thought a moment.

"No, I think I'll walk in. I want to buy a newspaper."

"Is that a good idea?"

"And why not?"

"You might find yourself in it. You never know who's been saying things."

"People are always saying things." Sam tossed the response but his son's words nested in the place in his innards where his fears, like so many worms, gathered.

"Yes, but some folks have more to say than others."

Sam eyed his son, sensing the subtle but marked shift in the power that flowed between them.

"You do remember what your grandfather said to you."

Isaiah nodded.

"I'm still thinking on it."

"Well, you just think real hard."

Isaiah shrugged and opened the door to the stove. He thrust in some kindling and lit it. He picked up an egg from a basket on the floor next to it.

"The last one," he said. "We'll have to find somebody else to buy them from. Or else get our own chickens."

The words cut, and Sam recoiled.

"That's more than enough," he said.

"I was just talking about eggs," Isaiah replied.

"Sure you were. You didn't mean for me to think of her, did you?"

Isaiah shrugged.

"Eggs," he repeated, "I'm hungry, and there's one egg."

"I'll see if I can buy some in town."

"What do you want me to do?"

"You could set out the lugs. Time to harvest the fruit. We'll be needing some cash."

"We always do."

"Yes, but I'm thinking more this year than usual."

Isaiah flipped the egg in the frying pan.

"I was only talking about eggs," he insisted.

As he walked into town, Sam tried to assume an uncaring, shambling gait, one that he would have employed not so very long as he joined his buddies at the baseball field, but those times now seemed like they had occurred to somebody else years ago. At the open air market where she used to go to sell her eggs was the table behind which she should be standing with her basket. Her spot was occupied by an old woman offering beans and cabbage. He quickened his pace.

Although it was still early, the streets were filling with activity, men dressed for business striding with purposeful steps, young women in twos and threes on their way to the shops and offices. In times past, he would have eyed them as though they were fruit he might purchase. But today, strangely, he felt none of the usual desire. He was as detached from the young women as he was from the men whose lives seemed so very different from his.

In front of a construction site where a building was being framed out, he paused and inhaled the scent of freshly cut lumber. Here was where he should have been. Things would have turned out so differently if he had been permitted to follow his own bent, to cut, shape, and join the wood from trees rather than attempt to grow them for their fruit. He heard the ring of the hammer as though it were the pealing of a church bell and the grating of the crosscut saw as though it were a bow stroked across the strings of a violin.

Union Street ran south from the river road, and it was even more crowded. He began to feel the eyes of those passing by him. He knew they were staring at him, while he struggled to maintain his carefree stride and a voice inside his head screamed at him to run. Up ahead he saw the general merchandise store he had been patronizing since his father had first taken him into town to begin to teach him how to handle money. These Howlands, his father had said, they're from New Hampshire, where I was born. I've still got a great nephew there. The Howlands are good people, careful with a dollar but honest. Treat them right, and they will treat you right. That's the key to doing business. Sam pushed open the door and approached the counter.

John Howland, still young enough to have difficulty growing the full mustache he aspired to, looked up from the packages he was stacking on the counter, and began to smile his welcome. Sam strode to the counter and offered a grin that used to be infectious but now felt contrived. His cheeks and lips were engaged in an argument, and he felt that he must look like the clown in the traveling circus that came to town every summer. John shifted his eyes, looked around the store, and then focused on Sam.

"Good morning, Mr. Logan," he said. "I haven't seen you in town for some time. Usually, it's Isaiah."

"I felt I needed to come in to check up on you," Sam replied.

"Well, you're just in time to look at our newest product." He pointed to the stacked packages. "Coffee in paper sacks lined with tin foil. Manufacturer claims it'll stay fresh."

Sam saw the young man's lips moving, and he heard his sounds, but he found it nearly impossible to translate the sounds into words. The clerk handed him one of the bags and indicated the text printed on it. Sam waited until the words stopped dancing.

"I'll take two," he said, "two bags."

"Yessir, that'll be fifty cents."

Sam reached into his pocket and felt only a couple of thin coins.

"Just put it on my account."

The young man pulled out a large account book from a shelf behind the counter and began to flip through the pages. At the end of the counter, Sam found a stack of the weekly newspaper, heard the door that led to the rear of the store open, and turned to see the senior Howland glance at him and then walk to his son's side. He whispered something into John's ear, then retreated back through the door. The clerk closed the account book and placed it back on its shelf.

"Sorry, Mr. Logan, my father says no more credit."

"Why, I always pay when my crop comes in."

"Yes. It's not that, it's..." the clerk flushed, "it's other considerations. And he'd like you to leave as soon as it is convenient."

Sam felt the urge to say that he'd leave when he was good and ready, but in a moment all resistance melted. His shoulders slumped. He held up the newspaper, and dropped his coins on the counter.

"You will take my money for the paper, though, won't you?"

"Of course." The clerk picked up the coins. "But you've given me too much."

Sam waved his hand as he turned away.

"Keep it. I don't need it."

He walked out the door and back onto the street with the newspaper rolled up in his pocket, turned a corner and began striding on unsteady legs without paying much attention to where he was going. The senior Howland, who used to pat him on the head and give him free penny candy when his father took him there, now treating him like a nigger! Between two buildings, he caught a glimpse of blue water. It glowed red. He shivered, remembering seeing the same fiery tint on the waters of the bay on that day, and wished with every fiber of his being that he could turn the clock back.

He stopped at that thought. What good would that do? She had been so insistent in her gentle, passive, maddeningly sure way. She would be his bride. Her head was filled with images of domestic tranquility, of bread in the oven and an infant crawling at their feet before a fireplace roaring its flame against a cold winter's night, an idea to which, twenty years earlier, he would have gladly assented. But now it was simply impossible. He could not make her understand. No. It was folly to want to turn the hands of the clock back. She would be thrusting that damned picture of a baby carriage in his face. Still, she didn't have to die, did she?

The water terrified him, brought to mind the burning lake that he now knew awaited him. He turned away from it and walked down an alley. It let out onto Washington Street, across from that same church where he had first heard about Satan and that lake of fire. Further along was the courthouse. He paused before the church entrance. Pots of geraniums in full bloom flanked the ornately carved wooden double doors, which opened, and the sexton stepped out. He had a watering can in his hand, and nodding at Sam tilted the watering can over the one pot on his left. Sam watched the stream of water, transfixed, as though witnessing a miracle. The man finished watering that pot and walked over to another. Again, Sam watched.

"Can I help you?" the man asked.

Sam wanted to explain how he needed somebody to help him, how he had never felt so utterly alone, how the blue waters of the bay and the river that flowed into it now seemed aflame, but he simply shook his head. The man pointed to the glass enclosed board on which were listed the times of services on Sunday. He walked into the building and closed the doors behind him.

Sam's eye caught another building, this one a simple white frame structure in contrast to the imposing masonry of the church. This more modest building was set back between the church and the courthouse with a large, six pointed star made of wood and painted white on the gable over its front entrance. He felt drawn to it, but unsure of what welcome he might receive, he moved on. Another glimpse of blue, the river, which like a serpent, seemed determined to encircle him. He expected it to rise and form the burning lake. In a strange way, it would be a relief if it did.

Unable to decide upon a direction, he put his hand to his cheek, but his fingers did not ease as hers had done. Behind him was the stone church in which he had first heard of the burning lake. He could not seek solace there. In front was the courthouse and its laws that would reach out and clutch him. To the left, and right, was the water.

In front of the white frame building he now approached was a small group of eight or ten men, all bearded, wearing some kind of tasseled shawls about their shoulders, and black felt hats. They were talking in a guttural tongue he could not understand, and discussing something with great heat, gesticulating with their arms, pointing their fingers at each other. Occasionally, one would raise his thumb up as if in triumph, and the others would nod or shake their heads. They glanced at Sam but did not stop their argument.

He stood and listened to their foreign words, at ease for the first time in days. They could not know his secret any more than he could know what they were talking about. After a few moments, one man separated himself from the others and approached. He had a full white beard that reached halfway down his chest. His eyes were a dark, fierce brown, his voice a gentle rumble with only a trace of an accent.

"Mister," he said. "Are you lost?"

"Yes," Sam answered without hesitation.

The man pointed to the building.

"It is still open. Nobody is inside but God."

"I wouldn't know..." Sam began.

"You do not need to. I'll take you in."

The old man lifted his hat, and removing the skull cap he wore beneath it, placed it on Sam's head. The cap was damp from his perspiration.

"You must wear this. For respect," he said.

Ascending the steps, he pushed open the door beneath the star. Sam followed.

"See," the man said as they stepped inside. He pointed to the rows of chairs. "Sit," he said, and left.

Dropping into a chair, he looked at how the sun coming through the windows illuminated the curtained area at the front. Somehow he knew that there was something of great significance behind that curtain. He was tempted to pull the curtain back, but feared the hand of their God would strike him down. But maybe he could have a conversation with the God who resided in this building that looked more like a house than a church. He sought the words to explain what had happened, how he had let her die, but what came to mind, his father, his circumstances, his ex-wives, his empty bank account, Isaiah, all of it sounded inane even to his own ears.

Half an hour later, he got up and pushed the door open, expecting they would be waiting for him, perhaps to accuse him of some violation of their customs, but they were gone. He began to wonder if they had been there at all, but then he felt the damp skull cap still on his head. He took it off and put it in his pocket.

Pulling the newspaper out of his pocket, he started retracing his steps, determined to reach his home where perhaps he could find a little peace. He scanned the front page as he walked. There on the right hand side was the headline, "Missing Woman Found Dead." The subhead said "Foul Play Suspected." He rolled the paper into a tight cylinder and threw out his arm as though to toss the paper away, but his hand refused to release it. Tucking the paper back under his arm, he increased his pace to a slow trot. He was sure everyone in town had read the story. It seemed people who approached him lowered their eyes until he had passed, and then he felt their eyes bore into his back. He began to run. A wagon pulled out in front of him, and he was certain the driver intended to block his path. He bent over to catch his breath. The wagon continued, leaving behind a steaming lump of manure.

Forcing himself to walk at a normal pace, he smiled at passers by and ignored the puzzled looks and half hearted smiles he received in return. He found himself in front of the building that housed a tobacconist on the first floor and a dentist's office on the second. He wondered if the constant pain in his jaw had somehow directed him here without his conscious thought. He considered his empty pocket, but the thought of relief convinced him to push open the door and walk up to the stairs.

Hugh Peterson, a man in his thirties, was a recent arrival in town from downstate where he had learned his trade. He had red hair, and a mole on the side of his nose out of which one red hair sprang. His own teeth were yellowed, as were his thick fingers. He kept a cigarette in his hand and waved Sam into the chair. Then he took a drag and exhaled a cloud of smoke. He kept the cigarette in his mouth, with his head cocked to the side and his eyes squinting against the smoke as he probed the area Sam pointed to. When the probe hit the bad tooth, Sam grimaced. Peterson withdrew the probe, and ground out the cigarette in an ashtray on top of the instrument cabinet.

"Well, Mr. Logan," he said. "It's got to come out, I expect you know that."

"I do."

"That will be five dollars. In advance."

Sam reached into his empty pocket.

"It seems I've left my money at home."

"In advance," Dr. Peterson repeated.

Sam pulled out his watch. The dentist held out his hand.

"It's beat up but it'll do."

He laid the watch on his instrument cabinet, and then opened the top drawer. He withdrew an implement that looked like an over-sized house key, with a rounded wooden handle on one end, and a small clamp like device on the other.

"Open," Peterson said.

Sam obeyed, smelling the tobacco on Peterson's fingers as the dentist rubbed something on his gum.

"Just to take your mind off it," he said. He positioned the clamp over the tooth and slid his fingers into Sam's mouth to turn the screw that tightened it over the tooth. "How are you feeling?" he asked.

His voice sounded further and further away until Sam was not sure what he was saying. He thought he heard him ask "Was this how she was?" but then the dentist's forearm was pressed against the back of his head, and he felt a yank as though his jaw bone were being pulled up through his gums.

Back on the street, he walked with a piece of gauze stuffed into his mouth over the hole in his gum, and knew he was swallowing his own blood. He tried to remember what the dentist had been saying as he fastened the instrument onto his tooth, and he was sure he was talking about her. Stumbling as he started to walk past S.E. Wait's pharmacy on Front Street, his head began to clear and his balance returned. He removed the bloody gauze and tossed it into the street. A woman passing by jerked her head away, but he didn't care. He was waiting to see if the pain would go away.

When he reached the road that led back onto the Peninsula, he began to breathe a little easier. He felt for the newspaper in his pocket. Looking behind him and ahead, he saw nobody, so he went off the road and into the woods that rose on a hill to his right. There he found a fallen log in a small clearing, and sat down on it and unrolled the newspaper. He spat out blood, as though it were an act of expiation, taking with it his pain and his guilt.

The article identified Margaret as the daughter of a farmer living in Archie in Peninsula Township, near the base of the Peninsula and indicated she had been found in a hemlock swamp within sight of East Bay after being missing for a day. Sheriff Clarence Billingham noted the empty bottle of laudanum found at her side. She was described as lying in a peaceful pose, hands clasped on her chest, and a flower in her hair. Suicide, he thought, that's what it looks like. But then he read on. The sheriff said that there was one troubling detail, marks on the young woman's neck. Sam turned his eyes away from the page. Maybe he only imagined that was what he read. He forced his glance back to the paper. No, there it was. Marks on her neck. He put his own hands on his neck and began to squeeze. He wondered if he could kill himself in this manner. He pulled his hands from his neck and tore the paper in half, and then with meticulous care continued tearing until he had a pile of shredded newsprint at his feet. Getting up, he made his way back to the road.

He walked with his head down, watching his feet kick up the dust. A wagon drawn by a pair of oxen approached him, laden with lugs, the wooden boxes into which the harvested cherries were poured. He looked up in time to see Wilson driving the wagon. The old farmer glanced at him, then urged his oxen forward. Sam stepped off the road until the wagon creaked by. He saw somebody on foot up ahead. He ducked onto a path leading into a potato field. He knelt among the plants as though he were inspecting them for beetles. The steps of the traveler came closer, and Sam scuttled back into the field. He lifted his eyes as the man passed and thought he recognized him. He lowered his head into the leaves of the plant.

Edward cast a glance at the field. You just have to find them, he thought, not eat them. He smiled. The movement of his facial muscles surprised him. He could not remember the last time he had felt joy, but today he was almost happy. He looked back over his shoulder at the man in the field and shook his head. He himself would not be doing that much longer, if at all.

He stopped the first person he met in town, a young man in a suit and derby hat walking at a brisk pace along the river road.

"I'm looking for the law," he said.

"The law?"

"Yes."

"Oh, you mean a judge or the sheriff."

"Yes."

The businessman's face flushed.

"Well, which?"

"Either will do, whichever is handiest."

"Look over there," the young man said. "Do you see that building with the clock tower?"

Edward nodded.

"That's the courthouse. And the jail. You'll find the law in there."

"Thank you kindly," Edward replied.

"And the state hospital is over that way," the businessman called after him, pointing in the other direction. "You might want to go there next."

Edward started to turn around, a curse on his lips, but then he just shrugged. There were more important things to take care of than teaching this rude bastard a lesson. He increased his pace to the courthouse and climbed up the masonry steps, pausing before the carved entrance door that reminded him of one on the parish church back in Cork. For a moment he was there, his small hand in his father's huge, rough grasp on a Sunday morning, thinking that perhaps he should return to his home town rather than go to California, for at least there he could use the name he was baptized with. He would not have to train his tongue to lose the accent he had learned as a child.

Opening the door, he half expected to see a priest in his surplice next to a bowl of holy water. But instead, he found himself in an entrance way leading to inner doors, flanked on one side by the flag of the country he had adopted, and another, which he could not identify. He bowed in the direction of the American flag, and walked through the inner doors into a hallway that led back to a rear door. Another hallway bisected it. He stood at the nexus.

"Can I help you?" The question came from a young woman carrying a stack of papers.

"I'm looking for," he paused to remember, "the sheriff. Or the judge."

"Well, which?" she asked.

He felt himself begin to perspire. He had to make a choice, but he had no idea.

"The sheriff," he said.

"Down that way," she said pointing to the hallway to the right. "Last office. Does he know you're coming to see him?"

Edward shook his head.

"I know something about that dead girl," he said.

"I see," she replied. "I'm going there. You can follow."

Edward hesitated. Was she taking him seriously? She waved toward the end of the corridor, and walked on. He followed. She opened the closed door, waiting for him to arrive, then motioned for him to sit on a bench against the wall to his right, and continued to another door that led to an inner office. She disappeared behind it.

On the hard wood of the bench, he leaned back and then forward. He placed his elbows on his knees. He started to count to a hundred and thought if she didn't come out by the time he reached that number he would just get up and look for the judge. He was up to seventy-three when she emerged from the inner office. She no longer had the stack of papers.

"The sheriff will see you now," she said.

He rose and walked past her. Sheriff Clarence Billingham was standing in front of his desk. He was a short but powerfully built man, with wide shoulders and broad chest. But his stomach had expanded over the years until it now protruded a good distance ahead of the rest of him. His face was framed by long sideburns and a walrus mustache. He extended his hand.

Edward did not respond right away because it had been years since anyone offered to shake hands with him. Billingham waited, then just as he began to drop his hand back to his side, Edward seized and held it for several seconds

"Well, then," the sheriff said, "Miss Wilkins says you have something to tell me about the Cutter girl."

"Not her, exactly, but about what happened to her."

Billingham settled his bulk behind his desk. The day was heating up, and warm air flowed in through the open window. He drummed on his desk surface with a pencil.

"Go on."

Edward sensed the other man's irritation. He was well used to being regarded as nothing more than an insect, a worker ant perhaps, but of no significance, one whose back could be crushed beneath the careless boot. As always, he slumped his shoulders and studied his feet for a few moments.

"It's just that I was wondering if there might be a reward for information about this case."

"Reward?" Billingham exclaimed. "For a suicide?"

"It weren't no suicide, I can tell you that," Edward said with an emphatic nod of his head.

"What do you know? Come on, man, tell what you know."

"I'm thinking on California," Edward said, his tone now that of a surly child being disciplined.

"California? What about the girl?"

"I work, or did work, for her father. He might be letting me go."

"Did you see her that day she disappeared?"

"I did, carrying that basket to gather flowers, but it weren't no flowers she was after gathering." Edward clamped his mouth shut. He had been tricked. He was giving away what he had intended to sell.

"Yes, go on."

"Is there a reward?"

Billingham expelled his breath in a burst and sat back in his chair. The perspiration now dripped down his nose, and he swiped it away.

"No, not yet," he said.

"Tell me when there is, and I'll talk with you further," Edward said. "I don't suppose the judge would know anything more about the reward than you do."

"Judge? There is no judge, man, until there is a case, and there won't be a case unless you tell me what you know."

Edward straightened his shoulders.

"I'll be back," he said, "when I hear about a reward."

Billingham rose heavily to his feet.

"Wait. If you are withholding information, that's a crime. You must tell me."

"I don't have no information," Edward said. "I told you what I saw that day."

"I'll want to talk with you again. What's your name?"

Edward smiled.

"Michael, sir, Michael O'Leary. You can talk to Mr. Henry Cutter about me if you like, but he won't recognize that name, which I haven't used these twenty years in this cursed country." He stalked out of the office.

Billingham leaned over his desk as though to grab Edward's sleeve, but then sat back down. It was so hot. Was this fellow lunatic? There was no sense in arresting him, or charging him with obstruction, but he would talk with Mr. Cutter, and see what he had to say. Why, it's likely that this idiot read about the case in the newspaper, if he could, in fact, read. He wanted to cash in somehow, and he probably doesn't even work for the Cutters. Miss Wilkins walked in and handed him a small, scented envelope.

"A woman just stopped by and handed this to me for you. She wouldn't wait or give her name. She said you would understand when you read what was inside."

Edward trudged back to the farm. He found Henry in the barn sharpening a plow blade with a whetstone. Edward waited for him to look up. When Henry didn't, Edward cleared his throat as loudly as he could manage. Still, Henry worked. Edward placed himself so close that Henry's arm brushed against him in its upward swing.

"I know you're here," Henry said, "it's just that I don't care."

"I spoke to the law," Edward said. "Told them where I worked and that I had some information. I expect they might come out here to speak with you."

Henry put the blade down.

"What about?"

"Me. Only I gave them a different name."

"Why?"

"My real name. Michael O'Leary." He thrust out his jaw. "I changed it after that time they said I was after that girl where I used to work."

"Well, Michael, if that's who you are, I don't give a hoot about you or your name, and I don't have anything to talk to the law about until they come to me and tell me they found who killed my daughter."

"Don't you already know?"

"Not for sure."

"I can make you sure."

Henry seized Edward's shoulders, and squeezed.

"The truth, that is all I want."

Edward shrugged off Henry's grip and stepped back.

"When the time comes, you just remember I'm your most important witness. Nobody else can say what I can say."

"Which is."

"What I saw. In the woods that day."

Henry fingered his revolver.

"Well."

"I saw Sam." He paused. "And Jim."

"Both?"

"Whichever you want. Or both."

Henry waved the revolver, pointing it first at one corner of the barn and then the other.

"Which one?" he demanded.

"Why, Sam."

Henry steadied the revolver as though he had Sam in his sight.

"I need to be certain before I shoot a man," Henry said.

"You can be certain. If it's Sam you want, then it's Sam."

Henry looked up at the loft where Jim slept, then whirled to face Edward.

"And if it's Jim I want."

Edward smiled.

"Then it's him you get to shoot."

"Don't you care?"

"No."

Henry sat back down and picked up the blade.

"If you're going to work for me, go on ahead."

"What about my information?"

"Save it," Henry said. "Maybe somebody else will want it." He started sharpening the blade again, moving his arm faster and faster until he achieved a furious pace. Edward watched him for a few moments, and then walked out of the barn.

"I'll go back to work on that fence," he called back to Henry.

For answer Henry plied his whetstone even harder, until his face reddened and sweat poured down his neck.

Heller studied the notes he had made from the autopsy report. He put a heavy check next to the mention of laudanum and another by the reference to ligature damage. He circled the description of the fetus. He heard heavy steps in the hallway outside his closed office door.

"Come on in, Clarence," he called out before the person in the hall had a chance to knock. The door swung open and Billingham filled the open space. His face was red from the exertion of carrying his weight up the steps and glistening with perspiration from the warm, humid morning air.

"The darndest thing..."

"I'm sure it was, to bring you huffing and puffing over here," Heller said. He reached behind him to a small sideboard and poured a glass of water from a pitcher. "Have a drink, catch your breath, and tell me about it."

Billingham took the water and downed it in a gulp. He pushed the glass back toward Heller. The district attorney filled it again, and the sheriff took another deep drink, and eased himself into the chair next to the desk.

"This fellow comes into my office, and says he has something to say about that girl who was found dead. He wants to know if there's a reward."

"And?" Heller leaned forward, his pencil now poised over a clean sheet of paper.

"And he says he's thinking about California. Then, he wants to know if the judge would know anything about the reward. I told him there wasn't a case yet, so there isn't a reward or a judge for that matter, and he should just tell me what he knows. He claims he works for the Cutters, and saw the girl on the day she died, but that's all he would say, and when he left he gave a name that he said Cutter would not recognize. I'm thinking he's a lunatic, or a desperate soul, looking for a way to put some money in his pocket. When I said I had no idea what he was talking about, he shrugged and left. I tried to stop him, but I couldn't arrest him for being a damned fool, so that's the end of the story. And yet he might know something."

"We'll want to talk to him."

"I'll check at the Cutter place, and if he's not there, I'll find him; if you think it's worth the effort."

Heller pointed to the report, and slid it over to the sheriff.

"I've just looked over the autopsy. It looks like we're dealing with a murder."

Billingham scanned the first page.

"Yes, the marks on her neck, but what about that bottle of laudanum? There was that young woman who nearly killed herself drinking that stuff, not two weeks ago."

"Yes, Miss Harriet Fuller, she and her friends at a party. Miss Cutter seems to have drunk some laudanum. But did she then strangle herself?" He leaned over the desk and turning the report to the next page, read upside down, and placed his finger on the paper. "Then, there's this. Here, do you see?"

148

"Fetus," Billingham muttered. His face reddened. "What a damned shame. Who would do such a thing, and why?"

"That's just it," Heller replied. "I don't think she killed herself. I think the father of that child was getting himself out of a situation. He gave her the laudanum, then choked the life out of her—and the baby."

"Then you'd better have a look at this," Billingham said. He held a perfumed envelope. "It came this morning."

Heller opened the envelope and read the note it contained, written in an elegant hand.

"Do you know her?" he asked.

Billingham nodded.

"Sure. She's living with her mother since the divorce."

"Why don't you invite her in for a chat?"

"You see that she doesn't want to be involved. Says it right there in the last line."

"She already is."

"I guess," Billingham replied. He heaved his bulk up from the chair.

"You'd think these people could be more considerate. If they've got to kill somebody, why not do it in the spring or fall. I don't do well in this heat."

Isaiah released the brake on the wagon and urged the horse forward with a shake of the reins. The huge animal eased into a powerful walk. In no hurry, he permitted the horse to find its own gait, which it did at a slow, steady pace. Empty lugs rattled on the wagon bed behind.

Without his direction, the horse found the farm road that led to the orchard on the hill behind their house, which traversed the southern end of their farm, crossing a field of corn before ascending the hill. An extension of this road that he and his father had been clearing traveled around the base of the hill, continued toward the bay on the west side of the Peninsula. As he reached the place where the new road branched off from the old, Isaiah pulled up on the reins. He sat looking up at the orchard, then flicked the reins to start moving again and pulled on the left rein to go down the new road. The horse resisted for a moment, unhappy with the change in its routine, but then turned and settled again into its slow walk. Isaiah studied the ground as they crossed it, remembering how it looked the last time he had seen it.

The brush had been cleared for about a quarter of a mile. He recalled working side by side with his father, each swinging an ax, clearing from the middle to the edge of the new road. They had started working together some ten or fifteen feet past the white birch where his father had begun clearing by himself. Looking ahead to the distance they had cleared together, he saw they had covered much more than double what Sam had done by himself.

Guiding the horse onto the old farm road and up the hill to the beginning of the orchard, he called "Whoa," and pulled the rein. He set the brake handle, then got down. He walked to the rear of the wagon and unloaded a lug. He wanted to lose himself in repetitious work. Otherwise, he would find himself thinking about why Sam hadn't cleared much brush that day, and if he did that, he didn't know what he might feel like doing.

Placing another lug at right angles to the one already on the ground, he looked up at the cherry tree beneath which he was placing the lugs to see the fruit round and red. It should be picked soon. Usually by this time, his father had hired hands from town to help with the harvest, boys or girls of high school age who would work cheap.

He looked down the rows of trees, each burdened with fruit. Stretching his fingers as though in preparation for the hours of picking, he realized he couldn't possibly do it alone, and he would have to get a crew somehow. He continued stacking the lugs in piles, crisscrossing them for stability. When the pile was as tall as he, he got back into the wagon and drove further up into the orchard. Working faster, he heaved the heavy lugs into place, and then moved on.

When he got to the crest of the hill, the last spot to place a stack of lugs, he was breathless, and dropped a lug onto the ground. Reaching for another from the wagon, he felt it slip as he placed it on top of the first. He held onto it too long, trying to right it, and it slipped out of his hand and started to fall. As he slid his hand beneath it to stop it, its weight brought it down on his fingers. The pain shot up his arm to his shoulders and into his neck. He thought he felt it in his jaw bone, reaching to his right ear. He stepped back.

"Damn, damn," he said. "What's the point?" He looked toward the sky as though expecting an answer. "Are you listening?" he asked. He waited a moment or two. "I guess not, must be too busy with more important matters than my poor fingers." He sat on the ground until the pain began to ease, then stood and thrust his injured hand into his pocket, walked a little further up the hill, past the last tree, and closed his eyes just before he reached the apex. He took a deep breath and opened them.

"There," he said, as he gazed out across the bottom of the far side of the hill to the azure waters of West Bay beneath a blue sky. White clouds, soft as pillows, scudded toward the horizon before a gentle breeze. Far out on the water, he saw a puff of smoke, and beneath it the shape of a steamer chugging toward Old Mission Harbor on the northeast side of the Peninsula. He watched its slow progress northward.

Forty miles south, Jim huddled in the rear of the boxcar. The doors opened and two railroad guards, burly men with short, vicious clubs, climbed into the car. Jim rose to his feet and shuffled toward them.

"Hello, sirs," he said.

"How far have you come, boy?"

Jim shrugged, as if in ignorance.

"Think we ought to send him back?" the other asked.

"Nah, let's just give him something to remember us by."

Jim bolted for the door but one guard put his foot out, and as Jim tripped, the other brought his truncheon down on his back. Jim put his arms over his head and staggered to his feet. The other guard rammed the end of his club into his stomach, and as he bent over, fighting the waves of nausea, he felt himself flipped out the door. He landed hard on his back. He lay still for a moment, and when he looked up he saw the two guards with broad grins on their faces looking at him, their hands scratching their groins. He got up and bowed.

"Good day to yuh, sirs," he said. He turned and hobbled away.

10

———

As Sam walked up his drive, he saw a buggy stop in front of his house. Its driver's wide shoulders seemed to extend from one side of the seat to the other. Sam recognized that shape, and thought about turning back but could not think of where he might go. Then the man on the buggy turned around and waved to him, so Sam trudged on toward him, cursing himself for shredding the newspaper. Like a student cramming for a test, he wished to review the story, see what was already known. He would have to depend on his wits. He held out his hand as he came abreast the driver of the buggy. Sheriff Billingham extended his own.

"Mr. Logan, how are you?"

"Just fine, sheriff." He spat a little blood onto the ground. "Except I just had a tooth yanked out."

Billingham clambered down from the buggy. His shirt was drenched in sweat. He ran his tongue over his upper lip, tasting the salty perspiration.

"Sorry to hear that. Must have hurt like hell."

"It did," Sam said.

"Sure is hot," the sheriff said, shading his eyes against the sun and looking out at the orchard on the hill behind the house. "Your crop looks good. You must be hoping the weather holds for you."

Sam nodded and waited.

Billingham shook his head, as though in sadness.

"Well, no sense talking small talk, I guess. Folks usually aren't too happy to see me come visiting. They figure I've got something on my mind."

"The last time you were here, you remember, it was not a happy occasion."

"That's what I mean, it's usually that sort of thing."

"And today?"

"Oh, I was just driving out this way, if you can believe it."

"Just like that?"

"Well," Billingham said in a drawl, "not exactly. You probably heard about that unfortunate young woman on the next farm."

Sam felt the blood rush to his face and he strove to stop his lips from quivering.

"Of course. Isaiah and I helped search for her."

"Oh, yes, your son. Where is he? I'd like a word with him."

"What about?"

"Oh, there's been some talk that she might have had a beau."

Sam felt relief tinged with nausea that he would be happy to see suspicion fall on Isaiah, yet he felt the urge to protect him as well.

"He's a good boy."

"Is he?" Billingham asked. "I didn't quite remember. But still he might know something."

"I don't think so. He's a good boy."

"Nobody's saying to the contrary." Billingham swiped the sweat from his eyes. "Say," he continued. "Would you have any idea who her boyfriend might be? Being her neighbor and all?"

Sam studied the sheriff's bland expression, one he might expect to see on his face in a conversation about the weather or the cherry crop.

"No, sheriff, I'm afraid not."

Billingham stepped closer and put his meaty hand on Sam's shoulder.

"You can be straight with me. I know what was going on when you were married. How your wife wouldn't even do the laundry, and you had to bring it over there." He gestured toward the Cutter farm.

"Isaiah took it over there mostly." The lie came easily.

"Why, there you have it," Billingham clapped Sam on the back. "That's why I think the boy might be able to help us out. Now where do you think I might find him?"

Sam hesitated.

"He's got his chores." He looked vaguely out over his farm. "He's out there somewhere."

Billingham sighed.

"Well, it's too darn hot. Just tell him to come in and see me when he gets a chance. You know where he can find me, don't you? My office. It's in the same building as the courthouse. And the jail. Convenient, ain't it?"

He climbed back into his buggy.

"Just don't have him wait too long," he said. "People are saying we've got a murder to solve here." He lifted his rein as though to urge his horse forward, but then let his arms drop.

"Say, while I'm here, you can save me some time. There's a question I have to ask everybody. It's just part of the investigation."

"What would that be?" Sam asked, although he was already preparing his answer.

"Where were you on that day, when she disappeared?"

Sam pointed to the west.

"Clearing brush for that new road to the resort that's going up."

"Oh, yes, the resort." He turned to the east. "And of course, she was found over thataway, wasn't she?"

"She was."

"Well, I guess I have got to go bother those poor folks. They're on the next farm that way, aren't they?" he pointed toward town. He didn't wait for an answer, but flicked the reins until his horse moved off.

Sam watched the dust rise behind the buggy as Billingham turned around and headed back down the track to the road to town. He dropped to his knees. Murder, he whispered. It was as though he had never thought of that word in connection with what happened. He tried again to remember how to pray. But for what, exactly? Of that he was uncertain.

Henry was sitting on the porch, rocking, although it was the middle of a weekday. He looked over his field of potatoes where weeds were growing between the plants. He held his hoe in his hands still sore from sharpening the plow blade, thinking *she* should be here to do the hoeing, repeating like a mantra, she should be here, the words echoing in his thoughts with each scrape of the chair's rocker against the wood planks of the porch. The words and the sound of the rocking calmed him somewhat. Sarah came out and placed a glass of lemonade on the table next to him and then retreated into the house. He didn't pick up the glass. He did not want to stop rocking.

He watched the cloud of dust approaching the house. He could not imagine that it had anything whatsoever to do with him, his distraught wife, or his dead daughter. When the buggy beneath the dust stopped in front of the porch, he glanced at it but did not stop rocking.

Billingham took note of the distracted, self-absorbed look in the grieving father's face and hesitated. This was a part of his job he truly disliked. He did not mind playing cat and mouse with a potential suspect as he had just done, but to intrude into the darkness of another's sorrow to ferret out a crumb or two of information struck him as repugnant. Yet, it was in precisely such situations where he might expect to confront a kind of naked vulnerability that often proved most fruitful. He swung himself off the seat, approaching the porch as delicately as a man of his bulk could manage.

"Mr. Cutter," he said in a stage whisper, better for use in church as a late arrival to a service.

Henry did not respond.

"Mr. Cutter," Billingham tried again, this time raising his voice a level. Henry turned his head toward the sheriff with great weariness, his eyes registering his slow recognition of the identity of his visitor.

"Sheriff," he said. "Have you got him?"

"Got who?"

"The man who killed my daughter."

"Well, now, Henry, I was hoping you could point me in the right direction to do just that. I do have my thoughts, and I'm hoping you can corroborate them."

Henry pointed to the north.

"Have you been there?"

"To Logan's place? I was just there speaking to the father, and looking for the son."

"It's the father, you want to talk to. His son..." Henry said, and then he stopped himself.

"What about his son?"

Henry waved his arm to dismiss the question.

"It's his father. He's the one. If it wasn't him, it was my man, Jim, but he's gone away. You can talk to my other man, Edward."

"Irishman?"

"Yes." He pointed again to the north. "He should be putting in a fence."

Billingham looked over the terrain, the hill he would have to climb and then the woods.

"Send him to talk to me. I think he came to my office the other day, talking like a crazy man. Said his name was Michael."

"That's him. He's working on a fence."

"Tell him to come see me." Billingham took a step closer, reached up and placed his hand on the heavy butt of the revolver still in Henry's waistband. "And there's no need for that." He started to lift the weapon but was stopped by Henry's hand.

"No need," Henry said, "leastwise not until you find him."

"Nor then neither."

But Henry had begun to rock again, eyes closed. The front door opened, and Sarah stepped out.

"Good day, sheriff," she said. "We cannot help you further." She placed her hand on her husband's shoulder. Billingham dipped his head as in the beginning of a bow, and climbed back into the seat of his buggy.

"Did you get those lugs set out?" Sam asked. That simple question, which not long ago he would have delivered with a patina of amusement layered over condescension, now caused him great difficulty as though his mouth were thick with molasses.

Isaiah continued unhitching the Percheron.

"What's the point if I did?" he asked without turning around.

Sam shook his head to clear it. What was the point, after all?

"Money," he said. "I couldn't buy the coffee, or an egg. We're flat."

"You mean you're flat. I always am." Isaiah spun around. "But to answer your question, yes I put the lugs there."

"Start picking tomorrow," Sam said. "Maybe your grandfather will help you get a crew. I don't think anyone is going to work for me, but they'll work for him."

"I guess that's right," Isaiah muttered. "Say, I thought I saw someone leaving as I drove up."

"You did."

"Well?"

"Sheriff Billingham. He wanted to speak to you about Margaret."

"Me? What about you?"

"I told him I didn't know anything. He wants you to come into town to talk to him."

"What do you suppose I should tell him?"

"Just what you need to. The sooner the better. I feel him breathing down my neck."

Isaiah began to lead the horse to the barn.

"I'll do that."

Edward Franklin's hands ached from driving the hole digger into the ground and then twisting it down. Looking behind him at the neat row of fence posts he had already installed, and then ahead at the quarter of a mile that still needed to be done, he began another hole, putting his weight onto the implement only to have it strike a buried rock. The shaft shook and sent waves of pain from his fingers up along his arms. He threw the tool down.

"No more," he muttered. "I think I know who I have to see."

He looked up at the sun and saw that he still had several hours of daylight. He began walking north.

"He's the one," he said. "I don't know why I didn't think of it before."

11

———

Usually Livonia would wait for her husband to look up before entering his study, but this time she did not hesitate.

"There's a man here to see you," she said.

Charles continued studying the map laid out on his desk, then placed a ruler on it, and drew a line.

"About Sam. He says he's got something to sell."

Charles turned toward her. His expression did not change, except for a barely perceptible raising of eyebrows.

"I think you ought to see him," Livonia said.

"I've already sent to Chicago to engage an attorney."

"I'll send him in." She motioned to the figure standing in the hallway. Edward approached. He was still breathing hard from having walked and trotted all the way. He felt that he was at the door of freedom.

"Go on in," she said.

"Yes, ma'am."

Edward walked into the study with his head bowed as though he were entering church or a courtroom. The stern, white haired man behind the massive desk could have been Jehovah himself, or at least a judge on the bench.

"Well, man," Charles said. "Mrs. Logan tells me you have something to sell us concerning our son."

Edward ran his tongue over his lips to bring it under control and then he spoke.

"Yes. I do. Very important, it is what I have to say. I'm Michael O'Leary." He pronounced his birth name with full pride and accent.

"Do you know my son?"

"Only from a distance, if you take my meaning." Edward's tongue now felt fluid. He could taste his liberation. "That's what I want to tell you. I saw him that day. But I could forget that I did. Or else I could remember that I saw somebody else as well."

"Well, which is it?"

"I want to go to California."

Charles lowered his eyes to his map. When he raised them he wore an expression of affected confusion.

"Do I look like a ticket agent?"

"No. It's the money I need. I know how to buy a ticket." He could not keep the anger out of his voice. Why did they always have to mock him as though he were a simpleton?

Charles folded his hands atop the map.

"What makes you think I might want to purchase what you have to sell?"

"It could be of great use to your son."

"Why not offer it to him, then?"

"Because everybody knows he has no money. And you do."

"Oh, so now you mistake me for my son's banker."

Edward took a step back. His shoulders slumped. He should have known better.

"It was a mistake, I'm thinking, me coming here."

"Maybe so. But as long as you are here, put your goods on the table. I'll decide if I'm your buyer or not."

Edward considered whether he were being set up for another fall, but this was, after all, his best chance.

"That day, when my boss's daughter disappeared, I saw your son, and somebody else, both in the woods. Either one could have been the one. The other one was black."

"I see. And your memory..."

Edward had rehearsed his answer all the way here.

"I got to settle on one or the other when I talk to the law. Or it may be that I won't even be here. I could get on a train for Chicago

159

tomorrow, or a boat right there on that dock." He pointed out the window in the direction of the harbor. "Why if I had a couple of hundred dollars I would leave and never come back."

"Such a ticket, even with another to California, does not cost that much."

"I'm selling my honor," Edward said. "That is worth something as well."

"Mr. O'Leary, I am interested in your proposition, no doubt. But I need to consult the attorney I have engaged, when he arrives in the next day or two."

"I was thinking of leaving tomorrow."

"Well, by all means..."

"I need the money."

"Then I'm afraid you may have to wait."

Edward felt his chance slipping away, and he tried to close his fingers on it.

"Somebody else might want to buy what I'm selling."

"A man with something to sell must find the right buyer."

"I thought I had when I came here."

"I'm busy, Mr. O'Leary. Where can I find you?"

"At the Cutter place. That's where I work." He turned and walked out of the study like a child who had been reprimanded for not doing his lessons well.

Livonia came in.

"I heard everything. I would have thought you would have done a little more with this man."

"He's not going anywhere. It's just another business arrangement."

"We're talking about our son."

"And I'm talking about how best to handle this creature."

"*Our* son," Livonia repeated, although she wondered, as sometimes she had done these many years, just how accurate it was to use that pronoun.

Charles watched her leave, then turned around in his chair to gaze out the window at the row upon row of trees, the Tartarian cherries, black against the green leaves where they had not yet been picked. Tomorrow, he would meet with the attorney. Now he calculated how many rows would have to be harvested to pay the attorney's fee. He took out his ledger and put down both the fee in dollars and the trees lost to it on the expense side of the page, with the notation "Sam's Folly. Again."

Standing at the intersection of the track leading to his father's farm and the road to town, Isaiah looked to the south and the courthouse where the sheriff was waiting to talk with him. He turned north. In a short distance, the road ran along the waters of East Bay, squeezed onto a narrow shelf by the hills advancing from the west on one side and the push into the shore line by the bay on the other. Making his way down a barely discernible path onto the beach, he saw sand littered with rocks.

Sitting down on a large boulder, he looked up at half a dozen gulls describing delicate circles while descending onto the sand. These creatures, so graceful in the air, on land lurched about on their webbed feet like Saturday night drunks trying to find the road home, their beaks poking into the sand. Finding nothing of interest, they rose again into the sky and regained their grace and style.

Small black specks they were against the white of the clouds and then they disappeared. Isaiah realized he had risen from his seat on the rock as they ascended, and he sat back down against the hard, irregular surface. A gentle breeze stirred the water's surface into ripples, moving with incessant repetition toward town. The movement of the water, not quite pronounced enough to be waves, the rhythm lulling but the direction of the wavelets reminded him of where he was supposed to go.

Climbing back up to the road, he headed toward town. At that point where the land widened again between the retreating waters and the hills, where there was that path he had crossed not long ago with the search party, he stopped as though he were an iron nail coming into the force field of a powerful magnet. He was, in fact, unable to resist the pull, and permitting it to draw him through the marshy ground and up the low rise to the very spot, he felt a chill wind descend on him just as he reached the place beneath the tree where she had lain. The impression of her body, he was sure he could see it, and he shivered although the sun still shone with full force on him.

Dropping to his knees, he closed his eyes to remember. He had to know. That day, after he had finished plowing the field, he was late to meet his father but he had not hurried to join him because he was angry. She was meeting his father, not himself. They had worked on the road together without talking much, and he recalled that his father's shirt was soaked through with perspiration, but that he hadn't made much progress clearing the brush.

He should have gone himself to meet her, but he hadn't. Now kneeling at this spot, he opened the door a crack to his deepest suspicion, and peeked in, and violently recoiled. It was just too horrible to contemplate. His father, he knew, was guilty of many things, and he could be thoughtless, even sometimes a little cruel, but no matter how hard he tried he could not force together in his imagination an image of his father with his hands outstretched, and Margaret with her bare neck vulnerable. The two images refused to come together. Could those same hands that had lifted him onto his shoulders in happier days, or led him into town where he could get his free candy in the store, or even, as he now remembered, bandaged his cut knee after his mother had left, as gentle, no even more gently, than she herself, how could those very same hands, so skilled with a piece of wood, fashioning a toy wagon for him, how could they close around a throat and squeeze? Although he would not enter that room for a full look around, he could not force the door closed. It remained ajar, with just a little stream of pale light streaming out onto his feet.

Sheriff Billingham eyed the young man standing in front of him in his office. It was now late afternoon and the sun poured in through the western window. Blinking against the glare, shifting his weight from one dusty boot to another, his hands jammed into his trouser pockets, he looked as fragile as an egg that would crack if pressed hard at all. And yet within that shell was the truth that Billingham was determined to retrieve.

"Isaiah, is it?" he asked.

"Yes, like the prophet in the Bible."

"Ah, yes, the Bible. I'm afraid I didn't pay as much attention those Sunday mornings as I should have. I guess I had my mind on other things like most boys do." He waited, looking for a smile, some sign of recognition of their shared experience of growing up male. All he saw, however, was a slight quiver of the boy's lower lip. He felt that he was very close to seeing that egg crack, and if it did he might never be able to reconstitute the oozing contents into the hard kernels of facts he sought before they slipped irretrievably through his fingers. "Have a seat," he said, pointing to the chair next to his desk. "You must have had a long walk into town, judging by the dust on your boots."

Isaiah sat down, and stared into the broad face of the sheriff, whose expression beamed at him with a specious benevolence.

"It's not that far," he said.

"Not for your young legs. But I take a seat on my buggy. As I did this morning when I rode out to speak with your father." Feeling his fingers press against the delicate shell, wondering if it would now break, Billingham held his breath.

"He told me you were looking to talk to me," Isaiah said. "But I don't know why." That was the line he had settled on just as he had reached town. After all, why should he know anything? He was just a hand on his father's farm, doing what he was told to do, going to church on Sunday with his grandparents. There was no need to reveal more, certainly not his hope that one day she might have turned her eyes from his father toward him.

Noting the stiffening of the boy's resolve, Billingham understood, of course, that the boy must know his father was the prime suspect. Perhaps the only way at the boy's knowledge was to crack that shell. He picked up a paper from his desk.

"Now, boy, I've got the autopsy report right here. It indicates two things. The first is that the young woman was strangled." He peered at the paper as though to refresh his recollection. "And, yes, the second is that she was pregnant." He slapped the paper down. "What it doesn't say, but what my experience tells me to a certainty, is that the father of that child is the killer of them."

Isaiah snapped his head back as though the words were blows.

"I don't think that was you. And if it wasn't, maybe you can tell me who it was."

"She used to help her mother do our laundry," he said. "That's where we got to know her."

"We?"

Isaiah nodded.

"I would go there with my father."

"And did you get to know her? Maybe in the biblical sense?"

"No. I did not."

"What about your father?"

"I never touched her like that."

"Your father, boy, what about him?"

"You'd better ask him that yourself."

"Oh, I will."

"Can I go?"

163

"Oh, sure, in just a moment. There is this one question I'm asking everybody. As part of the investigation."

"Yes?"

"Where were you the day she disappeared?"

"In the morning I was plowing, and then I went to help my father."

"Clearing the brush from the road?"

"Yes."

"Did you?"

"Yes. Later that day."

The answers were coming too quickly, the sheriff thought. The boy had been thinking about what he would say.

"Tell me about it."

"Nothing to tell. I got finished later than I thought and when I went out to join him, I met him coming back."

"From?"

Billingham rose out of his chair and leaned across the desk.

"From where, boy?"

Isaiah waited for the sheriff to ease his bulk back into the chair.

"From the new road, sheriff. Isn't that what he told you?"

Billingham waved his hand as though Isaiah were a buzzing fly. He leaned his weight against the chair back, and it squeaked loudly in the silence that filled the room. He noted the bead of perspiration on Isaiah's lip. The clenched mouth, though, wasn't going to open any time soon, unless he found a way to pry it. He narrowed his eyes and glared. Isaiah returned the look.

"That'll do, boy," Billingham said after a few more moments, and turned his attention to some papers on his desk. "We'll talk again another time."

Isaiah rose and waited. When the sheriff continued looking down, he left, and once outside, he felt lightheaded. He realized he was damp with perspiration.

"I did the best I could, old man," he muttered, and he realized he wasn't sure which old man he was referring to, father or grandfather. Maybe both, he concluded, and he trudged on out of town.

A man a head taller than any of the other passengers crossed the deck of the steamer and descended the gangplank onto the town dock in Old Mission Harbor. He was wearing a white linen suit over a striped percale shirt that hung on his bony shoulders as though it were still on a hanger, a red four-in-hand around his scrawny neck, and a red carnation in his buttonhole. His white captain's cap threatened at each step to slide down over his narrow forehead and reach his rimless spectacles. He carried a valise in one hand, a leather portfolio in the other.

Waiting on the dock were several passenger coaches. The man, climbing into one that bore the name of Old Mission Inn, was joined a few moments later by a white haired gentleman in a straw bowler, a younger man and woman, a little girl of about three, and a nurse holding an infant. The older man carried a cane, which he set on the floor in front of him and, while he held it with one hand, he tipped his hat with the other.   The coach lurched forward just as the tall man was about to lift his own hat, and thereafter for the rest of the ride he sat with his eyes closed, oblivious to the chatter of the family. When they arrived at the inn, he waited for them to get down, and then followed.

At the desk, he checked in, inscribing "Nathan Lowe" in a cramped, but neat hand in the register. "Tomorrow, my associate Mr. Benson will be arriving. Please see that he has a room near mine."

"Yessir."

Lowe pulled out his watch. "I imagine dinner is being served."

"It is," the clerk replied. "For another hour or so."

When Lowe arrived in the dining room a short time later, all the tables were occupied except one next to the family with whom he had shared the ride from the dock. On the other side of the room, however, he saw an older man sitting by himself.

"Do you mind if I join you?" he asked, with a glance across the room at the table next to the family where the infant had just bestirred himself with a loud cry. The diner smiled.

"Of course, sir, I understand completely."

Lowe pulled a chair out. As he did, he could see under the table. He sat down, and slid his chair back in.

"I believe I saw you preach some years ago in Chicago," he said.

"Well, sir, did you notice my face, my voice, or," he paused, and then brought his wooden leg down with a thump on the plank floor.

"Perhaps a combination."

"A very circumspect answer."

"It is my profession to be so, I'm afraid." He extended his hand. "Nathan Lowe, attorney at law."

"I do not think you have come all this way to hear me preach again," Reverend Lapham smiled. "Unless I miss my guess, you are here to approach the same subject of my recent sermons only from, shall we say, a more secular perspective."

"I have not yet met my client," Lowe replied.

"I hope you won't take offense if I ask you a difficult question."

Lowe smiled.

"I can anticipate you, sir. You are aware, no doubt, which side I represent, and you wonder about my conscience."

"Indeed."

"It is my profession, as you have yours."

Lapham flushed.

"I bring sinners to our Lord," he said.

"And I make sure Justice does not peek from behind her blindfold, or be deceived by a heavy thumb on the scale."

A servant girl approached the table, carrying the minister's dinner, roasted chicken, boiled potatoes, and peas. She looked at Lowe.

"The same, if you please," he said, "but I'll have a glass of sherry with it. Would you care to join me Reverend?"

Lapham shook his head.

"Temperance I preach, and temperance I observe."

"Please don't wait for me," Lowe said.

Lapham picked up his knife and fork.

"Ordinarily, I would, but I must get back to my room to work on Sunday's sermon. The people are troubled. I must try to soothe them."

The waitress arrived with a glass of sherry, and Lowe took a deep sip. "It is always so in cases that so touch their sensibilities: a young woman, in the family way, so suddenly to depart this world."

"Indeed," Lapham agreed.

Lowe looked out the window at the darkening sky.

"It looks like the Lord might speak to you in thunder tonight, Reverend."

Lapham smiled.

"I do not take offense."

"None intended. I was merely commenting on the approaching storm."

Lapham took a last bite of his potato, and wiped his mouth with a gesture delicate enough for a lady.

"Perhaps I will see you in church?"

"Undoubtedly."

Finishing his dinner, Lowe was thankful to be alone. He retreated to the wide front porch of the inn, lit a cigar and watched its smoke float in the brisk breeze that blew in from the harbor. He saw the steamer on which he had arrived was still tied to the dock. With his third glass of sherry in his hand, he was feeling just a little glow. The wind, he noted, seemed to be increasing and the sky was black.

He hoped the minister's thoughts were heading heavenward, far away from the sordid business of a dead young woman, pregnant with a child who would never be born. It would be well if the congregation's thoughts could be so directed before one, or several of them found themselves in the jury box.

Standing among his trees Charles looked up at the black sky. Atop the orchard ridge, the wind whistled hard from the bay not a half mile away. Storm clouds gathered, packed tight by the wind, as the temperature dropped, and he shivered. Heavy drops splattered his face. Lightning flashed, followed by thunder. He felt something harder than water hit his cheek, lifted his hand to the spot and felt his blood. Something glanced off his shoulder and bounced on the ground. The hail came down hard, big, multi-cornered chunks that cut and bruised his skin.

"Come on then," he yelled, "Lord, show me your power, your glory."

As if in answer, lightning struck the ground, thunder boomed, and a couple of seconds later, in a streak of fire, lightning split a tree not twenty yards from where he was standing. He raised his fist, as though in celebration.

"Yes," he howled, "is it fitting, the sins of the son shall be visited upon his father, isn't that so?"

The rain came down in torrents, interspersed with hail two and three inches in diameter. Many pieces struck him, but he felt nothing. He walked under the nearest tree and looked up into its branches, and saw the combination of hail and rain destroying his crop, cherries splitting under the deluge, flying from the branches and falling at his feet, as the wind slammed in, and the trees leaned away from it.

Into the house an hour later, drenched and bleeding from the hail, he found Livonia waiting for him with a towel, and she handed it to him.

"The Lord spoke," he said.

"Did He really?"

"Yes."

"And what did he say?"

"Your son," he said, "that is what he said, your son." He dried his face and hands with the towel. Somehow he felt cleansed as if the rain had washed away some stubborn, clinging bit of conscience. "In the morning, I will seek out Mr. Lowe. I will tell him what that Irishman has offered to sell. Perhaps he can put it to use."

Sam watched the same storm clouds whisk by to the north. The sky darkened directly overhead, but no rain fell.

"Come on," he said, "you can do it."

For days, ever since his trip to town, he had felt unclean no matter how hard he scrubbed his skin. Now, he looked up to the heavens for a deluge that would pour down on him and wash him clean again. He watched the black clouds rush by, skirting his farm and following the coast toward the northern tip of the Peninsula.

"Just like everything else," he muttered. "It all goes to him."

Charles joined Lowe at the inn as Lowe was finishing his breakfast, pouring himself a cup of coffee.

"Mr. Lowe," he said, "I am Charles Logan."

Lowe extended his hand.

"It's a pleasure, sir," he said.   "I arrived yesterday. My assistant should be here in the next day or two."

"I won't presume to tell you how to do your business, as I'm sure you wouldn't think you could tell me how to grow fruit."

"But..."

"But I need to tell you of a visit I had from a man who works at the girl's farm. He wants to sell information, so he can go to California."

"And his merchandise?"

"He says he saw my son and another man, a black man, in the woods on the day of the murder."

Lowe downed his coffee, and daubed his lips with his napkin.

"I see," he said, "and you think this other man, the black one, might be useful to us."

"Yes. And he apparently has fled."

"All the better," Lowe said. "We'll want him to stay wherever he is."

"I thought you would think so." Charles rose to his feet. "One more thing. The man offered to go away, if I gave him money to travel to California."

"That we can't do."

"My thought exactly."

"But the offer," Lowe said, "is most valuable to us."

12

Isaiah dragged his ladder to the first tree in the first row of the orchard that climbed the hill behind their house. Halfway up, he heard the thud of hooves. He glanced down to see his grandfather arrive in a work wagon pulled by two brown Belgians. Sitting next to Charles was a short, wiry man. Isaiah hopped down and walked over to the wagon. Charles shaded his eyes from the sun and studied the trees.

"Not a bad crop," he said, "and that storm the other night that dropped most of my fruit on the ground didn't touch yours."

"No," Isaiah replied.

"Do you have a crew?"

"No. Dad couldn't hire one."

"No wonder," Charles replied. He turned to his companion. "You may know Harold Jenkins here, he's my foreman."

"I've seen him," Isaiah replied.

"He's a good man, got a good crew, but the thing is now I've got half the work I usually have for him."

"We don't have any money, or any prospect of getting any," Isaiah replied.

"Boy, you've got fruit. You've got the promise of money."

"Dad says that promises don't do him much good."

"No, I expect they don't, but Harold here is a different story."

"I can have half my crew down here this afternoon," Harold said.

"I'll pay you when I get paid," Isaiah said.

"That'll be soon enough," Harold replied. "Your grandfather is who I work for." He walked to the tree where Isaiah had propped the ladder. He stared up at the branches and then continued on into the orchard.

"That man," Charles said, "knows his business. I offered him to your father, more than once."

"And now..." Isaiah began.

"Now, circumstances dictate. Your fruit must be picked. Your father's attorney needs to be paid. Harold's crew needs income."

"I see," Isaiah replied, and he thought, for a moment, he had a glimpse into his grandfather's mind, but was not at all sure that he liked what he saw there.

Isaiah felt that he and his father were living under a cloud of fear. One careless word, and the cloud would open up and spill ruin upon their heads. They both understood this, and yet they also realized they were powerless to dispel the cloud or to move from beneath its shadow. So they spoke little. Each morning Isaiah watched Sam pick up his ax and trudge off to continue work on the road. Then he would drive Chester into the orchard alone, past where Harold's crew was working. In the evenings, he cooked a supper. They sat across from each other, their cutlery moving food to their mouths, which opened to receive the food but not to let words out.

At night in his bed, Isaiah chewed the indigestible core of his dilemma, unable to swallow it or spit it out. His father would no doubt soon be arrested, and he, himself, would be questioned.

Staring at the cracks in the ceiling, he followed each line until it intersected another. Then, pausing, unsure whether to stay the course, or jump to the new line, he realized this mindless exercise replicated the problem he sought to avoid.

Meet me at the usual place, she had said.

I was clearing the new road, his father had said.

The note was tangible proof of an appointment.

The little progress his father had made working on the road at the time of the appointment.

Meet me, she had said. In the usual place. Would he not have gone?

The sheriff probed that spot. Did he know something?

His grandfather wanted him to lie.

His father had fallen into the sullen silence of a guilty man waiting to be apprehended.

His head ached. The cracks in the ceiling offered no solace.

At the breakfast table, across from his silent father, cradling a cup of coffee in his hand, Isaiah was looking out the window toward the orchard when he saw the air thicken and around a bend came the buggy. He didn't say anything, but a frown tightened his face, and Sam turned to see what he was looking at, then got up and walked around the table to stand behind his son. He squeezed his shoulders.

"You just remember whose son you are, and where you saw me that day, if you're asked."

Isaiah felt a chill run down his arms. He felt almost as though he should say something more, a farewell appropriate to his father who would be gone for an indefinite period of time, maybe, but he pushed away the thought, maybe gone forever. Searching for the words, his emotions seized his throat as unbidden memories flooded his mind: his father hoisting him on his shoulders, tossing a baseball, instructing him in how to drive a nail, a veritable collage of a mental scrapbook as though he and Sam, contrary to the facts, had enjoyed a conventional father/son relationship, not that they had most recently been in love with the same woman, who was now dead, perhaps at the hands of his father. He watched his father's broad shoulders fill the doorway, and then the door close behind him.

Sheriff Billingham stood on the steps leading up to the front door. He chewed on the stub of an unlit cigar, took the cigar out of his mouth, turned, and spat onto the ground. His face, as usual, wore its introductory expression of benevolence, as though he were just out paying a social call, or returning some item he had borrowed. But today the butt of a Colt revolver shifted in its holster as he ambled a step or two closer, the sun glinting off the handcuffs suspended from his belt opposite the gun. He opened a folded document in his large hand, and held it in front of him. Letting the hand holding the paper drop to his side, he smiled as though he and Sam were about to share a joke.

"Now, you know why I'm here, Sam. If you want, I can read this warrant, like I'm supposed to do."

Sam had, of course, prepared himself for this confrontation, but the harsh, legal word bearing the weight, as it did, of the community as expressed through the voice of its court, transcribed onto a piece of paper and thrust into the hands of a law enforcement officer, still shocked him. It was as though all the hushed rumors and whispered asides he had been actually hearing when he met people in the community, or even those that had appeared in his nightmares, were now reified in that single document. He had no desire to hear the words. His eyes shifted past the sheriff, and Billingham's free hand moved, ever so casually, to the butt of his revolver.

"Now, Sam, don't do anything foolish. I'm sure we can work this out once we get to town."

The door behind Sam swung open. Isaiah walked out and stood next to his father.

"That goes for you, too," the sheriff said.

"It's all right," Sam said to Isaiah. "Just remember what I told you." He held out his hands."You know, Sheriff," he said, "I understand what folks have been saying, the rumors and lies, none of it true."

"I'm not the judge of that," Billingham replied. "My job is only to accompany you back to town." He pushed Sam's hands down. "I don't think that will be necessary, will it Sam?"

Sam felt a flicker of his old insouciance.

"Just want to help a fella do his job," he said.

"You can do that by climbing on the buggy seat." Sam lifted himself onto the seat, and the sheriff looked to Isaiah. "You can visit him tonight, after his paperwork's been done." Billingham lifted his leg onto the step on the other side of the buggy and swung himself up. Isaiah jumped off the porch and reached up to seize his father's hand. They looked at each other for a moment or two. Then, Sam removed his hand from his son's and gestured toward the house. Isaiah nodded and turned his back. Hearing the snap of the whip, the horse's hooves against the hard dirt, and the creaking of the wheels on their axles, he waited until all was quiet again and then walked back into the house.

He wondered if his prayers were now answered, or whether he was now descending to a deeper circle of his personal hell.

Frederick approached the front desk of the Old Mission Inn. Behind it stood Martin Nelson who had been signing in guests for more than forty years. His shock of white hair and mustache set off his red cheeks, and he had a quick eye for sizing up customers: those who couldn't, or wouldn't pay, those who needed special services, and a finely tuned ear for bits of information he was only too happy to share. In another life, or another time, he would have been an old woman gossiping over the back fence.

"Hello, Mr. Gorschen, back so soon?" Martin turned the large register book around and slid a pencil toward Frederick.

"Why, yes, Martin, home for a bit, to see the wife and child, but a traveling man such as myself doesn't make any money sitting at his own table."

.   Frederick signed the register. Martin placed a thick finger next to the name above his.

"Now, that's Mr. Lowe, from Chicago, who just checked in a couple of days ago. Here to represent Sam Logan, they say."

"Is he accused?"

"Folks say the sheriff's gone out to bring him in."

"Are people so sure it's him?"

"Oh, he's the one all right, you just have to look at his past to know what he's capable of." Martin spun the register back around and took a key off a peg behind him. "Same room as last time, right down the hall from the minister, and now Mr. Lowe is on your other side."

"Perhaps I will make his acquaintance then."

The sheriff's buggy slowed. Beside him, Sam had been sitting with eyes closed, letting his body roll with the jolts while he worked hard to shut the door of his mind to the thoughts he knew would soon be demanding entry, for just about now, he figured, they should be reaching the track down on the east side of the road leading to the hemlock swamp, which would meet the one on the west running from the Cutter farmhouse. He snapped his eyes open and blinked in the sun. The sheriff had set the brake and was staring intently, the sun reflecting off of what he was looking at. Sam rubbed his eyes. When he took his hand away he could see the barrel of the revolver in the hand of Henry Cutter, who was standing before the boulder at the turn-off to his house.

Billingham reached to his belt for his handcuffs. "Hold out your right hand."

"What, so I can be a sitting duck?"

Billingham took Sam's right arm and snapped the cuff on it.

"That thought is why I'm doing this," he said, and then he closed the other end of the cuff onto the support for the seat. Swinging himself off the seat and onto the ground, he hoisted his belt over his paunch and laying his hand on the butt of his own gun he ambled toward Henry, making sure his body blocked Henry's line of sight toward Sam.

"Now, Henry, just what is your intention?"

"I saw you go by a while ago," Henry replied, glancing at Sam. "I figured you'd be bringing him back with you, and I could save you the bother."

"That's not the way of it, Henry, you know that," Billingham said.

"Just step aside Sheriff," Henry said.

"I can't do that. You know I can't."

Henry moved to his left, and then to his right, but each time the sheriff moved with him, so that it looked as though they were performing a silent dance, both of them kicking up the dust of the road, but neither saying anything. With each step, though, Sheriff Billingham also moved closer to Henry until he was standing only four feet from him.

"Now let me have that relic," he said. "It belongs in a museum. Probably blow up in your hand."

Henry backed up a step and Billingham followed. Henry repeated his backward motion like a crayfish scuttling across the lake bottom. Billingham lumbered after him, until suddenly Henry took two or three quick steps to his left and drew parallel to the sheriff. He raised his heavy weapon only to feel Billingham's strong grasp on his wrist, pushing the gun down. Billingham continued to press until the revolver was pointing at the ground, then the sheriff seized it with his other hand. Henry resisted briefly but released it. Billingham held it up.

"That was damned stupid, Henry. Do you want me to have to put you in a cell next to him?" He broke the revolver. "This has seen some action, ain't it, but none very recently."

"I was thinking on using it one more time," Henry replied, his jaw set in Sam's direction.

"I understand," Billingham said, "that's why I'll just take it with me for now."

"Can I just get a closer look at him?" Henry asked.

"Now what good would that do? You just go on home, and let the law do its work."

"Logan, "Henry shouted. "Here's for you," and he spat a large glob onto the ground." Billingham moved his foot out of the way at the last moment.

"Get on now," he said, and Henry turned and walked up the track to his house.

Daniel's cough brought his head to his knees, but then he sat back against the trunk of a pine tree on the bank overlooking the river. He gazed over the tops of the white blossoms of Queen Anne's lace to the water. Behind him, not more than a hundred yards, was the mansion out of which the young woman wearing yellow gloves had emerged and stepped up into the carriage. He recalled her face, framed in angelic curls, her eyes looking past him as though lost in thought. He chased the memory and chose instead to contemplate the fullness in his stomach, stuffed as it was with Mrs. Svensen's pot roast, potatoes, and apple pie. He thought now, as he had done so often in the past, about the paradox of his perfectly healthy appetite serving his fast deteriorating body. It was like loading wood into the firebox of a steam engine whose boiler had sprung a leak a long time ago. No matter how well the fire burned the engine could not generate much power.

Still, on a late summer afternoon such as this he was almost at peace, contemplating the waters of the river flowing gently by and he could just about convince himself that there was a benign deity above smiling down at His creation. But that happy thought had to contend with his recurring memory of the young woman, the one who had walked toward him that day not three weeks ago, distracted and emanating a despair so palpable that her death had come as no surprise.

Although his own frail grasp on life was a constant reminder of the general mortality, he yet distinguished between himself and Margaret. He had lived so long with the knowledge that he would in all likelihood die young that the fact seemed as natural and reasonable as the sure sense that the petals of the white flowers in front of him would soon drop there. Some already had, and the stalks themselves would follow, so that before long the plants would return to the dirt from which they had risen, just as he would when his flesh wilted and died. In contrast, the river would remain, its flowing waters suggesting an underlying constancy to all things.

All of this, and his own place in its context, made sense to him. The death of the young woman, though, did not fit. He lifted his eyes to thin clouds drifting above. Staring at them for a few moments, he shut his eyelids against the brightness of the sky. He had just started to doze, when he heard excited voices. Blinking himself back to awareness of where he was, he turned around and saw several people walking on the street. He got to his feet and made his way toward them.

"I heard he was being brought in this afternoon," one person, a well dressed businessman, said.

"And it's about time, I declare," the young woman beside him announced.

Daniel approached them.

"Pardon me, but can you tell me what you are talking about?"

The man pointed down the street toward the clock tower of the courthouse, visible between the trees.

"The sheriff has arrested that killer and is taking him to jail. We're going there to see if we can get a look at him."

"Who would that be?"

"That Logan, the one who was her lover."

"The father or the son?" Daniel asked.

The man looked perplexed.

"I can't say. I didn't know there were two. I guess we will have to see."

The young man tipped his hat and took the elbow of his companion and they hurried to catch up with the others. Daniel trailed after them. By the time he reached the courthouse his lungs were screaming their complaint. The small contingent he had joined now formed part of a much larger crowd, numbering forty or fifty, perhaps more. He took out his notebook to write, sensing the story was unfolding here, and he would need to record it.

Buzzing about how the murderer had been arrested, how there was ample evidence, and how he would soon get his just deserts, the people's talk began to diminish as the sun beat down on them. On the top step of the courthouse stood a boy wearing an engineer's cap, and next to him another boy, his arm in a sling, and a lean girl, barefoot. The boy wearing the cap rose on his tiptoes and stared down the road.

"They're coming," he called out. "The sheriff's got somebody with him. It must be him!"

A small face appeared in the window in the top floor of the jail. In a moment, it was joined by a larger one.

In the room behind the window, Deputy Allan Morgan looked down at his son. "Well, Billy," he said to the little boy at his side, "Daddy has got to go to work."

"Must you?" a female voice asked.

Allan turned to face his wife.

"I'm afraid so, Virginia."

"I never did want you to take this job." She walked to the window and looked down at the crowd. "Look at them. It won't be safe."

Allan picked up his badge from the shelf next to the window, and pinned it to his shirt.

"Are you going to wear your gun?" Billy asked. "Can I go with you?"

Allan hoisted him up and kissed his cheek.

"Yes, and no."

He took his gun belt down from its hook and put it on.

"Just in case," he said to his wife.

Virginia hurried to a small writing table and picked up a sheet of paper and a pencil. She handed it to him. "I read somewhere that somebody paid a hundred dollars for Charles Guiteau's signature, the one who shot Garfield."

"Logan didn't shoot no president," Allan said.

"What he did was worse if you ask me."

"Worse than what?"

They both turned to see Billy, who had crept out of his bed when he heard his parents talking, and had sat, unobserved, listening.

"You little pitcher..." Virginia said.

"With big ears," Billy smiled. "Worse than what?" he asked.

"Nothing you need bother about knowing," Allan said,

"Who did something worse?" Billy insisted. "The man you will put in the cell?"

"Yes, him," Allan replied, "he did something bad, that's why he's where he's at."

Billy lingered at the window, looking down.

"Get away from there now," Virginia said.

"It's funny," Billy said, "he did something bad and he's living in the same building as us."

He turned from the window and picked up a wooden wagon, which he began rolling on the floor.

"The child," Virginia said, "did you hear what he said?"

"I did. And I don't want to talk about it."

"You never do."

"That's right."

"Still," she said, "you know I've been saving what I can so we can move into a better place. And he's the first murderer we've had in the jail. Who knows when we might get another such chance?"

"I don't think..." he began.

"Try," she said.

As the buggy approached, the crowd fell silent. When it stopped in front of the courthouse steps, Sheriff Billingham stood up, balancing himself with one hand on Sam's shoulder and motioned to Allan, who was now standing at the front door of the building. Allan walked down the steps, and the crowd separated, reluctantly, to let him pass as he took his place next to the buggy.

"I guess you folks expected the circus to be arriving in town today," Billingham boomed, punctuating his remark with a broad smile. The crowd seemed to breathe out as one. Putting his hand to his forehead as though shielding his eyes from the sun, the sheriff swiveled his head as far as he could one way, then back the other, and finally peered straight ahead toward the distant horizon. "No sign of an elephant," he said. "Just me and my prisoner."

Daniel noted the mood of the crowd change. Before the arrival of the buggy, he thought he might be witnessing a lynching. Now, it seemed as though he were at a church picnic listening to the patter of an event organizer announcing that the horseshoe competition would soon be starting. There were smiles, and not a few chuckles as heads turned in the direction of the sheriff's gaze. But then came a deep bass voice belonging to a gray haired farmer, his cheek puffed out from a wad of chewing tobacco. "We don't need no circus animals, Sheriff. Just that murderer you have your hand on." This statement was greeted by first one and then a number of heads bobbing up and down in agreement, as an ugly murmur rose from the assembly.

Billingham's smile disappeared, replaced by a look of wonderment.

"I don't see no murderer here," he looked down at Sam. "If you mean this gentleman sitting beside me, why he's an innocent man who may be accused of a crime, but at this moment he is no more guilty of anything than that child over there." He pointed to the boy in the engineer's cap, who stood on the courthouse steps. Voices of protest lifted, but Billingham only repeated, "as innocent as any of you, that is until, and not before, a court of law decides otherwise."

"Then why are you holding onto him?" someone asked.

"Why to make sure he has the opportunity to appear in that courtroom in there. We wouldn't want him to miss that opportunity, would we?"

Sam sat sullen, head bowed. Willing his ears shut, so that although his mind registered voices, it did so like the buzz of bees circling his head, he hunched his shoulders as though expecting to be stung, but instead felt a tug on his shoulder.

Billingham lowered his head to him and whispered, opening the cuff attached to the bench support, and then closed it over his own thick wrist. "Now get up with me, I've got them calm enough for us to try to enter the building. Don't look at nobody, don't say nothing, you hear? Just walk along with me." He grasped Sam's arm above the elbow and lifted him up. "Stay close," he said. "Walk on his other side," he said to Allan.

Daniel slithered to the front of the crowd. He outlined a quick sketch in his notepad of the sheriff climbing down, holding onto Sam's arm, and then Sam himself almost falling off the buggy's step as he followed. Allan caught him and held his free arm. The trio passed within five feet of where Daniel was standing. Daniel focused his gaze on Sam's eyes. They wore the expression of a stunned animal, suddenly cornered by a pack of wild dogs. Daniel thought for a moment that Sam recognized him from the day of the search party, but then Billingham yanked him and they were up the steps and into the building.

Remaining for some minutes, the crowd was unwilling now that the spectacle was gone, to leave. Daniel recorded the comments he overheard, some indicating that it was a shame to have to wait for a court to decide what they already knew to be the truth. A strong hand clamped his elbow. He tried to pull his arm free so as to finish writing his sentence, but he could not.

"Are you a reporter?" Edward asked.

Daniel turned to face him, and Edward released his arm.

"I am."

"If you want to get it right," Edward said, "you should talk to me."

Daniel recalled seeing him before.

"You work for the Cutters, don't you?"

"I did. I'm my own man now."

Daniel held his pencil poised over the page of his notepad.

"What can you tell me?"

"What can you pay me?"

"Pay you? All I can do is quote you in my story."

"That won't get me to California, will it?"

"No, it won't but you'll be doing the right thing."

Edward shook his head.

"How's a man supposed to make a living when nobody will pay him for what he knows?"

"I'll tell you what," Daniel said, "you give me your information, and when I get paid for my story I'll give you a dollar or two."

"I'm afraid that won't do. I need much more than that."

Daniel snapped his notepad closed.

"I guess I'm not your man, then. Find yourself somebody with more money in his pocket than I have and maybe with a little looser grip on his convictions."

Edward raised a dirt encrusted hand to his head and scratched.

"I will do that, as soon as I can find him."

"Give me your name, in case I can get payment for you," Daniel said. "My editor might be willing to send some money."

"Michael O'Leary. You can spell that, can't you?"

"Sure thing, Mr. O'Leary. Where can I get in touch with you?"

"I'll find you," Edward said.

Daniel watched him walk away, and then wrote "Michael O'Leary" in his book.

The sun had set not long ago, and the shadows of the trees in the front yard had reached the porch as Charles Logan drove up to Sam's house. The house itself was dark, except for a pale glow visible in one window against the dusk. He got down from his wagon and walked up the steps. He knocked on the door. No one answered, and he pushed the door open. He searched for the light he had seen from outside, but he could not locate its source.

"Isaiah," he called out, "are you in here?"

A movement of a wooden chair leg across the floor, and then, "Yes, Grandpa, in here."

Charles walked in the direction of the voice and found him sitting at the kitchen table, his hands cupped around the stub of a candle.

"I cannot decide," the boy said. "The sheriff said I could visit him tonight. Should I Grandpa?"

"Perhaps not," Charles replied, pulling out a chair, its legs grating against the silence as he sat down.

"Why not? Shouldn't somebody see him?"

"Not you. I've hired the best lawyer I could find. He'll talk to him in the morning."

"I mean you or me," Isaiah insisted, "shouldn't one of us?"

"No. I don't need to see him in jail, and you should not. You need to keep your head clear. Seeing him might cause you to forget what you have to do. Remember?"

Isaiah lifted the candle and held it toward his grandfather. Charles sat in its light unblinking.

"It's not right," Isaiah said, "whatever I do is just not right."

"If that's what you think, then you must do what is practical."

Isaiah snuffed out the candle.

"Just as you would do."

"Yes."

Isaiah got up and threw his arms around Charles.

"It's so hard," he said.

"I know. And you know how hard it is for me. Let me tell you. This is only the second time I have been in my son's house, and it has to be at such a time as this."

Sam looked through the bars on his windows into the night sky. He held his breath and listened, thinking he could hear the river rubbing against its banks not a hundred yards away. It occurred to him with the force of revelation that he had not been swimming since he was a child even though he had spent his whole life within a short walk to the water. He shook his head, and turned his attention again to the sky. Seeking the familiar with the thirst of one whose thickened tongue, blistered by the desert sun, seeks the cooling drop of water, he would drink the familiar patterns of the dipper, of Orion, of all the stars and planets in their accustomed places, just as they would be if he were standing in his own orchard on this summer evening, or sitting on his porch, moisture beading on the lip of a glass of lemonade in his hand.

He seized these thoughts as hard as he could, for it came to him, as he stood with his hands on the iron bars, that he might never look at the night sky again except through such a curtain as he now gazed through.

So absorbed was he that he did not at first hear the steps approaching. When he did note them, his heart leapt. Surely, they were coming to release him. They must have realized their mistake, not of course that he was entirely innocent, but that their facts were too flimsy to hold him. What did they have to hold him on? The fact that he was known to have spent time with her? But where was he on the day she was killed? Wasn't he clearing the new road with his son Isaiah? And what about the bottle of laudanum? Everyone knew that she had never been right after her brother drowned. And he was, after all, the son of the wealthiest farmer on the Peninsula, not a man to be trifled with, fool sheriff with his gun and his handcuffs, he must even now be walking down that long corridor to the cell they had put him in at the end of a row of empty ones, as though he were some kind of leper, he would be holding the large iron key in his meaty hand and a look of utter chagrin on his face.

These ideas flashed through his brain, in time with the approaching steps, and as they did his conclusions seemed to strengthen. But something was wrong. The steps were too fast and light, not the heavy, weary tread of that elephantine sheriff. He turned and strode to the door of his cell.

"Good evening, Mr. Logan."

The man he saw in the dim light of the oil lamp in the hall outside his cell wore a tin badge, which reflected the feeble beam, and a gun belt about his waist, a young man, not yet thirty, of under average height and thin.

"Where's the sheriff?" Sam asked, still holding to his vision of Billingham's coming to release him.

"I'm his deputy, Allan Morgan. I helped the sheriff bring you in here this afternoon."

"Pardon me," Sam said, "if I don't recollect you. I was looking at the eyes of those folks who looked like they'd be happy to string me up on the nearest tree, like I was some nigger raped a white woman."

"They were in an ugly mood."

Sam waited for him to go on.

"Have you come to tell me I have a visitor?"

"No. I just came down from where I live." He pointed to the ceiling. "In an apartment on the top floor."

"Handy."

Allan took out a pencil and a folded piece of paper from his shirt pocket.

"Could you just sign your name?"

Sam put his hand through the bars.

"Some kind of form? I thought I signed everything I had to."

"Not exactly."

Sam looked at the paper.

"It's blank," he said.

"Until you put your name on it."

"Well, I'll be," Sam said. He crumpled the paper and snapped the pencil in half. He tossed both through the bars.

Allan picked them up. He smoothed out the paper, folded it and put it and the two halves of the pencil back into his pocket.

"It was my missus's idea," he said. "We could use the money."

Sam retreated to his window and looked up at the sky until he found the north star, gazing at it as the footsteps receded down the hall. Even after it was silent once again, he continued staring at its shine in the blackness. If only he thought about it hard enough, he would be able to reach through the bars of his cage and touch it.

After a while his neck began to ache from the strain of looking up, so he lowered his head and gazed below. For a moment, he was disoriented as he thought he saw a light, the star again, but now on the ground. Then he observed another light off to one side of it, and several others on the other. They flickered and moved, and he understood they were torches in the hands of people spending the night beneath his cell window. Anger rose in him like steam through a valve forced open. How dare they, what did they know of the circumstances, would they have done anything so very different? He lifted himself against the bars of his window, filling his mouth with saliva and spat. A sudden breeze blew the spray back into his face. He left it where it was and lay down on his cot. Let them stand out there, the fools, at least *he* knew enough to get some sleep.

"He wouldn't sign it?"

"No, Virginia," Allan said. "I showed you what he did."

She looked out of the window.

"They're still there."

"I know. I told them to go home, but they intend to stay."

"What on earth for?"

"I don't know. They didn't say. I guess they want him to see them."

She smoothed the paper.

"I just thought he might, it wouldn't cost him anything."

"Except his pride."

"He's got too much of that, if you ask me."

13

———

At eight o'clock as soon as the dining room opened, Frederick came down to breakfast, and took a seat at a table in the rear with his back to the wall. The only other person in the room was an elderly woman sipping a glass of water. Holding a napkin in one hand, and the glass in the other, each time she took the glass from her mouth she daubed her lips dry. A servant girl came walking toward him. Thin and plain, with close-set eyes above bony cheeks and a nose that narrowed to a point, her thin hand shook as it poured a cup of coffee.

"Do you know Mr. Lowe?" he asked.

She nodded.

"He has been having his breakfast here every day, always the same thing, a hard boiled egg, a piece of toast, and a pot of coffee on his table."

"Do you expect him soon?"

She glanced at the clock on the mantle over the fireplace. "Eight fifteen, every morning."

Frederick took out a business card and a pencil. He wrote a few words on the back of the card.

"Please give this to him when he comes in."

The clock chimed the quarter hour. Frederick looked up from his plate of pancakes and bacon as two men entered the dining room. The tall one stooped a little going through the doorway. He wore a white linen suit with a red four-in-hand and a white captain's hat. The sunlight coming through the east window glinted off his rimless spectacles. His companion's short and bulky body strained his vest and suit jacket. He had a bushy mustache and deep set brown eyes. The tall one glided over the floor while the other strode with rolling shoulders in advance of his body. They took a table near the window on the east wall.

The waitress placed a pot of coffee on the table and two glasses of water. The short one poured himself a cup, but the tall one contented himself with a sip of water. Handing Frederick's card to the tall one, the waitress pointed in Frederick's direction. The man nodded at Frederick, removed his spectacles, wiped them with a pristine looking handkerchief, and then settled them back on his nose, every motion precise. His associate seized his coffee cup as though he were afraid it might slip from his hand and brought it to his mouth with a jabbing motion of his arm. The tall one took his time reading the note on the back of the card. When he was done, he placed it on the table next to his companion's plate and said something, making the slightest, almost indiscernible movement of his head toward Frederick. The short one threw back his wide shoulders and turned a steady gaze on Frederick. Then they were served and began eating their breakfasts, a steak for the short one, a hard boiled egg and toast for the other.

Lingering over his second cup of coffee, Frederick was confident the lawyer would respond in his own time, and in his own deliberate fashion, to his note. He was not mistaken. Swiping his napkin across his mouth, the short one stood, and walked in his rolling gait toward Frederick.

"I'm Wendell Benson," he said in a gruff voice, just above a whisper. "I work for Mr. Lowe. And he wants to know what you can tell him about this case."

When Bill Heller arrived at his office, Richard Kelly, his young clerk, was waiting for him. Kelly's face was dominated by his buck teeth, over which he was attempting to grow a mustache. Currently, it was no more than a thin screen of scraggly hairs. Heller read the excitement in his assistant's face.

"So, it's true, is it?" Heller asked.

"Yes. I'm quite sure. My cousin Lizzy works at the Inn and saw him arrive."

"Well, I suppose I should be honored, as should our little town. It's not every day, or every attorney, who has the chance to go up against Mr. Nathan Lowe of Chicago."

"My cousin was struck by his dress."

"I've heard about his attire."

"Oh, and one more thing," Richard added, "another man checked in. He looked like..."

"An ex-Pinkerton detective, no doubt. Mr. Lowe spends a good fraction of his considerable earnings on his wardrobe and another sizable portion on his detectives." Heller settled back in his chair with a bemused expression on his face, then leaned forward, picked up a sheaf of papers, and set them in front of him on his desk. "Well, Mr. Kelly, we do have our work cut out for us." He shuffled through the papers. "Our man has motive, an unwanted pregnancy."

"The defense might stipulate that," Richard said. "And I've reviewed Mr. Logan's marital records. He has a history of getting women pregnant, and then marrying them. Besides Isaiah, he had another son, after his second wife left him. Both that one and Isaiah were born less than nine months after he married their mothers. Why wouldn't he be willing to do that again?"

Heller nodded, then furrowed his brows.

"I've been thinking about that. Trying to find a way to use that fact with more effect. You've read the autopsy report, haven't you?"

"Of course."

"The part about the fetus."

"Yes." Richard sucked in his breath. "You're not thinking about..."

"I am. Mr. Lowe is a formidable opponent. We will need all our weapons."

"But the judge won't permit it."

"No, he won't. But there might be a way."

"I don't know, sir."

"You're uneasy. That's understandable. But remember what kind of murderer we are dealing with here."

"Yes sir."

"Now, besides motive, Mr. Logan had opportunity, an ongoing relationship. But there are no witnesses, nothing to place him at the scene, and most important an alibi. He claims he was at least a mile and a half away on the other side of the Peninsula. If we can't break that down, we can't convict him. Did Mr. Logan leave anything at the scene?"

"Perhaps," Richard offered. "He didn't just land there. He must have walked, and the ground about there where the body was found is soft."

"An excellent thought."

Frederick rose from the table. He felt as though he had been undressed, his pockets emptied, and even his body cavities probed, all done without apparent malice, or even much interest. He walked by the table where Lowe and Benson were sitting, trying to read their faces. How had his idea been received? Benson's face registered absolutely nothing during his interrogation, and now Lowe offered a courteous smile that he might flash to a shoeshine boy snapping his rag over his boots. He wanted very much to sit down with them and reiterate, but his salesman's training told him that he had already made his pitch. Repetition would kill it. And so he continued out of the room.

"What do you think?" Lowe asked.

Benson nodded

"If I had a daughter, and this fellow was hanging around, I'd run him out of town before he could sell her some of his poison."

"But a legal poison," Lowe smiled.

"Legal or not, enough of it, well, you know, and he says he gave it to her because she looked so distraught."

"That's the point, isn't it?"

The woman outside of the sheriff's office was in her late twenties, slender with brown hair, blue eyes, and an aquiline nose that gave her face a look of delicacy. Clutching an envelope in her hand, she read over the note that it had contained. A toddler of about two clutched at her skirt. She put the note back into the envelope, slid it into her little beaded purse, and tapped on the door, so lightly as to hardly be heard.

"Go on, knock a little harder," said Miss Wilkins, "so he can hear you."

The woman first rubbed her left ring finger, which still bore the imprint of a ring she no longer wore, and then balled that hand into a tiny fist and struck the door harder.

There was the scraping of a chair from inside the office, and then the door swung open.

"This is the second Mrs. Logan," Miss Wilkins said, looking down at the child, "along with her son Jonathan." The woman hesitated. "It's all right," Miss Wilkins said.

"Come on in, Mrs. Logan," Billingham said, "I'm so glad you could stop by."

"That name no longer suits me," Eustace said, and again she squeezed her ring finger as though somehow it would betray her. The child stared up at the large man and then buried his face in his mother's skirt.

"I can understand," Sheriff Billingham said. He ushered her into his office with a sweep of his arm. "I served papers on Mr. Logan, must be two years ago." He looked down at the child.

"I was pregnant with him when you did."

"And a fine lad he looks to be," Billingham said. "If you like, Miss Wilkins can mind him while we talk."

The boy pushed himself further into the fabric of his mother's skirts.

"No, Jonathan will be fine with me." She walked into the office, laboring a little against the weight of the child, who dragged his feet across the floor. She picked him up and placed him in a chair. Reaching into her purse, she removed a piece of bread. The boy took it from her and began to chew, his concentration focused on the hard crust. Sitting down in a chair beside him, she took an envelope out of her purse, brushed off a few crumbs with a quick, efficient swipe of her hand, and opening the note, scanned it again. She had by this time read it so frequently she could probably have recited its contents from memory.

"You want to speak to me about Mr. Logan," she said, "but I thought I made it clear that I had said what I had to say. I wanted no part of his present trouble, which I could have predicted, if anyone had bothered to ask me." This speech left her a little breathless and she settled back in her chair, her thin chest heaving. She held up her ringless ring finger. "You see, don't you?"

"I hate to trouble you this way, but I'm afraid it's my job. You are part of our investigation."

"How is that possible? I know nothing more than what I wrote in my letter. I have not seen the man for two years since that day..." she stopped, then went on more slowly. "Since that day I climbed down from the buggy on the way to town, with my big belly, determined no longer to put up with his abuse. He had turned Isaiah against me, you know. I walked to the doctor because he would not take me unless I paid for the visit myself, knowing full well that I had not a penny of my own, and his child on the way. That is the last time I had anything to do with him, so how can I possibly be part of your present investigation?"

Billingham picked up a paper from his desk and slid it toward her. She glanced at it and shuddered.

"Do you recognize that?" he asked.

"Of course I do. It's the lies he wrote about me."

Billingham nodded and slid another piece of paper toward her. "And this?"

"Why of course I recognize my own words, in answer to all his lies."

"We are investigating a murder, Mrs. Logan, and we think Mr. Logan is the man we're looking for. Those documents tells us something of his character, which Mr. Heller, the prosecutor, has specifically asked me to look into."

"So you don't have him cold," she said. "I didn't think he was that clever. But if it's his character you are interested in, it's as black as his heart."

"We might need you to say that, or words to that effect, with specific details, at his trial."

She shook her head.

"I don't think I can do that."

Jonathan finished his bread and dropped down off the chair. The food apparently had fed his courage as well as his stomach for he now set out to explore that portion of the office that was available to his two foot height. Billingham crumpled a blank piece of paper and tossed it on the floor. Jonathan stepped unsteadily toward it, and sat down next to it. He scrutinized it as though expecting it to escape his grasp.

"Always worked with my own," Billingham said, "I don't know why."

Eustace smiled.

"Can I trust you?" she asked.

"Of course, just like your boy does now." He looked down at Jonathan who was holding the crumpled paper out toward the sheriff's knee, a big grin on his face.

"What do you want me to tell you?"

"The business about the laundry. Let's start with that."

"I have, as you no doubt know, a nervous condition, and sometimes I had to take to my bed, at which Mr. Logan would become impatient for clean clothes. He would not wait for me to improve, but he must carry the soiled clothes, mine included, how humiliating, to Mrs. Cutter, and her daughter, and pay them to wash them. Really, I don't know how that ridiculous affair made its way into our divorce proceedings." She pushed the papers back to him.

Billingham picked up one.

"It seems you said he wasn't giving the household enough money, so he replied by having Mrs. Cutter deposed to the effect that, based on your laundry, you had clothes appropriate to your situation."

"Nonsense. If you ask me he only took our clothes over there as a pretext to see that young woman you now think he killed."

"Well, why don't you tell me about that, and everything else you can think of." He leaned down and picked up Jonathan and sat him on his knee. "I'll just listen. And if you don't mind, I'll have Miss Wilkins come in and write down what you say. It may be that is all you will have to do, and we can keep you out of the courtroom." He watched her face, thinking he was pretty sure he had stoked her old, angry resentment enough to overcome her distaste at revisiting her short, unhappy marriage, just long enough to leave her with a child, little better than a bastard, and whatever money she was able to squeeze out of Logan.

"Very well," she said. "Let me tell you about the day he threw me down on the floor with his hands around my throat."

"I'm not your father confessor," Lowe said. He wiped the one chair in Sam's cell with a handkerchief, and sat down. "I am expensive because I do my job well. Your father wants me to win this case. We had only a brief conversation, you see. He said he wanted my services, I told him my fee, he agreed, and here I am."

"I see. What do you want me to tell you?"

"My job is to convince a jury that the case against you is not strong enough to convict you. I do not want you to lie to me, but I do want you to give me enough facts that will withstand the prosecution's best efforts to discredit them. These facts are the wall I will erect between you and a guilty verdict."

"Where should I begin?"

"Permit me to point you in a direction. We are dealing with facts that are incontrovertible, the bricks of that wall. There is the bottle of laudanum found at her side."

"Yes, the laudanum." He recalled how he seemed to have been floating while she had swallowed what was left in the bottle.

"Do you know where she obtained it?" Lowe studied Sam's face.

"That bottle, no. I had one in my house that I was taking for the toothache."

"Good. My man spoke to the drummer who gave her the bottle that was found next to her; we will have witnesses to testify to her distressed state of mind. Now, perhaps the most important fact, so be careful how you answer." He took a breath. "Tell me where you were on the day that Miss Cutter died."

Sam paused.

"Working on a new road from my property to a resort on West Bay."

"Do you have witnesses to support that."

"My son." The words came out easily, perhaps too easily, Lowe thought. "He will say so," Sam continued.

"Will he indeed? I will question him most roundly on that point. An alibi is a formidable brick in the wall, if one can establish it. Go on, then," Lowe said. "Tell me about working on that road, as much as you can remember. And when you're done, I will want you to respond to the facts the prosecution no doubt will present. They will be like a battering ram against our wall. We must see how we can deflect them or better yet turn them on the prosecutor himself."

"I was working on that road," Sam began.

"Tell me about it."

And Sam did.

Billingham found Heller having a bowl of chili for lunch in Johnson's Restaurant, sitting at a table outside overlooking the slow flowing river. He was working his spoon with his left hand, while his right held a pencil over a piece of paper.

"I've got a preliminary list of witnesses here," Heller said.

"Is Mrs. Logan on it?"

"Not yet. I was waiting to hear from you."

"Put it on with a question mark. I more or less promised her to keep her out of it. I have her statement. My secretary is typing it up."

"But you know we can't use that statement in court without giving Mr. Lowe a chance at her."

"That's my concern. I am not at all sure she would hold up."

"A bad witness is worse than no witness," Heller said. He wrote her name on the paper, followed by a large question mark. "We'll just think about that one."

The waiter stopped at the table.

"Just something wet," Billingham said.

"We have a fresh barrel."

"I was hoping you'd say that. Bring me a glass."

Heller pushed his empty bowl toward the waiter.

"The chili was excellent. A beer for me too," he said.

"Have you thought about who Lowe might call?"

Heller held up another piece of paper.

"The son."

"He must," Billingham agreed.

The waiter placed two mugs on the table. Billingham picked his up, took a deep drink, and smacked his lips. He peered at the paper.

"The man himself."

"Very likely. And he is a cool one from all I hear," Heller said, lifting his own mug. He held it in front of his lips, and then put it down. "What we need is a witness or a piece of physical evidence to place our man at the scene."

"You're not thinking of that crazy Irishman?"

Heller nodded.

"If he's all we have. But Mr. Kelly suggested there might be footprints."

"It rained the other day. That violent storm on the north end." Billingham paused. "Ah, but I don't think it did there." He drained his beer. "There's another angle, one I'm sure Mr. Lowe will hear about and pursue. Henry Cutter mumbled something to me about his hired hand who disappeared right after the murder, a black man."

"Lowe will find that very convenient."

"Especially if he stays missing."

"Try to find him," Heller said.

"I've sent telegrams to sheriffs in the neighboring counties."

"Excellent. He shouldn't be too hard to find. About the footprint..." Heller looked up at the sky where gray clouds could be seen on the horizon. "I wouldn't wait long."

"I need to talk to my deputy. I'll have him check it out."

Heller held his pencil poised over the first piece of paper.

"I'll put his name down and Richard's, as two testifying to the same fact would be better. If they do find something, that is."

"No doubt they will. What you find usually depends on what you're looking for. Thanks for the beer," Billingham said.

Isaiah's fingers were stained red from the thousands of cherries he had picked over the last few days. He got up with the sun each morning, had a cup of coffee and a piece of stale bread, and then trudged off into the orchard. He worked with only a brief respite at lunch time when he ate another crust or two of bread and a handful of the fruit from the basket hanging from his neck, washed down with water from a leather canteen. He loaded the lugs onto his wagon and hauled them to wherever Harold's crew was working. Returning to his empty house as the sun was beginning to set, he crawled into bed, often without the energy to fix anything to eat from the meager store of foodstuffs in the house.

Sinking into his physical exhaustion was something of a relief. But no matter how tired he was, how numb his mind, a little voice kept urging him to pick up the family Bible and open it to that place in the section that bore his name, where he had secreted her note. It called to him in her plaintive voice. And so at night, exhausted from moving ladders and lugs and repairing the wagon, he would approach the huge, leather bound volume, run his fingers over its spine, open the first few pages and glance at that old story of Adam, Eve and the serpent, vowing to himself that he would start to read, and not stop until he came to the Book of Isaiah, where he would again encounter her words, "Meet me at the usual place." But that's as far as he could venture. If he continued he would have to know what he was going to do. It was pointless to just read her note unless he had determined whether to publish it or to eliminate any trace of it.

When in spite of his weariness he could not sleep, and found himself pacing back and forth in front of the table on which the Bible sat, he would yank himself out the front door and walk north on the town road until it narrowed by the water, where he would clamber down into the sand, and sit, scarcely breathing while he listened to the wavelets lap against the shore. More than once he fell asleep on that beach only to be awkened by the sun and the morning cries of the gulls seeking their breakfast.

"What do you want my boots for?" Sam asked. He felt his palms begin to dampen.

"Sheriff asked me to trace them on a piece of paper," Allan replied.

"What on earth for?" Sam knew only too well why.

"I don't know, just procedure I guess."

"What kind of procedure would that be?"

"I'm only doing what I've been told."

Sam looked out the window and saw black, rain clouds. But still there was no guarantee.

"I'm thinking I should check with my lawyer about this procedure."

Allan had followed Sam's glance out the window.

"Sheriff told me not to wait. Something about rain coming. Said if you refused he'd get the court to order it, and make sure it was part of the record at your trial."

Sam sat down and pulled off his boot. He tossed it to Allan.

"Here, then, take it. I was just asking. There's nothing special about it or my feet."

In Cadillac, along the railroad tracks, Jim trudged toward the hut he was given to live in as the watchman at the lumber yard. The town was dominated by the sawmill that received the timbers from further north, arriving daily on the railroad's flatcars.

He knew he was conspicuous in this town. He slept with his ears open during the day. If a dog barked, or a cat yowled, or raised voices floated toward him from a distance, he would tense. He was ready at a moment's notice to wrap his few belongings into the blanket that served as his pallet and take off into the woods that ran across the tracks, and there wait for another train.

The owner of the yard, perhaps sensing his desperation and suspecting that he was fleeing from some trouble, hired him on the condition that he would not be paid until the first of the next month, three weeks away. Until then, Jim husbanded the few coins in his pocket, and scavenged for what food he could find, sometimes trapping a rabbit in the field beyond the yard, or gathering berries.

On this evening, he saw the tall, angular shape of a white man, and turned to seek the shadows a few feet to his right.

"Hey, there. You, boy. Where you goin'? I need to talk to you."

Jim looked at the man, as if in surprise.

"Yes, you. Come on over here."

Jim bowed his head and walked over with his subservient shuffle, then stopped, head lowered in front of the man.

"I'm Sheriff Malcolm Matthews."

Jim nodded.

"Do you know where you are?"

Jim shook his head.

"Are you mute?"

"No sir."

"Good. Well, you are in Wexford County of which I am sheriff. Now, I've got a telegram here from Sheriff Billingham up in Grand Traverse County."

Jim did not respond.

"He's looking for a nigger that used to work on a farm up there. That wouldn't be you would it?"

"No sir. I never do no farm work up there."

"Then where you from?"

"Way north of there, up near Canada. I cooked in the lumber camps."

"Then what are you doing down here?"

"I'm trying to get on home, back where I belong."

The sheriff took a step closer and peered at Jim.

"I don't know if you're him or not. Billingham didn't give much of a description, but he did give me a name. What's yours?"

"Moses, Moses Jones. You can ask the boss man here."

"Well, Moses, if that's who you are, don't you be traveling anyplace until I get a better description from Billingham."

"Goin' home, boss."

"Not yet, you're not, not until I tell you that you can. You want me to lock you up to make sure you stay put?"

"No sir. You don't need that. I ain't the man you're looking for. You'll know that soon enough."

Matthews started to walk away and then turned back. "Oh, but just to be sure you're not thinking about leaving us, look over there." He pointed to the entrance to the yard where two railroad guards stood, clubs in hand.

Allan Morgan braked the sheriff's buggy on the side of the road, and he and Richard Kelly got down. Allen pointed to the path that led toward East Bay.

"I think the swamp is over that way." He looked up at the overcast sky. "We'd better hurry."

Walking east along the two-track toward the bay, which they could see through a break in the trees several hundred yards away, they approached the edge of the swamp where the maples, birch, and pine gave way to a stand of hemlocks.

"There," Richard said, "see the hemlocks."

They took a few more steps, but then Allan threw out his arm to stop his companion.

"Slow down. We are close."

They were in the grassy area before the rise. After a few more paces, they left the meadow grass and the ground beneath their feet was now damp. Beyond the moist dirt was the rise, and beyond that the hemlocks.

"There's that huge old tree. She was found beneath it," Richard said.

Their eyes scanned the ground until Allan pointed, "There," he said. "See those impressions."

"And there," Richard said, pointing off to the right some ten or fifteen feet away.

They stopped.

"How can we tell which are his?" Richard asked. "There are footprints all around here. All those people in the search party."

"We just have to find a match," Allan said. He held out a piece of paper on which was drawn the outline of a boot. Richard took the paper. He balanced himself with one hand on Allan's shoulder and lifted his own foot to hold it against the outline on the paper. His shoe was clearly smaller.

"See," Allan said, "he has big feet."

Richard handed the paper back and then looked down.

"So do you."

"Fine, fine. Let's find a match. Here, I've got a copy for you."

The sky continued to darken as they walked about crouched over, each holding a copy of the boot outline over the various prints, being careful as they did so to walk on their toes so as not to add their own prints. Every once in a while one or the other would lose balance and come down flat-footed into the soft earth. It was a strange balancing act, which to an outsider looking on might have provided some humor. Allan stood a few feet from the tree beneath which Margaret's body had been found. He knelt with his paper.

"A match," he cried out, "just where the body was."

"But I have one over here," Richard called, pointing to a place well short of where Allan now stood. "The prints you found over there couldn't have been made by the same person who made the ones I found over here, unless he flew, because these don't continue in that direction."

"Mine match closer," Allan said. "They'll do."

"Would you swear to a match?" Richard asked.

"Of course. The man is guilty, ain't he?"

A few drops of rain splashed onto the ground. Allan folded his paper and put it back into his pocket, just as the black clouds released a torrent. The ground soon turned into mud through which broadening rivulets flowed, erasing the footprints.

"Well, then," Allan said. "I guess it'll be our word won't it?"

"I don't know if..." Richard began.

"Of course, you can. Just say what we saw. I'll do the rest. You might not even be called. And both our bosses will be pleased as can be."

In the telegraph office, Benson held a thick wad of bills out before the operator.

"Just a little information," he said.

"I couldn't," the operator said.

Benson peeled off a ten dollar bill, then another, and then still another, and put them on the counter.

"You see how thick this wad is. I can't give you it all, but I can keep going."

A middle aged, balding and timid man, the operator's eyes opened wider. But a sick wife and teenaged children made him open his hand, then grow bold.

"A little more, then, if you can."

Benson counted out two more tens.

"An even fifty. For what you can give me now. More later if you have something we need."

The clerk jotted down a few words on a piece of paper and then handed it to Benson. "I received this one from the sheriff in Wexford this morning."

The detective glanced at the paper and handed him the bills. He paused at the door. "I do hope your wife is feeling better," he said.

14

———

S am, pressing his thumb against his cheek at the spot where his tooth had been extracted, felt his gum throb. The pressure of his own thumb reminded him of her soothing fingers, but the pain remained.

Nathan Lowe sat across from him in his cell.

"Let's go over it again," Lowe said. "How you look is critical. You are a man anxious to set the record straight, yet respectful of the proceedings. Jurors listen to witnesses, and examine such evidence as is presented to them, they try to follow the arguments of the lawyers on both sides, but they also have a very natural human tendency to look at the fellow who is accused to see if they believe he could have done the crime. If they do, more often they'll convict, even if the prosecution's case is not all that strong. Now do you have it?"

"I must act like I am anxious to set the record straight," Sam repeated like a child reciting lessons learned by rote.

"No, damn it!" Lowe exploded. "You do *not* act. You *are*. Do you get it? You *are* anxious to set the record straight. If you act, they will see right through you. Now what are you? Do you not remember?"

"A respectable farmer."

"Do you smile?"

"No, I am serious, but not depressed."

"Because?"

"Because I don't want to appear like I am waiting for the inevitable conviction."

"Right, getting better. Do not look too somber, for that would suggest you are remorseful or just gloomy contemplating your conviction; don't smile too much, for then you will appear to have no moral sense. The prosecutor is going to paint a very ugly picture of you. You must look pained when these details are mentioned. He will no doubt dwell on the victim, and again you must show that you too regret her sudden death, even though you had nothing at all to do with it."

Yes, Sam thought, I do regret her death, with every breath I take.

Dressed in a new suit provided by Lowe, his hair cut, beard closely shaved, and fingernails trimmed, Sam stared up at Judge Horace B. Hightower of the Circuit Court. Hightower was tall and stern faced, with thin lips and gray hair slicked against his scalp. Lowe had told Sam that they could have worse luck, that Hightower was tough but fair, and he would control his courtroom. Sam looked past the judge to the windows on either side of the bench where pressed against the panes were the faces of people too late to get a seat in the courtroom. They looked back at him with the hostility usually directed at one already convicted. Although he had the muscular Benson on one side of him, and the elegant Lowe on the other, he felt naked and alone in his seat. Given the chance, the spectators, both those at the window and those sitting behind him, would not hesitate to subject his body to unspeakable indignities, before leaving his maimed corpse to rot unmourned, food for birds.

Prosecutor Heller rose to his feet. Sam shifted his gaze to the judge whose eyes were fastened on the district attorney. Sam dreaded this moment. Lowe had told him how difficult it would be to hear himself characterized in such a way, as Lowe had put it, that his own mother would not recognize him. Although Lowe told him not to, he now looked at the twelve jurors. He sat through the jury selection, not quite understanding the strategies motivating both attorneys for accepting or rejecting potential jurors. All he had been looking for during the process was a friendly face; finding none then, he saw none now.

Sitting in the back row of benches in the jury box was Wilson. He studied the grizzled face of his neighbor, wondering how the old farmer's memory of the times Sam borrowed his plow might influence his judgment. In front of him was Carl Matthews, with whose son Sam played baseball. Matthews' farm was further north, closer to his father's place. He knew Wilson and Matthews best of all the jurors, and he was sure that they, like everyone else, had heard all the gossip that had circulated during his troubled marital careers. No wonder they sat with stony expressions.

The other jurors were less well known to him, a blend of farmers, and businessmen from both town and the tip of the Peninsula, a store clerk from a dry goods store on Front Street, a dock hand from the harbor near the Old Mission Inn, a merchant who owned a shoe store on Union Street, and who would be the foreman, all of them sturdy, respectable citizens, and probably not a one with whom he would have wanted to sit down to share a beer. Lowe had said the idea of a jury of his peers was what he called a legal fiction. His own view was that it was a downright lie. For between him, sitting at this table next to his attorney, and the jurors in their seats on the slightly raised platform of the jury box, he saw an insuperable divide, wide as an ocean. As he held them in his glance, they faded into tiny little specks as though they were on a distant island, and not twenty feet away across a planked floor.

Pulling his eyes away from the jury, he knew that sitting not ten feet behind him, were Henry and Sarah Cutter. The heat of their rage scalded his back, and he wanted very much to turn around, though not to look at them, for there was nothing he could say to them now, but past them toward the back row.

"Take another look for me, will you?"

Lowe, dressed as always in his white linen suit and red four-in-hand, shrugged.

"I'm sure nothing has changed."

"Well, look, anyway. What do you see?"

Lowe swiveled his head in a quick motion.

"Isaiah is there, as he has been, sitting with his grandparents."

Relaxing a little, Sam turned his attention to the prosecutor. Heller paced back and forth before the jury box. He had started calmly enough, detailing what was not in question, that Sam's farm bordered the victim's that they clearly knew each other, and here Sam felt the prosecutor's noose start to tighten.

202

"But the most shocking fact, one which the defense will not, cannot deny, is one we hesitate to mention, yet it is our duty to do so." Heller leaned on the railing in front of the jury box. He towered over those sitting in the front row, and they looked up at him with rapt attention. Those in the back row were at eye level and leaned forward to hear what he would say next.

"You will hear from the doctor who performed the autopsy on this most unfortunate woman, not only that the cause of her sudden death was strangulation, but at the moment she died she was carrying in her womb the defendant's child." He whirled around to point at Sam. "That man is on trial for not one murder... but two. That man snuffed out two lives.

"And it is our responsibility to supply a motive for this heinous act. The defendant, faced with his lover's pregnancy, wanted nothing more or less but to remove the burden of his relationship with her, a burden cemented by the child she was carrying. This he could not tolerate. She, though, in her innocent and blind love could not understand why he would want to abandon her, and so she clung to him all the more forcefully. He decided he must free himself. Opportunity presented itself. They met at their trysting place. He plied her with laudanum to weaken her resistance. And then," he lifted his outstretched hands and brought them almost together, "he squeezed her neck until she could no longer breathe."

Dropping his hands, he waited while the spectators released their tension in an excited buzz. Hightower brought his gavel down once. The buzzing stopped. Heller looked at the defense table and brought his shoulders back in an exaggerated shrug.

"The defense, no doubt, will try to discount our evidence. They will say it is circumstantial and speculative, but as the judge will instruct, the law accepts the confluence of circumstantial evidence that points to guilt, as it is the rare murderer who has the good grace to perform his nefarious deed in front of an audience of potential witnesses." He looked at the jurors. Several of them nodded, while others permitted a small grin to crinkle their faces. Heller raised himself to his full height as though he were stretching to reach something on a high shelf.

"However, the state will not depend solely on circumstantial evidence. For we have the physical evidence that places the defendant at the scene of the crime."

Without turning his head toward Sam, Lowe jotted a note and slid it in front of him. Sam glanced at it, and wrote one word. "Rain." Lowe nodded. Then he folded the paper, and handed it to Benson.

Heller sat down, and Judge Hightower looked at Lowe.

"Do you wish to make a statement at this point, Mr. Lowe?"

Lowe put the flats of his hands on the table and lifted himself ever so slowly as if with an immense effort to rise against the wearisome nature of the prosecution's case. As he lifted his hands off the table, he turned them in front of him palms up. "Your honor, it is not necessary, as I did not hear anything in the prosecution's statement that justifies my client's presence here in court." He paused and then with great deliberation shuffled together the papers in front of him on the table. "I move for the charges to be dismissed for a palpable lack of evidence, for which the prosecution has been able to substitute only rumor and speculation." He sat back down with a movement that was the equivalent of an audible sigh.

"Motion dismissed," the judge said without hesitation. "Mr. Heller are you ready to proceed?"

"I am, your honor," the prosecutor said. "The state calls Dr. Rufus Rheingold."

Lowe looked down at the top paper in front of him, and put a check mark next to the first name. He looked over at Benson, who was thumbing through a thin sheaf of papers. He found the one he was looking for, and put it in front of Lowe. Sam peered at it. It was the summary of the autopsy report, signed at the bottom by Dr. Rheingold.

The doctor turned out to be a slight man of about forty or forty-five, with narrow, sloping shoulders, a thin, angular face and protruding front teeth that gave him the look of a rodent. He offered answers to the prosecutor's questions without hesitation, punctuating his responses with a sharp little nod of his head, as though he were agreeing with himself. Heller led him through the initial questions that established his credentials as county coroner, to which position he had been elected after five years in practice. Heller paused to glance down at his notes. Lowe nudged Sam because they both knew what was coming, and how Sam had been coached to react to the doctor's testimony.

"Did you perform an autopsy on Margaret Cutter?"

"I did."

"Did you establish a cause of death?"

"I did."

"Can you tell us what it was?"

"Strangulation. Her neck was bruised. I found no other probable cause."

Heller paced toward the jury box, pausing as though to consider what to ask next, and then turned his bulk around toward the witness chair. The movement of his large body seemed to cause a breeze to stir.

"Can you tell us what else your autopsy revealed?"

Sam thought he heard an intake of breath from the Cutters, and steeled himself.

"She was, uh, in the family way," Dr. Rheingold said. This time his head nod was even more pronounced. Sam stiffened in his chair, disturbed by this fact, which he had struggled to repress. He heard murmurs, the inarticulate outrage of all those sitting behind him, sounds that were not words and yet communicated pain and anger beyond the reach of language. He stole a glance out of the corner of his eye at the jurors, whose expressions, it seemed to him, had hardened. Perhaps the worst was over. But he was mistaken. Heller walked back to his table and reached beneath it to pick up something wrapped in paper.

"You are quite sure, Dr. Rheingold?" he asked.

"Yes," Rheingold responded, his eyes on the item in Heller's hands. The prosecutor peeled the paper from the top of the object, revealing it to be a bottle with a stopper in it. Lowe was on his feet, his mouth beginning to form his objection but he offered none. Heller pulled the paper down a little further. His body shielded the jury.

"Do you recognize this bottle?" he asked.

"Yes."

"And its contents?" Heller drew the paper all the way off.

"Yes."

"Can you tell the jurors what is in this bottle?"

"A fetus, an inch and three quarters long, probably eight or nine weeks. You can see the limb buds have begun to form," Rheingold said, but without his usual head bob. Sam averted his eyes. But then he opened them and leaned to one side, against Benson's shoulder, until he could see the bottle with its lump of flesh afloat, like a cork in the solution. He struggled to control the nausea that rose from his stomach. The spectators emitted a concatenation of sounds, high pitched screeches, middle toned mutterings, all against a counterpoint of bass groans. Hightower pounded his gavel. Sam raised his hands to his ears. Lowe pulled them down, and muttered just loud enough for Sam to hear, "He has been rehearsed well." Lowe rose to his feet, took off his spectacles, and wiped them with careful motions of his handkerchief. His nose revealed an angry red indentation where the spectacles rested, the only flaw in his impeccable appearance. "Your honor," he said, "I object to these obscene theatrics. Miss Cutter's pregnancy is not in dispute. What is the point, then, of the prosecutor's display but to inflame the minds of the jury against my client?"

"It goes to motive, your honor," Heller replied. "It is the people's theory that the defendant murdered the victim because he could not, or would not, deal with the consequences of his illicit relationship with her."

"We will not object to this object being introduced into evidence, if learned counsel for the people will adduce evidence to link it to my client," Lowe said.

"Why that is preposterous," Heller said, his face red, but he knew he had been had.

"Is it?" Lowe replied. "We know whose belly it came out of, but we do not know who put it there, do we?"

The courtroom erupted again, spectators shaking their heads. "Disgraceful," some said, "Who would suggest such a thing," others said, "She was a good girl." Hightower waited for the outburst to subside and then brought his gavel down just once, but hard enough to send a loud crack resounding through the crowded room.

"I will not permit this exhibit into evidence. We will recess for an hour for everyone to cool down," Hightower said. "The jury will try to erase this spectacle from their minds, and accept instead the simple proposition that the victim was with child, a fact both prosecution and defense agree to."

Sitting in the same row, but off to the side, Daniel observed Isaiah and his grandparents during the doctor's testimony. Charles's expression did not change. Livonia flinched when the contents of the bottle were described. Isaiah blanched. The three continued to sit. Spectators got to their feet to stretch while others shared their impressions. Daniel saw the woman sitting next to Isaiah rise and make her way out of the courtroom. He moved to her spot.

"Would you like to get some air?" he asked Isaiah.

Isaiah turned toward him, but his eyes did not focus.

"You do remember me?"

Isaiah nodded.

"Do you know this young man?" Charles asked.

"Yes."

"My grandson and I thank you for your interest, but he and we are fine," Charles said.

"Are you?" Daniel asked Isaiah. Charles turned a hard, cold stare at him.

"Yes, I am," Isaiah replied.

"I'll be sitting right over there," Daniel said, pointing to his seat.

Lowe's body language said that he was not to be hurried, and that he was not particularly impressed with the testimony he had just heard. He walked to the witness box and held out a document.

"Is this your autopsy report Dr. Rheingold?"

"Yes."

"Dr. Rheingold, how many autopsies have you performed?"

"Let's see, this one, two others, and of course one I witnessed in medical school."

"And of those which involved a suspected homicide?"

The doctor's lips twitched before answering.

"Just this one." He did not bob his head.

"I see. But you are sure of your results?"

"I am."

"Was there any evidence of damage to the hyoid bone?"

Rheingold slumped forward, and then straightened his shoulders.

"I did not detect any."

"Doctor, you do know where the hyoid bone is?"

"Certainly." He pointed to the juncture of his own throat and the back of his jaw. "It supports the root of the tongue."

"But it wasn't damaged?"

"I do not believe so."

"Oh, you do not believe so. Did you look?"

"Yes."

Lowe looked down at the autopsy report.

"It says here that you were going to follow up on the possibility that Miss Cutter had drunk laudanum."

"We sent a sample from her stomach to the laboratory downstate. The results were uncertain."

"Uncertain?"

"Some was found, but the amount was in question."

"You are aware, are you not, that an empty bottle of laudanum was found next to her?"

"I am. But we don't know how the bottle came to be empty."

"I see." Heller walked to the defense table and picked up a newspaper clipping. He strode back to the bench and showed it to the judge.

"I'd like to offer this into evidence," he said.

"I see no problem," Hightower said.

"Good." Lowe held the clipping in front of the witness.

"Do you recognize this?"

"I can't say I do."

"Pity," Lowe replied. "But you can read it, can you not?"

"Of course."

"It's a story about Harriet Fuller. Do you remember the name?"

Rheingold nodded.

"Now that you mention the name, I do remember."

"Well, of course you do, as you are mentioned in this newspaper story as the attending physician when the young woman almost died."

"That is a little exaggerated."

Lowe looked down at the paper.

"But that is what you said."

Rheingold shrugged.

"Perhaps I did."

"I see. And if she almost died, what would have been the cause?"

"Laudanum."

"Oh, so laudanum can kill you, if you drink enough of it?"

"Yes. But I do not believe that was the case in this instance."

Lowe strolled back to the defense table. He asked his question from where he was standing.

"Is it true that when you won election to be coroner, your practice was failing, and you were heavily in debt?"

Rheingold reddened.

"Objection," Heller cried out, "Irrelevant."

"It goes to competence," Lowe said.

"Sustained," Hightower ruled.

"Withdrawn," Lowe replied, "and I am through with this witness."

Sam was deeply troubled by the doctor's testimony, even though it did not reveal anything he did not know. As hard as it was for him to consider himself Margaret's murderer, it was even more difficult to deal with the unborn child who died with her. He had never taken his paternal responsibilities very seriously as they attached to Isaiah, but he somehow now deeply regretted the innocent life so needlessly snuffed out.

He spent the night in his cell standing at the window, staring at the immensity between the stars and wishing that somehow he could find refuge there between those most distant. He did not look down where outside on the jailhouse lawn the torches flickered in the steady breeze.

Sarah Cutter sat bolt upright in the witness chair the next morning.

"He was talking to my Margaret one evening on the hill across from our house. That would be in to the southwest of where I was standing. When she came in later, her face was all aglow, and I asked her what she was so happy about, and she said it was nothing more than the pleasure of being outside beneath the moon and stars on such a pleasant night."

"Do you think that was all there was to it?" Heller asked.

"I do not."

"Why?"

"She changed after she came to know him."

"In what way?"

"Careless with her chores. Why on the day she was murdered, she left her room untidy. She never would do that."

"Did you know she was pregnant?"

"Yes."

"Who do you suppose was the father?"

Hightower looked at Lowe, expecting an objection, which he thought he might sustain, as calling for an uninformed and biased opinion rather than a statement of factual knowledge. But Lowe sat with an expression of boredom on his face.

"That one," Sarah said, pointing at Sam. "Since she met him, she spent an awful lot of time in the barn, more than she needed to milk those cows."

"Is that all?"

"No. There was talk between Logan and my husband."

"Talk. What about?"

"Why, to provide a father for that bastard child."

Sam struggled to maintain his expression of equanimity. Lowe held up his hand, and whispered to him.

"I must be careful how I handle her. She has the jury's sympathy, of course."

Lowe uncoiled himself from his seat. He fixed a kind smile on his face and approached the witness chair.

"I know how difficult this is for you..." he began.

"No, it's not at all. Just as long as I see your client go to jail on his way to hell."

Lowe looked up at the judge.

"The witness will confine herself to answering counsel's questions," Hightower said.

"Yes, I am sure we understand how you feel," Lowe tried.

"You couldn't," she replied, "not in a million years."

"Let us try to begin," Lowe said in his gentlest tones. "Is it true you have two hired men working on your farm?" Lowe asked.

"We did. One has disappeared, and the other has gone crazy, going around changing his name."

"Tell us about the one who has disappeared."

"Not much to tell. Everyone knows who I'm talking about. Had been a slave, and we gave him a chance for a decent life."

"When did he disappear?"

"The night of the murder."

"I see. And where did he sleep?"

"In the barn. But that don't mean anything."

"Perhaps not. Perhaps yes. Tell us about the other."

"A crazy Irishman. He is still with us, but he don't work much anymore. My husband has told him he won't get paid if he don't start doing something useful."

"I see. And where does he sleep?"

"In the attic of our house."

"Above your daughter's room?

"Yes. But that don't mean anything either."

"Have you seen either of these two single, unhappy men paying attention to your daughter?"

"No."

"Are you sure?"

"Yes."

"I wish we could be as sure," Lowe said, and strolled back to his seat.

Henry leaned forward. His lip quivered. Lowe softened his voice.

"What did the defendant suggest as a way of dealing with your daughter's pregnancy?"

Henry turned his ferocious expression toward Sam, and then shifted it, without losing its intensity, to Isaiah, sitting at the back of the courtroom between his grandparents.

"Why, that he would convince his son to marry her."

Again, shock waves rose from a whisper to a loud murmur among the spectators. Hightower lifted his gavel, and the sound stopped. Lowe glanced at the judge, and then turned to Henry.

"Did she have any interest in Isaiah?"

"None, that I could see. I wished that she did. But she had eyes only for him."

"What was your response to the defendant's suggestion that your daughter marry his son?" Lowe asked.

"I saw that her life would be ruined. More if she married him than if she bore his bastard."

"Yes, no doubt. But did you not agree?"

"I said I'd talk to her. As a way out."

"But did you not agree?"

"I said I would talk to her."

"Tell us about your husband's relationship to the victim," Heller asked.

Eustace held a lace handkerchief to her nose as though it were being assaulted by a noisome odor.

"I would see him coming back from taking the laundry there. He would have a smile on his face, more than you would expect at such a time."

"Such a time?"

"He was doing a chore he detested, which he wanted me to do, not understanding my condition, how I couldn't bend over a wash tub. He said he was doing my woman's job. You would think he would come back carrying a laundry basket with a frown on his face, at the least, for that is how he left."

"But he didn't come back that way?"

"No, he did not. And I know it wasn't because of getting his clothes clean, or talking to Mrs. Cutter. It was the daughter he was after. And now we see where that has led."

"Objection," Lowe said, his voice heavy with irritation.

"Just answer the question," Hightower said.

"Now I know this is a painful memory," Heller said, "but tell us about the problems in your marriage that led to your asking for, and being granted, a divorce."

"Mr. Logan is a violent man of unsettled passions. He struck me more than once. It's all in the court records. I do not want to talk about it."

"I know," Heller soothed, "but we are trying to establish Mr. Logan's characters so that these good men in the jury box can understand how he is capable of doing the crime for which he stands accused."

"He is capable. I have felt his hands around my own neck."

"Tell me, Mrs. Logan," Lowe began.

"I don't use that name any more," Eustace replied.

"Do you have another?"

"Not yet. But I've filed papers to return to the one I was born with."

"But for now, it seems I have no other legal choice. You understand? The record must indicate whom I am talking to and you are, at least for now, Mrs. Logan."

"Sadly."

Lowe looked down at the papers in his hands, and then he handed one to her.

"Do you recognize this paper, which I intend to offer into evidence?"

Eustace glanced at the document and frowned.

"Of course. It is the lies Mr. Logan had his son offer."

"What you are saying is that this is a deposition from Isaiah Logan, the defendant's son, testifying to the time you held a knife to his throat, and was saved from possibly dire consequences by his father's prompt intervention. Is that not so?"

"Lies," Eustace said.

"Your honor?" Lowe turned to the judge.

"Please answer the question, as to whether you can identify this document. You do not have to verify its accuracy," Hightower instructed.

"It is what he says it is."

"That will do your honor," Lowe said. "One more question. Would you say your divorce was a particularly angry one?"

Eustace took a breath and straightened her thin shoulders.

"The day I left that man was the happiest day of my life."

"What is your name?" Heller asked.

"People know me as Edward Franklin. But I took that name to hide my true origin, of which I am deeply ashamed. I figured Franklin was a good name for an American. But I am Michael O'Leary, if truth be told." Edward had cleaned himself up for his court appearance, shaving with a dull razor that left his chin nicked.

"Well, Mr. O'Leary, as you are under oath, let truth be your guide."

"Except for me name change, done for necessity, it always has been the truth that Michael O'Leary tells."

Heller paused. He wondered if it had been a mistake to call this witness. Yet he could be valuable. He'd best keep his questions simple and to the point.

"Who did you see that day when you were digging fence post holes?" he asked.

Edward pointed at Sam.

"You are pointing at the defendant Sam Logan, are you not?"

"I am."

"Where did you see him the day Margaret Cutter disappeared?"

"I saw her too that morning."

Heller took a breath. They had not gone over this. But he couldn't let that statement just hang in the air.

"Tell us about that, about both."

"In the morning, when she was milking." He looked at the jury. He seemed to be enjoying his moment. "Then later. She walked past where I was digging. She didn't see me, but I noted her. The fence I was digging was to be on the line between his farm and ours. Then she went into the woods."

"You didn't see where she went after that?"

"I'd have had to follow her, now wouldn't I?"

"Yes."

"I didn't. I attended to my work."

"Tell us," Heller said, "about who else you saw."

"About noon, when I was waiting for the other hand to come..." Heller began to interrupt, but realized it was too late. He could hope that Lowe would miss the reference, but at the same time he knew how foolish that hope was. Edward had stopped in mid-sentence as he saw Heller's mouth begin to open, but now he continued. "While I was waiting there, I saw Mr. Logan at the edge of the woods on his side of the property line. I called to him, but he didn't answer."

"And did you see where he went next?"

"I know where he went, but if I am to tell the truth I can only do it in my own way, sir."

"Proceed," Heller prodded.

"I can only say I lost sight of him in the woods." Edward paused again, for effect. "But before he went into those woods I marked his direction. He was walking east."

"Did you visit Mr. Charles Logan?" Lowe asked.

"Who?"

Lowe pointed to the rear seat where Charles sat next to Isaiah.

"That gentleman back there."

"I don't think I can remember."

"Let me help you. Two weeks ago, on a Tuesday evening, you walked to that gentleman's house seeking an audience with him. Do you remember doing that?"

Edward scratched at the cut on his chin.

"Now you remind me, yes I do."

"Good. And is it not true you talked about your desire to go to California, saying you could if you had the money?"

"Yes. I thought he might be willing to advance it to me. I would have paid him back."

"Most certainly you would. But wasn't it understood that you were offering to either tailor your testimony to help his son, or leave before you could be called by the prosecution?"

"I wouldn't put it just that way."

"How would you put it?"

"I did mention California and his son's trial. But I don't recall putting the two together, as you just said."

"So you walk all that distance to talk to a man you've never met before to discuss your travel plans and his son's trial in the same conversation, while asking for money, and these ideas are not related?"

"They happened that night, that's all I can say."

"And that is the truth, Mr. O'Leary?"

"As my name is Michael O'Leary, it is."

Lowe paced back to his table. Benson handed him a document, which he glanced at it and nodded.

"Tell me Mr. O'Leary. Isn't it the case that eight years back, when you were working on a farm in Antrim County that you were charged with improper attention to the daughter of your boss?"

"Why she invited me, lifting up her gown to show me her leg."

"I see. And Margaret, did she ever do the same?"

"Not for me. That's for certain. I don't know what she did for others."

Heller approached the witness box, where Allan sat leaning forward, his eyes focused on the prosecutor's face.

"Tell us about how you went about ascertaining whether the footprints at the scene matched the defendant's."

Allan smiled.

"The sheriff asked me to find a way to get an outline of his boots. So I just went to his cell and asked him to take off his boots. Then I traced them on a piece of paper."

"Did Mr. Logan cooperate with your tracing his boot?"

"He did. After a little while."

"Did you take your drawing to the spot where the body was found?"

"Yes sir. Me and Richard Kelly from your office went out there a couple of days ago."

"And what did you find?"

Allan looked at the jury, then turned his head back to face Heller.

"Why, we found a print in the ground there that was just about the exact same as the one I had drawn from his boot."

"And where, exactly, was that print?"

"No more than three or four feet from where the body was."

Lowe waited while Hightower's gavel cracked against the spectators' noisy explosions of breath.

"Is this the paper on which you drew the print?" he asked when quiet was restored.

"It is," Allan replied.

"I see that your pencil lines are smudged as though the paper had gotten wet."

"It rained right after we found the print."

"I see. How very convenient. So, we cannot now go out there and verify your judgment."

Allan shrugged and offered a toothy grin, revealing the space between his front teeth.

"No, sir, it wouldn't do you much good. It rained and turned that ground into mud."

"Did your associate, Mr. Kelly, agree with your judgment?"

"He did."

"Will he so testify?"

"I guess you'd have to ask him that, but I don't see why he wouldn't since we both saw the same thing."

"Why not indeed," Lowe said. "But tell me, did you find other footprints in the vicinity of the ones you identified as belonging to the defendant?"

Allan shrugged.

"Some."

"Isn't it true," Lowe asked, "that a search party of some thirty or so went up and down that whole area before the body was found?"

"I wasn't there for the search."

"But you will grant that there was such a search party?"

"Yes."

"And that they did not arrive there by dropping out of the sky?"

"Yes."

"Do you know why Mr. Heller has not called Mr. Kelly to support your testimony?"

"No."

"Could it be that he is not as sure as you are?"

"I don't know."

"Just one more thing. Exactly where would you say were the defendant's footprints?"

"Right near where the body was found."

"Are you sure?"

Allan smiled.

"Yes."

"No further questions."

Heller shook his head and rubbed his eyes. It was well past midnight, and they were sitting in their shirt sleeves in his office. The air was hot, moist, unmoving.

"What do we have?" Heller asked.

"He's a violent man, from the ex-wife's testimony," Richard replied.

"She came across as angry, therefore less than credible."

"We have our witness placing him at the scene," Richard suggested.

"Would you believe our Mr. O'Leary?" Heller demanded. "I wouldn't. And I'm afraid our deputy didn't present that footprint evidence all that well. And you..."

"I'd rather not testify."

"Can't do it?"

"I'd rather not."

"Even if he were to go free?"

"Sir..."

"Never mind. What about the son? I just can't figure him. Would he support his father's alibi?"

"He might not."

"Pretty place the boy finds himself in, especially if he knows the truth. He's a big gamble for us, but I don't think I want to risk him. Could lose the whole case."

"We'll know if Lowe calls him," Richard said.

"Yes, but by then it will be too late, won't it."

"Grandpa doesn't want me talking to you."

On the other side of the bars, Sam nodded.

"I know." Sam reached his hands through the bars and seized his son's shoulders. "You are my son," he said. "You'll do the right thing."

Isaiah began to pull away, but part of him responded to the pressure of his father's strong hands, and he felt his eyes moisten.

"Yes," he replied. "But there were times I was sure you had forgotten you had a son."

"I can't deny it. I let you grow up pretty much on your own."

"That's why Grandpa..."

"Don't," Sam said. He squeezed hard, and then dropped his hands. "Well, I guess, no matter what happens, you'll still have him."

"No matter what," Isaiah replied.

Lowe and Benson were the only ones still in the dining room at the Inn.

"Can't you get anything on him, something?" Lowe asked.

"He's a good boy, goes to church with his grandfather, works hard, and lived with his father since the divorce from his father's first wife." Benson stabbed a piece of boiled potato and motioned to the waitress, pointing to his empty plate. "I'm still hungry," he said, as she slid over, balancing a tray of dirty dishes on her shoulder. She picked up his plate.

"I'll see what I can do. The kitchen is closed."

"Do," Benson said.

"If I put him on the stand, I've got to know what that boy is going to say," Lowe said.

"He talks about leaving as soon as he can, getting a job on a ship." Benson lifted his eyes as the waitress approached. "But if he has to testify, he says, he'll tell the truth."

"Which is?"

"That's all I can get out of him." The waitress slid Benson's plate in front of him with one more potato. He shrugged and sliced it with is knife.

"Our turn tomorrow," Lowe said. "We'll start with Frederick Gorschen, the drummer."

15

Frederick offered his best salesman smile, the one that says you can trust me, I only have your best interest in mind.

"Just a few questions, Mr. Gorschen, and then I won't need to keep you," Lowe said. "Did you have an occasion to talk with Miss Cutter not long before she disappeared?"

"Yes."

"Can you explain the circumstances?"

"The first time was in the cemetery behind the Old Mission Methodist Church. I was walking about before the service and wandered around behind the building into the cemetery. I saw her as she kissed the headstone and got up."

"What was her demeanor?"

"She seemed upset."

"Objection," Heller said. "How would the witness know her state of mind?"

"Sustained," Hightower replied.

"Very good," Lowe said. "I'll ask. Mr. Gorschen, how would you know?"

Frederick smiled.

"I'm a salesman. It is my business. If I don't read my customer's right, I don't make the sale."

"That's fair enough," Hightower said.

"Go on," Lowe replied. "What else can you say about this first meeting?"

"I was curious about whose grave she had been kneeling at, about the headstone she had kissed, so I read the inscription. It was for a little boy who died at two. I guessed it must have been her brother."

"And the second occasion?" Lowe asked.

"I was riding on the road toward town. It was a hot day, and I saw this willow beside a small brook. I thought I'd get a drink of water, then I saw her sitting on the grass next to the tree. She looked up at me and started talking about how her brother had drowned in that very same brook."

Lowe looked up at the judge.

"Will you allow me a little room?" he asked.

"A little," Hightower assented.

"I'll phrase the question with care," Lowe said. He turned to Frederick. "Can you describe how she looked and acted? Do not attempt to characterize her state of mind."

"She talked to me in a strange way, like she was explaining something I hadn't asked."

"And what did you do?"

"I offered her one of my bottles of Frederick's Elixir."

"Which is?"

"Laudanum, which is what I sell, but I add a couple of my own ingredients."

"Why did you offer your elixir to her?"

Frederick looked up at the judge.

"Go ahead," Hightower said. "There's no reason you can't explain your own motives."

"She looked so very unhappy. And my elixir does ease the nerves."

The prosecutor rose as Lowe took his seat.

"You don't sell your product as a means of suicide, do you?" Heller demanded.

"Of course not."

"And you would have told her how much of your elixir to take?"

"A spoonful I said."

"Would a spoonful cause any harm?"

"Not at all."

"Was the bottle full when you gave it to her?" Lowe demanded.

"It was."

"What would be the effect of drinking a whole bottle?"

"I would never recommend such a thing."

"Of course not, but the effect?"

"I hesitate to say," Frederick replied.

"Try."

"A whole bottle?"

"Yes."

"I wouldn't recommend such a thing."

"A whole bottle, Mr. Gorschen."

"If someone was so careless, that someone might not wake up."

The boy was about fourteen, tall and lanky, wearing an engineer's cap.

"You like to fish, don't you?" Lowe asked.

"Yes sir. Me and Carl, and his sister Susan, as soon as school was out, we would fish in the river. On weekends we would sometimes go out to the Peninsula to see if they was playing baseball. But during the week, we'd fish. That is, we did until last week when Carl fell out of a tree and broke his arm."

"Do you recall seeing a young woman walking along the river bank one day about three weeks ago?"

"Sure do. Carl told me to look at her. I didn't want to because I felt something on my line. But he kept poking me, so I handed the pole to Susan and took a look."

"And what can you tell us about this woman?"

"I dunno. She was just staring at us, kinda past us, at the water like."

"Did she talk to you?"

"No."

"What happened then?"

"She started walking again, and I watched her for a while until she started talking to this fellow. Later I saw them walking back the other way."

Daniel waited for Lowe to lead him through his time with Margaret on that day. He would answer the questions accurately, objectively, as a good reporter, but offer no more than he had to. In the back of his mind was the clear realization that this trial was going to come down to the testimony of the lovelorn young man he had met in the search party, the one he had mistakenly thought she was going to marry. He was anxious to take his seat again in the spectator section, his pencil poised above his pad.

"Daniel, please tell us the circumstances of your meeting with Margaret Cutter that day by the river."

"I was sitting on the river bank across from the Hadley mansion on Sixth Street, when she came wandering along. She fainted. She hadn't eaten, so I took her to a restaurant on Union Street."

"Which one would that be?"

"The Winston. It serves decent food at a price I can afford."

"I see. And why did you decide to take her there? You had just met her."

"I was afraid for her. And she looked like she so needed somebody to take a little care of her."

"What made you think that she was so, shall we say, desperate?"

"She was carrying a bottle of laudanum."

"And what conclusion did you draw about that bottle?"

"Objection," Heller interjected.

"I'll rephrase," Lowe said, his hand on this four-in-hand,, smoothing its ends. "Did she say anything about the laudanum?"

"She said she knew some girls like to sip it. I asked her if she knew what happened if she took too much of it. She said she hoped so."

"She hoped so. What do you think she meant?"

"I thought she might want to drink too much, and do herself harm."

"Did you get any indication from her," Heller asked, "concerning the cause of her unhappiness?"

"She mentioned something about getting married," Daniel replied, "but I sensed that there was a problem."

"A problem. Did she say anything specific?"

"About a problem? No. It was more in the way she talked."

"What way was that?"

"The way a child talks about something she wants for Christmas."

"Meaning?"

"That she knew, on some level, that she wasn't going to get what she wanted."

"Did she mention who she intended to marry?"

"She said Mr. Logan."

The courtroom buzzed until the judge's gavel hammered the spectators into silence.

Lowe strolled toward the witness chair.

"Do you know whom she meant when she said Mr. Logan?"

"Not at the time. But when I met Isaiah Logan during the search for her, I believed she had meant him, and I told him so."

"Did Isaiah Logan at another time give any indication that he was romantically interested in her?"

"He did."

"When was that?"

Isaiah was on his feet. The spectators turned to look at him. Isaiah looked about him like a hunted fox cornered by snarling hounds. The judge's gavel again came down. Charles's hand seized Isaiah's wrist.

"Sit back down, boy, it's the best you can do. Don't give them any cause, any part of that show."

Isaiah nodded, but remained standing. His grandfather tugged on his arm, a gentle pull, but enough to cause Isaiah to sit back down and he looked at his knees.

"No," Charles said, "you must look back at them."

With great reluctance Isaiah lifted his eyes. The gavel was still pounding, feeling like it was crashing down on his head, and then it stopped. The spectators turned their attention back to the witness stand. Lowe stood with a bemused smile on his face. Daniel held his handkerchief in front of his mouth on which red spots were now visible.

"Let us try again," Lowe said. "What indication did you have from Isaiah that he had a romantic interest in the victim?"

"It was the way he reacted when I told him I thought she intended to marry him. She had said 'Mr. Logan'."

"How did he react?"

"He grabbed me, his eyes were blazing, wanting, it seemed to me, to believe what I said very much."

"Did he?"

"I do not know. He said he didn't."

"Isn't it true," Heller asked "that there are other explanations as to why Isaiah was so animated when you told him that Margaret Cutter intended to marry him?"

"I wouldn't know."

"You are a reporter, are you not?" Heller turned his head to the jury and nodded, as though to share a confidence with those twelve stolid citizens.

"I am."

"Your experience as a reporter no doubt acquaints you with the complexity of human behavior."

"It does. That is why I only report what I see, not what I can speculate."

"I see. And you saw no other explanation for Isaiah's reaction, nothing, for example, to do with his father?"

"Nothing."

"Are you aware that laudanum is taken for many reasons, although suicide would certainly be at the bottom of the list?"

"I studied chemistry at college, so yes, I do know the properties of this opium derivative."

"Was it not possible that Miss Cutter had some physical ailment for which she was contemplating taking the laudanum?"

"Possible, yes. But what I saw was an extremely distraught young woman."

"You feared for her?"

"I did."

Heller half smiled as he arrived where he intended to be.

"As you should have. As she was about to go to a fatal meeting with that man." And he swung around to extend his arm toward Sam.

"Don't they ever go home?" Sam asked.

Lowe joined him at the bars on his window and gazed down to the sea of bobbing torches.

"The question is what does their presence tell you?"

"I know," Sam replied. "I've always known how people regard me."

"Well, the friends and relatives of those folks down there are sitting in the jury box. That's what we have to contend with." Lowe took one big stride away from the window and sat down on the bed. "Mr. Heller is going to ask you some unpleasant questions tomorrow. I can't prevent that. But what I can do is ask them first. To give them a certain context. Then I'll call Isaiah."

Sam sat on his bed.

"Are you sure of him?"

"Are you? He's your son."

Sam shook his head.

"I wish I was."

"Well," Lowe said, "let's go over your part."

16

⸺•⸺

The courtroom was silent, all eyes on Sam as he took his seat in the witness chair. He scanned the spectators, looking for a face not set hard against him. He did not find one.

"How did you come to know Miss Cutter?" Lowe asked.

"She lived on the farm next to mine," Sam said. "At a certain time when my wife was unwell, I would take our laundry there to be done, and Miss Cutter would help her mother do the chore, for which I paid them, to take the strain off my wife."

Good, Lowe, thought, but let's not be too polished. We don't want the jury thinking you are rehearsing lines I have written for you.

"Did you come to know her in other situations?"

"Yes."

"Tell us."

"As a neighbor. I would see her sometimes, in town maybe, when she was selling her eggs."

"No other way?"

Sam hesitated. He knew what he was supposed to say, but it was like rubbing salt into the wound that was his guilt, not just for what happened that afternoon, but for the whole sorry affair.

"After a while, she made her interest in me very clear."

"Her interest in you?"

"Yes."

"Explain."

"She looked at me a certain way, a way I have come to understand in a woman's eyes."

"In short, she seduced you."

A sound, something between a howl and a groan came from Henry. Hightower brought his gavel down.

"Mr. Cutter. I understand your distress, but you must control yourself."

"While that man spews his lies?" Henry demanded.

Hightower looked toward the bailiff. "I don't want to have to remove you."

"You had better not try that," someone said, and there was a rising volume of assent. Again Hightower brought his gavel down, pounding it on the bench.

"I'll have the courtroom cleared," he said above the roar. He waited and the spectators quieted. "Proceed," he said to Lowe.

"Were you seduced?" Lowe repeated.

"Yes. I was."

Lowe took a breath.

"Now, I must ask you some questions of a private nature."

Sam nodded.

"Did you know she was pregnant?"

"I did."

"Did you believe you were responsible?"

"Yes."

The spectators murmured their satisfaction. Lowe turned to them. His expression said, what more do you want from this man? He's exposing his soul as it is.

"Did you talk about what to do?"

"She wanted me to marry her."

"But you had no intention of marrying her."

"No. I tried to tell her that my son was more suitable."

"Even though she was carrying your baby?"

"Yes. I know how that sounds. But it made sense to me. As everybody knows, I am not much use as a husband. And my son loved her."

"Did you love her?"

Sam paused. Then he shook his head very slowly.

"No. I can't say that I did."

It was as though all the spectators as one spat a communal hiss.

"You didn't love her, and yet you made love to her. Is that right?"

"Yes. I'm not proud of what I did."

"Did you have conversations with Henry Cutter concerning his daughter's pregnancy?"

"I did. I said that he should convince his daughter, and I would talk to my son. He saw it, I think, as a way to work things out."

"So you talked about your children marrying."

"Yes."

"And did Mr. Cutter have any specific requests?"

"He didn't want me to marry Margaret. He told me that."

"Anything else?"

"He has a loan out with my father. It was understood that something might be worked out in that regard."

Henry rose to his feet.

"No more," he said. He squeezed by Sarah, and walked toward the rear of the room. Sarah followed.

"Disgraceful," one spectator, a plump, middle aged woman said, "selling his daughter like that. For a loan. Can you imagine." She lifted her arms and let them drop against her sides. "What was he to do?" asked her companion, a slim, balding man. "Would you have our daughter marry that man? Or have a bastard?" Others joined in until comments on both sides of the question filled the room. Hightower gaveled them into silence.

"We will recess for an hour," he said.

When court resumed, Henry and Sarah were back in their seats.

"Where were you on the day she disappeared?" Lowe asked.

"I was clearing brush for a road across my property to the new resort," Sam replied. "I had a contract from the builder, and I needed the money. I had to get it done by the first of the month."

"Where is that road that you were clearing?"

"It runs west from the main road, then across the southern boundary of my farm, then toward West Bay."

"How far had you gotten?"

"I was about half a mile west of where I had started."

Lowe seemed to be studying his shoes for a couple of moments as if his next question could be found in the reflection off his polished boots.

"What did you do when you heard Margaret Cutter was missing?"

"I joined the search party. Henry himself came to my door."

An inarticulate groan issued from Henry. Sarah lowered her head and shook it from side to side like the pendulum of a clock that was winding down.

"Where did the search party find her?"

"In the hemlock swamp near the shore of East Bay."

"East Bay, you say?"

"Yes."

"About how far from where you were working?"

"I'd guess maybe two miles."

"Your testimony is that her body was found two miles from where you were working on the new road on the day she disappeared. Is that correct?"

"Yes."

"And you do not have wings, do you?"

"No."

"So, you couldn't have flown to where she was found, and then back again?"

"No."

Lowe turned toward the jury for a moment, then back to Sam.

"Nor could you have flown across the ground to stand next to her body, as the prosecution would have us believe."

"No," Sam replied. "I never got closer than fifteen or twenty feet to her. I had no stomach to see her lying there."

"Is it not true," Heller asked, "that you and Margaret Cutter were lovers, and that the baby she was carrying was yours?"

"Yes. At least I believe it was."

"Do you have any reason to think the baby's father was somebody else?"

"No reason, in particular. But she was a very troubled young woman, ever since her little brother drowned."

"Did she talk to you about marriage?"

"She cut out pictures of baby carriages and showed them to me."

"Wasn't that to convince you to marry her and be a father to her child?"

"Yes."

"You have said you proposed a match between her and your son. Can you explain your thinking?"

"I think I already have."

"Try a little harder, if you please."

Sam knew he was being baited, as he had been so many times before. He looked up at the prosecutor's face. He was a big man, but that had never bothered Sam in a bar or on the baseball field. This was a different arena, however, one where his fists were useless.

"I was twice as old as she was. I didn't love her, at least not the way she wanted me to. I already had one son living with me, and another I have never seen, although I send money to his mother every month. I'm not much good at farming, but that is what I do, so I never have much money, and she was painting this rosy picture of us living together pushing our baby down the road in a carriage that she was going to pay for out of her egg money." Sam paused for breath. He had delivered these statements as though each was a blow to the prosecutor's midsection. He wanted to finish with a roundhouse knock-out blow, but he realized he didn't have one. "Don't you see," he continued, "it just didn't make any sense? But I couldn't convince her of that."

"And so you tried to hand her off to your son."

"He would have been a good match for her."

"Even though she would give birth to his own half brother or sister?"

"Even so. Better than me." Sam felt the veins in his forehead throb. "Mr. Heller, you are stripping me down to the bone, and I'm a proud man for all my failings. My solution wasn't very pretty. But her own mother and father agreed to it. The only one who didn't was her."

"Because she loved you."

"Yes. I guess she did."

"And so," Heller, who had been leaning over Sam, now raised himself to his full height, "you decided to extricate yourself, just the same way you had that tooth pulled out. You lured her to a meeting, had her drink laudanum, and then put your hands around her throat, just like your former wife testified you had done to her. Isn't that so?"

"No," Sam said. He was about to say that it wasn't like that at all, but then he bit down on his lip.

"What," Heller demanded, "were you about to say?"

Lowe was on his feet.

"Objection. The prosecutor is not only making his closing argument instead of asking questions, he is now baiting the witness."

"Sustained," Hightower intoned.

"Let's try a question, then," Heller said. "Do you deny the testimony of the witness Edward Franklin, or Michael O'Leary as he now calls himself, that he saw you walking toward East Bay at the time you say you were working on the new road?"

"I do," Sam said.

"You stand by your statement that on the day she disappeared, on the day rather when she was murdered, you were a couple of miles away clearing brush?"

"I do."

"And you were working there with your son?"

"I was."

"He will vouchsafe your whereabouts?"

"I am sure he will."

I'm sure he will, his father said, and the words knifed through Isaiah. He began to perspire, a cold sweat, and he found it difficult to breathe. So, it was going to come down to this, as he had feared it would. The weight of his father's defense would sit on his shoulders. But he was not at all sure of what he might say when Lowe called him to the stand. His grandfather's hand squeezed his, and then he felt the old man's breath on his ear.

"It will be all right," he said. "You will make it all right."

Isaiah nodded, feeling again as always how his own inclinations were drawn into the powerful field of his grandfather's will. His nod at this moment was not sincere. It was designed, rather, to release the immediate pressure. His grandfather's breath smelled slightly foul, as though flavored by decaying teeth, and there was a catch in its flow, indicative of some impediment in the old man's respiratory system. Isaiah, sensing all these things, was struck with the realization of his grandfather's mortality, and with the sadness that knowledge brought was the hope for liberation from the old man's control.

He heard the prosecutor bark that he had no more questions for this most unresponsive witness, and then the judge's gavel pounded out the days' adjournment. His father was led back to his cell, with just one meaningful glance at him. He forced himself to hold his father's gaze, and even to offer a small smile in response to the anxiety he detected in Sam's eyes. His grandparents rose, as they usually did at the end of a day's proceedings and started to make their way toward the rear door. Those sitting around them always waited, subdued, it seemed, by the palpable aura of authority emitted by Charles Logan.

But this time, Isaiah remained sitting. He knew his grandparents wanted to lead the way out of the crowded courtroom so as not to have to mingle with the other spectators, or worse be obliged to sit and endure the silent stares of their social inferiors.

"Come along," Charles said, but Isaiah shook his head. Charles started to reach for him, but then shrugged and walked out with Livonia, who first leaned down and pressed her lips to Isaiah's forehead.

Isaiah watched them leave, and then the other spectators. He felt their eyes on him, but he did not care. What ate at his marrow was far too private to involve the interest of strangers. He cared not what any of them might think of him. This, in the most fundamental sense, was between him and the man whose blood flowed through his veins.

That night, Isaiah sat again on the beach overlooking East Bay, listening to the slap of the water against the rocks embedded in the sand. He took off his shoes and socks, rolled up his pants and waded into the water. It was warm. He remembered how she had stood next to him on the porch of his house, and how she had gazed in the direction of this same water. He waded in further. The water now reached his groin and he felt it like a caress, like the touch of her hand. He was sure she was there with him. He dove in and angled toward the bottom only a few feet from the surface. He thrust himself forward with his arms and legs in a frog like motion. The water beneath the surface was still warm.

He rose to the surface for a breath and as he did he saw the round face of the rising moon. Looking out over the water, he gazed at the pale yellow reflection of moonlight across the surface. Beginning to swim with slow, powerful strokes along the ribbon of yellow, he kept his head in the water until his lungs ached, and he lifted his face up. Each time he dipped his head back into the water he marveled at its continued warmth in the moonlight.

But then, all of a sudden, the water turned sharply colder. He raised his head and saw that the yellow path was gone, the moon now behind a cloud. He angled toward the bottom but did not find it. Panic seized him. He felt he was going mad. He broke the surface again, and there was the golden path. The cloud had drifted away. He looked about, gauged the distance to the shore and realized he had reached that point in the bay where the bottom suddenly drops to forty feet.

He lay on his back for a few minutes in the cold water, and sensed that her presence was gone, so he turned and stroked toward shore.

On the pebbly sand of the beach, he looked out over the water. He felt as though she had just told him what he must do tomorrow.

17

—

He awoke the next morning when the sun shone through his bedroom window. For a moment he thought he was still in the water, floating on that golden, moonlit warmed lane across the bay's surface, rippled by a breeze. But then he felt the lumps in the mattress beneath his body and realized that the water had pooled off of his sopping wet clothes when he had thrown himself onto his bed the night before.

Rolling off the bed and stripping down to his bare skin, he spread the wet jacket, shirt, and trousers on the floor where the sun would bathe them, knowing that his grandfather and grandmother would be by to pick him up long before those clothes would dry.

Pacing back and forth in his room, and then out into the hallway, he saw the closed door to his father's room, which he had shut on the day the sheriff had come to take Sam away, and which he had not opened since. He turned the knob and pushed the door into the room and looked at the bed, half expecting his father to rise and greet him with his usual grin, as though he had just told a joke. On the wall opposite, hanging on a peg was the suit in which his father had married his second wife. Isaiah took it down and held it up against himself. It seemed as though it had been made for him, and it had not occurred to him until this moment how similar his body was to his father's.

Putting on the suit, though, seemed like putting on his father's skin, and he began to sweat. The jacket pressed against his chest until he couldn't breathe. Ripping the suit off, he threw it into the corner of the room. After a few moments, he lifted it up again, holding it with just the tips of his fingers as though it were the skin of a dead snake, and he hung it up. He shut the door behind him and retreated back into his own room.

Dressed in his collarless, sweat stained work shirt and his denim overalls begrimed with dirt and stained red from cherry juice, he walked down the hallway that led to the front door, and stopped. There next to the fireplace, on the small table, which he had watched his father fashion when he was little, was the Bible. Kneeling in front of the table as though it were an altar, he opened the Bible to the page he wanted as if it had been waiting all this time for him to request what it was holding. Picking up the note, he recalled how he had thought she had spoken to him the night before in the pale gold of the moonlight on the water, and he thrust it into his pocket.

He went out to the porch as his grandfather's buggy arrived. Livonia looked at him with disapproval in her eyes, and for a moment, he thought she was staring at the note, which had perversely risen to poke a corner out of his pocket. He slid his hand toward his pocket, but he did not feel the note.

"What happened to your good clothes?" she asked.

"They got wet. Last night at the beach."

"Well, I declare, what were you..." she began, but then just shook her head.

"Get on up here," Charles said. "There's nothing like showing yourself for what you are: an honest young man of the land. What got your father into this mess no doubt was his thinking that he was better than that."

Isaiah looked across the courtroom at Sam. The distance between them seemed to close and widen. One moment, Sam's face loomed at him with a fierce entreaty in his eyes, and the next it receded to a dot like a cold star in a black sky. Isaiah lifted his glance past his father and the other spectators to the back row where his grandfather and grandmother sat. Charles's face was set in that rigid determination that Isaiah had seen so often, whether the old man was closing a deal with a fruit processor for his crop or sharpening the blade of an ax. Livonia's expression, on the other hand, was like the caress of her hand wafted across the courtroom to his forehead, and he managed to smile at her. In between his grandparents and Sam was a sea of spectators, their eyes fixed on him as though he held the key to the door that would release Justice from the cell where Sam's alibi had imprisoned her. He imagined that if that door were to open, Justice would gather her robes around her, lift the blindfold from her eyes, and walk past Sam so that she could point an accusing finger at himself.

The bailiff came forward holding a heavy Bible, and for a second Isaiah thought it was the same one that had been on the table in his house. He realized he had his right hand in his pocket, his fingers pressed against the note that undercut his father's alibi, and wondered if he could lift his hand out without tugging the piece of paper as well since it seemed to have attached itself to his flesh.

The bailiff, a thin man, with hunched shoulders, waited. "You will need to swear on the good book," he said. It looked as though the book were too heavy for him to hold much longer.

Isaiah forced his fingers open and lifted his hand out of his pocket. He placed his hand on the Bible. The book, whose cover was frayed on the edges and stained by the hundreds of hands that had pressed against it, seemed to give off heat. After he swore and sat down in the witness chair, his hand began to move again toward the paper in his pocket, but he managed to stay it. He clasped his hands in his lap, almost as though he were a schoolboy waiting for the teacher to begin conducting class.

Lowe rose from his seat and walked toward him. Isaiah thought the attorney was moving in an exaggerated slow motion, as if he were under water, and his head appeared to be floating ahead of the body. Lowe fingered his red four-in-hand and Isaiah focused on the neckwear. He closed his eyes for a moment, and then snapped them open to find Lowe standing in front of him. He continued to look at the red cloth, fearful that if he moved his glance to the lawyer's face the head would once again float free.

"Now, Isaiah," Lowe said in his most gentle voice, "I can see how nervous you are. No doubt you understand the significance of the testimony you are about to offer. Is that not right?"

Lowe's voice seemed to be coming from a great distance. Isaiah now lifted his eyes to the attorney's mouth, and saw the lips move before the words came out. He strained to understand the question.

"Yes, I do."

"Good. Let us begin. Do you share the work on your farm with your father?"

"Yes."

"Did you do that on the day Margaret Cutter disappeared?"

"Yes."

Isaiah tensed.

"Tell us what you did on that day."

"In the morning I rode our horse over to Wilson's place to borrow a plow. I did some plowing on the southeast corner of our land until about noon, and then I met my father and we went to work on the new road toward the resort."

"At about what time would you say you met your father?"

"It was after noon. Maybe one o'clock although it could have been a little later, but not much. I don't have a watch. I usually just look at the sun."

Isaiah was feeling a little more confident. Lowe was leading him through a recitation of facts, and as long as he did that he would be able to answer.

"So about one o'clock, or in that vicinity, you met your father."

"Yes."

Lowe strolled toward the jury box and let his eyes pause on each of the faces. His expression said that something of moment was about to be offered them. He walked back toward Isaiah, and stopped a few feet from him.

"Think carefully now before you answer this next question. Can you do that? It's very important."

"Yes," and Isaiah felt his shoulders, which had been almost unbearably tense, begin to relax. This was the question he had lain awake thinking about until he decided that he would be able to tell the truth, a half truth to be sure, but truth enough to permit him to swear to it.

"Was he walking when you met him?"

"He was."

Lowe looked back toward the jury. He swiveled his head ever so slowly toward Isaiah.

"From what direction would you say he was coming?"

"He was coming from the west," Isaiah said, and his voice was firm and clear. "He was carrying his ax and told me I was late."

"Were you?"

Isaiah shrugged.

"I don't know. Maybe. Like I said, I don't have a watch."

"Then what did you do?"

"We worked on the new road until supper."

"You worked on the new road, the same road your father was working on at the time he was accused of murder." Lowe paused, and Isaiah realized that he was waiting for a confirmation. But such a statement would cross the line Isaiah had drawn in his mind. He did not reply. Lowe glanced at him as though to encourage a response. When he did not get one, he continued.

"At any *time* did your father show any *unusual* behavior?" He put a heavy emphasis on the words "time" and "unusual."

"No. He was short with me like he usually was, but no different from any other day."

"Did you both join the search party the next day?"

"We did."

"Again, from your observation, how did your father conduct himself?"

"Like everyone else."

"I took him as far as I could," Lowe said to Sam. They were in a small, holding room behind the courtroom during a brief recess requested by the prosecution. "If I had pushed him one step further he would have said something that would have sunk us."

"I imagine he did the best he could," Sam said.

Lowe shook his head.

"He could have done better. I had him set up to second my statement establishing your alibi, and he just sat there mute."

"Well he must..." Sam began, but Lowe waved his hand to silence him.

"Don't," he said. "I don't want to hear about what he knows, or thinks he knows. I tell you I squeezed the last bit of useful talk out of him. Our only salvation is that I'm damned sure Heller isn't going to have better luck. In fact, if he tries to shake him, your boy will just dig in his heels. I've seen that stubborn streak in him."

"He's a good boy, nonetheless," Sam said.

Lowe stared hard at him.

"I guess you know why you would say that."

"We have to try to rattle him," Heller said to Richard. They were sitting on a bench overlooking the river behind the courthouse.

"He's his son, the jury understands that."

"Yes, but they could see that he was being very careful in what he said for whatever reason. I think it was because he didn't want to out and out lie, and Lowe was smart enough to give him questions that he could answer, but the jury might just take a different view, seeing a young boy trying very hard to make sure he told the truth in a way that would be believed."

"What are you going to do?"

Heller stood up.

"Push him just hard enough to cast doubt on his credibility."

"How?"

"Don't know. I'll have to feel my way in."

"Tell us about the day your stepmother and you and your father were driving into town." Heller was holding a thin sheaf of papers.

Isaiah looked at his father. Sam shrugged and nodded. Isaiah's head throbbed. During the break he had entertained the thought of just leaving the courthouse and making his way to a ship, any ship, that would take him far away. He had walked through the front door, there to find the bulk of Sheriff Billingham standing with one foot on the street level, and the other two steps up. He was puffing a large cigar.

"Just getting some air," Isaiah had said.

Billingham had reached into his shirt pocket to take out another cigar. He held it out but Isaiah shook his head, took a couple of exaggerated breaths, and walked back into the courthouse.

"They were arguing," he said now, "my father and my stepmother."

"What about?"

"I don't recall. They argued pretty regularly."

"Did you all continue on to town?"

"No."

"Who didn't?"

"She got down and walked."

"Do you know where she was going?"

"I think to the doctor."

"Was she sick?"

"I don't know."

"Isn't it true that she was not feeling well because she was pregnant with your brother?"

"I don't know why she was feeling sick."

"Is it also true," Heller said in a rising tone, "that you have never seen your brother, who is living now in town with his mother?"

"Yes."

Heller peeled off the top paper from those he was holding, and showed it to Isaiah.

"Do you recognize this?" he asked.

"No," Isaiah replied.

"Well, then just read it, if you would."

Isaiah scanned the paper and then looked up.

"Please tell the court what you have just read."

"It's a statement from my stepmother. I guess it was part of the divorce."

"And what does it say?"

"It's about a time she says my father threw her down and choked her."

"Do you know anything about that incident?"

"No, I do not."

"Did you ever see your father assault your stepmother?"

"Like I said, they argued a lot. Sometimes they shoved each other."

"They shoved each other. Like your father and your mother? Did they shove each other as well?"

"Not that I recall."

"You don't recall."

"I was very little when she left. I remember her reading me stories at night. Not much more."

"Not how she and your father fought?"

"No."

"I've read their divorce papers," Heller insisted, with a turn to the jury. "They tell a different story. They tell..."

Lowe rose to his feet to object.

"I'll allow it," Hightower said, "as long as Mr. Heller shows relevance."

"It goes to the defendant's character," Heller said.

"But the boy does not remember, he says," Lowe interjected.

Hightower leaned toward Isaiah.

"Do you?"

"No, sir, I don't, any more than what I have already said."

"Mr. Heller you have your answer."

Heller walked back to the prosecution's table and handed the papers he had been holding to Richard. He strode back toward Isaiah and did not stop until he was close enough for Isaiah to see his chest heave and the saliva gather in the corner of his mouth.

"You seemed a little uncertain about the time you met up with your father on the day of the murder. Is that because you are avoiding telling the absolute truth?"

"No. I don't have a watch. I don't know what time it was."

"You say you looked at the sun. Was it straight up?"

"Not quite."

"So it was after noon."

"I expect."

"By an hour, or two, or three?"

"I can't say for sure. But it was after noon."

Lowe stood up.

"Your honor. The witness has answered the question. He did not construct a sun dial on the spot."

Heller spun on his heels to face Lowe.

"But perhaps he is now constructing a lie, a very delicate lie, but a lie nonetheless."

"Objection."

"Sustained." Hightower leaned down toward Heller. "Confine yourself to questions to the witness that the witness can answer, and when he has answered to the best of his ability, move on."

"You have no doubt heard testimony to the effect that not much progress seems to have been made clearing that road. Is that so?" Heller asked.

"I did hear that, yes."

"Would you say that characterization is accurate?"

Isaiah felt sweat drip down and pool at the base of his spine.

"Yes," he said. "But the work was slow going and difficult."

"Isn't it true that so little work seems to have been done on that road because your father, at the time he was supposed to be clearing brush, was meeting with Margaret Cutter with the express purpose of ending her life?"

The spectators nodded their assent. Lowe again rose to his feet.

"Your honor..." he began.

"Withdrawn," Heller replied. "I am through with this witness."

Hightower looked toward Lowe.

"Redirect, your honor," Lowe said.

Isaiah felt that his nerves were already strung so tight, that they might soon snap. He took a breath as Lowe approached.

"Just a little clarification, if you don't mind," Lowe said, his voice sugar. "You say you don't remember seeing your father choking your stepmother?"

"That's right. They fought a lot, but usually when I wasn't in the room. I would hear them raise their voices."

Lowe handed a paper to Isaiah.

"The prosecution has dug into your father's divorce papers and pulled out what he wanted. But I visited those same papers and found this statement. Do you recognize it?"

Isaiah glanced at the paper and nodded.

"Please answer out loud."

"Yes."

"Tell the jury, then, please what you are looking at."

"It's a statement I made to my father's lawyer. He asked me to tell about a time my stepmother had a knife in her hand."

"Where was that knife?"

"Near my throat."

"Was she threatening you with it?"

"I guess."

"What happened next?"

"My father grabbed her arm until she dropped it."

"Thank you," Lowe said, "for that clarification."

Hightower looked toward the prosecutor.

"Recross, Mr. Heller?"

"Certainly," Heller replied. "I'm afraid the clarification has only obscured the simple facts in this case. He strode to the witness chair. "Isn't it true," he asked, "that your stepmother was holding the knife to defend herself against the assault of your father."

"I don't know about that."

"I see. You don't know. Did you think she would use that knife on you?"

"I don't recall exactly what I thought. It was all happening too fast."

"Did you get along with your stepmother."

"Tolerably."

"Tolerably. Did you argue?"

"She sometimes said I was taking my father's side."

"Were you?"

"I just tried to keep out of their way."

Isaiah stepped down from the witness chair. He felt as though he had been in a boxing ring with his hands tied behind his back, being pummeled first by one lawyer and then the other. By the end of his testimony, he was no longer sure of what he knew or thought he knew.

"We need him, now," Heller said. He and Sheriff Billingham were standing on the steps of the courthouse. "I couldn't shake that boy enough, not near enough."

"I'll wire Matthews."

"We've got the weekend. Make sure he's here by Sunday morning. We'll need to talk to him to make sure what he's going to say."

Lowe strolled by. He nodded in their direction.

"My, my, I do believe you boys are cooking something up to surprise me."

"We wouldn't dream of doing that," Heller replied.

Lowe looked to his right across a field toward the railroad station.

"Some folks, I hear, don't even buy a ticket when they travel." He smiled and walked on.

"How'd he know?" Billingham asked after Lowe had disappeared around a corner.

"Just send that wire. Knowing's one thing. Doing something about it is another."

"This just went out," the clerk in the telegraph office said. He handed a folded piece of paper to Benson. The detective reached into his pocket and pulled out his thick wad, peeled off five tens and put them on the counter. He laid his hands on both sides of the little pile and evened the edges. Then he turned the bills lengthwise and evened them again.

"Are you being square with me?" he asked. "Tell me now if you're not. My boss don't like to be played for a fool."

"Why, what do you mean?"

"Just this. If there's been any other messages going out to the party we're interested in, or if this one ain't genuine, why then you wouldn't be being square."

The clerk put his hand on the bills. Benson seized his wrist with his thick fingers and squeezed just a little.

"Well?" he insisted.

"Mister, I'm no fool. This is all I have for you, the only message you'd be interested in, and it's genuine. The man sent it not more than fifteen minutes ago."

"I know that well enough," Benson replied. "I was watching from across the street there." He pointed through the window to an alley between two commercial buildings. "Right there in the shadows. I saw him go in, and watched him go out. But what I don't know is what he asked you to send."

"It's right there, like I said, on that paper."

Benson leaned over the counter, and spoke in the friendly tones he might have used to persuade a gunman to put down his weapon.

"I know you want to do the right thing. But maybe you're thinking this trial will soon be over, and you still have to live here after I'm long gone. Or maybe Mr. Heller has paid you more than I have. Is that it?"

"No, sir, it is not."

Benson released his grip on the clerk's wrist. The little man looked down at his skin, which still bore the imprint of the detective's fingers. He rubbed his wrist, then very slowly moved his hand back to the pile of bills.

"Go, ahead, now," Benson said.

The clerk scooped up the bills and shoved them into his pocket, and just then his receiving machine began to clatter. He looked at Benson.

"Write it down," Benson said.

The clerk listened, and wrote. When he was done, he showed the paper to Benson. The detective read, and nodded. Pulling out his money again, he peeled off another five tens.

"Very good," he said. "Now I know you're being square with us."

That evening Isaiah sat on a boulder on the shore of East Bay, looking up to the moon, in its last phase, a yellow sliver. It cast a reflection on the water, thin as a pencil line lightly drawn. He gazed at it until it disappeared into the blackening waters.

18

A train pulling out caused the floor of Jim's shanty to vibrate. The spoon in the coffee cup on his table rattled and then the cup slid toward him. He put up his hand to stop the cup, still half full and warm, from falling off the edge. He let it rest against his palm waiting for the last car to rumble by, counting them as they did, and when he had reached twenty seven, the rumbling noise diminished and the floor quieted.

Yet he sensed, more than he heard, movement outside his door, just as the sun was beginning to stream through his one window. He got up and walked on his toes toward the corner of his shanty. He crawled underneath the window next to his front door. Once past it, he stood up and grasped a piece of four by four lumber standing on its edge in the corner. He made his way back to the side of the door, again getting down on his hands and knees to pass by the window.

All this time he was listening. He heard no more than the slight scrape of the toes of his boots on the plank floor or the sound of the cloth on the knees of his pants as he crawled by the window. There was no noise coming from outside the shanty, and yet he knew somebody was there, and whoever it was intended him no good. He clenched the lumber and stood by the door.

It swung open. He watched it come toward him and stopped it with his foot. He raised the piece of lumber over his head. He saw a hat protrude through the doorway and into the room. He brought the lumber down on it as hard as he could. The lumber thumped against the floor and bounced up. He felt no resistance as it crashed against the hat, and started to lift the wood up again when an arm reached in and seized it. The arm was followed by the body of a man who held a cocked revolver in his other hand.

"I thought you might be expecting somebody unfriendly," Benson said.

"You could have knocked," Jim muttered.

"I'm pretty sure you wouldn't have answered."

"What do you want? I ain't bothering nobody and ain't done nothin."

"It ain't what you did or been doing. It's what you might have seen, and be willing to say you saw."

"You from up there?" Jim asked with a nod of his head toward the north.

"I am." Benson waved the revolver and Jim backed up a couple of steps. The detective knelt down and picked up his felt fedora and the stick on which it had floated into the room. The crown of the hat was flattened. "Good thing my head wasn't in this."

"What you want with me?"

"Maybe it's time for you to be moving on." Benson took out his wad. "Where you want to go?"

"Chicago."

"How much is the ticket?"

"It was eleven dollars from up there."

Benson counted out three tens.

"This'll take you there and give you a stake."

Jim stared at the bills in the detective's hand.

"Why you want me to move on?"

"I hear the climate's better where you want to go."

"That ain't the reason."

"No, it ain't. And you know what it is. You might have seen something. I could pay you to lie, or to forget, but let's just say this is a better way. You get where you want to go..."

"And what I might say goes with me."

"Right."

"I may change my travel plans. Go a little further. Stay in a nice place until I can get a job, better than this one."

"I see," Benson replied. He added two more bills to those in his hand.

"This ought to take you there. And that's all there's going to be."

Jim took the bills and shoved them into his pocket. He looked about the one room shanty, at the narrow bed, one wooden chair with its uneven legs pushed under the end of the crude table. There was a small wood burning stove in the corner. Next to it on the floor was the bundle containing his possessions.

"I can leave pretty much any time."

"I was thinking that."

"Except, they've got men watching me."

"I know that, too. I think I met one of them on my way here. There's a train going south in an hour."

Jim picked up his bundle, and walked to the door. Benson followed, his revolver now holstered.

"Just where do you think you're going, boy?" The voice belonged to a tall man with a gash over his right eye, and a revolver in his belt. Next to him stood another, shorter and broader, with a billy club in his hand.

"Why out for a little air, with me," Benson said. He stepped forward and turned so that his hand on the butt of his gun in his holster was clearly visible.

"Well, it does seem like we have us a situation here," the tall one said.

Emerging from the shadows was another man. He was dressed in a suit and held a folded piece of paper in his hand.

"Let's talk," he said.

Heller was not surprised to find Lowe at the train station.

"I expect you're waiting for the same train I am," he said.

"No doubt," Lowe replied.

"One of us will be disappointed."

"Or perhaps both."

It was late Saturday afternoon beneath a gray sky. A woman with a baby in her arms peered down the tracks. A driver sat drowsing on his buggy, a cigar in one hand, the reins in the other. He had his head on his chest, and the cigar dropped out of his clenched lips. A few feet away was a carriage with "Old Mission Inn" painted on its sides. Its driver was reading a newspaper. Lowe approached the woman.

"It should be here any minute," he said, "but why don't you sit down until it arrives." He pointed to the one bench on the platform.

"It's just that my husband, he's a soldier, has been gone so long," she said.

"I understand," Lowe replied. He tipped his hat and walked back to where Heller was standing.

"I don't suppose you know what this fellow Jim might testify," Heller said.

"No, I don't."

"And you didn't want to find out."

Lowe shrugged, a small smile playing at the corners of his mouth.

"I was winning," he said.

"Do you think so?"

"I do."

"The boy's credibility..." Heller began.

"Was good enough for doubt."

The ground began to shake and both men turned to look down the tracks.

"Is he on the train?" Lowe asked.

"I don't know."

Lowe looked toward the telegraph office.

"You shouldn't have had him fired. Then you would have known."

"And so would you have."

"We'll both know soon enough."

The woman walked to them.

"Is that smoke or a cloud?"

A gray column approached over the tracks.

"It's moving toward us over the track," Heller said. "It's the train."

"Thank the Lord," the woman said.

As soon as the train squealed to a stop, the door on the one passenger car opened, and a young man in the uniform of the cavalry hopped off. His left arm was in a sling. He trotted to the woman and embraced her with his good arm, kissed her, and then just stared at the baby in her arms.

"Oh, God, it was so awful," he said. "So many dead, women and children."

"Your arm," she said.

"An arrow," he said.

"Those savages."

He shook his head.

"We had repeating rifles. The women and children."

An elderly man walking with a cane in one hand and his valise in the other clambered down the steps at the end of the car and made his way toward the buggy. He tipped his top hat to the attorneys as he passed. When he reached the buggy, he poked the sleeping driver with his cane. The driver started awake and reached down for the valise.

"How's my wife?" the man asked.

"Not so well," the driver replied.

"Then get me home."

Lowe looked down the line of cars. "Maybe he's not on the train," he said.

But just then the door on the car opened again, and Benson emerged. He was followed by the tall man.

"Come on down," he called back up into the car.

Jim stepped out, looking about him as though for a friendly face or a place to run. The short, broad man nudged him from behind, and they both descended the steps.

"You've got your man," Lowe said.

"That I do," Heller said with a smile.

"Come on," Lowe said to Benson. "You can tell me all about it on the way out to the Inn."

"I almost had him on his way to Chicago," Benson said. "But then I would have had to shoot him or these two when they showed up."

"You did what you could," Lowe said. "But tell me the story as we ride. I understand we will have a fine English roast tonight." He led the way to the carriage.

"Well, Jim," Heller said, "what do you have to say for yourself?"

"Nothing."

"Are you going to try to run again?"

"Ain't no point," Jim replied.

"Good man," Heller said. "We will have dinner, and you will tell me what you know."

Jim cut a piece off his steak. He chewed it and speared the remaining piece. The waiter, wearing white gloves, stood near the table, a look of disgust on his face. Sitting across from Jim were Heller and Richard. Heller motioned to the waiter.

"What do you have for dessert?"

"Hot apple pie."

"We'll all have a piece," Heller said, looking to Jim. "I know you didn't want to get involved in this situation. But now you are. Can we count on you to testify as to what you saw?"

"If I do, you'll put me back on that train with a ticket to Chicago?"

"Absolutely."

"You want to know who I saw that day."

"Yes," Richard said, "but before you tell us that, we also have to know if you have anything in your past we should know about that could cause a problem."

"You mean something with a white woman?"

"Yes."

"I ain't such a fool."

"We've heard about your back," Heller said.

"That was from trying to run away."

"You slept in the barn where Margaret Cutter came to milk the cows."

"I kept my distance."

"Mr. Lowe is going to make something out of that," Heller said.

"He be making somethin' out of nothin', then," Jim said.

The waiter returned with the three desserts. He slid one in front of Heller, and another before Richard. He placed the third in the middle of the table. He started to walk away.

"Waiter," Heller called.

"Yessir."

"Finish what you started," he said.

The waiter returned to the table, leaned over Richard's shoulder and with his white gloved hand, pushed the pie plate to Jim.

"Go ahead, and eat," Heller said. "And then you can tell us what you saw."

Daniel sat on a fallen log as he waited for Isaiah after the service the next morning. Isaiah emerged, flanked by his grandparents, saw Daniel and started to walk toward him. He realized with a start that he had come to depend upon Daniel's support. What other friend did he have? But his grandfather seized his elbow.

"That's not advisable," Charles said. "That fellow's a reporter."

"And my friend, my only friend," Isaiah said. He took a seat next to Daniel on the log.

"Were you in court the other day?" he asked.

"Yes."

"I only said what I could."

"But not what you knew."

Isaiah shrugged.

"I'm leaving as soon as this is over."

"Where are you going?" Daniel asked.

"Grandpa wants me to inherit his farms, but that's not for me." He looked through the trees to the patches of blue in the bay.

"I see," Daniel said. "Well, I do wish you well. I hope you understand that I thought she was talking about you when she told me she was going to marry Mr. Logan."

Isaiah reddened.

"I wanted to believe that."

"Maybe she did, deep inside."

"No, sir," Isaiah declared. "I won't fool myself with that thought. It would only make what I had to do worse."

Daniel coughed into his handkerchief.

"Isn't there anything you can do?" Isaiah asked.

"Just live as best as I can for as long as I can." He held out his hand. "Good luck to you."

"Do you think I, you know, my father..."

"I'm no expert, but I think there's a fair chance."

A rueful grin spread over Isaiah's face.

"You know, I don't know whether I want to have saved him, or not."

Charles waved and Isaiah got up.

"Do me a favor, will you?"

"Anything I can," Daniel said.

"Wait for me after the verdict. I think I may want to give you something."

Daniel watched Isaiah walk away in the shelter of his grand-parents' prominence. He wondered what was the moral calculus by which to reconcile the imperfect hearts of men and women with their Creator who made them thus imperfect. How should the murderer be judged? The son who might have lied to protect his father?

19

The prosecution asks the court's forbearance," Heller said. "We would like to call a witness, whose availability has just become known to us."

Judge Hightower shuffled some papers in front of him. He waved his hand in a sweeping motion. "Approach. Both of you."

Heller and Lowe stood in front of the bench. Hightower looked from one to the other.

"Mr. Heller, Mr. Lowe has anticipated you and filed a motion asking that you be prevented from calling this witness. I assume we are talking about the same man." He turned to the district attorney. "You want to call this hand, this Jim Edwards. Is that right?"

"Yes," Heller replied.

"And you, Mr. Lowe, want me to rule against introducing this witness, as not having time to prepare for him."

"That is so."

"But," Hightower continued, looking at Lowe, my sources tell me that your man Benson knows all about this witness and was trying to spirit him away when he was approached by deputies of Sheriff Matthews."

"He had come to interview him, but was interrupted by the deputies."

"I see. Well, there was the train ride back to give him the time he needed. I'm going to allow this witness."

"Please note my objection," Lowe said.

"Done," the judge replied.

Deputy Morgan led Jim into the courtroom through the rear door. Lowe sat down next to Sam. "What can he say?" he asked behind his hand.

"I don't know," Sam replied, but with a start that brought a cold sweat to his face he remembered the noise he heard in the woods that afternoon.

"Is there something I ought to know?" Lowe demanded. Sam shrugged. Lowe patted his hand, and felt how damp it was. "Don't worry. Whatever he says, I'll make short work of him when my turn comes."

Heller raised himself to his full height, and as he stepped toward Jim clasped his hands behind his back.

"Tell us where you were at about noon on the afternoon Margaret Cutter, your employer's daughter, disappeared."

"I was supposed to help Edward, the other hand, dig fence post holes. Which I did, but I took my time getting there."

"And how, exactly, did you take your time?"

"I took a walk, way away from where I was supposed to be, going through the woods toward the shore."

"That would be the shore of East Bay, would it not."

"Yes."

"Did anybody see you?"

"Only Edward, but he was a ways away from me."

Heller paused and looked to Richard, who stood up and, carrying a large drawing pad to an easel, positioned it so the jury could see it. He handed a piece of charcoal to Jim. On the pad was the outline of a section of the Peninsula near town, with East Bay written on the right and West Bay on the left. The town road snaking up in a northeasterly direction ran by two rectangles with the name of Logan inscribed in the one to the north, and Cutter to the south. In each of the rectangles were smaller squares, with triangles to indicate the roofs of buildings. One square in each rectangle was labeled with a "H," for house and the other a "B" for barn. Where the two rectangles came together were the words "Fence" and to the north and east of that, curving on the other side of the road to the southeast "Woods," written with widely spaced letters toward but not reaching East Bay. Between the end of the word and the shoreline was an area with what looked like crudely drawn Christmas trees, labeled "Hemlock Swamp."

"Mr. Edwards," Heller said, "forgive the impertinence, but I must ask. Can you read the names on this map?"

"Yes. I got a little help from Mr. Cutter, who gave me a book, but mostly I learned myself."

"Good. Now, you see this road here, the town road, and the Cutter farm?"

"Yes."

"And this is about where their house and barn would be?"

"Yes."

"And this line here is where the fence was to be placed between the properties of Cutter and the defendant?"

"Yes."

"And here where it says "Woods," that's where the woods start at the beginning of Logan's property?"

"Yes."

"If you please," Heller said, "sketch the path you took, showing us where you went, and where you think you were when Edward saw you coming out of the woods."

Jim stood up and took the charcoal.

"Well, here, first," he said, "just north of that fence line is the woods." And with rapid strokes he sketched several trees. He drew the outline of a man's figure on the fence line. "Edward," he said. Then he drew another figure between the trees he had drawn, and took his time filling in the face with the black of the charcoal. "Me."

"How far would he have been from you?"

"Maybe thirty or forty yards."

"When did he see you there?"

"After I come back."

"Show us where you walked that day, before you arrived at the spot where Edward saw you."

Jim held the charcoal lightly in his fingers, as though he were accustomed to sketching. He placed the charcoal next to square labeled with a "B." "Mr. Cutter's barn," he said. Then he drew a dotted line going northeast and into the woods, through the woods heading to the southeast to a position near the shore line on the east, and then back through the woods to the spot where he had indicated he had encountered Edward.

254

Heller reached into his pocket and took out another piece of charcoal. He put an X in the area with the Christmas trees.

"Now, what is this area?"

"What folks call the hemlock swamp."

"And where my mark is?"

"Where that girl was found dead."

"Not far from where you had walked in the woods?"

"Not far at all."

Sam felt nausea spread up from his belly, and he knew his face must be white. The sound in the woods. He heard it again as he sat with his hands holding up his head, staring at the drawing pad.

"What did you see that day?"

Jim looked at Sam.

"I saw him heading into that swamp."

The spectators had been listening as if with suspended breaths. They now exhaled into a buzz of excited words. The gavel came down hard, until they all quieted. Henry's face was brick red, and the veins pulsed in his neck, but he said nothing. He just nodded, very slowly, up and down. Sarah lowered her head and sobbed in silence.

Sitting in the back between his grandparents, Isaiah felt a rush of conflicting emotions, lifted by the thought that his tortured testimony had now been shunted, if not into the shadows of irrelevancy, at least to the background by this new, much more concrete statement, but just as he reached the apex of his relief he was dropped into despair by the realization that he had failed not only his father, but his grandfather, that their name would now be forever sullied, and his father, whom he realized he still loved, would be locked away for the rest of his life.

And he would be known forever thereafter as the son of a murderer. And himself a liar.

"No further questions," Heller said and walked back toward his table.

Lowe got up and intercepted Heller. He held out his hand.

"I'd like to play, too," he said.

Heller looked confused.

"The charcoal, if you please," Lowe said. "I did not know to bring mine." Heller shrugged and handed Lowe the charcoal. Lowe held the charcoal between his thumb and forefinger and turned to Jim.

"Are you quite sure the man you saw was the defendant?"

"I am. I know Mr. Logan very well."

"As well, as you knew the victim?"

"Objection," roared Heller.

"Sustained," Hightower said, "I do not see the relevance."

"You will, your Honor, you will," Lowe said as though talking to a perplexed student. "But I will withdraw the question. For now."

"Be careful, Mr. Lowe, when you choose to revisit it," the judge said.

"You say you were standing here," Lowe said, pointing to a place on the map.

"About there."

"About there? But not here, nor here, nor there?" Lowe said, each time inscribing a thick X on various places in the area designated as the woods.

"About there," Jim repeated.

Lowe drew another X.

"Behind a tree?"

"Sort of."

"And you can see through the tree?"

"I looked around it."

"How far were you?"

Jim pointed to the rear of the courtroom.

"About fifty feet?" Lowe asked.

"About."

"And you saw the defendant."

"Yes."

"I see. So instead of reporting this to your employer, or the sheriff, you ran."

"Yes. If you was black like me, you'd run too."

"Are you saying blacks do not have the same sense of justice or civic responsibility as whites?"

"If you was black, you'd know what a crazy question that is."

"Explain, please."

"Anytime there's a dead white woman and a black man in the neighborhood, that black man's got trouble."

"Well, perhaps there'd be reason for that trouble. Tell us where you slept while working for Mr. Cutter."

"In the barn."

"The same barn that Margaret Cutter came to at least twice a day, when you and she would be in there alone."

"Not exactly alone, there was always the cows, and 'sides I made it my business not to be there when she was. I wasn't lookin' for no trouble."

"What kind of trouble would that be? The kind that explain those scars on your back."

Jim scowled.

"You don't know whatcha talkin' about. Got beat tryin' to run. I never mess with no white woman."

"Then why did you run this time?"

" 'Cause I know what folks like you gonna think. Soon's I see what happened, I hopped a train. 'Sides, I'm a free man, can go where I want."

"Of course, you can, although most free men would buy a ticket to ride the railroad."

"Didn't have the money."

"You could have waited to be paid, couldn't you?"

"I already told you what I was thinking."

"Then why did you come back to make this dramatic entrance and tell your story, the same story you could have told at the time?"

"Wasn't my idea to come back. Your man was givin' me train fare to Chicago, but the sheriff down there come along and put me on the train to come back. But I 'spect you know all about that."

"Indeed, I do. But we will have to let those fine men in the jury box decide in their own minds why you ran on that day," and here Lowe paused and turned toward the jurors, "on the very day the body of Margaret Cutter was found, the same young woman that came into your living space twice a day, and when she could no longer do that, because she was dead, you ran."

As he finished this rolling sentence, Heller was on his feet yelling his objection, the courtroom was abuzz, and Hightower's gavel was thumping down.

"I'm through with this witness," Lowe said. "May I approach?"

Hightower beckoned Lowe and Heller.

"What is it, Mr. Lowe?" he asked.

"Given the surprise nature of this last witness, I would like a brief adjournment to consider whom I might call to rebut."

"And whom might that be?" Heller asked.

"That's what I have to figure out."

"You have one hour," Hightower said, "and that's more generous than I feel I ought to be with you. Whoever you want to call needs to be available."

"I understand," Lowe replied.

Lowe could scarcely contain a smile as he sat across from Sam in the holding room behind the courthouse. Benson looked at him with a quizzical expression.

"Didn't we just get whipped?" he asked.

"No, not at all. I couldn't have planned it better."

"But..." Sam began.

"I know," Lowe replied, "you think we're finished. But don't you see, now we get the last word on the one issue that we have to stand on."

"He says he saw me there, where she was found."

"Well, then, we'll just have to have somebody say he's wrong, and see who the jury believes."

"Oh, I get it," Benson said. "You're right."

Lowe slammed his open palm down on the table. "Right," he exclaimed. The door flew open, and Allan peered in.

"Everything OK in here?"

"Couldn't be better," Lowe said. "But if you see Mr. Heller, do thank him for us."

"I don't know," Sam said.

"All he has to do," Lowe replied, "is repeat what he said before. It'll be enough."

The spectators stood. Some stretched. Most filed out of the courthouse, their faces red from both perspiration and the intensity of the drama. Isaiah remained sitting between his grandparents.

"I saw the look on the face of that lawyer," Charles said. "Like the cat about to put his claw on the mouse who's thinking it's safe to come out of his hole. He is good. Worth every penny I'm paying him."

"Why whatever can you mean?" Livonia asked.

"I understand," Isaiah replied.

"That's right, boy," Charles said. "There's only one rabbit he can pull out of his hat."

"Well, Mr. Lowe, are you ready to proceed?" Hightower asked.

"Yes, your honor." He turned to scan the courtroom, as though he were still looking for somebody he could question to undo the damage to his case just inflicted by Jim. "I call Isaiah Logan."

Isaiah did not get up.

"I don't know if I can do this again," he said.

"You must, boy," his grandfather said. He cupped his elbow and pushed. Isaiah leaned forward, looking almost as though he might fall, but then got to his feet and made his way to the witness chair. As he passed the defense table he glanced at his father. Sam offered him a pained smile. Isaiah's forehead throbbed, and he felt dizzy. He concentrated on taking one step at a time until he reached the chair and sat down.

"I remind you that you are still under oath," Hightower said. "Do you understand?"

Isaiah looked in the direction the voice came from but did not respond.

"Are you feeling well, son?" the judge asked, his tone now avuncular.

"I'd like some water," Isaiah said.

The bailiff poured a glass for him, and Isaiah drank it down. His throat still felt dry.

"I know how hard this is for you," Lowe said. "But it is very important that you answer my questions now. All we want is the truth."

No, Isaiah, thought, that is not what you want. You want a part of the truth, the part that might keep my father out of jail, and in the telling of it, it will become something I will have to live with the rest of my life. He thought again of the night he waded into the water along the golden path drawn by the moon, and how she seemed to be talking to him, telling him, that still she loved his father, even though that was so hard for him to hear, and she did not want to see him punished. And then that other night after he had testified when the golden path had narrowed to an insignificant line across the black water.

"Yessir," he said, his voice hoarse.

"Good," Lowe replied. "You see that map over there, that Mr. Heller has prepared, and how the last witness marked it up to show where he walked, and what he supposedly saw."

"Objection," roared Heller.

"I'll rephrase. What the last witness said he saw."

"Yes, I see," Isaiah replied.

Lowe reached into his pocket, and withdrew the piece of charcoal and handed it to Isaiah.

"Now, show us the road you and your father were working on. For some reason, Mr. Heller chose not to put it on his map."

I can do that, certainly, Isaiah thought. The road is where it is. He walked to the map, and drew a line for the road.

"Does the length of the line you have just drawn reflect your progress in clearing it?" Lowe asked.

Isaiah thought a moment. He hadn't consciously scaled his line, but now that he looked at it, and seeing how close it was to the shore of West Bay, he nodded.

"Yes, about right, I think."

"And you and your father were working on that road on the day Margaret Cutter disappeared?"

"Yes." Isaiah was feeling a little better. Just stay with the facts, he told himself, and you'll be all right.

"Now, this is very important. Show us the direction your father was coming from when you saw him that day, when you were going out to meet him."

Isaiah placed the charcoal on the left terminus of his line and moved it toward the right. He marked the direction with an arrow point from west to east.

"So, he was coming to you from the west and going east. But as far as you observed, he never got further east than where you met him."

Isaiah took his time processing that carefully worded question.

"I saw him come from the west to where I met him, and then we went back to work on the road." He drew another line heading back toward the west.

"Now, you do see the mark indicating where Miss Cutter's body was found, there near the shore of East Bay?"

"I do."

"How far away would you say it is from where you met your father?"

"About a mile or so. Maybe two."

"So, it is your testimony that at the time Margaret Cutter was encountering whoever it was that killed her, if she was indeed killed...."

"Objection."

"You can do that in your closing, Mr. Lowe," Hightower said.

"Well, I do have to ask," Lowe countered with a puzzled smile. "Let's do it this way. At the time she was there, where she died, your father, from your observation, coming as he was from the west where he had been working on that road, at that time your father was about a mile or two away."

Isaiah knew that Lowe wanted a prompt, sure answer. But he could not provide it. He had to parse the language, hold it up to the light to see whether it contained a palpable lie.

"Yessir," he said after a few moments.

"A mile or two away."

"Yessir."

"At that time."

"Yessir," Isaiah repeated, although he felt if he were asked again he would have to qualify his answer, say that there was a gap in the time, ample enough for his father to have met Margaret just as the note in his pocket requested. But to his immense relief, Lowe turned so that he was half facing him, but with his eyes on the jury.

"No further questions," he said. "Your witness," he nodded toward Heller.

The prosecutor strode to the witness chair. If he were troubled by Isaiah's testimony, his face did not reveal any misgivings. Rather, his expression was confident, as though he had seen the hole in the time frame that Lowe had so studiously avoided.

"You do love your father, don't you?" he asked. "As any son his father?"

The question struck Isaiah as absurd. As any son his father, what did that have to do with how he felt toward his own father? But he gave the simple, expected answer.

"Yes."

"And you don't want to see him in jail."

"No."

"And you would say anything to keep him out of jail, now wouldn't you?"

"No, not anything."

"Not anything, but some things?"

"Only the truth. What I testified to was the truth."

"As only a loving son could provide it." He smiled at the jury. "We understand. No further questions."

Isaiah stepped down from the witness chair. He was covered in perspiration, but then so was everyone else in the courtroom on this hot summer afternoon. But his sweat was different from theirs. His would have seeped through his skin if it were the middle of January with a howling blizzard blowing in through an open window, for the source of his sweat was the sickening fear that had gripped his belly as Heller had approached, certain as he was that the prosecutor would try to pin him down as to the time he had encountered his father. To his immense relief, though, the prosecutor had chosen the obvious rebuttal, short and dramatic, trusting his brief sequence of questions would discredit anything Isaiah might say in support of Sam. Isaiah made his way back to his seat between his grandparents and collapsed into it, leaning as he did against Livonia's shoulder, while Charles held and patted his hand.

"Fine, son, you did fine," Charles said.

Sam watched his son walk by. He saw the strain on the pale face, the collar damp from perspiration, and the unsteady step. He wanted to stand up and throw his arms around him. He started to rise in his chair, but Benson took his arm and eased him back down.

"I wouldn't," he said. "They might not understand."

"What do you think?" Heller asked. They were back in his office, the prosecutor sitting behind his desk, cigar smoke curling over his head, his assistant writing on a piece of paper.

"The boy hurt us. He was nervous, but he seemed credible."

"Damn it," Heller said behind an explosion of smoke, "and damn you for being right. To think we have come so far, and we might yet be beaten."

"You still have your closing," Kelly said.

"And I have public opinion. Not admissible but it comes in the back door anyway, and whispers in the ears of the jurors. Our best friend, maybe in this case. The man is twice divorced, abuse of his wives on the record, gets involved with a girl half his age and gets her pregnant. Even if that were all there was to the story, people would harbor a visceral dislike of him."

"You just have to put the two together, his character and the fact that the girl is dead."

"That's what's nice about closings, more freedom to color the argument," Heller said, letting out the cigar smoke in a smooth billow this time,

"Yes," Kelly nodded, "you don't have to stay between the lines drawn by the facts of the case."

"Especially, when Lowe has done a damned good job blurring those lines." He held out his hand. "Here, let me see what you have for the closing."

"It's just a start," Kelly said.

Heller read the first couple of paragraphs.

"And a very good start it is."

20

Dark gray clouds hovered over the courthouse the next morning. Heller rose to give his closing.

"A young woman is dead," he began, "and the people are convinced that she is dead, along with the baby in her womb, due to one person only, and that person is the man, Sam Logan, sitting right there next to his attorney, who has done a commendable job, as it is his right and duty, to obscure that simple fact. But no matter how well Mr. Lowe has managed to cast doubts about our evidence, it still stands, and it all points to the certain conclusion that the only verdict that matches the facts of this case is one that finds Mr. Logan guilty.

"These are the facts that lead irresistibly to that conclusion: Mr. Logan entered into a carnal relationship with his young neighbor, soon after, or perhaps even before, he separated from his second wife, who was at that time carrying his child. Mr. Logan seems to have a talent for procreation, but not for the responsibilities that go with that act. We have presented witnesses who confirm this relationship. I will take you through their testimony after I am through with this summary. But for now I am giving you, in effect, a table of contents for the book of evidence we have compiled pointing to Mr. Logan's guilt.

"Once it became known to Mr. Logan that his young mistress was pregnant he found himself in a untenable position. We can imagine his thought process at this point. Here he was, a twice divorced man, already paying to support the son of his second wife, an offspring he has never seen, faced with yet another child with yet another woman. Mr. Logan plays baseball, and perhaps he was thinking three strikes and the batter is out."

Sam squeezed his fingernails into his palms. How had the prosecutor come so close to the truth? Could his father have talked to him? But that was impossible. Isaiah? He must listen.

"He was faced with honoring his responsibilities, and he chose not to. It's as simple, and as ugly as that. He had the motive, he had the opportunity, and the physical evidence, and eyewitness testimony puts him at the very place where his victim was found. And there is no other plausible explanation. She went to meet him, carrying a basket to gather flowers. They must have argued. She begged him to do the right thing, to marry her, they would manage somehow, she was young, strong, and hard working, perhaps her parents would help. But he would hear none of it. He encouraged her to drink laudanum, to dull her resistance, and then he put his hands around her neck and squeezed the life out of her, and in so doing, terminated the growing life within her."

Heller walked to his table, picked up a glass of water, and took his time drinking it. Sam listened with growing fascination as this interpretation of events so central to his experience was fashioned into a chain of guilt to be tightened around his neck. He had to keep reminding himself that the man being described was, in fact, himself. He sat back in his chair and concentrated as Heller filled in the outline he had drawn from the testimony elicited from various witnesses. The telling was tedious, but absorbing, Sam found, in its cumulative effect. How, he wondered, was Lowe going to counter? Especially the part of the eye-witness testimony of Jim, who must have been, he thought, the one whose foot snapped that branch in the woods. That sound, now, echoed in Sam's mind like thunder.

Isaiah, too, had been paying rapt attention. When the district attorney mentioned the opportunity Sam had, he shuddered. That meeting, that note, why hadn't he just destroyed it and not mentioned its message to his father? What sense of loyalty or peevishness, he could not decide which, had motivated him to direct his father to that fatal tryst? Why, she would still be alive. He had seen how distraught she was, how tense his father, a dangerous combination, and he, like a fool, had caused these elements to unite in the noxious mixture that resulted in her death and his father, here in court. If he had destroyed that note, she would have picked her flowers, and gone home, and maybe even have given up her desire for his father, leaving her, what a thought, looking for an alternative that he could have provided. Heller moved on to other parts of his case, but for Isaiah there was nothing more to be said, and he paid little attention to what followed.

Sam noted, however, that in spite of the great lengths to which the prosecutor seemed intent on going the jurors' attention did not waver. They sat leaning forward, eyes fixed on him, occasionally offering a nod of agreement as one point or another struck a juror as particularly telling.

There, it was over, and Heller strolled back to his table. His face glowing, he smiled at Kelly as he took his seat, his expression indicating he was confident he had prevailed. Sam studied the jurors, the spectators in their seats, and those pressed against the courtroom windows. They all seemed to concur that Heller, yes, had made his case.

Lowe rose to his feet. It was hot and humid in the courtroom, yet he appeared cool in his white linen suit. Adjusting his red four-in-hand, hooking his thumbs in his suspenders, he strode to his position in front of the jurors. On his face he wore an expression of bemused indignation.

"The prosecution has just told you what we could charitably call a fairy tale, if that term itself were not so inappropriate for an argument that intends to put a man in jail for the rest of his natural life. But yet, Mr. Heller's case is as fantastic as any tale found in the Grimm Brothers' collection. It is nothing more, or less, than a hodgepodge of bits and pieces, by themselves indicative of nothing, tied together in certain ways to produce a patchwork fabric. I intend to show you the defects in that fabric, all of its rents, all its mismatched and improper seams.

"We acknowledge two facts: one, that my client was involved in a relationship with the young woman, and two, that she was pregnant. About these two facts there is no disagreement. My client has fully acknowledged them. But it is a very great distance from these two facts to the conclusion that the prosecutor would like you to draw, namely, that my client is guilty of murder.

"How does the prosecutor attempt to close the distance between the agreed-upon facts and the conclusion? He invents a motive. Perhaps he should be writing books of fiction rather than trying murder cases because he imagines that my client felt trapped by the fact of the pregnancy. How does he know this? What evidence has he been able to adduce to support this interesting speculation? The simple answer is none. He claims to know what my client was thinking, and ignores what my client has said under oath, namely, that he tried to negotiate a resolution to what was a mutual problem. And that negotiation produced an agreement with the young woman's father. It was not a pretty resolution, but it was an honest one. You cannot convict my client for murder because you do not approve of how he attempted to deal with the fact of Margaret Cutter's pregnancy.

"Having failed utterly to prove a motive, having relied on invention, in the rhetorical sense, rather than the necessary presentation of evidence, the prosecutor moved to opportunity. He would have us believe that my client, that man there," and he nodded toward Sam, "was in the vicinity of where the young woman was found. And what support has he presented to that effect? Why, the word of a man who tried to sell his testimony to the highest bidder, approaching both prosecution and defense to see who would pay him. And for what reason? So he could travel to California.

"But ah, you say, what about the last witness, the ex-slave Jim, whose testimony agrees with the perjurer. Why, what an upstanding fellow this is. He hopped a freight train right after the young woman disappeared." Lowe walked to the jury box and gazed at each juror, one at a time. "Is it not just possible," he said, "that the prosecution's star witness should in fact be sitting where my client is? Why else did he flee, if he had done nothing wrong? And it is well known that he slept in the barn where the young woman went twice a day. It is not hard to imagine that he might have taken advantage of her on one of those occasions." Lowe paused and stepped back. He stretched his thin frame to its full height, and then he reached out his right arm with the palm of his hand upward. "I ask you to consider a possibility, one that the good doctor did not testify to, and that is that the color of the skin of that fetus in the bottle was black."

He spun on his heel and walked toward the bench while the spectators erupted into excited murmurs. He waited while the judge's gavel pounded, and then he turned to face the jury.

"Ridiculous, you say, scandalous, you say, she was a fine young woman, you say, but I insist there is as much reason to believe my theory as the prosecution's." He walked to the defense table and poured himself a glass of water while the onlookers continued to whisper among themselves.

266

"The prosecutor also contends that he has physical evidence to place my client at the scene. And what is that physical evidence? A footprint that no longer exists, having been washed away by the rain, as the sheriff's deputy so testified. But the prosecutor's young assistant, who accompanied the deputy, would not take the stand. Why was that? Perhaps he was more concerned about his immortal soul, and would not place his hand on that good book and then swear a lie.

"Against the perjured witness, the runaway witness, and the less than credible witness, we offered the testimony of my client's son, a God fearing young man, who attends church every Sunday, who swore under oath before His maker that his father that day was working on the road leading to West Bay, while the young woman was found almost in the waters of East Bay. Now, you don't have to be a scientist to understand that a man cannot be in two places at the same time.

"That is the prosecution's case. I tell you it is nothing but air. And it ignores other possibilities. One I've already mentioned, concerning the ex-slave Jim. But what about the bottle of laudanum, and the testimony of the reporter as to the distraught state of mind of the young woman? You perhaps have noticed that I have not referred to her as a victim, because that word would suggest that she had been murdered, when it is just as possible that she is a suicide. We do not know how the supposed bruises came to be on her. But I find it plausible to think that her bereaved father, kneeling next to her, might have tried to shake her back to life. That makes as much sense as transporting my client two miles so that his hands could be around her throat."

As Lowe spoke, Sam found himself wondering how he would feel if Lowe succeeded in creating sufficient doubt to free him, how he would look at the man staring back at him in the mirror each morning. Would he be able to recognize him? And what about his memory of her, the touch of her hand to ease the pain of his infected tooth, the unadulterated love in her eyes for him? He had always thought of romantics as fools, who sought something more than the pleasures of physical intimacy, but now he began to understand, at least a little, what motivated them. He realized how precious her love for him had been, and saw, belatedly, how he had been willing to abuse it. He wrestled with the question of why he had permitted, even encouraged, her to die. He had come, reluctantly, to the unpleasant conclusion that it was his own cowardice, his unwillingness to bring down his father's displeasure on his head once more, to face a penniless future with a woman he did not know at the time that he loved, and her bastard child, his only in the sense of a biological accident, his seed planted in this field and not another, such as the fertile furrows of any of the girls who came to the baseball games eager to press their innocence against the sweaty virility of the players.

In short, he now understood that he had probably loved her then, and most certainly did now. He wasn't quite ready to say that he wanted to pay for his carelessness, but he wondered at the cost of his freedom, should Lowe succeed.

Finally, he knew that he would have to deal with his son, whom he had ignored for most of his life, whom he had shamelessly manipulated hoping to maneuver out of his responsibilities, whom he had taunted, and who, more than anybody else, contributed to his defense. How was he to reconcile himself to the savior he had so mistreated?

If he were a religious man, he would have seen parallels between himself and those who had turned on their savior. But he was not. Instead, he saw only that he had come of late to begin to understand and respect the bond of blood between himself and his son. And with a shock, he realized that his own deeply ambivalent feelings towards his own father had colored his attitude toward Isaiah, that he was guilty of passing from one generation to the next the mistrust and lack of support he had found so damaging to himself.

"You need not find my client innocent," Lowe was saying, standing in front of the jurors, his face flushed and moist with perspiration. "As the judge no doubt will explain in his charge to you, you must be convinced beyond any doubt that my client is guilty. That is not the same conclusion as finding him innocent. Finding him innocent is not your task. Your task is to render a verdict of guilty, which means you agree that the prosecution's case has been made beyond any question, or not guilty, which means you do not have the necessary degree of certitude to convict. That is your choice, and I believe if you examine both the evidence offered by the prosecution and the review of that evidence we have offered, you must return a verdict of not guilty."

Lowe sat back down next to Sam. His white linen suit was damp, and his four-in-the-hand seemed to droop.

"I had to go that road," he said. "They would never believe you were innocent. But maybe they'll have enough doubts now not to convict you."

"What a place I find myself in, if that's the best," Sam said.

"You put yourself there, my friend," and for the first time, Sam understood that his lawyer, just like everyone else, thought he was guilty.

This conclusion did not come as much of a surprise. He had been studying the jurors as they listened to the witnesses. Their faces had been imperturbable for the most part, but he could read their smallest reactions, their frowns, smiles, grimaces, the slight shake or nod of a head, the hunching forward of shoulders, all the while their expressions remained stubbornly neutral, and in these slight variations he had seen his fate, sealed even before the first piece of testimony had been offered. He had been convicted based on what they knew, or had heard, of his life up to this time, his divorces, his brawls, all his very public altercations, and they no doubt saw him as a blot on the fair name of their community. It was ironic, no doubt, that these men whose values he had scorned as representations of all that he had come to detest in his father, now held his life in their thick, work hardened hands. So, it was no surprise that his lawyer, seeing these attitudes had pitched his closing argument toward creating doubt of guilt rather than assurance of innocence. All that remained now was to hear announced, with all the formality of the law, what had been ordained from the onset of the trial.

"How long do you think?" he asked Lowe, who was sliding papers into his briefcase.

"Not long, I suspect. The longer the better for you. But if they come back tonight or early tomorrow, you will have been convicted. If that's what happens, we can appeal. I believe there are various grounds that might succeed."

"I doubt my father will pay for your services beyond today."

Lowe clasped his briefcase shut. He looked at Sam with a flicker of sympathy in his eyes, and then they resumed their usual, hard and cold stare.

"You are right about that. He told me that when he hired me, and confirmed it two days ago. He does not believe," he said, "in throwing good money after bad."

"Why am I not surprised?" Sam muttered.

"And you..." Lowe continued.

"Cannot afford you."

"Most cannot." He held out his hand. "I want you to know I did my best, and I believe nobody could have done better for you."

It was said in the tones a surgeon might use to tell his patient that the gallant life saving operation against impossible odds had, in fact, failed.

269

Exhaustion fell on Sam like a heavy blanket. He struggled to keep his head up. He wanted now only to return to his cell and be alone with his thoughts. But the judge was beginning to speak, instructing the jury at tedious length about how murder is the intentional taking of human life, the degrees, first and second, separated by whether the act involved deliberation or not, although both must show malice aforethought, and Sam tried to parse that distinction while the judge went on about the nature of this case being built by the People on circumstantial evidence, which could be, he said, sufficient for conviction, if all the pieces of evidence seemed to have been established, and here Sam thought of how Lowe had chipped away at each piece as it had been presented. The circumstantial evidence must, Hightower continued, also exclude other probable explanations, and Sam recalled Lowe's attempt to provide Margaret with another father for her baby, as well as to document her own enduring sadness. Yes, he must agree, Lowe had earned his money, had done as good a job as anybody could have in this case.

A fly began to buzz about his head, and he took a half hearted swap at it, but it continued undeterred. Its buzz blended with the drone of the judge's voice, and that combination along with the thick air in the courtroom deepened his weariness. He propped his jaw in his hands, no longer trying to project an attitude of confidence that his innocence would emerge from the confusion of the conflicting testimony.

He forced himself to listen as the judge expanded upon "reasonable doubt," and "moral certainty," and the words seemed so woefully inadequate to probe the emotions that had roiled in him, in her as well, that fatal afternoon, her insistence that they marry, his desire to escape that net, her despair, the laudanum that as much as anything had killed her while clouding his own judgment, none of that had come out because his defense was based on his alibi, supported by his son, that he was more than a mile and a half away from where she was found. Having made the decision to rely on the irrefutable contradiction between where he said he was as opposed to where she was, he had denied himself any opportunity to explore those ambiguities. Just as well, he thought, with another look at the stolid jurors. Never would they begin to understand, these men, to whom his passions and his weaknesses were as distant as the furthest planet to the narrow circuit of their lives.

Lost in thought for a couple of moments, he did not realize that Judge Hightower had finished, and that everyone had begun to rise as the judge exited the bench through the door behind it. Lowe nudged him, and he stood. Then Deputy Morgan snapped cuffs on him. They walked out, as they had each day of the trial. Sam felt, as he had each time, the hostile glances of the spectators, and more to the point, the jurors, his erstwhile neighbors whose minds, he was sure, had been set against him from the beginning. Strangely, though, he did not resent them. He would have felt the same as they if he were sitting where they were, and one of them was in his place.

They walked up the stairs to the prison floor. On the landing below it was a large, square window. Morgan looked through it as a loud clap of thunder was followed by a flash of lightning.

"Do you suppose that's a sign?" Sam asked.

Allan shook his head.

"I don't try to think of things like that. All it means is that I'm happy we're inside."

"I used to think like that, too," Sam said. "But I don't think I'll ever see rain in a sky only like that."

21

"Must I?" Isaiah asked.

"Yes," Lowe replied. "It's the last, best thing I can do."

" Isn't it too late?"

"Yes."

"But..."

"We'll do it anyway."

Sam permitted himself a little hope when the jury did not reach a decision that afternoon. He sat in his cell studying the flashes of lightning across the black sky. He wondered what he would do if the jail were hit. He decided he would hold onto the iron bars and hope to draw the current into his body. The thought was liberating.

The storm abated a couple of hours before dawn. His supper tray sat where he had placed it when it was pushed through the slot in his cell door. He looked at it with curiosity. He did not recall what it felt like to be hungry. It was as though he were already dead. He lay down and stared at the ceiling.

Just as the sun began to shine through his window, he heard approaching footsteps, and he knew he was convicted. It had been a little more than twelve hours since the jury retired.

"It's time," Allan said. "They're back."

The sun shone in a bright blue sky. Nature, Sam thought, was mocking him on what would be the darkest day of his life. He looked out the large window on the landing at the ground, now pocked with puddles from last night's rain. He wondered how he would feel if he were walking toward the gallows. Would he still avoid getting his feet wet in the standing water?

Lowe had changed his neckwear. Instead of the red four-in-hand he had worn since his arrival, he now had on a black cravat that contrasted with the crisp white linen of his suit. Sam raised his hand to his own collar as he sat down.

"Like for a funeral, is that it?"

Lowe shrugged.

"I told you what I thought yesterday. They're not looking at you. But we'll give them something to think about."

Sam saw that the jurors averted their glances from him, gazing instead at the bench where Hightower was holding his gavel. Sam turned around, as he had done every day, and looked toward the rearmost seats. They were there, their faces as grim as he now felt. He thought he had prepared himself for this moment during the long night of lightning flashes across the black sky, and the sound of thunder, as though it were God Himself talking to him, promising divine justice that would beggar that which the imagination of mere mortals could apply to his case. Lowe half stood and waved to the back of the courtroom. Isaiah walked forward. Benson got up, and Isaiah sat in his chair, next to Sam.

"You didn't have to," Sam muttered.

"I'm as much on trial as you, I figure," Isaiah replied.

"The defendant will rise," Hightower intoned.

Sam steeled himself. He got to his feet. Lowe lifted himself from his chair and leaned toward him.

"Steady," he said. "Don't give in to them."

Sam nodded. He stared at the jury foreman, the tall, thin shopkeeper from town. Sam recalled that he sold leather shoes and that Eustace often stopped in front of his window to look at boots with rows of buttons like a serpent uncoiled up the side. She had called them "darling," and asked that he buy them for her. But although they cost only two and a half dollars, he was short, as usual, and he had told her she would have to wait for a time he knew would not come. Somehow that memory confirmed what he expected this dour faced man was about to say.

"Guilty," the shopkeeper said. And then as though not satisfied with the one word, "We find the defendant guilty. As charged."

Sam's shoulders slumped, and he willed them straight. He felt a little dizzy, and the fly was buzzing about his head again. It landed on his ear, but he did not swipe it away. He saw the judge looking at him, and his lips were moving.

"Does the defendant have anything to say?"

Sam had rehearsed this moment in sleepless nights in his cell. He stood up.

"Only that I am innocent," he said in a steady voice.

"Mr. Logan, you have been convicted of murder in the first degree. The law requires a sentence, one with which I fully concur, given the heinous nature of your crime, life imprisonment at hard labor. You are to be delivered to the state penitentiary in Jackson, there to remain for the rest of your days." Hightower brought the gavel down, breaking the silence that had gripped the courtroom. An excited murmur filled the heavy air. First one, then another cheered. Those at the window added their voices. Hightower pounded his gavel again and again until the crowd quieted. Sheriff Billingham's large shape appeared outside the window nearest the judge's bench. He raised his arms and then brought them down as though he were pulling down a shade. He said something but the windows had remained closed from the rain the night before, and his voice was lost in the clamor. But then the noise stopped.

Sam cast a glance over his shoulder and saw the nods of satisfaction among the spectators. He looked past them to his parents, and gazed at their backs as they vanished through the rear door. The other spectators remained in their seats, staring at him. He did not know what they expected him to do. Isaiah stood and threw his arms around his father. Sam felt the strong, young arms of his son press against him.

"You don't have to visit me," Sam said.

A muffled cheer filtered in through the windows. Sam saw faces pressed against the glass, eyes bright with vindication. He wondered if anybody was carrying a length of rope.

"You see what I mean," Sam said. "It's not just me they hate."

"Bailiff, clear the courtroom," Hightower said.

With great reluctance, the spectators began to file out, each turning at the door to cast one more look at the convicted murderer and the son whose testimony had not saved him. The onlookers' expressions were solemn, self-congratulatory, declaring that they had known this would be the outcome from the very beginning.

Isaiah felt their hostility. He had not anticipated it. What did they think he would do? What would they have done in the same circumstance? Who were they to sit in judgment of him? One young woman looked at him with gentleness in her eyes, as though she might want to offer him a word of comfort. An older man, probably her father, took her arm and steered her out of the courtroom. He looked back at Isaiah with a fierce stare as though Isaiah's flesh were running with putrid sores. He hurried his daughter out of the door. The only one still sitting was Daniel. He mouthed the words "I'll wait for you," and he too went out the door.

Lowe pulled the straps closed on his leather portfolio.

"I need to talk with your father," he said. He extended his hand to Sam. His flesh was cool. And then he walked out.

Deputy Morgan approached.

"We'll wait a little while," he said. "The sheriff is out there talking to the crowd." Allan's hand rested on the butt of his revolver. "They've got the outside door jammed open. We'll have to walk past them to get to the stairs."

For a moment Sam's anger flashed, an insult to his pride and his dignity, the same sudden emotion that had propelled him into countless confrontations in the past, and he thought about marching out to face these people whose prejudices, more than anything they had heard in the court proceedings, had inflamed them against him. But then, just as quickly as it had risen, the anger was gone, replaced by a bone deep weariness.

"Do you mind?" he said, and sat down.

"Go right ahead," Allen replied. "I don't see the harm. No point in cuffing you either because you'd be worse than a damned fool to go rushing out there now."

"It has occurred to me," Sam replied, "but I'm not quite ready." He turned to Isaiah. "You go on out, now."

"No," Isaiah replied. "I can wait with you."

They sat in silence, the deputy, the convicted, and the son. Voices crept in through the window, the deep, ingratiating bass of Sheriff Billingham, and others, troubled and angry, various pitches and tones, all carrying the same message, saying in one way or another, "We want him now, he doesn't deserve to live another day." But after a while, only Billingham's words could be heard, although not clearly enough to be understood by the trio waiting at the defense table. Then the door opened, and Billingham's bulk filled the doorway.

"Come on, now," he said.

Sam got up and held out his hands. Allen snapped a cuff on Sam's right wrist, and the other end on his left.

"Just so they know you're not going anywhere," he said.

Sam looked at Isaiah.

"You stay here until I'm gone. I don't want you seeing what goes on out there."

Isaiah watched as Morgan walked his father toward Billingham, and then the door shut behind them as they passed into the entry hall. He heard the loud murmur of the crowd, punctuated by several sharp expletives, all ending with "Logan." He bowed his head and waited until the noise died down. Then, he made his way out of the courtroom and through the hall. The outside door was still wedged open with a piece of wood. When he emerged into the sunlight, he found Daniel standing on the top steps. Most of the crowd was gone. Those who had lingered stared their contempt at Isaiah. If they had stones, Isaiah thought, they would most surely now hurl them at him.

"I've been waiting for you," Daniel said.

"The crowd, how were they, when he came out?"

"Ugly," Daniel replied. "But the sheriff did his job, talked to them, and they quieted after a while."

Isaiah looked past Daniel, down the steps to the street where Charles and Livonia sat in their buggy, talking to Lowe. Charles handed a folded piece of paper to Lowe, and the attorney nodded his thanks.

"My grandparents are waiting for me," Isaiah said.

"What you did, what you said..." Daniel said.

"You are writing this up for *The Herald* aren't you?"

"Yes."

"Are you going to be fair? To him? To me?"

"I will write what happened. That's my job. What I might think I'll keep to myself."

Isaiah reached into his pocket.

"If I give you something, do I have your word that you will do what I ask with it?"

"Of course."

Isaiah held out an envelope.

"This is what I was talking about. You must not read it until I am gone."

"Gone?"

"I'm going to ship out on the next boat that comes into the harbor. I don't care where it's headed as long as it's away from here." Charles stood in the buggy and waved with both arms. "I must be going," Isaiah said. "Do you promise?"

"Yes," Daniel asked.

Isaiah pressed the envelope into his hand.

"I must trust you, then. Once you read it, I leave it to you what you might want to do with it."

Daniel sat down again on the steps, the envelope, unopened in his hand.

"Mr. Lowe," Isaiah said. "Is there nothing more to be done?"

Lowe looked at Charles.

"I could appeal. There are always possibilities."

"Will you?"

Lowe glanced at Charles, and then shook his head.

"I'm afraid not. Your grandfather doesn't approve." He glanced down at the folded paper in his hand. "He says I need to look elsewhere for work."

"Get on up, boy," Charles said. "It's time to move on. From here, and with your life."

Isaiah sat next to his grandmother. Livonia patted his knee.

"All is not lost," she said.

Sam stood at his window looking through the bars. The night was clear and the stars sprinkled the sky with points of light of varying intensity in their usual patterns. But he did not try to pick out the constellations. Instead, he lost himself in the immensity. He looked down, after a while, and saw just one torch. He studied it until its bearer walked away into the darkness. He turned his gaze to his six by eight foot cell, its bunk, its one chair and small table. On the table were a few sheets of paper, a pencil, and an envelope. He sat down at the table and began to write a letter to his son.

From the room next to his came the sounds of excited whispers. Daniel could not be certain, but he thought one voice must belong to a woman. He wondered how she had managed to slip by the watchful eye of Mrs. Svensen. He thought of Margaret, how she had appeared when first he met her by the bank of the river, and then again as she lay dead beneath the maple in the hemlock swamp. Had she ever sneaked into Logan's house, or he into hers? He realized that he had never seen her in health and happiness. His thoughts moved to Isaiah, and he regretted having misunderstood her declaration that she would marry "Mr. Logan." On the table next to his bed was the envelope Isaiah had given him. He would find a safe place to keep it, and he would not read its contents until he was sure that Isaiah was gone. It was the least he could do.

He took out his little notebook and looked over the notes he had scribbled as fast as he could as the verdict was announced. He had jotted down a physical sketch of each of the jurors, tried to record their facial expressions, and then strained to record the reactions of the spectators. He had been impressed by Sam's calm, although he had seen how tightly his fists had been clenched as though he would have enjoyed the opportunity to settle this matter with them. Still, there had been contrition in his voice, even as he insisted upon his innocence.

He held his pencil poised over his pad. He needed to file his story in the morning. Yet, its lead eluded him. He did not want to fall back on the simple declarative statement that Sam Logan had been convicted of the first degree murder of Margaret Cutter. That was a fact, of course, but it was both too simple and complex. Did the fact point to the truth? He was not so certain. There were layers and layers to all human actions and interactions. Of this he was sure. The verdict in a trial such as this was the beginning, and perhaps the end, of a story whose middle contained the marrow in which truth hid.

He stared again at the envelope on the table. Would its contents reveal or deepen the mystery?

Sam rested his head on the table. He had not been able to write the letter to Isaiah. There was both too much and too little to say. He could only hope that his son would not hate him. He heard footsteps approaching his cell.

Mary pressed her face against the bars.

"A fine fix you've got into this time," she said.

He found himself smiling in response.

"I guess so," he replied.

"Mrs. Logan sent me. She felt it would be unwise to come herself."

"I can understand. My father..."

"Yes, your father. That's part of what she wanted me to tell you. Your father is not well."

"I am sorry to hear that."

"She wants you to know that when he's gone, she'll remember where you are."

"Just like her," he said. "And it will be just like him to hang on for as long as he can."

Mary reached through the bars to press his hands.

"Such a fool," she said.

22

—◆—

Sarah knelt at Benjamin's grave this Sunday morning just as she always did. Only this time, on his knees next to her was Henry in front of the grave of his daughter. The other congregants walked around the church to the cemetery and passed by the couple before circling back to the front entrance. As people reached the grieving couple, they paused, bowed their heads, and sometimes offered a word of comfort.

Charles and Livonia waited in their buggy for the congregation to walk into the building. When the last person had done so, Charles got down, balanced himself on his cane, and offered his hand to Livonia. They climbed the steps and entered the sanctuary. Those already seated greeted them with a hostile murmur. They seemed not to heed, and made their way to their seats.

Sarah and Henry walked hand in hand out of the cemetery and along the side of the church. They stopped at the steps that led to the front entrance. Henry looked at Sarah. She shook her head, and they made their way to the road that led toward the southern end of the Peninsula. The sexton, who had been standing at the door watching them, hurried through the entranceway and into the sanctuary. He shook his head. Lapham, standing behind the lectern, nodded.

"Friends," he began, "open your hymnal to page one hundred and twenty five, and let us lift our voices."

Some hundred yards down the road, Sarah and Henry heard the voices of the congregation, "Softly and tenderly Jesus is calling, calling for you and me." The words floated after them, growing fainter as they continued to walk. When they could no longer hear, Henry stopped.

"I wonder..." he began.

"Don't," Sarah replied.

"Maybe we should go back," Henry said.

"Not today. I said my prayers over their graves. Didn't you?"

"I tried," he answered.

"That's all we can do, then."

She began to walk, and he joined her step for step.

Not far away, Isaiah stood before the town dock, his belongings in a sack over his shoulder. He watched the thin figure approach, pause, bend over, and then continue.

"I thought I might find you here," Daniel said. He looked up at the freighter tied to the dock, smoke billowing from its two stacks. "I heard this ship was leaving today."

"I read your report of the trial in the paper," Isaiah said.

"I wrote what I witnessed."

"I thought you did a fair job."

"I haven't looked at what you gave me."

"I know," Isaiah replied. "If you had, you might have written your story differently."

"Perhaps. But I don't think so. My job was to report what happened at the trial."

An officer standing near the gangplank leaned over the railing.

"It's time, boy," he called.

Isaiah held out his hand.

"I hope to see you again some time."

"I hope to be here when you return."

"That won't be soon."

Daniel shrugged.

"Well, good luck, then."

"Logan," the officer called.

Isaiah started up the gangplank, and then stopped.

"Don't think ill of me," he called back to Daniel, "or him."

That night, Daniel sat at the table in his room at the Inn. He took the envelope out of his pocket and removed the folded paper it contained. He smoothed the paper open with the palm of his hand. He moved his lips as he read its words.

"So, this is what you knew," he muttered, "you poor bastard. "Dearest, Meet me at the usual place at noon tomorrow. We must talk. I love you, now and always.'"

Now and always. Daniel traced the childish letters with his fingers. Meet me at noon. The usual place. The place usual at noon me meet. No matter how he moved the words around they added up to the same piece of irrefutable evidence that Sam Logan had an appointment to meet Margaret Cutter at the usual place, the hemlock swamp, no doubt, on the day she died.

But wait. Isaiah had this note. Sam did not. Daniel felt a chill, followed by a wave of nausea rising from his gut. What if Isaiah had that appointment? He looked at the note again. No name, just "Dearest" as the salutation. Who was dearest? Was it possible that the father had taken the fall for the son? She had said she intended to marry Mr. Logan. Which Mr. Logan? The one in jail, or the one who is now headed out onto the lakes, and thereafter who knows, maybe Europe, the far East, any place the broad highway of the ocean can lead to?

His head began to ache. The chill and nausea had passed, replaced by the warmth of a fever. He folded the note and started to slide it back into the envelope. But the tips of his fingers found another piece of paper still in the envelope. He pulled it out and unfolded it. It was written in pencil, in a neat, plain hand, the hand of someone accustomed to labor and unaccustomed to moving a pencil over a piece of paper, so that the motion was done with great care.

"In case you are wondering, my father never got this note. I've kept it all this time. But I told him what the note said. I do not know why I didn't give him the note itself. Would it have made any difference? I don't think so. Maybe if I hadn't told him about it, though, she would still be alive. That thought enters my mind without my asking every night when I close my eyes to sleep, and it's there when I wake up.

"We only spoke about the meeting once, and he said he hadn't gone there. I chose to believe him. He is my father still."

So that's it, Daniel thought, he's your father still. Easier to believe him against your better judgment and then do what you felt you had to do. Daniel folded Margaret's note over Isaiah's and put them both back into the envelope. He took out another piece of paper.

"Just what happened beneath that tree?" he wrote. "The jury had its answer. God only knows what Isaiah now believes in his heart. Foolishness! To think that anyone, any observer can ever plumb those secret places. Why, Sam himself might now have told himself what happened so often that he no longer knows, in any real sense, the truth."

He craned his neck to stare up at the ceiling and past it.

"Maybe you know, you bearded old man. Nobody else does." He wrote these words, and underlined them. "I hope you can sleep, both of you, but I doubt you can."

23

———

He had a wool cap on his head, his face was unshaven, and his feet were little unsteady finding purchase on land after weeks on the water. His shoes kicked up yellow, brown and orange leaves as he walked. He had a small bundle over his shoulder as he made his way up the dirt path to the little house he now owned on Fifth Street in town. His face was still youthful although the skin was weathered. His eyes, though, were those of a man much older than his thirty years.

He opened the door. The aroma of freshly cut wood greeted his nose. A new table sat in the little room off to the side of the short foyer. The top of the table was inlaid with strips of walnut and maple, waxed to a high sheen. The legs had been turned to a graceful taper, punctuated by a ball half way down. Four matching chairs were pulled up to the table. On its top was an envelope propped against a book. A grizzled man sat in one of the chairs.

"I see you've been busy," Isaiah said. He swung his bundle off his shoulder and placed it in the corner of the room.

"Nothing much else to do," the old man muttered.

Isaiah leaned over the table.

"You haven't forgotten," he said.

"It's what I thought about these past years, what I'd do if I got out, what I should have been doing all those years before," Sam said.

"Well, I suppose you can take what you've made with you when you get a place of your own."

"Haven't been thinking about moving."

"This was supposed to be temporary," Isaiah said.

"It was generous of you to offer. I give you that. You could have had much more than this little house that your mother left you."

"I didn't want it."

Sam shook his head.

"All that land and those trees, and he wound up not having anyone to leave them to."

"He gave the farm to a great nephew in New Hampshire."

"Funny thing," Sam said. "I thought I wanted it, but it was more the idea of it than the land itself." He walked to the window. He ran his hand over the frame, and found a place where it had pulled away from the wall.

"Needs some work," he said.

"I could hire a carpenter," Isaiah said.

"You could," Sam replied.

Isaiah picked up the envelope.

"When did this come?"

"Just last week."

Isaiah opened the envelope.

"Who's it from?" Sam asked.

"An old friend."

"What's he want?"

"I'll know when I see him."

The clerk in the administration building of the new state sanitarium in Howell slid his finger down a large register containing a list of patients. His nails were neatly trimmed, and he squinted through thick glasses that sat uneasily on his nose. His finger stopped.

"Yessir," he said. "Your friend was admitted only a couple of weeks ago. I remember when he came in." He leaned forward and lowered his voice to just above a whisper. "He waited much too long."

"Can I see him?"

"Surely. Just walk down that corridor and through the door. You'll see a building with two wings. The one on the left is for men. He'll be in there."

Daniel was propped up in his bed. His eyes were rolled back into their sockets in his gaunt face, which looked as though the flesh were peeling off the bones. His thin arms clasped a blanket to his chest, and he shivered as though he were sitting naked in the middle of the winter, although a warm breeze floated through the men's wing of the building. He lifted one skeletal arm from the blanket and pointed to the openings between the columns supporting the roof.

"They want us to have fresh air. They think that'll help." He forced a smile. His teeth looked preternaturally large against his thin lips. "I won't be around long enough to find out."

"Don't talk like that."

"I've already beat the odds. By years. But I knew I had to get in touch with you. So I wrote. An old friend at the newspaper gave me your new address in town."

"I wish I had known, sooner."

Daniel shrugged.

"It doesn't matter, not now. But I had to talk to you, once I heard about your father." He started to lean over to reach for a newspaper on the floor next to his bed, but he stopped. "I'm afraid I can't."

Isaiah picked up the paper and handed it to him.

"It's right here," Daniel said, holding up the newspaper, his finger pointed to a headline in modest type face on the lower right hand corner. "Governor Pardons..." he began to read but stopped as a coughing fit wracked him. He daubed his lips with a cloth that was spotted with rust colored stains. "I'm sure you know what it says." He put the paper down. "But I never understood why. I guessed you had a hand in it."

"No. My grandmother, after my grandfather died, hired Lowe again with the money he had left her. Lowe filed appeals, something about the testimony of that ex-slave being bought with a promise of money. I guess the governor was convinced."

"I see. And you?"

Isaiah shrugged.

"I'm not unhappy. Or happy. We didn't have a welcome home party."

"Yes, he's still you're father. You wrote that."

"I did. And he still is. But there's more, something, you don't know."

Daniel rolled onto his side. He lifted himself up, resting his weight on his elbow. His eyes were a paradox, glassy yet brightly focused.

"Tell me."

"He's living with me."

"In your house in town?"

Isaiah nodded.

"My mother moved away years ago, right after the divorce. I don't know where to. But her family owned that house. She left it to me when she died. It had been vacant for some time. He wants to fix it up."

"In a strange kind of way," Daniel said, pausing on each word, "his living with you makes sense." He reached under his pillow and pulled out a leather notebook. He handed it to Isaiah. "It's all in there, my thoughts, which are not important, but what is, is that piece of paper you gave me. It has weighed on my mind all these years. I have struggled to understand."

"Do you?"

Daniel shook his head, and collapsed back onto his pillow.

Isaiah opened the notebook. He began reading.

"It's all there," Daniel said. "From the day I met you with the search party. I was going to write the whole story up, make a book out of it, tell the world the truth but I couldn't because no matter how hard I searched I couldn't find truth, couldn't entice it out of the shadows in the corner where it was hiding. I thought I could look into the human heart, but I discovered that what I was good at was recording what I saw. Nothing more."

Isaiah flipped the pages until he came to the folded note. He opened it as though expecting it to burst into flames.

"Can you explain?" Daniel asked.

"No. Why did you keep it?"

"I wanted to give it back to you myself. But tell me, did you ever find somebody else?"

"No. Did you?"

"There was this girl," Daniel said in a whisper, his eyes closed. "She was wearing yellow gloves, and she was in a carriage."

"What about her?"

"Girl with yellow gloves," Daniel repeated. He seemed to nod off, but then he sat upright as though infused with energy. His eyes snapped open. "Promise me something."

"Anything."

"Do not come back for me."

"But why? Do you have anyone else?"

"No." He lay back down. "Don't need, don't come back." His eyes closed. His breathing was labored. Isaiah watched his thin chest rise and fall, saw the spasms as he fought to pull air into his lungs. He watched until he was sure the breathing would continue at least for now. And then he left.

Isaiah put the note on the table in front of Sam.

"What's that?" Sam asked. "Something from your friend?"

"He was holding it for me. I gave it to him right after your trial."

Sam placed his large hand over it.

"You should read it," Isaiah said. "So you understand."

Sam shook his head.

"I don't think I want to."

"Pick it up and read it!" Isaiah said, his voice informed by a cold fury that surprised him. He tried to pry Sam's hand off the note. "I'll read it to you. It's been my nightmare these fifteen years."

But Sam pulled the paper away. He lifted it up to his chest. He peeked at the first line.

"Dearest," he read. "Who is dearest? Why are you showing me this?"

"You know damned well," Isaiah said.

"No."

"Don't you recognize the hand?"

"No."

"How can you not?"

"Because she never wrote me."

Isaiah collapsed back into his chair.

"Then you do see, don't you?"

Sam's eyes glistened. He held out the note and read.

"You had this all that time?" he managed to ask, his words wrenched out one at a time.

"I was supposed to give it to you."

They sat in stunned silence, years of pain, guilt, anger lying between them.

"What should we do?" Sam asked. His voice was plaintive, as though he were now the child.

"What I should have done a long time ago," Isaiah replied. He held out his hand and Sam gave him the note. "The stove is still lit."

"Are you sure?" Sam asked.

"What else am I going to do? Go to the law now? Have you forgotten you were convicted anyway?"

"I didn't kill her," Sam said. "Leastways not in my mind."

"Why didn't you tell me?"

"I couldn't. I couldn't tell myself. How could I tell you?"

Isaiah walked to the wood stove, and opened its door. He stood there for several moments, but then with a sudden movement he hurled the note into the stove. Sam joined him. They watched a tongue of flame begin at its corner and then flare. The paper curled up, turned black and then collapsed into glowing embers. When all that was left was a small pile of ash, Isaiah slammed the stove door shut.

"Now, it's over," Sam said.

"No," Isaiah replied. "It will end when we are both in our graves. As she is."

The next morning, Isaiah packed again his little bundle of clothes. Sam was at the table, drinking a cup of coffee.

"I'll be back in two or three months," he said.

"Can I stay here until then?"

"Do what you want."

"I'm going to open a carpentry shop, I think. I should have..."

"Yes, you should have, but you didn't."

Isaiah swung the bundle over his shoulder and walked out the door.

Sam sat at the table, running his fingers over its surface until he found a small dent that he had not been able to smooth.

"Should have," he muttered.